# DARLING MINE

Also by Romy Hausmann

*Dear Child*
*Sleepless*
*Anatomy of a Killer*

# DARLING MINE

## ROMY HAUSMANN

*Translated from the German by*
*Jamie Bulloch*

QUERCUS

First published in the German language as *Himmelerdenblau* by Penguin Verlag,
a division of Penguin Random House Verlagsgruppe GmbH, München, Germany, in 2025
First published in Great Britain in 2026 by Quercus
Part of John Murray Group

1

*Himmelerdenblau* by Romy Hausmann © 2025 Penguin Verlag,
a division of Penguin Random House Verlagsgruppe GmbH, München, Germany
English translation copyright © 2026 by Jamie Bulloch

The moral right of Romy Hausmann to be
identified as the author of this work has been
asserted in accordance with the Copyright,
Designs and Patents Act, 1988.

Jamie Bulloch asserts his moral right to be identified as the translator of this work.

All rights reserved. No part of this publication
may be reproduced or transmitted in any form
or by any means, electronic or mechanical,
including photocopy, recording, or any
information storage and retrieval system,
without permission in writing from the publisher.

This book is a work of fiction. Names, characters,
businesses, organizations, places and events are
either the product of the author's imagination
or used fictitiously. Any resemblance to
actual persons, living or dead, events or
locales is entirely coincidental.

A CIP catalogue record for this book is available
from the British Library

HB ISBN 978 1 52944 670 8
TPB ISBN 978 1 52944 671 5
EBOOK ISBN 978 1 52944 673 9

Typeset in Swift by CC Book Production

Printed and bound in Great Britain by Clays Ltd, Elcograf S.p.A.

Papers used by Quercus are from well-managed forests and other responsible sources.

Quercus
Carmelite House
50 Victoria Embankment
London EC4Y 0DZ

John Murray Group
Part of Hodder & Stoughton Limited
An Hachette UK company

The authorised representative in the EEA is Hachette Ireland,
8 Castlecourt Centre, Dublin 15, D15 XTP3, Ireland (email: info@hbgi.ie)

*'No man chooses evil because it is evil;
he only mistakes it for happiness, the good he seeks.'*

—Mary Shelley

At some point in the course of history, a few fish strayed into the deep, dark caves along the Mexican coast. It ought to have been their death sentence, but instead of perishing they adapted to the conditions, to the cold and darkness. For orientation, these fish increasingly relied on their sense of balance rather than vision, which had major consequences for their future development. First they lost their colour, their pigmentation. Then their retinas withered away until they no longer grew any eyes.

They're ugly and blind.

But, in spite of everything, they've survived. They are what their environment has made them, what nature has forced them to become. I wonder what would happen if one of them managed to swim free from the deep, black labyrinth. If it reached the surface that reflects the sun's rays. Would it feel the light, the warmth? Become used to this again, over time? Get its eyes back, be able to see again? Or would it—

My train of thought falters. The firm grip of the hand on my shoulder from behind jolts me back into reality. I take another deep breath in the hope of calming my quivering fingers.

*Give him his peace*, is the instruction. I know I mustn't go over the top. All the same I want to try. I have to.

'Do you think . . . I mean, could you maybe sort out the light at the weekend?' I look up at the ceiling, from the middle of which two bare cables dangle like dead plant shoots.

'Yes, maybe,' is the answer I get, and the grip on my shoulder tightens again, as if a reminder of what's at stake for me. Lowering my fingers on to the keyboard, I type.

*You've got to stop looking for me.*

In any case, you won't find me down here, in my deep, dark cave, I add in my mind.

# 1. TRANSCRIPT

## TEN DAYS EARLIER

### THEO

*Click*, it goes inside my head. *Click*, like an old-fashioned toggle switch.

Light on, orientation. I'm in a chair. I didn't sit down on a chair. Around me are white walls, in front of me a whatsit, a desk made of cherry, perhaps mahogany. To my left a window, sun, dancing dust. Don't lose yourself in details, Theo. The details are just a distraction. From him, the man. Gaunt, pale skin, pointy nose – an arrogant nose. He's wearing a white goat. I pat my chest and look down. I'm just wearing a shirt and a cardigan. That's my white goat the man's wearing.

'Theo?'

How does he know my name? What's going on? I leap up and the chair wobbles. I know for certain that I didn't sit down on a chair! The gaunt man lunges, grabbing the chair before it goes crashing to the floor.

'Everything's alright.' His voice sounds calm and monotonous, an audible sedative. I throw my hands up and hold my droning head. Anaesthetic, ten letters: sufentan. Synthetic opioid, the strongest permitted in hun List number: 641-081-8. Now I understand. He seda put me on a chair.

I need to go, I need to get out of here at once. The gaunt man hobbles after me, catching me up at the door.

'You see,' he says, as if by way of proof. Not that I know what he's trying to prove to me. I don't know him, the man is a stranger. No, not a total stranger. The man is a hazy feeling. He is pain.

'Please!' I say, reaching awkwardly for the handle. 'I have a wife. Her name is Vera and she'll be waiting for me to come home for dinner.'

The gaunt man touches my upper arm and shakes his head slowly. His monotone voice again: 'Vera's not waiting for you, Theo. She's been dead for four years.'

'Dead,' I repeat in a brittle voice. And before I can come up with an adequate insult for this man, the tears are already streaming.

*Arsehole.*

Now I remember what I was going to say. And I'm annoyed that it didn't occur to me at the time. This gaunt man with the arrogant nose is Claus, Claus Dellard. He wants to be a luminescence in the field of neurology and psychiatry. He's an arsehole. A pompoms old snitch. Instead of leaving me in peace he called Sophia and now we're in a pickle. She humiliated herself by coming to collect me from Dellard like a mother picking up her wayward son from the headmaster's office. *Sorry, Claus. He's clearly having a bad day today, Claus. Yes, Claus. I'll look after him, Claus.*

*Claus*, pah!

'I mean, it's possible that you chose to sit on the chair in the consultation room,' she says now. 'You did have a check-up with him, after all. It's quite normal to sit down in these things.'

I growl. I'd have preferred her not to come. I'm seventy-four years old and can take the bus. Any fool can take the bus. How else did I get to the hospital in the first place?

'Dad?'

'What else did that idiot say about me?'

'You mean Claus? Nothing! Nobody's said anything about you.'

'Don't lie, Sophia.' I bet he mentioned the Vera thing too. As if I didn't know she'd died. As if I wasn't there, holding her hand. I mentioned the dinner as an excuse to be rid of Dellard. In all the hoo-ha, it was just a minor slip of the tongue. When I look at the clock in Sophia's car I see it's 12.43, the middle of the day. I meant 'lunch', 'lunch' was what I meant.

'Someone at reception called and asked if I could pick you up. That's all, Dad, believe me.' A sideways glance and the sort of smile she thinks is encouraging. I hate it when she does that.

'Maybe he told you—'

'Dad, please! You were there the whole time. When could he have said anything to me about you?'

I peer over at her. She looks like Vera when she was young, only a harsher version, with narrower features and a V-shaped groove between the eyebrows. And the hair, the hair colour is different too. Dreadful, by the way. I do a calculation. Sophia must be thirty-four now. That's how old Vera was when Sophia was born. She was 2,876 grams and 47 centimetres small. A little mite. Ha! Forgetful, me? Rubbish!

I have to know. I have to know if Sophia's telling me the truth. And I'm certain she won't be able to keep it to herself if Dellard said I didn't remember the death of her own beloved mother. How about a little test? I'm going to test Sophia.

'Your mother.' I stop at that, waiting for her reaction.

'What about her?'

'Who?'

'Mum. You were going to say something about her.'

My Vera. I smile. 'She was so beautiful.' I look out of the side window up at the sky. 'Do you remember how beautiful she was? Do you remember that?'

'Of course, Dad. She was gorgeous.'

'And not just on the outside, eh? She was gorgeous on the inside too. She believed that a person's true nature was in their heart.'

'Yes, she was a very special woman.'

'Every day all I did was cut open people's chests – and why? Because the heart is an unreliable lump of tissue. But your mother, she was a hopeless romantic who trusted this lump all her life.' I sigh when it occurs to me again why I even started talking about Vera. It's probably a good thing she can't hear any of this anymore. Because a person's true nature is actually located elsewhere. Not in the heart, but right behind the forehead. In the frontal lobe, *lobus frontalis*.

'Yes, she did. Even so, she'd now suggest you give Claus a chance – sound advice. He's highly skilled and he's also empathetic.'

I look at Sophia behind the wheel. Her long, dyed-black hair is wet and it's left a damp patch on her blue T-shirt. Maybe the clinic called while she was in the shower.

'What makes you think he's skilled? Just because he's wearing a white goat?'

'Coat, Dad.'

I've already opened my mouth when she adds a 'Sorry'. 'I just thought you'd feel more comfortable with him than some stranger for whom you're merely another name on a list. After all, you were colleagues for many years. And he's your friend.' It sounds like a question. Which doesn't deserve an answer from me. Claus Dellard was never my friend. An arrogant bastard at most. I couldn't bear him back then, and now . . .

For quite a while we continue driving in silence. Until she says, 'I've spoken to Richard about your car. He's going to collect it after work.'

'Oh.' So I can't have taken the bus to the hospital. No, I didn't. The dark green Saab, 2011 model, is in the thing, the hospital parcark.

'Richard is—'

'Your husband. I'm not stupid, Sophia.'

'That's not what—'

'Shut up, now!'

Sophia obeys. Silence is better. Two traffic lights further on I feel sorry for what I said. She was so tiny when she was born, a little mite. I peer to my left again.

'You're very beautiful too.'

'Thanks, Dad.'

'I just don't like your hair.'

'I know, Dad.'

Once more I gaze through the window, up at the blue, the sky. Are you there somewhere, Vera? Can you see me? Then please look away. Dellard says I'm changing. Sophia says I already have. I rub my eyes and, in the same movement, my forehead too. I want

Sophia to think I'm sweating, that's all. Just sweating, perfectly normal in high summer. If you don't sweat you die. Or you've got anhidrosis, a generalised absence of sweating, often a genetic condition. Those with severe anhidrosis can suffer thermoregulatory disorders or, in the worst-case scenario, heatstroke. And then death. I remember all this. So I give my face another wipe. Not because I'm crying – no way, I'm not crying. I never cry! I only cry very seldom! – no, simply because I'm healthy, a perfectly healthy, vigorous, sweating man. So there! I look over at Sophia again, but she doesn't notice; she's concentrating on the traffic. That's good because her driving is as dreadful as her hair.

'I'll come up with you if you like,' she says, when we stop outside a six-storey block of flats in Spandau. 'We could have a coffee.'

I shake my head and open the passenger door.

'Floor two, bay sixty-eight, between a silver Audi A6 and a red Mini Cooper, assuming they're still there this evening.'

She looks at me in confusion.

'Richard,' I remind her. 'You said he was collecting my car after work.' I feel in the pockets of my trousers and cardigan until I've found the keys. Just as I'm about to put them in the central console, Sophia says, 'Maybe we should keep the car in Weissensee for the time being.'

I gawp, my hand still hovering over the central console.

'You shouldn't drive anymore, Dad.' Her eyes flicker; I can see she's finding it hard to hold my gaze.

'Legally, the fact is, that in the early stages—'

'Dad, please!'

I drop the keys into the console, get out and head for the door. Behind me I hear Sophia turn off the engine, then her door shut.

'Dad!'

I turn around. She looks sad. Her wet hair is hanging limply, just like her narrow shoulders and the corners of her mouth. She comes over and squeezes herself so tightly up to me that it feels as if her heart is beating inside my chest. I try to tolerate this behaviour without getting angry. At Sophia, who probably thinks that a hug is enough. At Claus Dellard, the arrogant bastard. At the world, which is conspiring against me, and even at God, who I don't believe in, to be honest, but who might exist anyway and who's trying to prove that he does by robbing me of everything. The thing is, until today I was sure there were two things that would stay with me, no matter how some idiot classified my condition. Two things that don't sit in the wobbly grey mass inside my head. Which might not even sit in the unreliable lump of tissue Vera had placed them in. Two things that have burrowed their way deeper, into my bones and my entire self. Which I breathe in and out, every day, every hour, every second.

First, Vera's death.

I think back to Dellard's consultation room and have to admit that he caught me off guard. For a teeny-weeny moment at least.

But if that could happen to me, what does it mean for the second thing? What does that mean for you, Julie? What if I wake one morning and forget that you ever existed? That would probably be the day I'd kill myself, as if on remote control, without the slightest inkling why. Pushing Sophia away from me, I say, 'Go!'

## LIV

LIV: Julie Eileen Novak is born on 6 June 1987 in central Berlin, the eldest daughter of Vera and Theo Novak. Theo is a world-renowned surgeon as well as the director of the clinic for heart, thoracic and vascular surgery at Berlin's Charité Hospital. This provides him with a tidy family income. Indeed, the Novaks live in sheer luxury in their huge house in the leafy suburb of Grunewald. Vera used to be a teacher, but gave up her job after marrying Theo to devote herself to the family. These days we might think of that as old-fashioned, but we're talking about the 1980s here, and at the time there was still widespread acceptance of this division of roles. In short, Dad brings in the money and, in return, Mum cooks him something nice for dinner and looks after the kids. In the longer term, however, it isn't enough for Vera; she wants to feel useful in a wider sense. So she volunteers to help with children and young people with psychological disorders. This is ahead of its time because, again, we're talking about the late 80s, when depression, for example, or bipolar disorders were treated very differently from how they are today. Little Julie is the Novaks' pride and joy, and this joy becomes even greater when, two years later, Julie's sister Sophia is born. Also part of the family are a cat and an au pair, who looks after Julie and Sophia when Vera is busy. And one of the two, either the cat or the au pair, is called Feline . . . Ha ha, Phil, the look on your face – it's pure gold! But it's not clear from the sources. Sometimes the cat's referred to as Feline, and sometimes it's the au pair.

PHIL: Wow, just imagine you're that au pair and your name is,

I don't know, Nicole or Jacqueline. All of a sudden you find yourself in the papers and they've given you the cat's name.

LIV: On the other hand, you might be quite pleased if nobody knows your real name, because what the papers are reporting on here is a crime. It's very possible you don't want to be in the spotlight. At any rate, as so often in our podcast, the Novaks are the absolute – what?

PHIL: Perfect family. Sure, it's classic.

LIV: Precisely. And just to give you a better idea, Phil, I've brought along a photo that was taken, I guess, around 1997. Julie must've been ten years old and her sister, Sophia, eight.

PHIL: Wow! Where did you get hold of that?

LIV: Well, my dear, I have my sources.

PHIL: Yes, I can see what you mean right away. At first glance this looks more like an ad for a washing powder than a family photo. We've got Mum, Dad and two little red-haired girls, sitting on a picnic rug on a jetty and gazing at the camera. The whole thing looks – well, how should I put it? – totally unreal, almost kitsch. The girls have pigtails with little ribbons and they're wearing identical pink dresses. The father looks like your typical doctor. Charismatic, but also very sleek somehow, a neatly combed Teflon-type. He's wearing a light-blue shirt with rolled-up sleeves and a stand-up collar, beige shorts and dark blue deck shoes. The mother? Exceptionally pretty, I'd say. She could be a famous actress. She's got long red hair and is wearing a bright yellow dress.

LIV: Anything else?

PHIL: Hmm, I'm assuming the photo was taken on the Novaks' property, because it's right by a lake, with its own jetty. In front of them, on the picnic blanket, are plastic containers with sandwiches, fruit and vegetable batons. And they're all laughing. Well, all of them apart from one.

LIV: That's exactly what I was getting at. Julie doesn't look particularly happy, does she?

PHIL: You're right. Because of its age, the photo isn't so sharp anymore. But it's clear to see that her face is a bit twisted. As if she'd just been crying.

LIV: And if you now take a closer look, maybe you'll notice something else.

PHIL: Oh my God! You're right. There are a number of red stains on her dress. Is that . . . blood?

# THEO

I don't want Sophia to come up with me. But she's just as stubbly as her mother used to be, and won't take no for an answer. I've tried everything, even insulting Richard, who I don't trust to get my car out of the parcark without scratching it. I insulted Sophia too with her dreadful hair and matchstick-man figure. I told her it's not surprising she has to wear long trousers even in summer. She's so thin she's always freezing and keeps shivering like a crapping dog. Despite this, she's on my heels as we climb the stairs to the third floor. I remember the humiliating sticker on the loo door, but not whether I did the whatsit, the washing-up this morning. Or yesterday. I feel ashamed. Ashamed that I can't remember about the washing-up, ashamed about the smell of goulash soup in the stairwell, which I can't do anything about. I'm ashamed about the small puddle beside Sophia's left shoe, which could be water, but also beer or dog pee. But most of all I'm ashamed about the flat where I'm going to make my daughter a coffee. The flat is small and dismal. Nothing like the house she grew up in, but a merciless testament to failure. I suddenly spin around and flail my arms like a huge startled bird might its wings. Sophia gets out of the way just in time.

'Shh, Dad,' she says after the initial fright. 'Your name is Theo Novak. You're at home, on the stairs in your block of flats in Spandau. I'm Sophia, your daughter. I love you, you don't have to be afraid.' With each of her words, her hand carefully moves closer to my cheek until Sophia, one stair below me, touches my face.

'Please go.' It sounds like I'm pleading.

Sophia shakes her head.

'Go!' This time I hiss the word.

She hesitates.

'Shall I take your dirty washing at least?' There is something swimming in her eyes that I can't immediately pin down. All I know is that no child should ever see their father like this.

'Not necessary,' I say, turning my back on her and climbing the rest of the stairs up to the third floor.

My world consists of disorder, anger and small yellow stickers with Sophia's handwriting on them. One of them says 'Kitchen' and logically it's on the door that goes into my kitchen from the narrow hallway. On the fridge is another sticker that reads: 'Fridge – only food in here!' That was after someone accidentally put a newspaper in it. I don't know how many of these stupid yellow stickers I've ripped off, scrunched up and thrown into the bin. Not because I've forgotten in some pathological way, but because even someone who hadn't been diagnosed wouldn't be able to count them all. I always do it when I'm anxious that Sophia might make one of her house calls – you can't call them 'visits' anymore. I don't want her thinking she's right with her stupid stickers; I don't want her thinking I can't get by in my own flat. I mean, I'm not an idiot, just a bit absent-minded, perhaps. But that's nothing new. Back in the day Vera used to tease me whenever I'd left my briefcase at home yet again. Oh, my Vera. She cooked the best beef whatsit in the world. Name of a famous Russian aristocratic family with ten letters: Stroganoff. Yes, that's it. As I walk in I pull the sticker off the kitchen door and squeeze past the dining table to the window. If I strain hard enough, my view of the buildings becomes transfigured into the glittering expanse of a lake on which a gentle breeze ripples the sun's rays. Those are no longer walls blighted by graffiti, but deep green trees sprawling up into the kobold-blue sky. That's no longer Sophia about to get into her car, pausing for one final glance up at my kitchen window. In place of her I see Julie, who's about to jump on her bike, and who pauses when she sees me standing here, at the window to my study. I can see her smiling, putting a finger to her pursed lips in a conspiratorial gesture and waving at me. Shaking my head in mock resignation, I smile back. 'Look after yourself, my angel'; my lips shape the words silently. Julie, who understands me even from afar and through walls, like she always did, answers in the same silent yet intense way. 'I love you too, Dad.' Then, dressed in her favourite flared jeans with holes in the knees, and one of Vera's old 70s blouses, she gets on to her bike and cycles away. I shake my head once more and move away from the window. Vera would read her the right act if she knew our daughter was meeting her friends rather than revising for her biology exam tomorrow. Or is she meeting a boy? No, I think. She would have told me.

With a chuckle I sit down at my desk, pick up a pen and open a patient file. Member of the carp family, three letters: Ide. River of forgetfulness in Greek mythology, five letters: Lethe. Flower of (spiritual) awakening, five letters: Lotus. End of life, five letters – I make a noise that sounds strange even to my ears. I'm not sitting at my desk in my house in Grunewald. I'm in the kitchen of the poky little flat in Spandau. And the patient file is actually the morning edition of the *Berliner Rundschau*, open at the page with the crossword. I harshly sweep the paper from the table. And then I howl like a baby for the third time today.

I'm so sorry, Julie.

I'm so sorry.

## DANIEL

'... There are a number of red stains on her dress. Is that ... blood?'

I can't help but roll my eyes. Just the way they're pretending that they've got exclusive possession of that photo of the Novaks. *Well, my dear, I have my sources.* You have nothing, Liv Keller. No respect, no ethos, no idea – at most you've got Google and that's it. The photograph is all over the internet because at the time there was hardly a newspaper that didn't reproduce it. I even think that Theo Novak himself made it available to the papers. At the very least he showed this photograph once in a television interview. They also talked about it in another true crime podcast last week. That infantile pair of presenters likewise kept dwelling on the weeping Julie with the red stains on her dress, only to conclude that these were probably from the cherries in one of the Tupperware boxes in the photo. What price on these ones now talking about an omen?

'... and yet it's a bit sinister, don't you think? Like a glimpse into the future—'

I press pause and yank my earphones out. I knew it: an omen. Things weren't going to end well for Julie. If you're ever in a bad mood as a child and get stains on your Sunday dress – that's a death sentence. You're repulsive, you and your trashy podcast, do you know that? You're repulsive and so transparent! It's only when my knuckles start hurting that I realise how tightly I'm gripping my phone. I shake my head and relax my grip. You can't change people's minds; they don't let you. They construct the truth out of an opinion, and from the supposed truth, they tie a noose. On impulse, I reach for my collar and undo the top button of my polo shirt. It's warm today, oppressively sticky. A storm is forecast for the evening, which means I need to clock off punctually to make sure I get home on time. I glance up at the sky, then back down at the phone in my lap. What I would give to hear the story as it really happened, just for once. I'm aware that people like that Liv whatevershescalled and her colleague won't manage that – but there's hope, each time there's hope: that whore with her purred promises. No, I decide. I'm not going to fall for it this time, as I did in the past. That's never going to happen to me again. I look up from my lap at the garden. One of my colleagues, Anna, is out with Frau Lessing from room 316.

They're going at a snail's pace, Frau Lessing supporting herself on her walking frame. Anna occasionally checks her watch while her eighty-two-year-old charge is busy coordinating her careful steps as well as taking in her surroundings. I watch her smile as she points at one of the trees, a bottlebrush buckeye, with its long panicles of white flowers, while Anna's eyes are back on her wrist. No patience, no manners, no sympathy. When Frau Lessing sees me sitting here, she gives me a friendly wave. I slip my mobile and earphones into my pocket, smooth down my parting and get up from the bench where I was actually going to spend my lunch break. With a few steps I've sprinted across the gravel path, and am offering to accompany the old lady on the walk she's clearly keen on having.

'I'll take over, Anna.' She doesn't need to be told twice. Without a 'goodbye' or a 'thank you', only a nod, Anna hurries off. I shake my head again, then hold out my bent arm to Frau Lessing as if I were going to take her on to the dance floor.

'May I?'

'I don't know,' she says, looking hesitantly at her walking frame.

'You don't need that, you've got me.'

Frau Lessing looks at me, still somewhat uncertainly. Inside her is a generation that doesn't want to put anyone to any trouble. Or whose right to put someone to any trouble has been drummed out of them after a few months, at most, in the old people's home. When the family's promise to visit at least twice a week has faded and the reality kicks in that they've been abandoned here to die, in the care of the Annas of this world, who themselves are steamrollered by their own reality on a daily basis. Once upon a time, maybe, they had good intentions, wanted to do something meaningful, but then they realised just how far apart theory and practice are from each other. A carer's wage is just enough to pay the rent and the work is demanding on all fronts. Not only physically but psychologically too. You have to be able to face decay and death, day in, day out. Perhaps you have to do more than just put up with this, perhaps you need to recognise the gift in it too.

'Surely you're not going to turn me down, Frau Lessing. That would break my heart.'

'Oh, my dear Daniel,' she says with a smile, then she does take my arm. We get going, slowly, cautiously, step by step. 'If I didn't have you . . .'

'You'd have another admirer.'

Frau Lessing giggles. It strikes me that nobody appears to have combed her hair this morning or helped her with her clothes. It's not just that she's dressed far too warmly – there are also stains on her long-sleeved, dark grey top: bits of egg yolk and something else light, maybe the cream from yesterday's coffee afternoon. Stains – which brings me back to the podcast again. Julie and the cherry juice on her dress.

'All the same, I've got a bad conscience about taking you away from your lunch break.'

'You don't have to worry about that,' I say, patting her pale hand which has locked itself beneath my elbow for support. 'I wasn't doing anything anyway.'

'Really? You looked so preoccupied sitting on the bench over there. You haven't got work worries, have you?'

'No, not at all. You know how much I love this job.'

'Everything alright at home, is it? Is your doggy better now?'

I can't help but chuckle at the way Frau Lessing always calls my Queen a 'doggy'. That's only because she's never seen a photo of her.

'Much better, thank you.'

'What about the seizures?'

I momentarily turn serious again. I should never have told Frau Lessing about the seizures, because now she asks me about them at every opportunity, and at once the image shoots into my head of Queen spitting and screaming as if the devil had got inside her. A painful sight, it's unbearable.

'They've eased up.'

'Thank God. We had a doggy once, too, my husband and I, after the children moved out. A little Bolognese.'

'Yes, you told me about him. Jimmy, wasn't it?'

'Yes, our darling little Jimmy. He gave us such joy before he became terribly ill.' She looks at me. 'You have to take your Queen for regular visits to the vet, Herr Daniel. You really must.'

'Queen is on top form,' I say emphatically. 'I just mustn't do any overtime today. They've forecast a storm for later on and that always makes her a bit frightened when she's home on her own.'

'Oh, I sympathise with that. I don't like it either when there's thunder and lightning outside. My husband always used to make fun of me. Just imagine, he used to even go out walking in it!' A brief laugh is followed by an expectant look. 'So? What was on your mind?'

I shrug. 'I was just listening to a podcast. Nothing I wouldn't happily swap for a stroll with you.'

'I see,' Frau Lessing says, nodding. 'That's a sort of radio programme on the internet, isn't it? My granddaughter's forever listening to podcasts. She's planning to visit this weekend.'

'I'm very pleased to hear that. She hasn't been here in a long while.'

'Well, she's thirty now and has her own family. She's always got a lot going on.' Her lips simulate a smile. 'What was your podcast about?'

'True crime. Every week the presenters discuss a real criminal case. What usually happens is that one of the presenters tells the story and the other one reacts to it spontaneously – or that's how it's meant to sound.' I shake my head. 'In truth there's nothing spontaneous about it. I reckon the whole thing is scripted.'

'That's what my husband always used to say when we watched telly. Elly, he said, don't believe everything you watch. They've got a script for everything, including the news.'

We wander a little further. The garden is the nicest thing about the St Elisabeth old people's home; here humanity bows down to nature rather than the other way around. The trees stretch and shoot out, notwithstanding their age or the weather conditions. Even those ones that take the occasional year off and are marked by the caretaker with spray paint for felling. It's precisely then that, in an act of defiance, they waken again to new life, and the caretaker has no option but to back off with the chainsaw. How does the saying go? There's life in the old dog yet.

'Well?' Frau Lessing asks after a moment. 'What case were they discussing today? My husband and I, you know, we often watched that programme with Eduard Zimmermann on a Friday. Elly, my husband, always used to say, the world is full of weirdos.'

'Quite right.'

'So?'

Stifling a sigh, I steer her in the direction of the main building. My lunch hour is almost over and I'm sure my companion could do with a nap so she's rested enough for the OAP gymnastics later on.

'It was about a young girl,' I reply. 'Her name is Julie.'

As if on command, Frau Lessing stops and gives me a searching look. I wonder briefly if she noticed anything. Did I hesitate? Maybe I sighed unintentionally or sounded a bit strange when I said Julie's name?

I clear my throat, ready to change the subject. I'm forty-two now, an age at which you start losing your hair and putting on weight. An age at which youth and its possibilities have become a distant shimmer. Sometimes this is sad and sometimes not, because it's also an age at which you've understood people and how they tick. With people like Frau Lessing, for example, it all revolves around one thing: they're lonely. They only ask questions in the secret hope of being asked questions in return. They don't really want to listen; they're waiting for the opportunity to talk about themselves, because they know they don't have much time left to do so. Their stories have an expiry date; they have to tell them to people while they have the chance, so that there's still something of them left at the end. A small memory at least, a short anecdote that brings a smile to the lips of the person who's heard it long after the room where it was told has found a new occupant.

'I'd be interested in knowing what you were like as a young girl,' I say, to give Frau Lessing her opportunity. 'I bet you were a right little tearaway.'

She narrows her alert eyes, effortlessly dissecting me, and says, 'Stop trying to change the subject. I'd like to know what happened to that Julie.'

## LIV

LIV: Let's jump forward a bit to summer 2003. Julie is now sixteen years old and after the summer holidays is going to start in Year 11 at the Walther Rathenau School in Grunewald, Berlin. She's been a very good pupil till now, with a remarkably quick grasp of things. She takes after her father, Theo: she loves the natural sciences. She dreams of studying geophysics and oceanography after school, preferably abroad. In keeping with the future career she's aiming for, Julie's very drawn to water in her spare time too. She does her first diving certification at the age of ten and gets her boat licence at fourteen. Diving has now become one of her favourite hobbies, along with canoeing, sailing and swimming in general. She and her sister, Sophia, also attend martial arts courses and dance lessons. And, if I'm being really honest, I have to say, how the hell does she fit it all in? This girl must be a machine rather than a human being! For not only does Julie have an insane number of hobbies, she's also got a whole host of friends she's always out and about with. They go shopping, to the cinema, or the group meets up at Julie's house – more accurately, at the old boathouse in the Novaks' grounds. Here they listen to music and no doubt down the odd beer in secret.

PHIL: And smoke weed and snog.

LIV: There's no proof of that, but maybe.

PHIL: At that age, surely.

LIV: Sixteen, you mean? Although some of Julie's friends are in fact older. One person stands out in particular: Daniel W. He's already twenty-two when he meets Julie in early June 2003. And guess how?

PHIL: Tell me.

LIV: It's a total cliché. Julie gets a puncture while on her bike, Daniel happens to drive past and immediately plays the knight in shining armour.

PHIL: Ugh!

LIV: Yup, that sums it up nicely, given the age difference. Anyway, the two of them soon become a couple, which leads to conflict in the Novak household, because Julie's parents are not happy bunnies at all.

PHIL: Completely understandable. I mean, he's a grown man while she's still in the middle of puberty. Who wouldn't hear the alarm bells ringing straightaway?

LIV: Right, but it's not just the age difference that causes the parents concern. Because Daniel W. – look, I've brought along another photo for you – doesn't only look like James Dean, he's also exactly the type of guy that James Dean used to play on-screen: an outsider. He comes from a very disadvantaged background and has already dropped out of his studies. Obviously this doesn't go down well with the posh Novaks. Besides, his influence on Julie soon becomes noticeable too. She starts neglecting her schoolwork which, given the plans that Julie has for her future, could spell trouble. And she suddenly starts neglecting her family and friends, because she spends almost all her time with Daniel W. He deliberately isolated her from the people she was close to, one of Julie's best friends later said in a newspaper interview.

PHIL: A toxic relationship.

LIV: Which Julie's parents soon put a lid on. They forbid her from seeing Daniel W. And to everyone's surprise, Julie actually seems to comply with this. She begins the new school year in August 2003 full of enthusiasm. She's also spending a lot of time with her friends and pursuing her numerous hobbies once more. In short, she seems to be the old Julie again. But then...

PHIL: Da-da-da-da, ominous music.

LIV: That sort of thing. It's now Sunday, 7 September 2003, very early in the morning and not quite light yet. Julie's mother, Vera, has just got up and is about to make breakfast for the family. As she passes her husband's study on the way to the stairs, a bluish-white light angling through the chink in the door catches her attention. Vera goes into the room and sees that the source of this light is the computer screen. A Word document is open: the longest ransom demand in German criminal history. Before we take a look at this in all its detail, I'll first give you and our listeners a quick summary. The document basically says that their daughter has been kidnapped and her abductors are demanding 30,000 euros in exchange for her life. Vera immediately checks Julie's room, where indeed there is no sign of the sixteen-year-old. In total panic Vera races into her bedroom and wakes up her husband...

## THEO

The dream goes like this: Vera's standing at the foot of our bed. She's flailing her arms, and words are shooting out of her mouth like missiles. They don't reach my brain; they come crashing into my head and stick there.

Julie, something about Julie.

Vera has darted around the bed and is now tugging at my arm. I'm a doctor, always geared for an emergency, for a prompt reaction. Anything else could cost a life.

'Calm down, Vera,' I say. I always say, 'Calm down,' because keeping calm is essential in an emergency too.

'Julie!' Vera screams.

'Calm down!' This earns me a slap.

'Don't you understand, Theo?'

At that moment Julie enters the room. Her face is smeared with blood, her hair dark red and stuck together. A piece of paper is fluttering noisily in her hand.

'Have you got the money, Dad?' she says as tears cut tracks through the blood on her cheeks. I nod several times quickly in succession.

'That's good, Dad. I can go and wash my face now.' She leaves our bedroom. Shaking Vera off, I rush to the bathroom after our daughter.

But Julie's not there.

I spin around, again and again, as if it's seriously possible that I might have missed her. It's only when Vera appears in the doorway that her screaming brings me to an abrupt stop. I look at Vera, her eyes wide open, her trembling right hand that she puts over her mouth to stifle the screaming. Then I follow her gaze to the tap. From which blood is dripping. And I wake up.

It isn't the first time I've had this dream. I can't know this for sure, but I can sense it; it's a feeling lurking inside me. I sit up and at once my back makes its presence felt. Vertebrae lumbales, a vulnerable region of the body. I should think about some ibuprofen. $C_{13}H_{18}O_2$. A non-steroidal antirheumatic. Besides paracetamol and acetylsalicylic acid, the most frequently used analgesic for pain, fever and inflammation. Or a new sofa. This one is saggy, its leather cover full of scratches and tarnishes. In our old house, it used to be in my study and was used for conversations, intimate moments when you looked each other in the eye and held each other's hand, for confessions, plans, decisions. Only once in all those years did I sleep on it, after an argument with Vera when she booted me out of the bedroom. She thought it was outrageous that I'd left Julie's school ball early, but an emergency is an emergency. Now the sofa is in my kitchen, which really isn't big enough for it. But quite apart from the fact that I don't have the money to reburnish the place more appropriately, this is one of the few pieces I was able to take from the house. I'll opt for the paracetamol after all. I rub my brow. There's still a flicker of the dream in my head, but apart from that, the afternoon nap seems to have done its job. Apart from the slight back pain, I feel good. I know exactly where I am and I can name all the objects in my field of vision. Chair. Table. Cupboard. Coffee machine. A pile of dirty... whatsits – I screw up my eyes to concentrate – dishes. I nod in satisfaction; an eagleness is flowing through my limbs. I get up. I want to do something. I want to get moving. I want to visit Vera and bring her some fresh flowers. My Vera. She loved flowers. Not those swanky bouquets, but the flowers that simply grew wherever nature gave them space. Siberian irises, marsh gladioli, cuckoo flowers. Vera never bought flowers; she always picked them, in our garden or down by the lake. All the same I'll get her some from the shop by the cemetery. I don't want her thinking I've become stringy. Anyway I wouldn't know where to go picking flowers around here. On the narrow strip of grass outside the block where I live, the most you'd find is the odd stray daisy amongst discarded wrappers, empty drinks cans and dog turds. Then it dawns on me that Sophia has confiscated my car key. Has she? Just to be sure, I feel my trouser pockets and also check the key rack in the hall. Ha! I was right, I remembered – which I'm happy about, but it doesn't solve my problem. I have a think and remember the bus. Any fool can take the bus. I go into the bedroom. There, my desk is wedged beneath the window, another relic salvaged from the past. On it is the computer. It's a slightly old model; in terms of capacity and speed, no comparison to the things people use these days, but it does its job. When I switch it on, I immediately hear a buzzing – the fan. I'm going to find out about buses to Grunewald Cemetery when it occurs to me to check my email inbox first. I used to get dozens of inquiries – invitations to symposiums, interviews for journals, or applications from young people who'd just finished studying and dreamed of working on my team. I pause when I recall how those sorts of inquiries steadily decreased, to be replaced by others, each of which felt like the thrust of a dagger in words – requests for interviews about my daughter's disappearance. When these finally abated, too, I was glad to begin with. Until I realised what this meant. Nobody believed that Julie could still be alive. She'd been written off.

Now I've been similarly written off.

I know I've got an illness. I know how this illness usually ends. I can read a goddamaged MRI and I'm familiar with all the studies. And yet I get the feeling that it isn't *my* MRI when Dellard shows it to me, and that the things he says don't apply to me. Maybe he really is mistaken, or he's only doing all of this to take revenge on me because, because, whatshisname, Dellard was always an idiot.

The cursor wanders down special offers and warnings to renew the antivirus software for my computer. Until I come across a subject heading that sticks out from all the others. It says: 'Request for interview about the case of your daughter Julie'. Breathless, my hands shaking, I click the mouse on the relevant message.

Dear Herr Novak,

My name is Liv Keller and, together with my partner, Philipp Hendricks, I have been producing the podcast Two Crime – The True Crime Podcast since 2020. With monthly hit totals of more than 800,000 listeners, we are one of the most successful true crime podcasts in the German-speaking world. We're currently planning an episode about your daughter Julie – a case that is twenty years old this year and which we've really been moved by. We can't believe that after all this time, nobody has been able to come up with an explanation of what happened to Julie, and we'd like to do our bit to help get the case back in the public eye and reawaken the interest of the investigators. As it goes against our ethos of journalistic responsibility to rely on half-baked information cut and pasted from the internet, we would very much like to interview you for the episode. Only that way can we be sure of getting a reliable, first-hand statement.

The recording would need to take place in mid August in our studio on Knesebeckstrasse here in Berlin, and we plan to release the episode in the third week of August. I'd be delighted if you could give me a call (you'll find my number at the bottom of this email).

Best regards,
Liv Keller

'But this email's already two weeks old – it's well out of date,' is Sophia's first reaction, though I'm not particularly interested in what she thinks. When she realises this, she stands beside me, legs apart, hands on hips, and snarls, 'No! Forget it! There's absolutely no way you're giving them an interview!' Now I regret having called Sophia and asked her over. Just her tone and the way she's standing there while I'm slouched on the saggy leather sofa. And Richard, who she just brought along without asking, clattering away behind her with my dirty clockery. All of this makes me furious. So I get to my feet. However much she tries to puff herself up, Sophia is considerably shorter than me and as thin as a rake.

'It's not for you to decide whether or not I meet this journalist,' I growl back at her.

'Oh, yes, it is!' she retorts. 'Because this decision doesn't just affect you, but me too, and, by extension, Richard as well.'

Confused, I look past Sophia at her husband, who briefly interrupts the washing-up to glance and sigh over his shoulder. Richard's family comes from Brazil. With his slim, muscular, almost perfect body, he looks like a sculpture from an expensive art collection, as if his creator had taken exorbitant care in fashioning him. Personally I find him too handsome for a man you might think in any way competent.

'I don't know what he—' I try to say, but Sophia doesn't let me finish.

'In case you've forgotten – and please let's entertain that possibility seriously – Richard and I are in the middle of an adoption process. And we're not, I repeat *not*, prepared to give up our chance of having a child just because you think it necessary to bring the whole thing up again after all these years!'

'The *whole thing*, Sophia?' I take a step towards her to make the size difference between us a little more obvious. 'Julie isn't a *thing*, she's your sister! The girl who used to sit in the garden with you and organise whatsits, tea parties, when you didn't have any friends to play with! Who took you along to her gymnastic courses and adjusted her ballgown for you because you thought it was so beautiful! Who—'

'I see. So you remember all that. But the fact that Richard and I have been trying for almost a year to adopt a baby is of course not important enough for you to store somewhere where you can access it again.'

'Sophia.' Richard, a dripping plate in his hands, turns from the sink towards her and shakes his head. 'Come on, it's not intentional.'

'Oh yes, I forgot,' she replies sarcastically, slapping her forehead. 'He's ill! Sometimes he can't get out of bed for days!' She whips around to Richard, grabs the plate off him and waves it under my nose. 'He can barely keep his own house in order, let alone . . .' With her free hand she reaches for the button flap on my cardigan and tugs at it. The second button from the top is in the third buttonhole. 'Just look at him! He looks like he's homeless! The hair! The beard! Have you taken a look in the mirror recently, Dad?' She lets go of my cardigan but keeps brandishing the plate. 'He has moments where he loses it, thinking he's been abducted by a stranger, when in fact he's sitting in a consultation room, and the supposed stranger isn't just his doctor but a long-time friend and colleague! That happened only today. Do you remember, Dad?'

I look at the floor, but Sophia isn't finished with me yet. 'Mood swings! Problems finding the right word!' She throws her arms in the air, the clean plate still in her right hand. 'But, yeah, what the hell? Let him do an interview and make a complete idiot of himself in public!'

*Click* –

## LIV

LIV: It's still not quite light on this Sunday, 7 September 2003, when a convoy of police vehicles stops outside the Novaks' house. Within half an hour of Vera having notified the police of her daughter's disappearance, many officers are already at the scene – which is astonishing when you think about what it says in the ransom note that Vera found on her husband's computer. This reads, and I quote: *Dear Herr and Frau Novak, please read this through very carefully and follow our instructions precisely. We have your daughter. For the moment she is safe and sound in our custody, but this could change very rapidly if you fail to meet our demands. You will put 30,000 euros into the black sports bag that your daughter usually takes to her karate class. We will call you during the day to provide you with further instructions for the handover of the money. Don't think about calling the police. We're watching your house and have also taken every technological step to monitor your channels of communication. If, despite this, you decide to involve the police, you will have to reckon with immediate consequences. We will send your daughter to her death. And she will leave this life in the knowledge that you abandoned her. We will dispose of her body, depriving you of the opportunity to bury her. For the rest of your lives, we will remind you of the fatal outcome of your decision. Do not underestimate us. Unlike you, we are familiar with this type of situation. We've been working for a long time in the 'barter' business. Some deals have been successful, others not – it all depends on whether our 'business partners' stick to our rules. No tricks, Herr and Frau Novak! We've got the upper hand. And we know what we're doing. Be ready.*

PHIL: Wow, OK. I need to let that sink in.

LIV: Unlike the Novaks, it seems, for, as I said, they immediately get the police involved, defying the express warning of the kidnappers.

PHIL: That's one hell of a decision.

LIV: And they have to accept that it might cost their daughter her life. I get it – at that moment the parents probably feel completely overwhelmed – but would you really take that risk? Particularly as the note says that their channels of communication are being monitored. So wouldn't you – if you did decide to contact the authorities – do it in such a way that nobody found out?

PHIL: You're referring here to the police convoy outside the house?

LIV: I mean, you couldn't be more conspicuous if you tried.

PHIL: True. But putting aside the fact that the parents are clearly going against the kidnappers' instructions, how strange is that ransom demand? Who goes to the trouble of writing something so long when it can basically be boiled down to four short sentences: *We've kidnapped your daughter. We want 30,000 euros. No police, otherwise she dies. We'll be in touch during the day* – done.

LIV: I gave it a go yesterday, timing how long it would take to type. We're talking about 237 words here. Obviously I'm not a professional typist, but I do use all my fingers and I fancy I can get it done fairly snappily. And yet it took me around five and a half minutes, while I made four typos. More importantly, I was just copying the letter, meaning that I didn't have to think about how to phrase anything. So let's assume that the person who originally wrote the document took considerably longer than *just* five and a half minutes. Let's be serious here: who does that? I mean, imagine you're one of the kidnappers . . .

PHIL: I certainly wouldn't sit down in the father's study and take my time over the note, running the risk of being discovered. I would have already written the ransom note at home and brought it with me. Then I'd have made my way into the Novaks' house, grabbed the girl and got away again as quickly as possible.

LIV: You and presumably every other rational-thinking person in this world. Especially if you're supposedly a *professional* in this strange sort of *barter business*.

PHIL: And what I also find strange is the ransom amount. Surely a family as rich as the Novaks could pay 30,000 euros from petty cash, no?

LIV: Erm, yes and no. Maybe the kidnappers assumed that the Novaks had that much sitting around at home, under a pillow, as it were. To get hold of a six- or even seven-figure sum, on the other hand, Theo Novak would've had to contact his bank, which probably would have involved questions being asked, and also taken some time.

PHIL: OK. But if I'm so certain that Novak keeps cash at his house, why don't I just go looking for the money? I mean, I've got into the house anyway and I don't seem to be in such a hurry or particularly anxious about being discovered. So why do I go to all the bother of taking the girl with me?

LIV: Are you implying that from the very beginning it's actually been about the girl rather than the money? But that doesn't make sense either, does it? Because if you just wanted to take the girl, why bother wasting time on the ransom note?

PHIL: Do you think, then, that Julie's abduction has definitely got something to do with money?

LIV: It has to play some part, yes. Otherwise you wouldn't risk being caught unnecessarily, would you?

PHIL: Listen, Liv. I think I'm a liar. I'm not a group of people as I claim to be in my ransom note. This isn't a job for me. I'm an insider, someone who knows the family well enough to be aware of the money. I'm an individual with a very personal motive.

LIV: That's possible. At least it's the line that the police soon take too. For in the Novaks' house that morning, something crucial is missing – apart from Julie, of course.

## THEO

Light on, orientation.

Whatsit. Kitchen. Table. Man opposite, hands together as if in prayer. Me: open mouth. Words stuck. Only sound comes from throat. Man: pushes hand across table. His hand on mine.

Voice: 'Everything's alright, Theo. You're at home in your flat in Spandau. I'm Richard, your son-in-law. Do you recognise me?'

More sound from throat. Hand balls into fist.

'It was a bit too upsetting for you, I know.'

Me: Want to get up. Want Richard out. Not sitting, not his hand on my fist.

'Would you like something to drink, Theo? Shall I get you something?'

Me: Shake whatsit, head.

'Maybe a glass of water?'

Shake, shake. Image in head. Young Vera. Word trickles out: 'Sophia?'

'I told her to go home. She needed to calm down, just like you.'

Me: Look at floor. There: Broken thing.

'It's not always easy for her, you know? She really wants to help you, but she gets the feeling that you're not prepared to let her. And that hurts her, Theo. It really does.'

Me: Keep staring at broken thing. Words trickle: 'Did . . . I . . . ?'

'You got angry, yes. But don't worry, you didn't hit her or anything like that, if that's what you're thinking. You'd never hurt her, not in a thousand years.' Richard: Gets up. Goes around table, bends down, picks up piece of broken thing. 'Broken dishes bring good luck, don't they?' Laughs a bit. 'You snatched the plate from Sophia and threw it on the floor.' Tears.

'Hey, it was just a plate. You've got tons of them. Some of them have just been washed up. Come.' Richard helps. Get up, walk, little steps, ten, eleven, twelve. Yellow note: 'Bedroom'. Bed. Me: Sit. Richard: My shoes, my coat, my whatsit, trousers, my shirt. 'That's better, isn't it? Now have a rest and a bit of a sleep. The world will look different when you wake up.' Liar. Still, word trickles: 'Thanks.'

## DANIEL

'... in the Novaks' house that morning, something crucial is missing – apart from Julie, of course.'

Some advertising is threaded between the pseudo-cryptic introduction and the revelation of the crucial thing that's missing. Liv Keller claims to be an enthusiastic reader, but who often lacks the time, while her partner is the saviour who of course has an immediate solution. Which is ... an audiobook platform that reduces thousands of books to their essence. I feel my temple throbbing. Because that's the problem, isn't it? People just want everything reduced to its essence. They don't want to truly understand anything, because that would mean having to get to grips with the reasons, understand developments and consequences. They would have to exert their intellect and their humanity.

It's not as if I didn't try to make myself understood. After everything that was done to me, I nonetheless bit the bullet, willing to tell my version of the story. And? Hope at first, but hope's a whore, so in the end, just more disappointment. People out there have no interest in thinking independently. They satisfy themselves with the morsels that others give them because it's more comfortable that way.

I take my left hand off the steering wheel and massage my throbbing temple. I'm feeling rock bottom. Fittingly, the big blue sky has tensed into a low-hanging, grey mass. It's not the advertising that makes me angry, I have to concede, it's the deception, which is indescribable. The outrageous hypocrisy. Because it's clear where this story is going. As always. Julie's feckless, crude, semi-paedophile ex-boyfriend. As always, always, always. I slam the palm of my hand on the steering wheel; the horn gives a succession of pitiful faint sounds, while Liv Keller, undeterred, repeats the name of the audiobook platform, as well as giving a discount code that's exclusive to the listeners of the podcast. Fifteen per cent off the monthly subscription. I can't believe it. As advertising partners, they're also filling their pockets with the podcast's disgraceful claims. Calm down, Daniel. You have to calm down. You can't arrive home in such a state, it's not fair on Queen. If you can't bear listening anymore, you've got to switch it off, simple as that.

'Don't forget, the code is *twocrime15*, all one word and lower case,' Liv Keller says, then she finally relieves the unpleasantly artificial suspense created by the advertising break: 'There were no fingerprints, no intruder's DNA, and not least, the Novaks' house showed no signs of a break-in. All the police were able to find was a broken window in the cellar. But whether this was actually smashed on the night in question, or had been broken on an earlier occasion for a different reason, has remained a puzzle to this day. Either way, the lack of any other traces was a clear sign for the investigation team that a stranger couldn't have been responsible for Julie's disappearance on 7 September.

'Further support for this theory is that Julie didn't scream when the kidnapper abducted her,' Liv Keller adds, but of course her partner can't leave it at that. 'Well, he could've threatened her with a weapon to stop her from screaming.' Yeah, right. You've just been questioning the kidnapper's preparation and professionalism, and now he's got a gun up his sleeve. Where's he got hold of that, then, you smart-arses?

'You know, the more I think about it,' the guy continues, 'the more certain I am that whoever kidnapped Julie from her parents' house that night was definitely no stranger.'

And so begins the part that the two of them – as you can clearly hear from the excitement in their voices – have been looking forward to all this time. It's in front of them like a hunk of raw meat and they pounce on it like two starving hyenas – finally, finally we're here. It's time for the only conceivable scenario. It's time for the chop. My finger shoots to the screen and taps wildly. A break, I need a break, a brief reprieve, just a few minutes. Six, to be precise. Six minutes and eleven seconds. That's the length of David Bowie's 'Heroes', the first in the playlist of my favourite songs. I press play and then reach for the glovebox to get the packet of cigarettes. I light one, wind down the window and inhale deeply. It's only six minutes and eleven seconds, but during this time I'm the hero rather than the scapegoat. Queen, I think, spurred on by the lyrics. I smile. I'll be home very soon, my girl.

## LARA

I should sleep, I should sleep all the time. For many years, like Sleeping Beauty. And, if it were up to him, many more years on top of that. I should sleep to allow me to forget, finally. That was the reason for the pills too, the tons of pills. They wrapped themselves around my thoughts like a sticky film, around each one until my head was nothing but a viscous porridge. I had to forget who I am and where I come from.

He was the devil.

He wanted to take away my knowledge, my identity and all my colours. All that should be left of me was an empty white surface that he could refashion as he liked.

It began with my name, back then, shortly after he'd brought me here, to his hell. My name, which I insisted on, after which he said I was 'uncooperative'. A trait he intended to rid me of as soon as possible.

'What do you think of Lara?' he suggested, his calm voice seemingly friendly. 'It's a lovely name. Don't you think so?'

'No.' I looked him in the eye with determination. The devil just sighed. Then he silently passed me the small plastic mug with the pills ready, as he would always do if I said something he didn't like but he didn't want to come back at me. For a while I thought he did this to avoid an argument. Over time, however, I realised that he regarded his silence as a disciplinary measure.

To begin with, it was just a few pills, two or three, then more and more over the course of years. Years full of numbness, fatigue and feebleness. At the same time – no matter how good he thought he was at dispensing my medicines – there was something, right at the back of my mind, which he couldn't get to, despite it all. I didn't know what it was exactly until one morning I heard a noise. Awkwardly propping myself up, I looked over at the window. It was locked, as it always was for 'security reasons'. The noise was so loud, however, that it didn't only penetrate the thick glass but the sticky porridge in my head too. It was the cry of a crow whose family had a nest in the tree right outside my window. I watched the crow perch in the nest and regurgitate a worm. Fascinated, I cocked my head and felt the twitch of the tiny little thing buried deep inside me. Like a shoot trying to push through the soil. And when it finally succeeded, growing with this shoot was the first clear thought I'd had in years: *home*.

Ever since, I'd been protecting it, this little thought, this delicate ward of mine. I knew that the medicines would kill it; one little pill and it would perish. So, from that moment on, I copied the crow with the worm: I regurgitated everything the moment I was alone. To do this, I had to be good beforehand, swallow everything without complaint; no drama, no shouting. As soon as he'd gone, I'd spit the pills out again and hide them under my mattress. Luckily I was beyond the stage where I'd been tied to both sides of the bed; he'd realised it wasn't necessary, in combination with the medication, with my head full of porridge and the sluggish, washed-out movements I was still able to make, but only on good days. I didn't have a clue why it had taken me so long to come up with the idea with the pills, the plan as a whole. Had I been too frightened before? Had I been too weak? I had no answers to these questions. I knew only one thing, and by now knew it word for word again: 'In Celtic mythology the crow is a symbol of the supernatural and the connection between the worlds.'

It was you, Mum, wasn't it? You sent me the crow as a sign. You wanted to tell me that it couldn't go on like this. That I'd never get out of this hell if I didn't come up with an idea. You wanted to tell me that it was time for a plan.

## LIV

LIV: Let's summarise again. Julie Novak disappears from the family home in the middle of the night without any of the three other family members noticing. There are no traces of a break-in, no unknown DNA or fingerprints in the house, and the ransom demand has been typed on the father's computer in his study. The note says that the kidnapper or kidnappers will get in touch some time over the course of the day to arrange the handover – but this never happens.

PHIL: At first glance, that's unusual.

LIV: Yes, but as your *at first glance* implies, there are plenty of other cases of kidnapping where something similar has happened. Besides, the ransom demand states that the kidnapper or kidnappers are watching the family. This means they would have seen that the Novaks did get the police involved.

PHIL: And got cold feet, so the handover came to nothing.

LIV: Correct. After the initial shock, it dawns on the Novaks that it must've been a mistake to call the police. Because instead of looking into one or several kidnappers from outside, the investigation team focused on possible problems in the home environment; there's even talk of abuse. Theo and Vera Novak are shocked and end their cooperation with the police.

Especially as it's perfectly obvious to the parents which lead ought to be followed now with the greatest urgency: Julie's connection to – Phil?

PHIL: That's right, Daniel W., the ex-boyfriend.

LIV: Exactly. But because the police don't do that, it's the distraught father himself who really takes Daniel W. to task. There's even a photo of the incident, which then of course gets into the press. Look at this.

PHIL: Hmm. You can see Theo Novak lunging at Daniel W.

LIV: Exactly. And then we've got another picture, showing Daniel W. a few days after being attacked by Novak. His right eye is dark purple and completely swollen.

PHIL: The swelling is as big as a grapefruit!

LIV: And his lips appear to have been stitched too. By all appearances, Theo Novak went berserk. In some ways understandable – we're talking about his daughter, after all. But on the other hand, I find it shocking how even supposedly civilised people can get so badly carried away.

PHIL: *Anyone* can get carried away, Liv. It just depends on the situation.

LIV: Or people have always been like that behind closed doors and are just good at concealing it. I mean, would you have thought that lurking inside our good doctor is a thug?

PHIL: A *thug?*

LIV: Take another look at the photo!

PHIL: Are you now feeling sympathy for Daniel W.?

LIV: What do you mean, *sympathy*? I just think that taking the law into your own hands is not the right way.

PHIL: So, what is the right way, Liv? The police had called Daniel W. in for questioning several times. If only they'd kept him in a cell. That wouldn't have happened to him in a cell.
LIV: Are you saying that's where he belongs? In a cell?
PHIL: I didn't say that. All I'm saying is that Daniel W. came away from it quite lightly.

# THEO

So there you are, wrinkling your nose, as the morning sun caresses your skin. You keep your eyes closed and imagine it's Vera's long red hair tickling you. You imagine her pressing her face into the hollow between your neck and shoulder and saying, 'I love you.' Then you think how damned lucky you are. And it is damned, your luck. You used to be a big man, Theo. You had it all. Now look at yourself. The only thing still big about you is your stature; all the world's misery stretched across 1.9 metres. Your daughter, your wife, your money, all of it gone. And, if you're not mistaken, the mattress beneath you feels sort of wet. You're lying in your own piss. It's not funny but you laugh anyway when you realise the irony. Today actually seems to be a good day, your mind functioning properly. You know where you are. You can put a name to everything around you, your mind is clear and the past so tangible, as if it were right beside you in your piss-stained bed. You don't have much time left, Theo. You've got to make use of what remains. You owe this to Vera and Julie. So get up. Go to the bathroom. Face up to the misery in the mirror and grab your razor. The shaving cream is long past its sell-by date, but it does its job nonetheless. You get rid of the thicket growing over your mouth, chin and cheeks and are astonished by the sight of yourself. You wet a comb, draw it through the stubborn grey strands to work out how long they are, then take the scissors to them. You're not a barber, you're under no illusions there. Your cutting is angular, crooked and ungainly, and yet it's probably ages since you've looked as good as this. Almost human, a perfectly normal human being. You pull the stained vest over your head, get rid of the damp underwear and have a shower. You couldn't say with any certainty when the last time was that you did this; like many other things in your life, it's a vague feeling of 'a long time ago' – too long, probably, seeing as how unfamiliar it seems to feel the sponge on your skin. You turn the tap off, dry your wet body and dodder into the kitchen to check the temperature. It's too warm for a long-sleeved shirt and cardigan; it probably was yesterday too when you went to the funfair with Sophia. All it needs are a couple of rides on the merry-go-round and a red toffee apple, and then she's not so sad anymore. You put on some fresh clothes, sit at the computer and find the interview request again. You forward it to Sophia without comment and check the public transport connections. Underground to Jungfernheide, then overground to Greifswalder Strasse where you change again on to the tram. Sophia and Richard moved recently from their old flat in Kreuzberg to a small house of their own in Weissensee. They want the child they're trying to adopt to grow up with green spaces around. You smile because you've remembered all of this. Because it came to mind without too much effort. You smile because perhaps not everything's too late yet.

*

'Dad?' Sophia opens her eyes wide, a mixture of surprise and concern. I offer her the bag with the rolls I bought on the way here and say, to get things straight from the outset, 'It's Saturday, 26 August. Olaf Scholz is our chancellor, he's still pretty relaxed about the rise of the AfD in the opinion polls. You recently had your first wedding anniversary, 9 July to be precise. At your wedding there was chocolate soufflé for pudding that I found too sweet. But I bet your mother would have liked it.' My gaze darts across Sophia's petite figure. She's wearing a top and long pyjama bottoms with a flowery pattern, and her black hair is tied up into a messy, whatsit, er . . . bun. 'You must've just got up.'

Sophia blinks a few times in succession as if she'd actually just woken up that moment, but it's more likely down to the fact that the last thing she was expecting was to see me here. And certainly not shaven, my hair combed, and in clean clothes. A few more seconds pass before she finally takes the bag of rolls and steps aside to let me into the house.

'You're right,' she says. 'It took me ages to get to sleep last night.' She closes the door behind me. Sophia doesn't mention what it was that kept her awake, but that's not necessary. I look around. A decorating table runs along almost the entire right-hand wall of the hallway. On it are a pile of old newspapers, two tins of paint, brushes, masking tape and a tin of turps. The house is old, but presumably it was a good deal. All the same, I'm surprised. Sophia's not exactly the type for such big challenges. Julie was different in this respect.

'Dad?' Sophia asks.

'Yes,' I say, thrusting my hands into my trouser pockets, somewhat embarrassed. In the left-hand one, I can feel paper, three of the yellow stickers from the pad that's on my shoe rack at home. On them I had jotted down the route to Weissensee, the same thing three times over, all identical. I clench my fist, scrunching up the notes. I wouldn't admit this to Sophia, but the moment I put my hand on the door handle to my flat, I was seized by anxiety. What if I got lost? If my mind went black somewhere en route? Irrespective of how well I feel today, I didn't want to take any unnecessary risks that would only end up validating Sophia's concerns. So I wrote the first note. The only problem was: what if I lost it? To be on the safe side, I wrote the second and, because silly things sometimes happened, the third.

'I just wanted to make sure that everything's fine between us again.' I smile. 'You had a nice time at the funfair yesterday, didn't you?'

Sophia sighs. 'That wasn't yesterday, Dad.'

'Wasn't it?'

She shakes her head.

'Well then, I must've come to apologise.'

Sophia raises her eyebrows. 'Really?'

I nod.

'Uh-huh,' she says, pushing past me to go into the nearest big room, the living and dining room. I follow her. She puts the bag of rolls down on the rustic wooden table and sits on one of the four chairs. 'After I got up this morning, I briefly checked my emails. Guess what I found in my inbox?' With her hand, she makes a gesture inviting me to sit down too.

'I'm going to do it, Sophia. I'm going to meet that journalist. I have to.' I'm relieved when I hear how calm my voice sounds. Shouting is for people who are in the wrong.

'Why, Dad?' Sophia keeps her composure too, which comes as a relief. 'It's almost twenty years ago.'

'That's exactly why. So much time has passed.' I look at my hands, the thick, bluish-purple veins sticking out from my thin skin. My hands that used to have meaning. They were strong, controlled, precise in every cut, no matter how challenging. They saved thousands of lives and they were the first thing Vera noticed about me. She loved my hands. 'I don't want to die without having given it a final attempt, Sophia.'

I look at her and notice her scraping her bottom lip with her top teeth. 'Yes, I understand that, Dad,' she says after a moment. 'But what do you think has changed? There are no new leads or openings. There are just these podcasts, and they're not revisiting the case because there's something new to say. They're just doing it because twenty years have passed now, a sort of anniversary. They're doing it because the labels "cold case" and "mysterious" drive up their listener numbers, not because they're seriously interested in Julie. Or in us, for that matter.'

'So what? If Julie's disappearance enters the public consciousness again and maybe someone remembers seeing or hearing something back then, I can live with that. The end justifies the means.'

'Machiavelli said that and ended up in prison.'

'Because of a conspiracy, Sophia, not because of those words.'

She rolls her eyes and is just about to come back at me when the terrace door behind her opens and her husband comes in. Judging by what he's wearing and the sweat on his brow, he's been jogging.

'Reinhard!' I get up from my chair and go over to clap him on the shoulder. Surprise at my visit is written on his face too.

'Richard,' Sophia says, sighing. 'I'm glad you're back, darling. Dad's here.'

'Thanks for the info.' He laughs and copies my friendly gesture. 'You look great, Theo, really fantastic. Coffee?'

'Lovely.'

'Alright then, let me just quickly get changed, then I'll make us some.'

'Terrific!'

'Terrific,' Sophia echoes after Richard has left the room and I've sat back down. With narrowed eyes, she bends down to me. 'I'm really happy that you're having a good day and are sharing it with all of us. But don't think I don't know what you're up to with your behaviour.'

'I'm not up to anything, Sophia. I already told you that I'm going to do the interview. I'll call the woman straight after and arrange a meeting. If there is any purpose to my visit here, it's to signature to you how much it would mean to me to be able to count on your support. If you don't want that – fine, I'll accept your decision. But it doesn't change anything for *me*.'

'*Signal*, Dad. Not signature, *signal*.'

'What?'

'You said *signature*.'

'No, you must've misheard.'

Sophia chews her bottom lip again for a while. Then she suddenly jumps up from her chair and dashes over to the coffee table where her mobile is.

'Do you want to know what sort of a podcast it is that wants you to do the interview? Do you want to know what they call you? Here!' With her fingers on the screen, she comes back and tosses her phone on to the table in front of me. 'I hope you've enjoyed your good day, Dad. Shame it was so short.'

## DANIEL

The storm has passed over the city like an empty threat, which on the one hand is good because it spared us a restless night, with Queen just tossing and turning, keeping me awake too. On the other hand, we've still got the oppressive mugginess, the tension like after an argument that hasn't been brought to a close. I'm already back at work, weekend shift. Usually at this time I would be helping out with lunch in the dining hall, but now I'm sitting on a chair beside Frau Lessing's bed, watching her sleep. She doesn't cope well with the weather either; it really affects her circulation. I think of the woman who was so fit and curious on our walk yesterday, and how there's suddenly nothing left of her. Frau Lessing's clever, alert eyes are shut as if the plug has been pulled on her. But this is what it's like at that age. A tiny change in the air pressure is sufficient to switch her off. Sad, but not unusual, and that's why there's no reason to page any of the medical staff as my colleague Anna suggested. My astonishment at her suggestion given the ignorance she normally displays threw me only briefly. Then I convinced her that our doctors had better things to do. Admittedly, Frau Lessing was a little pale and her blood pressure slightly low, but her chest was rising and falling at healthy intervals, and from time to time she opened her eyes and said something. Not long ago she asked for a drink, which in itself was a good sign. Dying people don't want to drink anymore, and from that point, you can literally see them drying out, their lips chapping and their eyes dulling because the body doesn't even have enough liquid for the tear ducts. All the same, Frau Lessing needs to be monitored in case her condition does deteriorate or she makes an unfortunate attempt to get up. Of course Anna had no objections when I offered to look after Frau Lessing, because it meant that, after overseeing lunch in the dining hall and the washing-up afterwards, she could enjoy her break in peace instead of wasting her time sitting here with the curtains drawn.

I, on the other hand, don't mind at all. On the contrary, after last night there's something restorative about the sight of the sleeping old lady, a welcome peace. I know it was stupid to switch on the podcast in the first place, and even more stupid to listen to the end. I'm aware of what it does to me. I know that in moments like that I get this feeling I never want to surrender to again. It's not the pure form of hatred, not that. It's not the one you might be able to take something good from, which over time could turn into something positive, like determination. No, it's a different form of hatred, adulterated and much more dangerous: hatred laced with despair.

And yet I simply couldn't help myself; I listened to the episode all the way through to the final second. After all, it's not just Julie's story they're discussing, but mine too. Even when it's told wrongly, in such a malicious way. The only thing that surprised me was that they took a pop at Theo Novak as well, at least for that brief moment when they called him a *thug*. I can't say I feel sorry for him. Theo Novak, formerly God, the man who believed he could control everything and everyone through his will and his words alone.

I immediately remember that phone call. It was at the end of June 2003, shortly before the start of the summer holidays, around two and a half months before Julie disappeared – a Friday evening.

My mother, who was still alive then, knocked on my bedroom door. I remember I was standing in front of the mirror that rested above the chest of drawers, on which I'd lined up everything I needed for my evening with Julie: a comb, hair cream and a can of beer. I didn't actually like beer but I drank it because I told myself it would make me more chilled, funnier and a little less nervous. Because that's exactly what Julie made me – nervous, with her sheer presence, her looks and the way she smiled. I still couldn't believe that someone like her could be interested in someone like me. She was so beautiful, so clever, so special. And me? The newspapers, television programmes, internet forums or podcasts could say what they liked, but all I had in common with James Dean were, very hazily, my looks and the values that were popular in his day but are now outdated. Also at the ready on the chest of drawers was the bottle of aftershave Subtil Pour Homme by Ferragamo. Too expensive given my measly apprentice's pay, and yet I'd bought a whole load of the stuff when Julie told me how much she liked the smell of it on me. We'd arranged to go dancing that evening. Or Julie had. There was this club near the main train station where she'd been dying to go for ages. Some of her friends often went there because nobody at the place got around to checking their IDs. I couldn't dance and had only gone out two or three times at most in my life before. But the idea of holding Julie, moving with her in time to the music, and feeling her face on my neck, really close because she was taking in my scent, excited me so much that I would do whatever it took.

'Turn the music down, this sounds important!' Mum's voice sounded forced when she came into my room holding the phone, and so loud that it was cracking. She was competing with David Bowie's 'Heroes' that was on a loop while I got myself ready. Julie's favourite song. Another thing we had in common: we both seemed to belong to a different time. Whereas Julie loved the 1970s, with its fashion, music and ideal of freedom, I had a weakness for the 1950s, no doubt in part because our house was still furnished as it had been when my grandparents brought my mother up here. Nonetheless, Julie and I didn't find it hard to strike a compromise – in the middle of our two favourite eras, the 1960s, which produced a very particular film that we went to a special showing of for our first date. *Doctor Zhivago*. Julie had always wanted to see it. She said her parents had called her after Julie Christie, having also seen this film together on their first date. And they'd also kissed for the first time, like us. I realised what this meant. What Julie saw in us. And even though I felt a bit uncomfortable when she spoke about her parents – especially her father, the seemingly infallible Theo Novak – the fact remained that the two of them had been happily married for many years. That was what I wanted, exactly that. The sort of deep connection that lasts a lifetime, which was so much more important than the mundanely physical – even though Julie and I had often discussed whether we would sleep together for the first time soon. I thought we ought to wait a bit longer. We had our intimacy and our kisses, which meant the world to me. Maybe I secretly feared that nothing else would be able to match up. Or perhaps it was simply my own lack of experience that unnerved me.

I turned the music off and took the phone from my mother. On the other end of the line was Theo Novak's secretary. He wanted to speak to me, she said. I was too dumbfounded to ask why he was going via her and whether the famous doctor wasn't capable of pressing a few numbers himself. Only later did I realise that this wasn't the point at all. It was a pure demonstration of power: he was someone who had a secretary and much more besides. He was superior to me, of that there was no doubt. I'm still annoyed today that this trick, this little psychological poke, actually worked. My heart beat in places it had no business being, even in the ends of my hair, it felt like. With a quavering voice, I asked my mother to leave the room. Then I sank on to the edge of the bed, my knees trembling. His secretary put me through to his office, but not without putting me on hold first. When Theo Novak finally took the call, I was exactly the way he wanted me to be: a wretched little worm. It didn't help that he didn't use my first name; in fact, it almost made it worse.

'Listen, Herr Wagner,' I heard him say very calmly on the phone, 'just to avoid any misunderstanding, I'd like to clarify that what I'm about to say to you is neither a request, recommendation, piece of advice nor the basis for discussion. You will keep away from my daughter. You will not see her again – not in my house, not in my garden, nor anywhere else. And to prevent you from succumbing to the temptation of defying my wishes, you will delete her telephone number right now. Have we understood each other?'

I could do nothing but stammer inanities, which didn't stop

Novak from dissecting me with relish like a fillet steak at dinner he'd been looking forward to all day long. It didn't bother me that he had a go about my age; I was well aware that I was six years older than Julie. But I also felt that, over time, the gap would narrow and nobody would be shocked anymore when she was eighteen and me twenty-four, or she thirty-four and me forty. But I was hamstrung by the doubts I harboured, my own insecurities and complexes, which he toyed with – and won. Because he was right when he said I wasn't good enough for her, I had nothing to offer her. I was a ne'er-do-well from the underclass, with an apprenticeship in *arse-wiping*. 'Don't get me wrong, young man. Society needs people like you, and when the time comes, I'll be very happy for you to wipe my posterior. But until then, you'd be well advised to keep out of my sight. Understood?'

I promptly gave the wuss's reply of 'Understood' and was still shaking for a long time after the call was over. Afterwards I finished the can of beer and dialled Julie's number. Surely her father wouldn't want her to be wandering alone around the city on a Friday night just because I lacked the decency to call off our date. And I didn't want her to be doing that either. It was a dangerous world out there.

Frau Lessing groans, a sound that wrenches me from my thoughts. My gaze darts over to the bed then to my hands. One is holding a spoon, the other a small plastic bowl. Just a few brown marks are evidence of the chocolate mousse that was in it. Within seconds I put both of them back on the tray beside the bed, where the rest of the lunch is. On a plate covered with a plastic cloche are three half potatoes, a pile of peas and a small piece of turkey. Everything from tins, jars and the freezer. I bend over Frau Lessing. Judging by the rapid eye movements beneath her closed lids, she's dreaming. After feeling her brow, I take the flannel I wetted a while ago and dab her face with it. Very carefully I also moisten her lips. I miss my mother, something I often think in situations like this. I even miss caring for her. It's possible that's what I miss the most. So long as someone is healthy and independent, they have enough strength to maintain their façade, and words are just words, meaningless filler. My mother always assured me that she believed me about Julie's disappearance. She stuck by me even when reporters found our address and laid siege to our house. Mum was convinced that the whole thing would die down at some point. But the longer it went on, the more I fancied I could see the accusation in her eyes. Why could we no longer lead a normal life? *Me.* Why did we hardly dare go out anymore, not even to shop, and subsist mostly on tinned food? *Me.* Why did we have less money because the apprentice's contract had been rescinded? *Me.* Why were total strangers creeping around our block at night and leaving threatening letters in our mailbox? *Me. Me, me, me,* and the silent accusation in her eyes, which said precisely that: *you, you, you.*

It was only when she became bed-bound that something changed. Her face, when I sat beside her and held her hand – there was no more accusation in it, no doubt, no regret, merely love and gratitude. I promised her that I wouldn't ever submit to that feeling again, that desperate hatred, but that I would believe. If not, like her, in a Holy Father in heaven, then at least that the truth always triumphed in the end. That rumours, all the wickedness and lies, might have staying power, but ultimately never endured.

Another image flickers in my mind, another memory that slips over the one of my mother. I see a lean, pale boy in front of me with thick glasses on a thin nose. I seize him and scream: *Why? Why did you do that?*

This is what hatred does to you: it grabs the past by the hair and adjusts your gaze to what you've still got left and what you ought to be grateful for, even in the most adverse circumstances. And the worst thing about this is that it often affects those who can't do anything about it. Take yesterday evening, for example. Queen would have loved to have gone for another walk, in the darkness that belongs to us alone. When the world is peaceful and quiet. But after I'd listened to that podcast, not even her sorrowful face could move me; I sacrificed her to the feeling of hatred. Now I'm sorry, but what good is that? The moment has irretrievably passed.

I hear a quiet knock and then Anna enters the room.

'Everything OK?' she asks, pointing her chin towards Frau Lessing.

I nod, put the flannel down and take a step back from the bed. 'She's better, she's just a bit tired.'

Anna approaches the bed and glances at the sleeping woman in it. Then she picks up the tray.

'She even had something to eat,' I add, unsolicited. 'The mousse.'

Anna merely nods; she doesn't care. At 12.30 the dining hall will be cleared up, at 12.50 the rooms. That's what the schedule says.

'Good. Just let me know if there's anything I can do,' she says before leaving the room. For a moment I keep watching the closed door, then I turn back to Frau Lessing. Her eyes are now half open; her gaze is dull.

'I ate your pudding,' I say.

'That's alright, Herr Daniel.' She smiles feebly. 'The main thing is that you're here.'

## LIV

LIV: Did they ever really rule out the possibility that Julie might have staged her own abduction because she couldn't bear it at home anymore and simply wanted to get *away*?

PHIL: I see what you're getting at, because after Novak's attack on Daniel W., people were asking whether Novak might have been violent towards Julie in the past too. There was even talk of possible sexual abuse.

LIV: Wow... you know quite a lot about this case. Even though I'm the one who's been doing the research.

PHIL: I just remember. I mean, the case hit the national headlines for a long time. But back to your theory that Julie might have run away from home of her own accord. Seriously? I don't think so. For one, no proof was ever uncovered that Theo Novak could've been guilty of domestic violence. And then there's the practical aspect. Look, running away isn't enough in itself. You've got to succeed in *staying* undetected too. And in Julie's case, this means for twenty years. How could a sixteen-year-old have pulled that off? Where might she have hidden and how could she have looked after herself?

LIV: You're right. She would never have been able to do that without help.

PHIL: And this brings us straight back to Daniel W., our wannabe James Dean. Also known as Grapefruit Eye. I hope you've got some background information on him for us.

LIV: Some, yes. What we know about him is as follows: Daniel W. grew up on his own with his mother. She, as well as her parents, were very Christian. And when I say *very Christian*, I mean going to church on a Sunday, church choir, the whole shebang. Nothing is known about his father, on the other hand. And as his mother kept her maiden name until she died, we can assume that Daniel was born out of wedlock.

PHIL: Or he was an immaculate conception. That sort of thing happens in those circles, supposedly.

LIV: What were you saying about implausible theories?

PHIL: Touché.

LIV: What we do also know is that after finishing school, Daniel W. embarked on an apprenticeship as an electrician, but soon dropped out. His former colleagues and boss later described him as a loner and slightly eccentric. He didn't really fit into the team. When he met Julie, Daniel had just started his second apprenticeship as a carer for old people.

PHIL: A good Samaritan, on the surface at least.

LIV: I can already see that you've taken a dislike to the guy. But let's not forget, this *on the surface*, as you put it, could apply to Theo Novak too. There must be a reason why the police checked whether there could have been incidents of domestic violence within the family. And just because nothing could be proved, that doesn't mean it didn't happen.

PHIL: Forget Novak. Think instead about the interview Julie's best friend gave the newspaper, in which he described the relationship between Julie and Daniel W. as toxic! Whatever happened on 7 September 2003, I believe it was exclusively between the two of them.

LIV: But Julie had already separated from Daniel W. by the time she disappeared.

PHIL: Yes, and that's exactly why! What if W. refused to accept her decision, then got her back violently by kidnapping her?

LIV: Then the ransom note would make sense, that's true. Daniel W. was an apprentice, I'm sure he could have done with some extra pocket money.

PHIL: He was the one who blackmailed the Novaks. But when he realised that the police were involved, the whole thing got too much for him and he aborted the handover of the money.

LIV: Maybe. But in that case, why weren't his fingerprints and DNA found in the Novaks' house?

PHIL: I'm sure they were, but that wouldn't have proven anything. Don't forget, he and Julie had been a couple. All he had to do was visit her once at home and your point becomes invalid.

LIV: Sure, but ... I don't know. Surely the police wouldn't have let Daniel W. go that easily if they thought he was Julie's kidnapper.

PHIL: It's not about what you think someone might be, what counts is that you've got sufficient proof to turn your suspicion into facts. And if you don't, then you're unlucky and the other person concerned is lucky. But of course you're right. From a legal point of view, we're obliged to point out that we're just imagining a potential scenario here and we're in no way claiming that Daniel W. actually had anything to do with Julie

Novak's abduction. To make it a bit clearer, let's go back to referring to the 'kidnapper'.

LIV: Yes, I think we should do that too. All the same, I'm surprised that the case remains unsolved today. Particularly as the strategy of the kidnapper or kidnappers, including that strange ransom demand, was so amateur.

PHIL: Or – let's say I'm the kidnapper now – I'm anything but the dilettante everybody thinks I am. Maybe I'm even really smart! Maybe I've been playing my game for twenty years and the other players haven't realised.

LIV: But twenty years is a hell of a long time to avoid making a single mistake.

PHIL: Well, I said I was smart, didn't I? And I'm patient.

LIV: Do you think Julie's still alive, then?

PHIL: Do you?

LIV: No. Simply because, as you said earlier, you can't just disappear, you have to stay hidden. And to my mind, twenty years is just too long for this as well.

PHIL: Which makes it even more important to reopen the case and finally give the relatives some certainty. You ought to know, guys, that Liv asked Julie's father, Theo Novak, to do an interview for this episode. Unfortunately he hasn't yet responded to the request.

LIV: Well, he's over seventy by now, and you know what old people are like with technology. Or maybe he's been too busy beating people up again, ha ha. Whatever the case, sadly we're not going to solve the puzzle of Julie's disappearance here and now. That's why I think we should say goodbye to our listeners at this point. We'll be back for you next week with a new episode of *Two Crime – The True Crime Podcast*, with me, Liv Keller and . . .

PHIL: . . . me, Philipp Hendricks.

LIV: Until then, stay happy and alive! Ciao, ciao!

# THEO

I've done it. I've seen it through with strength and determination, like the front crawl with which I became three times junior runner-up when I was with SV Albatros. The only difference is that the resistance I had to battle this time wasn't the water but my daughter Sophia. But I was undeterred. I called Liv Keller and made an appointment to see her.

And now I'm going to meet her, I'm going to meet her at a place where there are no more misunderstandings. Only mangled hearts, shattered dreams, realisations that came too late. A place which appears unfamiliar for most of your life, until you yourself are the person with the mangled heart. On top of this is the fear, because you know you're going to be the next one. Is it death itself that scares us? The inevitability? The inability to imagine an absolute ending? I was a doctor, and for the whole of my professional life, I had to make decisions that made the difference between life and death. And now I'm at the mercy of my own death. No doctor can help me, I don't have the whiff of a chance.

I'd like to tell Liv Keller about Vera, my Vera, who lies here and who firmly believed that our body was merely a sort of vessel. After all, she said, we needed some sort of solid form to be able to move in this world. I used to laugh at that sort of thing. My Vera, such a clever woman spouting such nonsense. But right now, standing here at my wife's grave, I catch myself wishing that I were the one who'd been mistaken and simply got carried away in my argumentation about biochemical processes. For the possibility of an end as I'd always conceived of it now scares me even more.

I want to tell Liv Keller about Julie too, especially about Julie. I'd like a person to emerge from the things Liv has said about her in the podcast, from the character in the transcript. I want Liv to hear her laugh, as if it were real, as if Julie were standing right beside her. This laughter and how we always teased her about it. When she was embarrassed, she sounded like a little guinea pig. And when she found something so funny that she couldn't control herself anymore, she sounded like a drunken sailor, throaty, almost filthy, after too much whisky and too many cigarettes, even though she'd never touched a drop of alcohol, let alone tried smoking. Liv compared Julie to a machine because of all the things she achieved, but I want her to understand that Julie was anything but a machine.

On the contrary, Julie was pure life. She was wild and inquisitive. The things she did came from the urge to keep moving in every respect, physically as well as mentally, and try everything out. I want her to see not only Julie's red hair, but every single one of her freckles too.

And most of all, I want her to help me. Because although I've never given up the hope that Julie might still be alive, equally I realise that she could be dead. And if that's the case, if it's really true, then she belongs here, by her mother's side.

I'd be damned if I'll admit it to her, but Sophia's concerns are anything but misplaced. I'm almost no longer capable of fulfilling this final task that life has thrown at my feet in the form of Liv Keller's interview request. Sophia's right when she says I've become slightly more unpredictable, and this would be very easy to exploit. Nonetheless she's accompanied me to the meeting at the cemetery, to her mother's grave, where I've asked Liv Keller to come, to establish the ground rules for our interview. I will give my account to Liv, and in return, she will help me find out what happened to my daughter. I'm well aware she can't promise that we'll find Julie. But I want her to promise to try, with everything she's got, with all her commitment, her time and her best, most honest intentions.

I want to tell her all of this in the clearest way I can, without stammering, without 'whatsits' and without the slightest slip of the tongue. All of it is inside my head somewhere, in exactly this clarity, and I take another deep breath, open my mouth and look at Liv Keller, who's standing opposite me in her grey trouser suit with red hair that tumbles down to her shoulders and then I hear – *click* – myself bellowing like mad across the cemetery: 'We need to intubate, shithead!'

## LIV

'We can't do it.' Liv has been waiting for hours to utter these words. She's been sitting on the edge of the sofa like a tense patient urgently needing to speak to the doctor, while outside it's gradually been getting dark. She hasn't even taken off her blazer even though the buttons dig into her tummy when she's sitting down, not to mention the tight waistband of her trousers. Silly clothes, especially in these temperatures. She looks over at the open door to the sitting room. A man's black silhouette stands out against the dazzling light of the hallway. It freezes when it hears Liv's voice. Apart from the brief clinking of the bunch of keys, it's deathly silent for a moment. Then the silhouette touches the switch on the wall beside the door, flooding the sitting room with light.

'Does that mean Novak's cancelled?'

'No, Phil.' Liv tugs awkwardly at her blazer to get more air. 'It means *we're* going to cancel. It's just not possible.'

Phil lets out an exaggerated sigh, then moves through the room to the sofa to sit next to her.

She immediately shakes off the arm he puts around her shoulder.

'Novak's not well. He's got dementia.'

'Even better.' Phil raises his hand and writes an invisible headline in the air. '*Shortly before his death, Theo Novak, suffering from dementia, musters the last of his strength in an attempt to clear up the mysterious disappearance of his daughter Julie.* That's prizeworthy.'

'Do you actually understand what I'm saying?' Liv wriggles out of her blazer. 'I can't interview him! Besides, we sent out the interview request before we recorded the episode. And why? Only because the girls at *Murder Talk* got the case before us and we wanted to go one better by cutting in a few real soundbites.'

'And now we will go one better.'

'I ought to have told him that we've already done the story.'

'Just think about it, Liv. Why should we throw away this extraordinary opportunity just because it's come our way a little later than expected?' Phil tries to hug her again. This time she lets him; she's too exhausted to put up a fight. It wasn't just that

Theo Novak suddenly started shouting in the middle of the cemetery, but that his daughter Sophia was also there. While she had her arm around her trembling father in an attempt to calm him down, she explained everything to Liv. She told her that he was ill and broke, having spent his entire fortune on his wife's cancer treatment. That he spent most days in his small flat in Spandau, staring torpidly into the distance. And she certainly wasn't going to let him be paraded at his expense in the dubious entertainment format of a no less dubious podcast. Sophia's right, Liv thinks, it would be wrong. The fact that a few minutes later Novak had gathered himself again, and appeared to be totally clear-headed when he asked how and when she was going to begin her search for evidence, was irrelevant.

'I'll say it again: I can't do an interview with him.'

'But you're not going to do an interview with him,' Phil protests, removing his glasses and massaging his nose with thumb and forefinger. Liv is about to sigh with relief when he adds, 'It's going to be more than an interview.' He looks at her, his gaze focused far away, his eyes sparkling with the vision that's just taking shape in his mind. 'You'll see, this will go viral on every channel as an exclusive piece of reportage!' He opens out his arms and groans as if he's having difficulty grasping the magnitude of his idea. 'We will be the ones who, after twenty years, are finally responsible for justice! We will succeed where the police failed! It's going to be us, Liv! Us!'

'Haven't you listened to a word I've been saying? Even if Novak's health allowed him to go through with it, we have no idea what we'd be unleashing. His daughter told me that reporters besieged their house and crazy people kept getting in touch – some were women who thought they were Julie and others claimed to be the kidnapper. Just imagine that! Her father almost lost his job because the hospital management didn't like their director appearing in the papers all the time. So they put him on leave for a whole eighteen months and only recalled him when they realised that the hospital couldn't cope without him. And now there's his illness, his wife's death. All of that has left its mark, Phil.' Liv lowers her gaze.

'You called my father a *thug*,' Novak's daughter had accused her. 'Is that what you consider to be serious journalism? Did you actually read through your hypocritical email before sending it to him? *Ethos and journalistic responsibility*, my arse! It's repulsive, the way you talk about people in your podcast.' Liv had rarely felt so ashamed before.

Phil stands up. He goes to the counter in the kitchen area, switches on the light there too and noisily picks up glasses and bottles.

'You don't deny a dying man his last wish.'

'Oh, come on, you can't be serious?'

'Go looking for clues with him. Open up the case again like nobody has done in twenty years. Win us a prize, Liv.' Phil fills their glasses with gin and then takes a large swig from the bottle. 'I'll look after the podcast for as long as you need and do the standard episodes,' he continues when he's put the bottle back down. 'Look, I've got the Vlado Taneski case earmarked for next week. That's easily a double episode.'

'I don't know.' Liv sweeps a strand of hair from her brow. Her hair. She feels like an idiot. Of course she'd seen photographs of Julie Novak beforehand, of her mother and sister too, all with the same hair colour. But she's forever looking at photos, and in such numbers that the faces and the individual features eventually blur into a single mass, a sea of people, a pool of licence-free images. The podcast has been going for three years, and each week Phil and she discuss a different case. That's a total of 147 episodes so far, which in turn means a huge amount of faces encountered over the course of the research. Those of the victims, the perpetrators, the relatives or sometimes investigators too, if they've played a key role in a particular case. The fact is, last week Liv was still a brunette and she only realised how bad the timing was to change her hair colour when she saw the look on Theo Novak's face. 'He must've thought I was taking the piss,' she mutters.

Meanwhile Phil comes back from the kitchen area with their glasses. One he hands to Liv, with the other he toasts her.

'This is our big chance, Liv,' he says. 'And now, chill.'

'You know what, Phil? You do it! I mean, you're the journalist out of us two. You've studied journalism, I haven't.'

Phil laughs. 'Look, that internship I did at the paper was one big joke. And second, you've been a journalist for ages! For three years now you've been researching and documenting criminal cases for the podcast. The reportage isn't any different. Perhaps a touch bigger, I suppose. But see it as a challenge that you can grow with and prove yourself. It's time for the next step, Liv. Believe me, you're ready.' He toasts her again, puts his glass to his lips and downs half of his gin and tonic in one. Liv copies him with a large chug. But the uncomfortable feeling that's been nagging at her since earlier today won't go away.

## LARA

So, this was the plan.

First of all, obviously the devil mustn't realise that I wasn't taking my tablets anymore. When he was in the room, I had to act sleepy, peaceful and willing, and even force the odd little smile. It's what the devil had wanted for ages, but I wouldn't dream of it. There wasn't much power I had left, particularly not given the state I was in. 'Give me a smile, Lara, eh? You look so pretty when you smile.' And he would smile himself to show me how to do it, just in case I might have forgotten. Once, right at the beginning of my captivity, I summoned all my energy and spat in his face. He took a cloth handkerchief from his trouser pocket and wiped the corner of his mouth where I'd hit him. He did this with such blatantly slow movements, as if to give me enough time to understand what I'd done. And he said nothing, which was the worst – the silence again, his way of disciplining me. Nor did he say anything when he left my room. I suspected then that there would be consequences. With my defiance, I realised, I'd made a critical mistake. I'd been stubborn, I'd refused and, in his eyes, probably left him with no other option than to sedate me with his medicines.

Now I had to make him believe that this was no longer necessary. I had to make sure that he began to trust me. Trust, I hoped, meant that I'd finally get out of here, finally get out of the place he'd locked me up in for so long. I didn't imagine that he'd let me leave the house, but I absolutely had to make it out of the room. For beyond the door must be something without which there was no point in me fleshing out my plan any further: a means of communication, a telephone or a computer with internet access. I had no idea what was going on in the world outside, and this was precisely what stoked my worst fears. A lot of time had passed, in which much could have happened. What if nobody out there was waiting for me anymore? If they'd forgotten me? No, I mustn't think like that. After all, that was what the devil had been trying to convince me of for years. And for a short moment, I'd believed him. For that alone I'd never be able to forgive him, for that alone. And for this reason, I realised, nor would it be enough for me to regain my freedom.

I wanted the devil to pay. With his life.

## 2. THE NIGHT, WHEN

### LIV

Liv is sitting on her chair as if a corkscrew had bored into her coccyx. A piercing pain shoots up her spine. Everything about her is stiff, even her fingers that are clenching the glass of matcha latte. Liv knows this feeling. The feeling of being not only out of place but utterly wrong. Wrong as a person as well as in the wrong place. Liv is a fraud. And, as much as she loathes this thought, Phil is just as bad. She looks over at him for help but he doesn't notice her. Instead all his attention is focused on the guy from the *Abendblatt* – Max, who he did his internship with, though that was at a different newspaper. They know each other well, Liv thinks, perhaps slightly too well, judging by the looks they're exchanging, even though this Max keeps glancing down with a touch of uncertainty.

'What do you think, Liv?' Phil asks, his eyes still fixed on Max.

*That they've gone too far*, is what she thinks. Even before they've properly begun. And, in any case, how do you *begin*? Where do you start with a case that has already been told hundreds of times from start to finish? At the same time, everything about it is so confusing, so tangled up like a string of fairy lights carelessly pulled from the tree the Christmas before and stuffed in a box.

Now, one year later, you're standing there with this huge knot and don't know where to start.

'You need to talk to the people. You need to know how to put the screws on them correctly,' Phil said the evening following her meeting with Theo and Sophia Novak at the cemetery.

She doesn't want to disappoint him; she doesn't want him to think she's stupid and incapable. *Stupid, stupid, stupid little Liv*. No, that mustn't happen.

So she arranged the appointments for the interviews, and for the past few days has done nothing but sit in front of her laptop, researching. She's read, watched and listened to everything that was ever published about the Julie Novak case. Something she ought to have done a long time ago if she really wanted to be a proper journalist. Not that she uncovered anything new in her research. But at least now she'll have a sense of what she's talking about when she meets Konrad Bergmann tomorrow afternoon, the chief investigator on the Grunewald task force at the time. Before that, in the morning, she's got a meeting with Theo Novak. For this too, she's spent the last few days working her fingers to the bone and doing her head in, researching the topic of dementia. How do those suffering from it think? How do you deal with them? Can you make serious mistakes? Two things from her research have really stuck in her mind. One, that you've got to have patience. Not a problem for Liv, who regards herself as a highly patient individual. She almost sees a weakness in this; she's never learned when you ought to stop being patient. The second thing is that those suffering from dementia sometimes forget how to behave properly. In medical articles, she's read about 'abnormal social behaviour', 'brutalisation', 'compulsiveness', 'sexual disinhibition'. Terms that her head immediately turns into images, which in turn are accompanied by ugly laughter that nobody apart from her can hear.

Again she seeks to catch Phil's eye, like an anchor – in vain. Not only does he not look *at* her, he's also stopped looking *into* her. Her fears and needs are unimportant. Yesterday evening she wanted to discuss the whole thing with him again, but Phil was too preoccupied with reading test reports and reviews of video cameras. The dictation function on her mobile won't be enough if Liv begins her interviews tomorrow, he insisted. 'We need images, Liv! We need to get really close up!' Now he's thinking that, if things go well, they could sell the reportage straight to a TV channel or a streaming platform. Liv feels sick when she thinks of it. Phil and his scenarios. Phil and the invisible headlines that he draws in the air with his grand gestures and his gin-enhanced ego. But most of all, Phil and the huge mistake.

'Liv?' Finally he does look at her.

'Sorry,' she replies, tapping her right ear. 'I didn't get what you were saying. It's pretty loud in here.' She's right, it's not a lie, *that* isn't. The little café in Kreuzberg is jam-packed, the background noise indescribable.

'You see, Max,' he says as if to prove it. 'We're not open to any attempts at bribery. You'll have to wait until we've published our research findings ourselves. But after that, you'll be the first person we'll talk to, I promise.'

To Liv's relief the newspaper guy doesn't appear convinced. But Phil wouldn't be Phil if he let him off that easily. 'This time it's going to be the breakthrough in the case, Max. The breakthrough, finally, after twenty years.'

Max seems to be in two minds. 'You've got to give me a little teaser Phil,' Max tries.

But Phil won't budge.

'The deal is, you run an item on our Novak investigation in the *Abendblatt*. For that you'll get an exclusive interview with us later.'

Liv feels queasy. Phil has already posted on social media, promising unpublished insider information and a supposedly red-hot new lead, and asked the question, 'Is it possible that, after twenty years, we – Liv and Phil from *Two Crime* – have succeeded in getting to the bottom of what happened to Julie Novak?' followed by a winking emoji. If that were not bad enough, he'd also called his old journalist mate from the *Abendblatt*, and so now they're sitting here with Max in a café in Kreuzberg. *Two Berlin Podcasters Reopen Decades-Old Cold Case* is the headline Phil wants.

'Just tell me one thing. There are two camps when it comes to the theories about the case. Are you more on the side of those who believe Julie Novak disappeared of her own accord, or those who think it was a kidnapping?'

'Julie was the victim of a crime,' Phil replies like a shot. Liv can't believe it. Although he aired his doubts on the podcast that Julie could have lived twenty years under the radar, that was something different, she thinks. Just a personal opinion, a little bit of harmless speculation. Just like they've been speculating all the time on the podcast, for 147 episodes. But now he's announced the reportage and the existence of new leads, he's made it public on social media, and tomorrow morning, if he gets his way, it's going to appear in black and white in the *Abendblatt*. Now his speculation creates a very different impression: it sounds like a fact. Liv wants to stick her oar in, to at least qualify Phil's comments. Because what if they fail? What if Phil's promise is hollow and they fail to come up with a groundbreaking new discovery? There might be another headline, but this one would read: *Berlin Podcasters Exposed as Liars*. And normally Liv would open her mouth now. But much worse than the prospect of them not being able to make good on Phil's promise and forfeiting their reputation is the fear she's feeling. She could live without the podcast, but not without Phil. So she keeps quiet.

Liv and Phil were given the silver Fiat 500 to use by a car dealership in spring, in return for regular plugs on their show. They're on their way to the electrical retailer to get the video camera. Liv is driving, Phil in the passenger seat. He's on his phone. Liv catches herself taking the opportunity of every red light to look over. Is he writing to Max? Someone else? She feels wretched. The wonderful Liv Keller, known for being so confident and quick-witted on the podcast. Who even comes across as superior to Phil sometimes, almost a bit cheeky. Girl power, that's what it must be. The point is, almost ninety per cent of their audience is female and they want to identify with a strong woman, not this picture of misery sitting here. In truth this is what she's always been. *Stupid, stupid, stupid little Liv.* Phil chuckles; another sideways glance reveals that he's still staring at his phone. Liv clears her throat – fuck it!

'That was a huge mistake,' she rants. 'You're putting everything at risk here! We don't have any new leads, we've nothing at all!'

She's amazed by how calmly Phil reacts to her outburst. Apparently unfazed, he drops the phone into his lap and turns to her.

'But we haven't even begun yet.'

'Exactly!'

'So? You're going to start with the interviews tomorrow.'

Liv abruptly puts her foot on the brake, more out of anger – or at least agitation – than for any reason to do with the traffic. It earns her an irate honk from the car behind.

'Chill,' Phil says. She raises her right hand in front of the rear-view mirror in apology and speeds up. For a while it's quiet again, then she makes another attempt, more composed this time. 'What are you actually hoping to get out of the interviews? That someone suddenly remembers a detail that passed them by twenty years ago? That one of them may have even been involved in Julie's disappearance and now gives themselves away by mistake?'

'It's possible.'

'Phil . . .' Liv sounds as if she's begging.

'You need to take the next left.'

'I know.' Silence again. Liv hopes that Phil will say something that feels like from *before*, that feels intimate and light-hearted. But this doesn't happen.

'Have you found out how to get in touch with Julie's ex-boyfriend yet?'

'No, but I don't think he'd be interested in getting involved in the investigation. Why should he?'

'We have to make him realise that it would give him a unique chance to clear his name, shake off the old accusations for good, simple as that. Unless, of course, these accusations were justified.'

'I imagine the police would have found that out by now, Phil.'

'As we well know, the police failed miserably. So buckle down. The guy's important.'

'I can give it a go, but . . .'

'You'll manage. Let's get the video camera and then . . .' When he makes no attempt to finish his sentence, Liv takes her eyes off the road and looks at him.

'And then?'

'We'll check out how it feels to kidnap a girl,' Phil says, smiling.

## THEO

you're nice and warm, so your bones won't start aching again, there's someone taking off their cardigan and handing it to you without you having to ask, someone who knows you so well, almost better than you know yourself, is julie here with you, is she wearing your old blouse and the jeans that are tripped at the knees, or the dress from her school ball which she looked like a princess in, but no, that's not right, that's impossible, she passed that dress on to sophia when she had her school ball and she looked pretty in it too, it's not true that she didn't look really pretty in it, you saw the way the boys looked when it came to the last dance and now i really don't know why i'm being snapped at here, i'm the director of the clinic for heart, thoracic and vascular surgery, that's my job, no, it's more than a job, it's a responsibility and if i'm paged because there's an emergency i have to go, i have to drop everything and go to the hospital, and the rest of you know this full well, you know that death doesn't care if it's christmas or easter or holiday or the school ball, i have to go at once and be quicker than death—

'Dad?'

'Shhh, Sophia, I'm talking to your mother!'

'Dad!'

'I said . . .'

*Click.*

The flat in Spandau, bedroom, sitting room, kitchen, bathroom, separate loo. Fifty-seven square metres, exactly 243 fewer than we used to have. But there are four fewer people than before, four Novaks and an au pair, as well as a cat and most of the whatsit, the furniture.

'Sophia,' I say. Sophia is standing with her arms crossed in the door to the bedroom, Reinhard behind her. I'm sitting on my bed, in my underpants, an open shirt and brown socks. Now I remember. Sophia and Reinhard have come so we can practise together at supper. But I don't want to practise, I'm a grown man, once I was even the head of the clinic for heart, thoracic and vascular surgery at the Charité. You don't get a job like that if you're a fool. But that's exactly how Sophia treats me. As if I were a fool. So I said, *Rubbish, you must be crazy, you've lost it*, and stormed into my bedroom. Sit down first; if you can sit down you shouldn't stand.

Sophia nods. I can't stand the expression on her face. 'I know, Dad.'

'Yes, you know, you know. You always know everything better, don't you? What do you administer in such situations? Adumbran, really? So then you must know what effect that can have on the circulation? And we're talking about your mother here!'

Sophia shakes her head, Reinhard stares at the upper-left corner of the door frame.

'No, I mean I know you're having a chat with Mum. She came into the bedroom and woke you up. She said she found a ransom demand on your computer and that Julie's gone. Then the two of you searched the entire house for Julie before trying to call her on her mobile. But her phone was on her bedside table; she didn't have it on her.' Sophia cranes her neck like a tortoise and her eyes stare at me until I slowly nod. Then she nods and continues, 'You remember, don't you? Then you called the police. Why, Dad? Why did you call the police even though it said in the ransom note that you shouldn't do that?'

I close my eyes and Vera appears before me. She's standing there, trembling and pale, dressed only in her thin nightie, and her beautiful red hair looks completely dishevelled, partly from sleep and partly because she can't stop pulling at it, pulling at it really hard as if she were trying to set her head straight again. I reach for her hand to stop her and squeeze so that she can feel I'm there. It's cold around us, walls are moving in. But I'm here. I'm here, Vera. I hold her hand very tightly and place it on my chest. A lion's heart never stops beating, never, do you hear me? I'm here and I'm not going away.

'We were afraid,' the voice of an old man says, while his younger self holds the hand of his crying wife in a different place. 'And sometimes you can be driven mad by fear. Then you have to watch out that fear doesn't destroy logic. It can happen very easily.'

Vera slobs, her whole body is shaking. I place my free hand on her back and pull her petite body towards me. I'm crying too but differently. Like I cried at my mother's funeral, inwardly. And Sophia, she's crying as well; she's still so young and she's crying the loudest. We ought to get her over here, with us, but not right now, not yet. Vera and I have to stand here without her for a few seconds, just us.

\*

'Dad?'

Opening my eyes, I find myself back in my bedroom, in the hovel in Spandau, sitting on my bed. Sophia comes slowly over, then kneels right in front of me. She touches my left leg and says, 'You didn't call the police immediately, do you remember? You went outside and looked for Julie. You went around the entire property, all the way down to the lake, while Mum called a few of Julie's friends. At least the ones whose numbers you had.'

'We did everything we could think of in the moment. Only then did we notify the police,' I say.

Sophia nods and gives me an urgent look. 'Can you remember the evening before too?'

I'm outraged. 'Of course I can! I remember everything!'

Sophia narrows her eyes like one cowboy eyeing up another, his fingers twitching by the holster. I copy her.

'Me too,' she says, when she appears to realise that, despite my claim, there's not going to be anything else from me.

'Would you like me to tell you about that as well?' I push her hand off my leg and get up from the bed. The cheek of the girl! The brazen cheek! I need my trousers. While I go looking for them, I hear Sophia's voice behind me.

'Mum cooked boeuf stroganoff.' She chuckles. 'She was pretty pissed off, at the both of you. You because you'd been working overtime again without telling her. And Julie because she hadn't come straight home after karate. I didn't go to karate that day because I had a terrible cold. I was hunched over a bowl of camomile flowers in hot water, inhaling the vapour, while Mum was grumbling the whole time that the stew was drying out. The two of you turned up in quick succession just after eight and Mum really let you have it.'

My trousers, I've found them. They were under the bed.

'And how!' I agree, putting my left leg into the trousers.

'Yes,' Sophia says. 'Surely you knew, she said, how much extra work there'd been for her in the house since our last housekeeper had left. And that you hadn't yet sorted out a replacement like you'd promised.'

'She gave me hell for that,' I say, now getting into the right trouser leg.

'Well, not exactly, I mean she didn't scream or anything like that. But she did criticise you, that's for sure. Very good, Dad.'

I try to pull the zip up. Sophia's 'very good' is not appropriate; I spin around. She is on her feet again too and standing there as if she couldn't give two sprigs how short she is compared to me.

'I don't have to practise,' I growl.

'Yes, you do, Dad.'

'Sophia.' Reinhard from the doorway – oh, he's still there.

'No.' I take a step towards her, one hand still on the zip that's stuck. Sophia isn't going to help me, no way. I fling my arm in the air and call out, 'Reinhard!'

'Richard,' my daughter hisses.

Whatever his name, her fiancé comes closer. I bet Vera would have liked him.

'All Sophia wants is for the interview not to be such a strain for you tomorrow, Theo,' he says, looking up from my trousers and smiling. He has incredibly white teeth. Vera would have said that he looks like a work of art. But, then again, she was a work of art herself. Personally I find him too handsome for a man you might think in any way competent. At least he understands something about zips, I have to give him that.

'Thanks, *Richard*,' I say, with one eye on Sophia.

'No problem. Anyway, the pasta must be ready by now. Shall we go to the kitchen?' he says, pointing the way and looking at me, then my daughter. I briefly think, why pasta all of a sudden? We were going to have boeuf stroganoff. I'm about to open my mouth but then I remember, I remember perfectly. Sophia and Richard have come to dinner. It's penne all whatsit. Richard cooked. He's a good cook, my son-in-law. 'All'arrabbiata,' I warble at Sophia and get moving. 'Your mother always found it too spicy with the garlic and red chilli. But your husband, she would have liked him.'

'Dad?'

I'm almost out the door, but I turn back.

'I know you only mean well.'

I nod. For a moment I feel sorry that we've had another argument. She's a good person and she was so tiny when she was born, no bigger than a shoe. Vera and I were terrified we might lose her.

'We'll go through it again,' is my peace offering. 'But only once, OK?'

Sophia nods again. This time there's a smile, but it looks strange. Has Sophia always smiled like that? I rack my brains but it's too much of a strain. I need to concentrate on more important things. I have to prove to her that I can do it, the interview. That I might forget some things, but there's a lot more that I can remember if I make the right effort. After all, I can still solve any crossword puzzle and I know the list numbers of all medicines. Adumbran, the trade name for oxazepam, $C_{15}H_{11}ClN_2O_2$, from the group of benzodiazepines, relieves anxiety and tension, list number: 604-75-1. Too strong for Vera, also because of her weak circulation, and it can quickly become addictive. So there's still capacity in the wobbly grey mass in my skull. I just have to store the things in the right place. And I mustn't forget that this is what I intend to do. I decide to secretly write one of those silly little notes and stick it on the headrest of my bed so that I wake up with this decision tomorrow morning and it really etches itself on my memory.

'I wanted to give your mother an opipramol,' I tell Sophia, who looks at me in surprise. 'At least half a tablet. Just to calm her down a bit. But she refused, she wanted to keep a clear head. She said: *We have to call the police, Theo. There's no other way.*'

'And nobody could've known, of course, that Inspector Bergmann and his team would make so many mistakes,' Sophia says.

'Yes,' I reply. 'They made a lot of mistakes, didn't they?'

'And perhaps that's what cost Julie her life in the end.'

I swallow. I don't want anyone to tell me that Julie is dead. Maybe it's true. Maybe she's with Vera, up in heaven, or under the earth, buried somewhere. But nobody must say that, those words mustn't be spoken until we know it's absolutely certain.

'But what if she's still alive?'

Within seconds Sophia is beside me, giving me a firm hug.

'You think so,' I say to the side of her head. 'You think she's dead.'

Sophia lets go of me, puts a hand on my cheek and caresses it softly. Her eyes are glassy. 'No,' she says, 'forget what I said. It was stupid of me. We never gave up hope then, and we're not going to now, either. OK? Let's keep hoping.'

I nod.

'Let's keep hoping, Dad,' she repeats and smiles again. This time it looks whatsit. It goes better with her face. Just her hair colour is dreadful. Vera wouldn't have liked it either.

## LARA

I'd imagined it would be simple, gaining his trust so he'd let me out of the room. Out where I might not find freedom immediately, but perhaps a telephone or computer with an internet connection. But I didn't seem to get through to him at all. I was good and willing, as he'd always wanted. I even smiled, opened my eyes like an actress in a film, and when he was there, I touched myself as if oblivious to the fact. I would slowly caress my neck or décolleté and sigh. I even thanked him for anything I could. For helping me and protecting me from the world outside. Or, just before he left my room, for having visited me. I asked him how his day had been, whether he'd like to brush my hair or put his arm around me, just for a bit because I longed for some warmth in my cold, austere room. He didn't respond to anything, not to anything at all, and I soon decided that I had to be careful. Maybe the change in my behaviour had been too rapid and thus achieved the opposite of what I'd intended. Maybe I'd made him suspicious. Or the appeal had suddenly gone, now that I no longer appeared to be resisting him.

I needed to think again. If he wouldn't voluntarily allow me to leave my room, I had to force him to. A weapon. I needed a weapon. But I couldn't find a bloody thing I might use as one. The mirror in the bathroom – that was my first thought. If only I could smash it and take a broken shard. But I wasn't allowed into the bathroom unsupervised. Not even when I was on the loo did he take his eyes off me. No doubt there would've been a needle with a sedative in my neck before my fist crashed into the mirror glass. And the cutlery that came with my food was useless too. It was made of silicon, like for babies, and bent the moment the pressure became too great. It couldn't cut meat and so my meals were already portioned into mouthfuls when I got them. If I'd tried ramming the ludicrous baby knife into his stomach, it wouldn't have even left a scratch; at most it would have caused him to burst out laughing. The crockery was no different. All silicon, everything meticulously thought out, from the start. That devil! I was in despair. What was the point of my new-found lucidity if I couldn't do anything with it? What did it bring me, apart from memories that played back ever sharper images in my mind? All of a sudden even the minutest details had returned, and when they forced themselves on me, they felt like pinpricks. Favourite colour: sky blue. The poems. The music. My favourite film and Yuri riding in the spring to Yuriatin, where he meets Lara in the library and they become lovers soon afterwards. My mother's scent: wildflowers and Chanel No. 5. My father's favourite tie: dark grey with white dots. Weaving daisies into the little one's hair and jumping into the water from the jetty in my blue bikini, laughing, laughing, only ever laughing.

Would things ever be what they once were again? Would my family recognise me? I'd changed, both on the inside and outside. My body had become thin and bony, my hair was dull and matted. And I was so ashamed, I was ashamed of my ugliness and my weakness. But growing alongside this feeling of shame was my rediscovered anger and determination. I had to get out of this room, I had to force him to let me go. If I didn't have a weapon, I had to be one myself. I thrust my hand beneath the mattress, felt all the pills that I'd collected over the last few weeks, and took a deep breath.

## LIV

Liv and the night conduct a relationship that isn't totally dissimilar from the one she has with Phil. There are nights that feel like an embrace, reminiscent of closeness and intimacy. Or those, mostly in combination with a cocktail and a pounding rhythm, that beat every constraint out of mind and body, making her feel alive in a different way. And free. Then there are those in which the night's embrace feels like a vice, seeming to crush Liv's ribs. Nights when her memory whispers: *You can't fool me. Stupid, stupid, stupid little Liv.* Tonight is like that, a rib-crushing night. Phil, who's just parked the Fiat in a side street, gets out. Then he closes the driver's door and opens the boot. They've got a sports bag, black, just like the one Theo Novak was supposed to put the ransom money in, according to the note. But that's a coincidence. They've had the bag for a long time; Liv often takes it with her to yoga. A coincidence, yes, yes. Or perhaps it's a sign, a harbinger of impending disaster? *Stop*, she tells herself silently. *You're working yourself up into something.*

'Are you coming?' she hears Phil say before he shuts the boot. Liv closes her eyes briefly then gets out too.

The walk there drags, even though it's only a few hundred metres. Only every second street lamp is working, a cost-cutting measure by the city. Although this is a residential area, the individual properties have the luxury of being on large plots of land you hardly ever find in Berlin. They stop in front of an opulent wrought-iron gate. Phil gives it only a slight shake, but that doesn't stop Liv from flinching. The metallic squeak sounds to her like a cry.

'Locked,' he says, and for a moment he's lost in thought. Restorative moments of silence in which all she can hear is the lake in the distance, a few waves roused by the night wind. More importantly, these are moments in which Liv hopes Phil will come to his senses. What they're doing here is totally idiotic. And reckless to boot.

'Have you got your purse?' Phil asks.

'Why?'

'Maybe we can open the lock with a card.'

Liv shakes her head.

'Hmm,' Phil says. Liv follows his gaze, which is now sizing up the wall. Flanking the gate on both sides, it's overgrown with ivy and about two metres tall – not insurmountable, Liv fears. A thought that's evidently occurred to Phil too, for now he stretches, and on tiptoes he's able to touch the top. 'Leg-up,' he whispers to Liv, bringing his hand back down. 'Get your phone ready.'

Despite all her inner opposition, Liv feels in her back pocket and takes out the device that's attached to a cord. She hangs it around her neck and then puts a foot on Phil's crossed hands. Once he's helped her up on to the wall, he tells her to switch her phone torch on.

'I don't want to jump,' she whines, phone in hand, the torch pointing downwards. Beneath her, undergrowth and dead leaves hide the true state of the ground. 'I really don't fancy breaking anything.'

'Shh!' Phil says, then whispers, 'Is there ivy on the other side of the wall too?'

'Yes,' Liv whispers back. A mistake for, according to Phil, decades-old, solid ivy makes an excellent ladder. And he's right.

'We're getting into very hot water here,' Liv says, after Phil has thrown the bag over the wall and now, the toes of his shoes hooked into the ivy, climbs over too.

'Just give it a break, will you?' he replies. 'We've gone through this a hundred times already.'

They had indeed, for the whole of the rest of the afternoon and late into the evening. It's now just after twelve o'clock. The night has swallowed the city and, with it, every ounce of reason, it seems. This is a residential area, for Christ's sake. Yes, the gardens are extensive, but people live here nonetheless. People, on either side of the street. These people could look out of their windows at any point, spot them and call the police.

'This is just bonkers,' Liv says.

But Phil just takes the phone from her neck, puts it in her hand and then angles the hand so that the torch function is pointing at the sports bag and he can take out and assemble the equipment. When he's done, he points the lens at Liv and says, 'Let's go.' Then he presses the record button, just as Liv presses a button, an internal one. Operate. Putting on a faint smile, she clears her throat in preparation for her professional speaking voice.

'It's Thursday, 31 August 2023. In exactly one week, it will be twenty years since the puzzling disappearance of the then sixteen-year-old Julie Novak.' She throws up her hands in a hammy gesture of bafflement. 'How often has this case been discussed? How many investigators, journalists and amateur detectives have dabbled with it? The answer is: countless. And yet none of them has ventured as deeply into this case as we're doing now. All of them have eventually given up, out of frustration and maybe out of fear too. For one thing is clear: anyone investigating a crime like this has to accept they might be putting themselves in danger. Are we ready for this? Well, I am. What about you, Phil?'

'You bet!'

'No surprise there! And as for you, dear crime gang, you're coming along too, right up close to the action. For as you can see, we've decided to produce this reportage not just as a podcast to listen to. No, this time we're also equipped with a video camera so that we and you miss nothing – and I mean absolutely nothing. So get ready to explore with us the mystery surrounding Julie Novak's disappearance.'

The smile on Liv's face locks and the enthusiasm in her face gives way to uncertainty as she waits for Phil to approve her performance.

'Perfect!' he says, pausing the recording that he now reviews on the display. Liv hears her own voice and how indifferently she reels off the script. Phil wrote it; Liv finds the text slightly overblown, especially the bit about the fear. It sounds as if they're exposing a drug ring or poking around in other dangerous domains. But she keeps the objection to herself; it seems ridiculous in view of everything else: Phil's ill-considered promise to solve the case, his plan for tonight and, not to be forgotten, the tense mood between them.

'Perfect,' he says once more, giving Liv a kiss on the side of the head. 'The image is a bit dark, but maybe that's a good thing. *Blair Witch* vibes.' He laughs and Liv does too. She doesn't want to brood any longer; she wants to focus on the fact that Phil's with her and that what they're doing here might bring them closer together again. *We'll check out how it feels to kidnap a girl.*

Liv takes a deep breath and says, 'OK, then, let's go.'

The trees cut contours in the night and the odd root sticks up out of the ground, tripping Liv up a few times. Nobody has looked after the garden for a long time, a fact not even the darkness can hide. In front of them the house rises as a massive black fortress, the moonlight reflecting in its windows as if in dead eyes. Phil wants Liv to do a commentary as they approach the house. He lets her go ahead, capturing every step and stumble with the camera. They go to the right around the house, where the window to the cellar is. They know this from a diagram that was published on an internet forum for amateur sleuths, a ground plan. Liv stops right in front of the window, her phone torch pointing at the opening. The glass is missing; just a few shards jut out from the plastic frame like tiny sharp teeth. On a nod from Phil, Liv describes her impressions.

LIV: So, as you can see, it could be pretty tight. It's not so much the width of the window that's the problem, which I guess might be around, er, eighty centimetres. But the height! What do you think, Phil?
PHIL: Thirty, forty centimetres, I'd say. This window was clearly put in afterwards, because if we go on to the next one . . .
LIV: Yes, OK, I see what you mean. Guys, I hope you can sort of

make this out. Unlike the first window, here we have a steel window with bars in front of it. Getting in here would surely be a bit tricky. Which means that the first window – come on, let's go back – was basically the only possible way in for the kidnapper. At any rate, we can see very clearly that the window has never been repaired, even after twenty years. But this doesn't necessarily mean that (a) it was smashed, or that (b) this must have happened on the night that Julie disappeared.

PHIL: But how would the window have broken if someone didn't smash it?

LIV: Oh, I dunno. In a storm, perhaps? The fact remains, the police were unable to find any traces of a break-in anywhere else in the house. So, if someone really did get in, it looks like it must have indeed been through this window.

PHIL: Don't be fooled by Liv's highly professional window analysis. Can you see how she's trembling? She's shit-scared.

LIV: So? I mean, we're virtually breaking in ourselves here.

PHIL: Just like the kidnapper.

LIV: Or kidnappers.

PHIL: Yeah, yeah. What's far more interesting is that they – just like us – must've run the risk of getting caught. I mean, there were people living in this house. Which means the kidnapper was absolutely hard-nosed. They knew exactly what they were doing. And what – or *who* – they wanted.

LIV: Another possibility is that he – or she – didn't climb in through this window. For if someone had smashed the windowpane that night, surely this would have woken the Novaks.

PHIL: Not necessarily. This is a big house and all the bedrooms are on the upper floor. They're also on the side facing the lake.

LIV: OK, you've got a point. But the question remains of whether the dimensions of the window would allow someone to get in this way.

PHIL: Which is exactly what we're about to find out.

LIV: Oh God. You're going to land us in prison.

PHIL: You have to go in backwards, on your tummy, feet first through the opening.

LIV: Yeah, yeah, I get it . . . Hang on a sec . . . Ow, my knee.

PHIL: Wait, your gloves! I mean, we don't want to leave any fingerprints behind, either.

LIV: Yes, gloves, almost forgot them. They're in my coat pocket. OK, let's go. Take my phone.

PHIL: Backwards, I said.

LIV: I know.

PHIL: Slowly.

LIV: Ow! Shit! The shards are digging into my hip. This is anything but pleasant.

PHIL: Tonight on the menu, we have slices of Liv. Watch your head!

LIV: The problem is that my legs are hanging in mid-air. I'm trying to feel for the floor, but . . . Wait, my left foot has knocked something, something narrow. A pipe or something. Maybe I can stand on it.

PHIL: Have a go.

LIV: Yes, I will. OK, wait . . . yes, it's taking my weight, now I can—

PHIL: Mind your head!

LIV: Yeah, yeah, I'm through. Give me my phone.

PHIL: She's through, guys! It worked.

LIV: Now I'm keen to see how you manage. I mean, you're a fair bit taller than me and you've got a more muscular body.

PHIL: We're about to find out. Here, take the camera . . . Liv?

LIV: Shit, Phil, it's completely dark down here.

PHIL: Yes, that sort of happens with cellars. Use the phone torch again. Watch out, I'm on my way.

LIV: Stand on the pipe first.

PHIL: OK.

LIV: Seems like this is the boiler room. Something's dripping. And it smells a bit mouldy.

PHIL: The house has been empty for a long time. Careful . . . Oh, my head, shit!

LIV: Do you know what I'm wondering? Why *is* the house empty? Supposedly Theo Novak has financial difficulties, but from what we've been able to find out this house was never sold. Why not? It must be worth millions.

PHIL: Definitely, given the size and location. But no idea. Ask him tomorrow in your interview. OK, give me back the camera. Guys, you can see that I managed it too. So, assuming the kidnapper wasn't two metres tall, didn't weigh a hundred and fifty kilos, and was in reasonable shape, they can certainly have got into the house this way.

LIV: Or *kidnappers*.

PHIL: If you want. Look, is that a door?

LIV: You want to go on? Seriously?

PHIL: Of course. It's a shame that our community can only see this afterwards. Because I'm sure that if we were live and took a vote on it, everyone would be in favour.

LIV: I really do feel like I'm in *The Blair Witch Project* right now. The door's stuck.

PHIL: Let me try. One, two, three ... There. OK, on we go. You go ahead with the phone torch. Describe for us what you see.

LIV: We're in a corridor. There are two further doors, probably leading to other cellar rooms. Shall we take a peek?

PHIL: Later. Let's go up to the living area first.

LIV: I don't know ... Can you smell that?

PHIL: Yes, nobody's aired this place in ages. Come on, up the stairs.

LIV: Ugh, the stairs. The way they creak is so creepy.

PHIL: It's an old house, for God's sake. Don't get your knickers in a twist.

LIV: I hate you, I really do. OK, the next door. Are you coming?

PHIL: Don't worry, I'm right behind you.

LIV: Ah, that's the kitchen.

PHIL: Wave the torch around a bit so we can see something.

LIV: The units are still there, but one of the doors to a wall cupboard is off its hinges. The cooker is covered with a plate. And look, the marks on the floor here. You can see exactly where the dining table and chairs were.

PHIL: Wait a sec, I have to adjust the focus. Shine the phone torch on it.

LIV: There's a cup on the work surface.

PHIL: Wait, I'm panning.

LIV: Sort of sad, isn't it?

PHIL: The cup?

LIV: Well, yeah. Maybe Theo Novak made himself one last coffee. Then he sat here somewhere in silence, going over in his mind all the years he spent with his family in this house before he finally left it forever.

PHIL: Tissue alert!

LIV: What? It might have happened like that!

PHIL: All I'm saying is that it sounds a bit melodramatic. But who knows . . .

LIV: Phil?

PHIL: Yeah, I just want—

LIV: Phil!

PHIL: What is it?

LIV: There's still coffee in it.

PHIL: Well, maybe good old Theo was in a bit of a hurry to get out of here.

LIV: No, that's what I'm getting at. After so many years, the coffee would've evaporated by now. Come here, for God's sake!

PHIL: Alright, alright. What's wrong?

LIV: The . . . the coffee! It's still warm!

# DANIEL

On the journey to work, I stopped by the supermarket, even though I was already late. So what do we have now? An idiot with a four-pack of chocolate mousse in one hand and a bunch of roses wrapped in cellophane in the other. I stand in the doorway and I feel my left eye twitching, my entire body stiffening under this disagreeable feeling. It's hatred, despair. It's never going to stop. They're all the same. How could I even for a second be fooled into believing that there might be the odd exception amongst people? How could I be taken in by them? Fucking hypocrites!

With slow, cautious movements Anna gets up from the edge of the bed and strokes Frau Lessing's upper arm. It's not news to me that Anna is a snake. But it tears me apart to see Frau Lessing getting close to her. Even though it was me who went to the supermarket because I wanted to do something nice for the old lady. Then I came to St Elisabeth, signed in for work, and went straight to room 316 in the expectation of finding Frau Lessing lying in bed, weak, pale and asleep, like every day lately. I was going to wake her gently and show her my presents. The mousse and the roses. I was going to feed her. Arrange the roses in a vase on the bedside table so she'd have a good view of them all the time and know that she wasn't alone. That there's somebody here who cares about her deeply. How much I've looked after her this last week! How much I hoped she'd get better! Just enough so we could chat again, that would have sufficed for me. Like I did with my mother when she lay in bed, too ill to hold on to any sort of ego, but well enough to address what really mattered with a clear mind and a meek heart. What a wonderful time that was and I'd love to have something similar with Frau Lessing. But she's fine. She's sitting upright in bed, a pillow at her back, a cardigan over her nightie, glasses on her nose and a newspaper in her lap. That's how I found her when I opened the door to her room. And in deep conversation with Anna too. They didn't hear me; I was extra quiet because I thought Frau Lessing might still be asleep. And I'd have probably gone in unsuspectingly had I not immediately heard my name and, in the same breath, Frau Lessing saying, 'It's him, I'm sure of it. He was telling me about the girl only last week when we were out walking.' I froze, my hand stuck on the handle, holding the door in position, about ten centimetres open.

'I've always found him a little odd,' Anna's voice then said. And Frau Lessing agreed: 'My husband always said, "Elly, you can never really know what's going on in another person's head."'

Anna hummed thoughtfully. 'Well, I've definitely heard of the case. But it would never have occurred to me that the dodgy ex-boyfriend might be Wagner.'

'He didn't say he was a suspect. Only that there was once a girl called Julie he liked very much and who disappeared just like that.'

At first I thought they were talking about the podcast. That Anna might have listened to the episode too. But then I thought this was an overestimation of Anna's powers of deduction and Frau Lessing certainly wouldn't have heard it. All she knew was what I'd told her about Julie's story. I never once mentioned the role I played publicly in the case that followed. Then I looked again at the newspaper in Frau Lessing's lap and it struck me. That's what must've happened – some grimy editor had been swayed by Liv Keller and Philipp Hendricks digging up Julie's disappearance again just before the twentieth anniversary.

'Since then he's only loved his dog,' Frau Lessing went on undeterred, and an image immediately flickered in my head: my Queen. I thought Frau Lessing was making a fool of herself. And that was the moment when I gave the door a nudge. 'Morning,' I was going to say as I swung it open, determined to put on a brave face. But my voice failed. The feeling – the hatred, the despair – was choking me.

Anna grins. As if we'd fought a battle that she's won. My eyes bore into Frau Lessing's, in search of answers. Is this what loneliness has done to you, Elly? Are you so desperate for the attention your family has failed to give you that you're prepared to take Anna's? That Anna, by the way, who doesn't give a toss about you and treats you like a tiresome job she needs to get done? Like a basket full of dirty washing or a tax declaration. Anna, who's usually glancing at her watch the moment you open your mouth just to breathe, let alone utter a single word. And what about me? Am I not good enough for you all of a sudden? Have you forgotten the devotion with which I've looked after you? How much time I've taken for you? How much patience I've shown you?

*The main thing is that you're here*, I hear you say inside my head.

Yes, I have been here. I've always been here for you, Elly. Is this your way of thanking me?

Frau Lessing looks away, but her words are addressed to me when she says, 'Herr Daniel! What a nice surprise!'

Meanwhile Anna is rather awkwardly fluffing up the pillow behind Frau Lessing's back. 'We want you to be comfortable.' She takes the newspaper from her lap, quickly folds it and tucks it under her arm as casually as possible. That's confirmation, I think. There must be something in that paper about Julie, about me, or Anna wouldn't behave like that. I note that it's the *Abendblatt*, and for a moment I'm tempted to grab it as Anna squeezes past me out of the door. But what good would that do? What difference would it make now whether she spreads the news in the staffroom with or without the additional evidence in writing? By the lunch break, all our colleagues would have stormed the little kiosk opposite St Elisabeth to get hold of the paper.

'You seem to be much better,' I say, approaching the bed.

'Yes,' Frau Lessing says, beaming. She still can't bring herself to look me in the eye; her gaze is angled slightly past me. She knows what she's done. Or at least I hope she does. 'Thanks to your excellent care, my dear Herr Daniel.'

I merely nod, then place the roses on the bedside table. The breakfast tray is still there, full of its clutter. Sure enough, Anna had forgotten to take it with her because she couldn't wait to leave the room with the newspaper under her arm. On the plate is a slice of black bread with margarine. Only one bite has been taken, which is hardly surprising. Nobody in the home likes the bread. Beside it is a half-empty cup, the teabag still dangling in it. Camomile, good for the stomach. I take the little spoon from the saucer and sit on the chair beside the bed. I've often sat here this past week, watching over Frau Lessing's sleep. I've been speaking or reading to her. *Doctor Zhivago*, by Boris Pasternak, the novel that the film was based on. It made me think of Julie and how we once met at her house in a previous life. We hauled the little old boat from the shed to the lake and spent the entire afternoon in it, me on the oars and Julie on the narrow bench facing me, with that very book, reading passages to me. I'm sure I can't read as well as Julie did, but I tried my best. I tried my best for a woman who slept, who occasionally sank into a delirium, who perhaps couldn't take anything in anymore. All the same I made an effort. I held her hand, from this chair. I leaped up at every gasp and every pained sound to moisten her chapped, pale lips, to cover her if the blanket had slipped and cool her forehead if beads of sweat had appeared. I did everything for her, even overtime, though I've got my own responsibility at home. I have to look after my Queen. Care for her and feed her. Always remember to close the doors so that she doesn't open them and do herself an injury. Just like my mother when she once made a crazy attempt to leave her room without my help and fell down the stairs. I have to be with her when there's a storm, hold her when she has a seizure. As if that weren't enough to do; instead I'm wasting my time with Frau Lessing. I inhale deeply and breathe it away, the hatred that's trying to impose itself on me again. And it works. I sit down on the chair, suddenly embraced by an astonishing calmness. I like the way it flows through my body. I break off one of the mousse cartons and open it; the rest of the pack I put on the windowsill behind me.

'So then, *Elly*,' I say as I slowly lower the spoon into the carton, 'how has your morning been? Did you have a nice chat with Anna?'

# THEO

I'll manage, it's going to be a doddle. Any idiot can answer a few questions. I'm not ill. Or at least I'm not an idiot. Vera and the dry boeuf stroganoff. Julie and I and the roasting we got. Closing my eyes, I run through the text in my mind. But all that comes to mind is Goethe's 'Erlking'. We had to learn it by heart in the sixth year. I was thirteen. It was 1962. The Cuban Missile Crisis, Franz Josef Strauss's resignation, the worst storm tide in a century over the North Sea. In May Marilyn Monroe sang 'Happy Birthday, Mr President', and in August she was dead. Unlike many of our neighbours, we already had a television set at home – a Philips Leonardo with a shiny, varnished hazelnut-look casing that only showed one channel. But one channel was enough. In fact it might have even been better than today. More broadcasters mean more versions of one and the same story.

Vera and I were on television once. We sat close together on a red sofa; I was wearing a light-grey suit, white shirt and dark grey tie with white dots, Vera a houndstooth suit. She was crying. She'd just told the interviewer that a crow had landed on the kitchen windowsill that morning and pecked in her direction while she was making coffee. Could that be a sign from Julie? she asked the interviewer. As if he might have an answer. I mean, he wasn't even wearing a tie as you would expect when it's a serious matter. And so it was down to me to get things back on track. I put one hand on Vera's knee to make her stop the crow nonsense, while I pointed the index finger of the other hand straight at the camera and addressed my daughter's kidnapper: 'Whoever you are, we will find you. You will never have a moment's peace until you bring my child back!'

'Does this mean,' the interviewer now said, 'that you're no longer going to rely on the police's work alone, but launch a private investigation?'

I looked at Vera and she looked at me. Clearing my throat, I said, 'Please understand that we don't wish to comment on that.' Then I showed the photograph of my family that I'd brought especially to the studio. I wanted people to understand how happy Julie had been and there was no reason why she might have run away from home, as the police had started suggesting. And that I had never laid a finger on my daughter. I loved her more than my life; I'd never have hurt her.

No, no, no.

I slap my forehead. It's as if someone had been leafing through a book and got the wrong page. This is not what we're doing here. Lisa Keller had switched on her camera and asked me to introduce herself. My name: Professor Doctor Theodor Novak. I insist on the title so that everyone knows from the start who they're dealing with. That's to say, not a fool. Age: seventy-four. Then she asks me to say something about our family. I said that we were happy.

'But then something happened, didn't it?'

I nodded.

On the night of 7 September 2003, our daughter Julie was abducted from our house. A ransom demand was left behind, typed on the computer in my study. Thirty thousand euros that nobody ever collected. This was the police's fault, without doubt. The police made so many mistakes.

Lisa Keller's last question was about the evening before Julie's disappearance. Yes, that was it! That's what I was going to talk about before the 'Erlking' stole into my thoughts, then the police, their failures and their outrageous aspersions.

No, no, no.

'Dad!' Sophia is bent over me, clutching my hand that's having a go at my head. Hers is still very white and wrinkly. But that's her problem, not mine. I didn't ask her to clean my flat. On the contrary, when she turned up here at five this morning, with her plastic bucket and all those bottles of detergent, I sent her packing and simply went back to bed. But clearly she wasn't having any of it, for when I left my bedroom again around three hours later everything was smelling of lily of the valley, and Sophia was standing beside the kitchen table, ironing a tablecloth.

'You're hurting yourself!' She looks terriblyfied, almost like she did when Julie disappeared. Yes, now I remember.

'Shall we take a break?' Lisa Keller has got up from the chair she was sitting on opposite me.

'Turn the camera off!' Sophia barks at her. Poor Lisa already looks so pale and jittery this morning. She even knocked over the cup of coffee Sophia gave her while she was waiting for me to get dressed. Now the freshly ironed tablecloth has got a big stain on it that looks like the former USSR. It doesn't bother me; there are more important things. The reportage is important. Julie is important. Sophia, on the other hand, she's pissed off, I can see it. Who knows how long she spent ironing the tablecloth and how difficult that was? Vera always said I didn't have a clue about such things. That it took an extraordinary amount of time if you had to do all of it on your own without a housekeeper. I expect she too would have been against the idea of having the interview take place here in my flat. Like Sophia. And me too, in fact, because the flat is such a hovel. No comparison to our old house. Three hundred square metres, huge garden, right next to the Hubertussee with our own jetty. When the sun shone, refractioning the water, you could see nothing but blue, an endless blue surface as if there were no difference between the sky and the earth anymore. Siberian irises grew there, as did marsh gladioli and cuckoo flowers. Vera never bought flowers, she always picked them and then arranged them in a vase on the kitchen table. Once, when Sophia knocked the vase off the table, Vera started crying bitterly. Her flowers were sacred.

But Vera's no longer here and so she can't object to my having let Lisa Keller into my flat with her camera equinoxment. And as for Sophia, she shouldn't always be in the right, like with those yellow notes. It's not good for her. Educationally it's completely wrong. So I told her, 'That's how I live. If you're ashamed of me, why don't you just stay at home when Lisa Keller comes to do the interview?'

'Alright, alright,' I say now, quickly putting my hand down. But Sophia still won't let go of it; I have to shake really hard before she releases her iron grip. 'Let me go! I can remember, I remember very well!' I look over at Lisa Keller and give her a nod, inviting her to sit down again. 'I remember,' I say once more. 'Don't worry.' And I really do, even if it's not part of the text I practised with Sophia yesterday. 'Everyone was annoyed that evening, not just Vera. Julie must have come into the kitchen, dropped her sports bag on the floor and given it a kick. I wasn't much after Julie, but by the time I arrived, an argument was already in full swing.' I look at Sophia, who's also returned to her original position: by the window next to the sofa where I'm sitting for the interview. This way she's not in the picture but close enough to make sure that Lisa Keller doesn't try to pull a fast one over me just to get a soundbite. 'Even you were irritated. I mean, it was your sports bag that you'd lent to Julie for karate. The strap on hers had broken. And you didn't need it that day because you weren't well enough to go to karate.'

Sophia gives a slight wince. 'That's right,' she says, as if my words had pressed a button in her head.

I grin. Ha! Even Sophia forgets things sometimes, even though she's young and the wobbly grey mass in her skull is still in good working order.

'You're right, Dad. Julie was pretty pissed off when she came home.'

'Can you remember why?' Lisa Keller has got to her feet again and she slowly turns the camera on its tripod towards Sophia. My daughter purses her lips. I can see that she doesn't want to be filmed and I'm surprised that, despite this, she's not objecting.

'I think she had problems.'

'With her ex-boyfriend? Daniel?'

'That Wegner,' I growl. Just hearing the name makes my fists clench. *It's got nothing to do with me, Herr Novak! Please believe me!* I'd grabbed him by the collar, that Wegner, grabbed him so tightly that he started wheezing. I punched his face with powerful blows only a former junior runner-up in front crawl could manage. Yes, I remember that, I remember vividly. Vera, my Vera, usually so piecemeal, had encouraged me to deal with him, right outside his house, even if – or because – it was teeming with journals. Vera said, *Any loving father would do it. We're desperate and the police have let us down. We need to set an example.*

'No,' Sophia replies to Lisa Keller. 'As far as Julie was concerned, the thing with Daniel was well over. It was something to do with the karate class. Something was going on there.' She clamps her bottom lip between her teeth and thinks. 'I think it was because of our instructor.' Now she shakes her head. 'But it was just a minor thing, no big deal. I think he wasn't going to put her in for the next grading.'

'Arsehole!' I shout out as if on cue. Exactly! That was the first word I heard when I came into the kitchen. Julie saying *arsehole!* But somehow that got forgotten because Sophia immediately started whingeing about her bag and then Vera let rip about how dinner was ruined. 'Sophia's right. Julie was complaining about this, this . . . what was he called again, the karate instructor?'

Sophia shrugs.

I get impatient. 'Are we going to have to X-ray your head too?'

'Dad, that was ages ago. I think he was called Jason.'

'Jason,' Lisa repeats. 'Surname?'

Sophia shrugs again. 'Sorry, I really can't remember. We had class once a week at KSVG, normally on a Wednesday.'

'KSVG?' Lisa says.

'Kampfsportverein Grunewald,' Sophia says. 'But that week the Wednesday training had been cancelled because our instructor was ill or something. Yes, that's it, he was ill. Which was why the class had been rescheduled for the Saturday evening.'

'Correct,' Lisa says, more to herself than us. 'It *was* a Saturday.' She looks at me and the voice of my wife suddenly blends with her face. Vera asking, 'Can't you at least be at home at the weekend like any normal father?' Goodness knows how often I have to explain to her that I'm the whatsit, the director of the clinic for heart, thoracic and vascular surgery, that's my job, no, it's more than a job, it's a responsibility, and if I'm paged because of an emergency I have to leave, I have to drop everything and go to the hospital, and the rest of you know this very well, you know that death doesn't care if it's Wednesday or Saturday or a school ball, I have to go at once and be quicker than death.

'Death doesn't bloody well wait!' I roar at Vera, before realising that she isn't here. Lisa Keller is looking at me, her eyebrows raised. 'As a clinic director you're always on duty, even at the weekends,' I explain to her.

'Yes, I can imagine,' she says, nodding. 'How about a karate instructor?'

Sophia takes a step over from the window. 'What's that supposed to mean?'

'Nothing, it's just . . .' Lisa shakes her head, then fiddles with her camera again. 'What's happening with your old house? Why haven't you sold it?'

What a rude question. 'The house belongs to the family! And it will always stay that way! Our financial situation couldn't be—'

'He did,' Sophia interrupts me. 'To my godfather. Why do you ask?'

'To your . . . what? But I thought . . .' I can't grasp it, but they're ignoring me.

'I think I ought to show you something,' Lisa says, now looking paler than she has done all morning. Lack of red blood cells, seven letters: anaemia. It occurs when you don't have enough iron in your diet or if you lose a lot of blood, as in childbirth or in an accident. Adults can die if they lose a litre and a half of blood.

'Are you a vegetarian?' I ask, but Lisa Keller doesn't hear me because she's discussing with Sophia the best way to get to Grunewald at this time of day, avoiding the traffic. I bet she's a vegetarian, just like Sophia. They often suffer from anaemia because they're missing the iron you get from meat. Liver, for example, is a good provider of iron. 'You ought to eat beetroot. And oats.' But she still doesn't hear me. 'Beetroot!' my voice thunders and finally this shuts the two of them up. It works, then.

They let me sit in the front because I'm so tall, 1.90 metres. My Vera particularly liked this about me, my size. I was her protector. It suited both of us to see me in this role, yes, it was nice. Behind my seat, which has been put back as far as it will go, is Sophia. On the seat next to her is the bag with the camera equinoxment. Lisa Keller is driving her silver sardine tin along the A100. This isn't a car for grown-ups, at best it's for young girls who've just passed their test, or petite types like Sophia. Besides that I would have taken the B2. That's how I always used to drive home from the clinic. It's faster, fewer roadworks. Lisa's right hand presses the button for the radio. She switches from one station to the other.

'That one!' I call out when she gets to a classical music station that's currently playing Tchaikovsky's 'Warts of the Flowers'. I turn to Sophia. 'That was the last song at your school ball, do you remember?'

Sophia doesn't react; she merely stares out of the window. She's obstinous, just like her mother. She's not happy we're on our way to Grunewald, but she wouldn't let us go without her.

'One, two, three,' I count out loud, to remind her of that evening, the school ball. It was a lovely evening, I remember that very well. Sophia was wearing Julie's dress, which she looked pretty in too, though it fitted Julie better because she was taller than Sophia and a touch slimmer. 'You have to begin with your left foot to the side,' I told her, in case she'd forgotten the steps. 'Pull in your right foot, to the side, then the left, it's quite simple.'

Sophia still isn't reacting. Is she angry with me? I'd practised specially for the occasion because traditionally the girls had the last dance with their fathers, and the boys with their mothers. I mumble to myself. Sophia is a hard nut to crack. Then I look at Lisa. She's got a nice profile and I like her long red hair. I turn back to Sophia and say, shaking my head, 'I don't like your hair. The black is ugly.'

Sophia sighs but keeps looking out of the window.

'I know, Dad.'

'Your mother wouldn't have liked it either.'

'I know.'

'Look at me when I'm talking to you, young lady!'

Finally she obeys.

'But we still love you, you understand? And nothing's ever going to change that. No matter what happens.'

Sophia smiles, not properly, but it's something at least. 'I know,' she says, now for the third time, then she turns back to the window.

It's not as if I don't understand her. It's because of Grunewald. We were happy there and that's where Julie disappeared. It's not easy to decide whether it's a nice place or a bad one. All the same, I'd never— Hold on!

'Sophia!'

She gives a start, as does Lisa, even though this is none of her business.

'Why would I have sold the house? We always said we had to keep the house. What if Julie comes home? What if she rings the bell and strangers open the door to her? That mustn't happen!' I can feel pain in my neck vertebrae from turning round to the back seat. And now my heart is beating far too quickly too. 'No, we're not going to sell the house, Sophia! Over my dead body!'

My daughter shifts forward and lays a hand on my shoulder. 'We had to do it, Dad. Mum got ill, remember? We needed the money to pay for her treatment. Besides, Claus promised we could go back there any time.' She smiles again, differently this time. 'He'd never let strangers move in there. He's a good man.'

'Claus,' I say through gritted teeth.

'You know the new owner, then?' Lisa pipes up.

'My godfather. Mine and Julie's. He was a long-time colleague of my father's and a close family friend.'

I shake my head angrily and dislodge Sophia's hand from my shoulder. Sophia, she's lying again! She's lying!

'I'd never have sold our house to that arrogant bastard.'

'You had to!' Sophia insists.

'We have to,' Vera agrees with her from somewhere.

I rub my brow.

'We have to,' Vera says again. 'Because there's no bloody alternative!'

Now I can see her, my Vera. My head has found her, Vera and the moment in question. I see her sitting in our old kitchen. On the table in front of her is the vase with flowers we'd picked together that morning. She wasn't to go on her own anymore; she had low blood pressure. Also on the table are boxes of pills. Within me there is a nasty sense of unease and anger. I had to get moving but I knew it would make Vera nervous if I kept racing around the kitchen as if I'd been wound up. She even felt dizzy watching, so she looked away. But I wanted her to look at me; we had to talk about it. I forced myself to make calm movements, I wandered slowly over to the kettle. A cup of tea would do Vera the world of good right now. Or at least she'd believe it would, having read a magazine article about how the high proportion of plant compounds in green tea supposedly reduced the lymphocyte count by at least twenty per cent. Of course I'd talked to her about plant compounds, so-called polyphenols, especially epigallocatechin gallate, which had an antioxidant effect. I must have explained this a hundred times. Yes, antioxidants could render free radicals in the body harmless. However – and this was something Vera's article hadn't mentioned – antioxidants could also affect cancer treatment by neutralising the impact of other medicines.

I usually saw to it, therefore, that she didn't drink too much green tea. But right now I realised she needed one, just like I could've done with a schnapps. Claus called himself a friend and then this happened. This!

'The price, Vera!' I shouted above the roar of water from the tap. 'The bald-faced cheek of it!' Vera waited with her response until I'd filled the kettle, put it on to its base and switched it on.

'For one thing, you'd have to find a buyer who could come up with the money quickly. And second, Claus has promised not to sell the house on for the time being.'

*'For the time being,'* I echoed then shot my hand out towards the kitchen window. The lake was peeking out from behind the trees with its blue shimmer. 'Out there, Vera! That's where I intended to sit and die one day!'

'I know.'

'It's what I said the day we moved in. This is the place we're going to live for the rest of our days. This here is our home!'

Vera began to cry again. Both of us knew the truth: if she didn't start the new therapy in the US quickly enough, the rest of our days was now. I lowered my arm. The water was boiling. We needed the money. We needed Claus.

*

'We needed the money,' I repeat in Lisa Keller's direction when the present moment superimposes itself on my memory. We're in a car, on the way to Grunewald, to our old house. 'I'd always earned very well, but we lived our lives accordingly. We had everything – the house, two boats, three cars. We employed a gardener and for long periods of time had an au pair or housekeeper too. Vera supported a few charitable organisations. The girls got everything they wanted. Twice a year we'd jet off somewhere. We couldn't go more often because of my job. But when we did go on holiday, it was to the Maldives, the Bahamas, Sri Lanka. You know, I don't think there was a sea Julie hadn't swum in. She was a real water lily.' I can't help laughing, an exhausted laugh triggered by the memories that, all in all, are merely testament to my failure again. On the other hand, I'm relieved by how well my mind is working right now. Nothing is woolly or hazy. Everything is clear, and yet a massive pile of crap. I sold our house. To Claus Dellard, of all people. That can't be true! I want to get out! I don't want to see Claus, who's now living in our house and who takes away everything that belongs to me! I jiggle the whatsit, the whatsit for the passenger door. I hear Sophia scream and the other woman, the one who's sitting next to me, screams too. She grabs my arm and tells me to let go of the door. Of course I let go of the door, I mean, I'm not mad. We're driving down the A100 at 120 km/h and we're swaying, swaying. What the devil is she doing?

'Steer straight, you lunatic!' I yell at Lisa. 'Are you trying to kill us?'

'Dad,' I suddenly hear Sophia gasp behind me.

I spin around in shock. 'What are you doing here?'

Sophia doesn't reply; she just stares.

'Changed your mind then, have you?' Typical. First she's against the interview, then she wrangles her way in. She even hides in Lisa Keller's car so as not to miss anything. I turn back and flip the sun visor down. Sophia is really so predictable.

'We're driving to Grunewald,' I explain to her. 'Frau Keller wants to show me something important. It's . . .'

It's? I peer to my left. Lisa Keller doesn't look well. She's totally pale, like a ghost.

'Lisa?' I ask cautiously.

'Liv,' Sophia mutters from behind.

'What are you, Sophia? A parrot?'

'You called her Lisa.'

'No, I didn't!'

'It's fine,' Liv says. 'The thing is . . . Phil and I were there last night. In your old house, I mean. And in the kitchen I found a cup of coffee that was still warm. But that's not all.' She looks over at me, her pupils are bickering, hard to tell why. Fear? Pity?

'Out with it, woman!'

Liv Keller takes a couple of deep breaths, then says, 'We think Julie's kidnapper has returned.'

# LARA

Thirty-four. Sum of the digits: seven, a particular number in mythology, the connection between the spiritual and the worldly. The three stood for the sky and the four for the earth. Mum, is all I thought. She'd always been interested in these sorts of things. She believed in fate. In symbols recognised only by those who were open to them. She believed that there was more than only what you could see and touch. She believed in connections that went far beyond demonstrable chemical formulae. In things that only the heart could grasp.

Thirty-four, sum of the digits: seven. This couldn't be a coincidence. It was my mother. She was trying to encourage me. *Do it. Trust yourself.* I did the reckoning again, just to make sure. And it was right: thirty-four. Sum of the digits: seven.

I waited for supper. I didn't plan on eating anything but I had to drink, I needed a large glass of water. When the tray was finally in front of me, I knew the time had come. I had around half an hour before the door would open again.

Thirty-four, sum of the digits: seven.

Each time I carried out the procedure – brought my hand to my mouth and took a tiny sip of water from the glass – I sent a quick prayer to heaven. I was aware of the risk. There was only living or dying, nothing in between. One way or another I would get out of this room tonight – that much at least was certain. I'd swallowed all thirty-four tablets that I'd stored under my mattress over the past few weeks and was now waiting to see what happened.

## LIV

Getting into the house through the cellar window. Finding the cup of still-warm coffee in the kitchen. Standing there speechless for a moment and hearing a noise break the silence. A thump, it sounds like a dull thump. As if something had fallen on the floor above them, something heavy. Liv, instinctively grabbing Phil's arm, and the camera almost slipping out of his hand. Wobbly images, no, not proper images but a black judder, interrupted by the quivering beam of light from the phone torch. Anxious whispering – Liv wanting to leave at once, and Phil, for whom this is out of the question. Neither of them says this outright, but it's not necessary, for the noise was too loud, too obviously here in the house. Both of them know, they just know that they're not alone in here. The camera view steadies, it's now pointing at Liv's face with her panicky, wide-open eyes. Phil's voice can be heard whispering, 'Let's go upstairs.' Liv protests, but she does follow him, judging by the heavy breathing in the background. The picture is still dark, the camera moves slowly and carefully forward, on and on, out of the kitchen, through the hall to the wide, old staircase. Then upwards, step by step, a brief hesitation each time one of the old stairs creaks. Halfway up, the camera does a surprising pan back to Liv, who's a few stairs behind. She looks tiny from this elevated perspective, like a little girl with inexperienced legs, holding on to the handrail to her left. As if each new step were demanding bags of energy from this delicate body.

'You go in front,' Phil whispers and Liv freezes for a few seconds. But she behaves, of course, as ever. Gingerly she pushes past the camera and goes on ahead. At the top of the staircase a corridor runs to either side; the camera pans left, then right. It's hard to make out much in the dark – only once does the shot pick out the irregularities of the walls. It appears as if picture frames once hung there. If you look more closely, the marks are still visible.

'What do you think?' Liv whispers, and the way she's standing there shows she's unsure of which way to go.

Phil seems to think about this for a bit, then answers, just as softly, 'To the left. It sounded like it was in the room directly above us.'

With a nod, Liv takes the way he's suggested, then stops again outside the first door. She waits until the camera is behind her, then tentatively presses the handle.

An empty room, all black.

'Go on a door,' Phil's voice says. Liv obeys.

The same routine: a close-up of her pressing the handle down, the door opening, a cautious step into the room. A gasp from Liv, then the camera shot jerks abruptly because even brave Phil seems to have had one hell of a shock.

The room is furnished, or at least to an extent. Liv's phone torch skims a bed with a bare, stained mattress and a canopy made of flowery curtain fabric, a desk with chair, a wardrobe with white veneer. It skims a film poster on the wall, *Doctor Zhivago*, a poster of David Bowie and then is briefly reflected in a full-length mirror.

'Do you think this is Julie's room?' Liv says, but before Phil can answer, the camera suddenly stops by the bed. The beam of light follows and likewise comes to an abrupt stop. A large blue rubbish bag is on the floor; it appears to be partly full. To the right of it is a vase with a bunch of wildflowers that no longer look that fresh, and next to these, on the wooden floor, is a fat white candle, from which a trace of white, a few centimetres wide, winds its way to the nearest gap in the floorboards.

'What the hell . . .' Phil exclaims as he focuses the camera on the scene. His hand, still wearing a black glove, can be seen touching the candle. Something is dripping, molten wax. 'Fuck, it must've just been alight!'

'Shhh!' Liv says. 'Not so loud!'

Now Phil's hand reaches for the rubbish bag and pulls out several candle stumps, one after another, as well as other bunches of flowers in various stages of withering. Some are so dry that they crumble.

'What *is* all this?' Liv asks, sounding shaky.

The camera turns and Phil's face is now in focus. 'In all honesty? I think this is some kind of altar. Someone was just clearing up in here when we arrived.'

'What?' Back to Liv. 'Do you really think so?'

Between her question and Phil's answer is another sound. It comes from a distance, a creaking.

'Someone's on the stairs!'

Movement, more wobbly images alternating between pitch-black and bright flashes of the phone torch. Phil, running out of the room to the stairs, Liv in tow. Then a crash – the front door. The door immediately again when Phil opens it. They run outside, further and further, often stumbling in the overgrown garden. They run till they get to the iron gate. Despite Phil's feisty efforts, it won't give; it must still be locked.

'That fucking bastard!' Phil pants. The next moment he stands beside Liv and turns the camera so that they're both in the picture. His crooked grin runs across his face, mascara across Liv's.

'I want to get out of here,' she whines. 'Please, Phil!'

He ignores her plea. 'Guys, you've just been with us live. He was here. Julie Novak's kidnapper was here.' He turns to Liv, his expression displaying at once disbelief and fascination. 'We've just been in the same house as Julie Novak's kidnapper! She didn't run away, she was abducted, or maybe even killed . . .'

*

Liv fiddles agitatedly with the camera until she finds the button that stops the footage. She looks up timidly, first at Theo Novak, then at his daughter Sophia, both of whom are standing close to her. Seeing the images from last night on the small screen and in bright sunshine have mitigated the terror somewhat, but she's still not feeling great. She wanted to call the police but Phil was against the idea.

'Think about it,' he said. 'If we get the police involved now, everything will have been in vain. They'll take over and stop us from researching anymore. And in the end they'll fuck it up again, just like they have been doing for the past twenty years. Or, even worse, they'll solve the case, but nobody will know it was us who gave them an important lead. No, Liv, no way.'

In the end Liv let herself be persuaded, partly because Phil was being so attentive to her again after a long time. After their experience in the Novaks' house, he did everything to reassure her. He let her sleep in his bed, holding her tightly in his arms for the rest of the night. This is what happiness felt like, even in such circumstances.

Phil had also been against Liv telling the Novaks what they'd found. Liv realised that here too he wanted to remain in control. And she hadn't intended to, really she hadn't. But then she'd come to Theo Novak's flat that morning, which was jam-packed with old furniture, all of it probably from his former house. Post-its stuck everywhere, noting everyday stuff, which was revealing about the state he was in. The worst one, she thought, was the note on the bathroom door: 'Only pee here'. She mustn't tell Phil about this. He'd have a real go at her for not having taken a close-up of the note. Overall she'd tried to film only those parts of the flat that evoked a somewhat normal life. The kitchen, for example, which was clean and tidy. The sparkling stainless-steel sink or the lovingly set table for coffee, where Sophia invited her to sit while Theo Novak was getting dressed in the bedroom. Then he came out and Liv saw at once that he'd tried to make himself look smart. He was wearing a shirt that had been wrongly buttoned up and was tight over his tummy, a tie that dangled crookedly from his neck and flared suit trousers with ironed creases. Her stepfather had worn trousers like that back in the 90s. By the time Theo Novak had sat on the battered sofa, smoothed his parting once more with his hand and straightened his back like a schoolboy determined to follow the lesson as attentively as possible, she'd grasped the seriousness of the whole thing in a very different way. Sitting opposite her was an unwell old man, who was putting all his hope in her. A father ready to do anything to get to the bottom of what had happened to his daughter. Even if that meant ruthlessly exposing himself by allowing the outside world to share in his decline.

Liv didn't have a father like that. She only had her stepfather, whose voice still happily tormented her after all these years. *Stupid, stupid, stupid little Liv.* Of course, it wasn't easy with Novak. He would often start babbling nonsense. Such as the thing about beetroot, which must have made some sort of sense in his head, but not for outsiders who had no access to his thoughts. Or when, for no apparent reason, he tried to jump out of the car on the motorway. Or his surprise at the fact that Sophia was suddenly in the car, even though she'd been with them all morning.

*

So now they're standing here, by the iron gate to the Novaks' former property. Liv, Theo and Sophia, having just watched the footage from last night. With one hand Liv is still holding the camera, with the other she sweeps a red strand of hair behind her ear. The ongoing silence embarrasses her; not even Sophia, who's usually quick to go on the offensive, is saying a word. Maybe Liv really has made a mistake here, maybe the Novaks are silently agreeing to turn on their heels and immediately storm the nearest police station to report Liv and Phil for trespassing. Maybe Theo is having his next meltdown because the situation is too much for him and Sophia is going to lay into her. Either way, that might be the end of the reportage and the same could be the case with Phil.

'I'm . . . I'm really sorry,' Liv stammers and it's as if these words break a spell: the Novaks awaken from their stupor. Sophia takes a lunge to the side and puts a hand over her mouth as if she's about to be sick.

'No, no, no!' Theo cries, pulling his daughter into his arms. Right now he seems perfectly lucid, which Liv wasn't expecting. Just as she wasn't anticipating Sophia's tears, which Liv can only guess at from the way she's convulsing and twitching in her father's arms.

'They're wrong,' she hears Theo mutter to the top of Sophia's head, and again: 'Don't worry, they're wrong.' Now he looks at Liv. Shaking his head. 'That means absolutely nothing. What you've found isn't proof that—' He breaks off. Even from a metre away, Liv can see the panic in his pupils.

She'd said the same to Phil last night, finding his conclusion terribly hasty. Julie was killed? What if they'd just interrupted a few young people having their own little *Blair Witch* evening? Or, given the candles and flowers, holding a séance? After all, the house had stood empty for years – though it was a mystery why – and it wouldn't have been the first of its kind to attract some sort of people. Young adventurers, abandoned-places tourists, dopeheads or the homeless. 'Possibly,' Phil conceded. 'But you saw it for yourself, Liv! That was a bloody altar! And who would have had a reason to construct an altar like that, if not the . . . *killer*?'

Although Liv, despite the fright, felt that Phil had got carried away with his theory – and it wasn't surprising he did, seeing as he was desperate for their project to be a success – his words are exactly what she now repeats to Theo Novak: 'But you saw it yourself! That looked like a bloody altar! Who would have had a reason to build an altar like that, if not—'

'Don't you dare say it!' Novak hisses over Sophia's head to Liv. She shuts up momentarily. He's right. How often did she correct Phil when he talked of *a* kidnapper, insisting instead on the possibility of the plural? And now? Now she's trying to utter the word *killer*.

'Sorry,' she says quietly. 'All I'm trying . . . I'm just wondering who might have reason to put flowers and candles in Julie's bedroom. Or . . . was it you, maybe? If so, oh God, obviously I didn't mean to . . .'

Theo opens his eyes wide. 'Why would we do that? Julie isn't . . .' He breaks off, pushes Sophia away slightly and looks at her. 'We've got hope, haven't we?'

Sophia nods.

'Show us!' Novak's voice has become forceful. He lets go of Sophia, who's still crying, and moves over to Liv, who automatically takes half a step back. 'I want to see it with my own eyes.'

'Yes,' she replies, slightly breathless. 'No problem. It's just . . . I had no idea you'd sold the house and so I assumed you'd have a key.' She looks at the iron gate. 'We can get in, but in a rather unconventional way. Or you could give the owner a quick call.'

Novak follows her gaze to the gate. 'If I remember rightly . . .' Instead of finishing his sentence, he reaches for the gate and performs an absurd combination of pulling, pushing, pulling again and finally a mighty shove with the shoulder. It opens and Novak marches through. 'Come on, then!' he calls, without turning around.

The next hurdle is entering the house. The cellar window is too small for Theo. Despite this, he won't have Sophia and Liv go in alone. Nor does he want Sophia to call her godfather Claus to ask him for the key. The discussion that ensues seems to be endless to Liv. But then Sophia remembers there's a spare key, well hidden beneath one of the loose stones on the steps leading to the front door. Her mother kept it there for emergencies.

'No, Sophia,' Novak says, 'your mother would never have . . .' He falls silent when he realises that Liv has switched the camera back on. They follow Sophia to the front door where first she pulls a scrunched tissue from her trouser pocket to wipe her nose, then – finally composed – bends down, feels around and eventually shows them the key she's found. Novak chunters away.

They go straight upstairs, to Julie's room. There's her old bed, the desk, the wardrobe. But there's no sign of any candles, flowers or a rubbish bag. Two pairs of eyes look searchingly at Liv, who lowers the camera.

'That . . . that's impossible,' she says.

## DANIEL

'Frau Lessing's going to die,' I say to my Queen, who is curled up and returning my gaze from half-open, bleary eyes. She's not happy with her new cage, even though it's more than a metre long and thus big enough to tolerate being in it for a few hours at a time. It's a precaution for when I'm at work since her seizures have got worse. I open the lock, then the grille door.

'Come on, you can come out now.'

Queen lifts her head sluggishly, but puts it straight down again and otherwise seems to be in no hurry to move. Normally she loves lying on the bed with me for a cuddle when I come home in the evening. She can hardly wait. Usually. I sigh. She's really stubborn. But she'll get used to it, the new cage, I'm sure of that. She'll realise that all of this is only for her own good. I switch from my kneeling position by the grille door to sitting cross-legged.

'It often happens that shortly before they die, people perk up one last time,' I explain to her. 'It looks like they're getting better. A mean little trick of nature to spark hope in relatives. Or maybe not. Maybe nature deliberately arranges it this way to give dying people the opportunity to sort out their affairs. That needs energy and a clear head.' I think of my mother and how she was suddenly sitting upright in bed again. She had regained her appetite, let me comb her hair and looked through old photo albums. We talked a lot during this phase, including about things that were normally taboo. About my father, for example, who I'd never met. And I didn't recognise it either, this little trick of nature. I thought my mother was recuperating and would soon be as good as old. Maybe, as the person who knew me best, she'd give an interview and tell people what I really was like. Maybe she'd call Theo Novak and give him hell. The black eye was no longer swollen and had healed, but sometimes when I looked in the mirror I could see it again. I knew, of course, that it wasn't there anymore, but the memory of it, the shame, remained. This black eye had been seen on television and the front page of newspapers. And it made no difference that I sued Novak for bodily harm and won my case. Nobody was interested. To the outside world, this black eye was proof that I was guilty. Because something like that would never have happened to an innocent man, and a loving father knew better than the police because he could sense the truth in his heart, even if the facts said something different. After all, I had an alibi for the night Julie disappeared, at least to begin with.

My mother was a strict woman, no question about it. Sometimes she was even cold. Only when she had to lie in bed, so ill and weak, did she become affectionate. Now she realised she had nobody left apart from me; she realised what she had *in* me.

It's different with Frau Lessing. I'd have thought she'd known this for ages. And I'm bitterly disappointed that she's not using her last days to spend quality time with me rather than getting involved in Anna's smear campaign. Of course I've tried to put on a brave face. To simply ignore the looks and whispers of my colleagues. Clearly it didn't take Anna long to spread the news. I realised this after hearing her conversation with Frau Lessing this morning. And yet I'd still harboured the absurd, miniscule hope that nobody would fall for it. Innocent until proven guilty. That's what they say. I clench my fist and hit my forehead. It's only when Queen makes a sound that I stop. She's raised her head again and there's fear in her eyes. I quickly wipe my face. I don't know when I began crying.

'Don't worry,' I say and attempt a smile. 'We'll get through this too. Like we've got through everything together in the past.' I close the grille door and stand up. 'I'll sort out dinner now. I bet you're hungry.' Queen curls up again. I feel a pain in my heart. If I were to lose her I'd have nobody. I'd be all alone in the world. I shake my head. She's here. And her seizures will get better soon. I'm taking good care of her. It'll be fine.

I leave Queen in the bedroom, shut the door and go downstairs to the kitchen. The house isn't particularly big. My grandfather, who built it, was a man of modest means, who hadn't expected his daughter, my mother, to go on living here, with a child to boot. When there were four of us – my grandparents, my mother and I – it felt cramped, almost stifling. Now I'm happy that the house is so small, or at least not any bigger. I'm familiar with how loneliness makes every space bigger, sometimes so much that it feels like the whole world. As if nothing else existed, nothing at all save for the vacuum of loneliness. Before I begin peeling the potatoes, I turn on some music on my phone. 'Heroes' by David Bowie. He can still make me happy with those opening chords. The six minutes eleven seconds, during which time goes backwards and everything is still in front of us. We're young, in love and unsuspecting. I fill a pot with water and take a peeler from the drawer, but then decide to take out the rubbish first. The lid of the bin is gaping open already; if I tried to chuck in the potato peelings too, it would end up a holy mess. Just before I carry the bag out, I notice the newspaper on the kitchen table, the *Abendblatt*, and I feel like scrunching and ripping it up, and stuffing it in with the rest of the rubbish. But I don't. Although I know the article by heart now – it fills an entire page! – I might wish to read it again later, and again, and again. I don't know why. Is that a human thing? Scratching the fresh scab over and over instead of allowing the wound to recover? On the other hand, *I'm* not the one who opened it all up again. I realise my wound is still some way from being healed, but I'd learned to live with the injury.

But that's not all. It's not just about the article, more about a certain name printed in it. The name jumped out at me immediately when I opened the paper to the relevant page, having picked it up at a petrol station on my way home. And I screwed up my eyes as if there was the serious possibility that I'd got it wrong, that I might have gone a bit mad or paranoid. But the name was still there in black and white. I persuaded myself that I could subdue the sheer anger brewing within me merely by taking slow, deep breaths. I failed miserably and that makes me feel ashamed. Right now I don't want to think about this anymore. I can't. I want to listen to Bowie and do something useful. Take out the rubbish. Make dinner, for me and my poor, sweet Queen. *A man living a perfectly normal life.*

In one hand I've got the rubbish bag, with the other I turn the key in the front door. I always lock up, always, even when I'm at home. Better to be safe than sorry. I step out into the darkness and close the door behind me. The bin is in a lean-to behind the house. David Bowie echoes through the open kitchen window; I hum along. In my mind Julie is dancing, her long red hair flying through the air, her beautiful body moving as if it had been made exclusively to dance to this song. I lift the lid of the bin and the rubbish bag goes thumping to the bottom of it. A second later it's me who thumps to the ground. My knees hit the concrete mercilessly; my wrists grate in the attempt to somehow cushion the blow. Bright lights explode before my eyes. The blow to my head came from behind, unexpected and fast. I hear myself groan, the pain. I roll awkwardly from my tummy to my side. Footsteps hurry into the distance, Bowie sings, I close my eyes.

## LIV

Liv was expecting to find Phil at home. Particularly as it's just gone ten o'clock. But from outside she saw that no light was on. She calls his name nonetheless when she enters their flat, in case he's already gone to bed and fallen asleep. Only when there's no answer does she remember that he'd planned to spend the day at Coworking Space in Knesebeckstrasse, where they've rented their studio. He was going to write the script for the Vlado Taneski case. A huge amount of research that Phil thinks will provide enough material for a double episode; they intend to record the first part tomorrow. Liv goes into the large open-plan area accommodating both kitchen and sitting room. She switches the lights on above the dining table and beneath the extractor, takes a glass from the top cupboard and the open bottle of orange juice from the fridge. She briefly considers making a bit of pasta because she's had nothing to eat all day, but soon dismisses the idea. She hates eating on her own. Besides, it would just be a refuelling measure; she's not hungry. She puts the glass and juice bottle back down on the dining table, then unpacks the camera and notebook from the small black sports bag. Exhausted, she sinks on one of the two kitchen chairs, stretches her legs and for a few moments simply stares into the distance. She feels as if she's run a marathon over the past thirteen hours. Only she hasn't just completed this marathon with her body; it's taken place in her head too. And unlike her legs, which can now rest, her thoughts are still racing. Liv has to sort herself out, prepare for tomorrow. Also so she can report back to Phil later and plan their next steps.

First: Spandau, the meeting with the Novaks and the conversation about Julie's final evening. The new information about Jason, the karate instructor who Julie had clearly locked horns with before her disappearance. The strange fact that the class had been rescheduled for a Saturday. Liv picks up her notebook, takes the biro from the rubber loop attached to the side and writes: *Jason, karate instructor*. She'll google him afterwards, in the hope that even without a surname she might find his contact details by adding *karate* and *KSVG* to her search. She has to talk to him for sure.

Liv puts down the biro and continues reviewing her day. The drive to Grunewald, to the Novaks' old house, and showing Theo and Sophia the footage from the previous night. But most strikingly, the fact that the candles, flowers and rubbish bag had suddenly vanished from Julie's bedroom, which at first made Liv look like a liar, a complete idiot. But she had it all on video. The video footage was the indisputable proof. The candles, flowers and rubbish bag *had* been there. Someone must've returned to the house to clear up once Liv and Phil had left. Why would a random squatter do that? Or a group of young people who'd just come to smoke some weed or for the adventure? And how had they got in? It made no sense – that had to be obvious to the Novaks too. You could argue over whether the person who'd constructed the altar, then taken it down again, could be called Julie's *killer*. But what any sane person had to agree on was that no outsider could have had a reason to do something like that. This was exactly what she'd told the Novaks in Julie's bedroom after the initial shock, and she'd hit a nerve. Theo dropped on to Julie's bed and Sophia went over to the window, and Liv saw her shoulders begin to twitch again; she was crying.

It took quite a while for anyone to speak again. Luckily Liv had this recorded too. The moment when father and sister seemed to realise that something unusual had happened in this room. And then Theo Novak suddenly squared his slumped shoulders, lifted his hanging head and said, 'This is a lead, right?' This question – tentative and yet so full of hope – along with his wrinkled face and the tears that had welled in his eyes but didn't dare stream uncontrollably down his cheeks: this was an image that Liv already knows Phil is going to praise to the roof. Unlike Sophia, who suddenly turned around and screamed at Liv, 'Stop that!' But it remained unclear whether she was just referring to the fact that Liv had kept the camera running during this very personal moment or that she'd given Theo a modicum of hope. Novak himself seemed to know the answer. He got up from the mattress, wandered over to the window and put his arms around Sophia once more. Another scene Phil would be very happy with.

'You've got to calm down,' he murmured, his lips pressed to the top of Sophia's head. 'We promised that we were going to remain hopeful, remember?'

'Dad,' Sophia sobbed, but she couldn't say any more. Liv

understood; Sophia wanted to spare her father any disappointment. In view of his age and condition, it would probably be the last major emotion in his life. And it wasn't a good one, not one that you'd like to depart this world with. But Theo Novak seemed to be lucid and composed at that moment; he came across as healthy and steady, and most of all, determined.

'We're going to see this through, Sophia. Do you hear me? We're going to find out what happened to Julie.' He looked at Liv, straight into the camera. 'This really could be a lead.'

Notify the police. The idea was aired only briefly, as if it had to be articulated for the sake of decency, only to be rejected again. Back at the time, Novak had complained vociferously in the media about how, in his eyes, the investigation team had failed under the leadership of its head, Konrad Bergmann, and Novak's opinion hadn't changed after all these years. He called Bergmann a *bundler* – that was the word on Liv's recording. Novak had probably meant to say *bungler*, but this didn't alter the fact that he was against informing the police about what had happened inside his old house. Liv hadn't been anticipating that Sophia would agree with her father, but perhaps emotionally she wasn't up for her obligatory resistance. Liv was relieved by the family's decision, because she was well aware of Phil's take on this too. On the one hand, he agreed with the Novaks that the police had failed. But he also said that involving the authorities might put their project at risk.

'What happens now?' Novak asked, after Liv had checked the time and realised she had to be off to her next appointment.

'I'll take you home and I'll be in touch later.'

\*

Liv switches on the camera and flips open the display. Her next appointment was with the *bundler* Konrad Bergmann. She wants to review the footage she took just to make sure that she didn't miss anything. On the drive to Bergmann's flat in Teltow, it had struck her how much she'd been affected by her meeting with the Novaks. Two people who'd lost so much and didn't know how to deal with their contradictory emotions. It had taken half a day, and Liv's opposition to the reportage had shifted into something that felt like a duty – to Phil, of course – but especially towards the Novaks. Theo, whose hope touched her heart. Sophia, who she didn't find particularly likeable, but whose resistance she could certainly understand. Liv mustn't screw up. She didn't want to be the reason for the last great disappointment in Theo's life. Even if ultimately she didn't succeed in uncovering the truth behind Julie's disappearance, she was keen at least to give it her best shot.

Liv plays back the footage, the interview with Bergmann. She presses PLAY and picks up the biro to take notes. Bergmann, now retired, is sitting in an armchair in front of the bookshelf that occupies the entire wall of his sitting room. Ironically he reminded Liv of Theo Novak, the way he tried to dress for the occasion. He's wearing a shirt that's bulging slightly at the tummy, and a double-breasted jacket with dropped shoulders. He doesn't appear to have gone shopping since the 1990s either. He's combed his thin snow-white hair back; on his lap is a file. Now that Liv is looking at the images again, she finds the file astonishingly thin given that the Julie Novak case has been ongoing for twenty years. But Phil was probably right when he said that the police set the case aside at some point and no longer bothered with it after that.

Bergmann's wife served them coffee in their best china: flower pattern, gold rim, coiled handle. After he takes a sip of coffee at the beginning of the interview, Bergmann doesn't put the cup on the table beside his armchair, almost as if he were glad to be able to hold on to something. In the course of her research, Liv had discovered that the Julie Novak case had left its mark on him too. Bergmann, now seventy and a keen amateur fisherman, had been head of the Grunewald task force from 2003 to 2015, which had investigated Julie's case. He'd been sent straight to the Novaks' house on the morning of Julie's disappearance, after Vera had rung the police and told them of a suspected kidnapping – but had not mentioned, according to Bergmann, that the ransom note explicitly warned against involving the authorities. 'Otherwise we would've definitely been a bit more subtle in how we turned up there – plain clothes and without bells and whistles,' he explains on the recording.

'But isn't this what every ransom note says? *No police*,' Liv can hear herself ask in the background. Bergmann grins.

'For people who watch too many crime shows, perhaps, but in real life that's not necessarily the case. OK, normally I wouldn't criticise the mother for not having gone through all the relevant points when she phoned the police. You're distraught in a situation like that, and also the officer who took the call ought to have been a bit more thorough with their questions. But then you join up what appears to be a minor point with lots of other things that, even at the beginning, I felt were rather strange, and a picture emerges. And with all my years of experience, I said quite clearly: something's not right here.' It began, Bergmann continues, as soon as he arrived at the Novaks'. Half the neighbourhood was already assembled in the house. 'At a potential crime scene!' he says, visibly angering. 'After calling the police, the parents had – I kid you not – let their neighbours into the house. You could hardly move! I don't need to tell you what this meant for forensics – any potential traces of the kidnapper or kidnappers hadn't only been contaminated, but possibly destroyed altogether. While the mother was sitting listlessly on the sofa in the sitting room, in the company of her friends, the father and one of his mates were running around outside, screaming his daughter's name. And then later, Theo Novak had the temerity to stand before the press and claim that the police had scared off the abductors when they arrived with their lights flashing and sirens wailing, ultimately aborting the handover of the ransom money.' Bergmann is getting into his stride. The bizarrely low ransom demand. The lack of evidence for a break-in. And then the thing with Sophia.

'Wait,' Liv interrupts him. 'Not so fast. One thing after another. You say there were no traces of a break-in. What about the cellar window? Isn't it possible that the kidnapper or kidnappers came in that way?'

Bergmann laughs. 'The cellar window, really?'

There's a short silence on the recording. What can't be seen is Liv nodding vigorously behind the camera.

'So this is what we found,' Bergmann says, 'when we examined the window. Yes, the glass was missing. But we couldn't find any shards in the boiler room, not even any splinters of glass. We thought it was pretty unlikely that the abductor or abductors would have carefully picked up all the little pieces of glass afterwards. Much more interesting, we thought, was the fact that there were no deposits of dust on the window ledge and remains of spiderwebs in the window opening. Just remains, no intact webs. And guess where we found the matching threads—'

'Anyone at home?' The voice and the noise of the door closing tear Liv from her concentration. She hastily stops the recording, cutting Bergmann off mid sentence. Phil has come back, just at the right time. Liv leaps up from her chair and runs over to him.

'You're not going to believe it, Phil! The footage is awesome!' Even as she's moving, she gives a start. She's struck by her own outburst of enthusiasm because it feels wrong the moment it's left her lips. Then she winces again when she gets to Phil, who's standing motionless in the hallway, his features hardened, his eyes narrowed and full of incredulity.

'Is . . . is everything OK?' Liv puts out a hand to touch his arm. But Phil is still standing there stiffly, just staring at her. In the end he shakes his head agonisingly slowly and hisses, 'What the hell have you done?'

## LARA

With heavy lids I squinted at the sun, a blinding light. I heard a rustling, the wind in the trees above me and a soft rippling, the lake. It was soft where I was lying, so wonderfully soft, in the grass beside the jetty. *Home*, I thought, when suddenly another sound forced its way into my head. A persistent, relentless beeping, far too high-pitched. I tried moving my lips. But they didn't obey me, just like the rest of my body. I felt my heart begin to beat panicked salvos, at which the beeping took on a jittery rhythm.

'She's back with us,' a woman's voice said as if from far away. *Mum?* 'There, there, sweetheart.'

Mustering all my strength, I opened my eyes. It wasn't my mother bending over me, it was a woman I'd never seen before. My gaze flitted around. I wasn't lying outside at the lake but in a bed. And the light I'd thought was the sun was coming from a neon tube beneath a white panelled ceiling. It took me a moment to understand: I'd actually done it, I'd got out of my room. And now I was in hospital.

Before my eyes the woman filled a syringe. As torpid as my mind was, I realised that the out-of-control beeping was coming from an ECG machine. And that the syringe contained a sedative to counter this. No, I thought, no! Because I realised too that the moment the needle hit its target, I would drift off again. Straining harder than I ever had in my life, I managed a croak, and with it the most important words: 'Wait . . . Kidnapped . . . Please!'

The woman – a nurse or doctor – bent over me. 'What did you say, sweetheart?'

Once again I opened my mouth. I wanted to tell her my name. Tell her that she had to inform my family.

'Isabel!'

That wasn't my voice. Nor was it my name. I flinched, just like the woman, but more acutely. The shock, like a kick to the chest, then my heart stopping momentarily. It was his *voice*. The devil was here, in my hospital room. The woman turned around and I lifted my head too. My sight blurred, but I was still able to make out a silhouette in the doorway. Now it came closer, slowly, ominously. I tried to keep my head up, but my body was too weak. I sank back into the pillow, fighting myself. *Up again! Scream! Kick! Punch!* My body merely lay there like a lump of meat.

'She needs rest,' the devil's voice said, reminding the woman of the syringe in her hand. I saw her nod.

No, no, no, no!

In vain.

The syringe. The sedative.

I felt dizzy. I teetered back into that familiar state of torpor, in a faraway place where I belonged to *him* alone, his property forever. No way out, never. The devil had won again. My thoughts disintegrated. I disintegrated.

'Please, help me!' I whispered. But nobody, nobody could hear me anymore.

## LIV

*Stupid, stupid, stupid little Liv.*

Because she only ever makes mistakes and is one big disappointment. Every time she sees this in someone else's eyes – disappointment and resignation – she's twelve again. She's standing there, head bowed, in her parents' house. She's wearing a denim skirt, her sweaty hands clutching its white seam, and staring at her bare feet in the sandals she'd wanted for so long until her stepfather Heinz bought them for her. She shouldn't have accepted them. But she did, she accepted them and even thanked him. Sitting on the sofa facing Liv are her mother and Heinz, like a tribunal. And her mother's weeping, that's the worst thing of all, because now she's finally happy, after all those years bringing up a child alone, Liv's biological father having died in a motorbike accident during the pregnancy. Yes, there had been a few men along the way, but none who'd stayed for any length of time, because she was a mother with all the obligations this role entailed. In short, because of Liv. Because she, Liv, existed. But then came Heinz, twenty years older than her mother and the owner of an advertising agency. A good catch. A man who cared and never lost his patience – not even with such a ghastly child as Liv, who clearly couldn't bear sharing her mother's attention and thus didn't shy away from making up stories. Vile stories that had to be nipped in the bud before they got around. No, her mother hadn't deserved that and certainly not Heinz. He had given them a home and a future. And Liv was ruining it all – *shame on you, girl, shame on you!*

Disappointment, resignation.

That's how Phil's looking at her now too, as they stand opposite each other in the hallway of the flat they share. And it finds its mark, that look. It hits her right in the heart, like the fucking blade of a fucking sharp knife. Phil means everything to her. For where would she be now without Phil? Maybe not here at all, because she couldn't have stuck it out forever. Because eventually she would have come to the conclusion that it would be better to be lying under the ground than under Heinz's heavy, sweaty body.

Phil rescued her from that, Phil saved her. And how does she thank him? By putting their entire life together on the line.

Disappointment, resignation.

*Stupid, stupid, stupid little Liv.*

'Do you know how many messages and comments we've got on social media from listeners who cannot believe that you lifted the transcript of the Julie Novak case almost word for word from another podcast? I checked it out, Liv! I listened to both episodes, ours and the *Murder Talk* one! You even copied the experiment to see how long it would take to type that incredibly long ransom demand! This can hardly be explained away as a coincidence!'

Liv doesn't know what to say. She fiddles awkwardly with the hem of her T-shirt and stares at her feet, as she had back then in her stepfather's sitting room.

'What the hell got into you? Were you just too lazy to do the research, was it too much like hard work, or have you simply forgotten that it's the podcast that fucking pays the rent here! Have you forgotten that, Liv? Are you suffering from dementia too?'

'But you knew that *Murder Talk* did an episode on Julie Novak. I told you,' Liv says softly. Phil cocks his head; he doesn't need to do any more. Yes, he knew that *Murder Talk* had featured Julie's case, but he hadn't listened to the episode beforehand. He'd just instructed Liv to send the interview request to Theo Novak. And of course it hadn't crossed his mind that Liv would simply copy their rivals' content so brazenly.

'How are we going to salvage this now? Hmm?' he keeps grumbling. 'How are we going to explain it? And Max! Oh God, Max! Max and the newspaper article! We're finished!'

When things calm down for a moment, Liv cautiously looks up, just slightly, to find out what Phil's going to do next. She sees him take off his glasses and massage his nose. She's ashamed, she's so ashamed, in a way she wouldn't have thought possible anymore.

'I need to think.' Putting his glasses back on, Phil pushes past her towards the kitchen. She hears him open the cupboard, glasses clinking, followed by the fridge door. Gin, she thinks, he's pouring himself a gin. And she also thinks she's got to do something. She needs to calm him down, she has to find a way to make him look at her differently again, not full of disappointment and resignation like her mother back then.

So she follows him into the kitchen, picks up the video camera and, ignoring for the moment the issue of her having copied the other podcast, starts playing the interview with Konrad Bergmann. When after a few minutes Phil still hasn't shown any reaction and, what's worse, even looks bored, Liv stops Bergmann mid sentence to summarise the interview in her own words. Konrad Bergmann told her that there were no DNA traces on the cellar window that didn't belong to the family. But that dust from the window ledge and bits of spiderwebs were discovered on some tracksuit bottoms and a sweatshirt from Julie's washing basket. The police presumed, therefore, that Julie had gone through the cellar window herself in the past, maybe to secretly creep out of the house. To see her boyfriend, perhaps – although he vehemently denied this – or friends of hers. But it was impossible that a kidnapper had used the window opening, as they concluded from the lack of other DNA traces, including Daniel Wagner's. In Bergmann's opinion, Julie vanished of her own accord, a theory only supported by the fact that it looked like she'd often done a secret bunk through the cellar window. Maybe that night she'd run away for good to punish her parents for the breakdown of her relationship with Daniel Wagner. Or because, behind the apparently perfect middle-class façade – and at this point Bergmann quoted various statistics – Julie had been forced to put up with things she wanted to escape from once and for all. Although Bergmann kept things very general when he spoke about domestic abuse, the fact that he'd had Julie's bedclothes checked for traces of sperm, and had also had a sample from Theo

Novak analysed, speaks for itself. Liv doesn't know what to make of this. Not much, probably, after she saw how Theo comforted Sophia today. And who, if not Liv, could tell a loving father from a man like Heinz?

Bergmann's first theory, on the other hand – that Julie did a runner because of Daniel Wagner or another boy – seems more convincing. And if Julie really had been her own abductor, she must have written the ransom note herself too, in an attempt to set them all on the wrong track. Maybe because she wanted to keep open the possibility of coming back home at some point. She could have claimed to have escaped her abductors and wouldn't have had to confess to her own hand in the matter. But then something – or someone – had thwarted her return. Phil is poker-faced and his voice remains monotone when he asks Liv what's groundbreakingly new about any of this, apart from the fact that Liv wasted valuable time on an interview. OK, the kidnapper didn't get into the house through the cellar window. So what?

'But how, Phil?' Liv is getting increasingly desperate. 'How else could they have got into the house unnoticed and then left it again with Julie, also undetected?'

'That house has a fucking door, Liv!'

'But they found no traces of a break-in there!'

Phil's response is no more than an angry growl. A second later he grabs Liv's arm, drags her through the flat, and with his free hand opens the door with such force that it goes crashing against the wall. He continues pulling Liv out into the stairwell. She doesn't know what's happening; she gasps his name in horror. But it's as if he's numbed by his anger. Still clutching her arm tightly, he drags her up the stairs until they get to the top, to the attic, where one of the areas used to be their former recording studio. Letting go of Liv, Phil shakes the handle of the heavy metal door that divides the stairwell from the attic. The handle moves, but the door doesn't. Liv points to the key hanging by some string on the wall beside the door frame, for all the residents to use.

'No!' Phil says, fishing his wallet from the back pocket of his trousers and taking one of the credit cards from it. Pulling his right sleeve over his hand, he then slides the credit card into the narrow gap between the lock and the metal frame. Liv hears a soft click. Phil transfers the card to his other hand and with his right, still covered by the shirt sleeve, pushes the handle again. This time the door opens.

Liv shakes her head. He's right if he's trying to show her with this crude stunt that it's perfectly possible to crack the lock of a door without leaving scratches or fingerprints. But she thinks that he's likewise proving how much objectivity he's lost. He's convinced that Julie was kidnapped. That there was a perpetrator, a crime, a clear direction that should steer the investigation's narrative. Liv thinks this is questionable. Not because Phil is wrong in her opinion. No, his theory that Julie – even if she vanished of her own accord to begin with – was ultimately the victim of a crime, might be right. After all, she never *did* come back home, this is an indisputable fact. It's just that Liv believes Phil is basically doing exactly what he criticised the police for: plumping for one theory and thus preventing himself from entertaining other possibilities. That on her way to what she might have regarded as her freedom, Julie had an accident with a fatal outcome. That the person responsible for this accident tried to cover it up by getting rid of her body. Or that she is in fact still alive somewhere, with no pressure, no fear, happy and under a different name. Or, or, or. Phil is categorically disregarding all of this, even though he's a trained journalist, a bastion of impartiality. But now isn't the right moment to point this out. He's pissed off with her because of the *Murder Talk* thing. He's so pissed off that he grabbed her far too hard, really hurting her in the process.

Liv feels like howling. As a sign of appeasement, she circumspectly holds out her still-shaking hand to him. But Phil just leaves Liv standing here and makes his way back to the flat. A sad smile flickers on her lips when, instead of following him, she goes into the attic. She's craving a moment to herself, a moment from *back then*, when the sticky, cramped partition at the back of the attic was her little realm. The trestle table is still there, where they used to put the laptop and microphone for their recordings. And the two camping chairs are still facing each other. A grey film has covered the seats while the arms are shrouded in spiderwebs and dust. Beneath an old sheet, a plastic shelf from the DIY store is bravely bearing the weight of some rather fat ring binders where they keep their research findings. Beside it, folded up, is a hastily wiped whiteboard, on which they jotted down names, theories and ideas for titles. In a corner is a small fridge for drinks so they didn't have to interrupt their work unnecessarily. The plug is lying idly beside an extension reel, and next to this is some carelessly coiled orange rope, also from the DIY store. They'd bought it when they were discussing a case in which a young woman had killed herself by hanging a rope construction for her neck, hands and feet from a balcony. They wanted to find out on-air if it was possible to tie yourself up this way, and already failed at the tying the hands behind the back stage. This, even though Phil had knowledge of this topic – remotely, at least. His father had been in the navy and taught him all the knots when Phil was a boy. But there was clearly a difference between mooring a ship and tying yourself up.

*Back then*, it was nice. *Back then*, when they spent their nights up here, like two adolescents who pitched a tent in their parents' garden to tell each other horror stories.

Liv allows her gaze to roam the room longingly once more, then she leaves the attic and goes back down to her flat. Phil's in the kitchen on his second gin and tonic. She'd best leave it, she thinks. Let him go to bed and, if she's lucky, the night will clear away the worst of the debris. Tomorrow the world might look quite different, if he's had a few hours' kip.

She can't leave it.

'I might have another lead. Sophia told me that shortly before she disappeared, Julie had a bust-up with her karate instructor.'

'Really?' Phil replies. 'Did she tie her belt wrongly?'

Liv swallows but she's not prepared to give up. 'No, I . . . I intend to find him, this karate instructor.'

'Did you ask Bergmann about him, seeing as you think he's so important?' Phil takes a last sip then puts his glass in the sink. 'Or about Daniel Wagner?'

'Not about the karate instructor, no. I sort of . . .'

'Forgot? Maybe because the *Murder Talk* podcast didn't mention him?'

'No, I . . .' Liv swallows again. 'But I did ask him about Daniel Wagner. Of course I did! Bergmann says that as far as he's concerned, Wagner was wrongly on their radar. A boy who was just unlucky.'

'*Unlucky,*' Phil echoes tersely. How unprofessional is that of him? What proof does he have?'

'Well, the fact that Daniel Wagner had an alibi for the night in question. One of Julie's friends saw him. Apparently he was in a disco until gone five in the morning.'

Phil laughs. 'You don't mean the alibi that was later retracted?'

'Yes, but according to Bergmann that was irrelevant because Wagner still had the faded entry stamp for the disco on the back of his hand when he was questioned the day after Julie disappeared.'

Phil narrows his eyes. 'Do you know how long one of those fucking stamps lasts if you don't scrub it off, Liv? It could've easily been a day older, so long as there wasn't a specific date on it. And I would love to see a disco stamp that has a date.'

'Hmm,' Liv says, quickly wiping her right eye, which a tear is trying to come loose from. Seemingly there's nothing she could say or do to mollify Phil's rancour, not at the moment at least. She briefly considers showing him the footage from the Novaks' house, more specifically the scene when she was in Julie's room with Theo and Sophia, and the intense reaction of both of them to the altar, or the fact that it was no longer there. But she's worried she'd only wind Phil up even more. Because his instruction was specifically *not* to do that: let the Novaks in on what had happened to her and Phil the night before in the house. He'd decided that they should keep all their research findings to themselves for the time being, to avoid giving a heads-up to anyone potentially harbouring a secret. Insanely, this included the Novaks, even though they couldn't have had anything to do with Julie's disappearance. So Liv keeps quiet and just stares at her feet again. Like in her parents' sitting room. Disappointment and resignation. Another hurried wipe, this time over her left eye. Liv can't cope, that much is certain. And Phil isn't making any pretence out of the fact that he thinks the same: struggling and, more than this, not up to shouldering the responsibility for the reportage. Once again she wonders why he gave her this task in the first place. Why didn't he take it on himself from the start? Of the two of them, he is the journalist, after all.

'You can't simply assume that people will tell you everything they know,' he says, to cap it all. 'You need to ask the right questions.'

Yes, Liv thinks. Just like a real journalist would do effortlessly and automatically out of experience and instinct. She feels like screaming at him. But how often did she feel like screaming at Heinz back then? Or her mother? And she never did, not once. She alwaysalwaysalways remained silent.

'I'm going to bed,' Phil says, leaving the kitchen. Liv stays where she is, with the video camera, her notebook and the feeling of being a loser. Alwaysalwaysalways a loser.

*Stupid, stupid, stupid little Liv.*

# DANIEL

### TWO BERLIN PODCASTERS REOPEN COLD CASE
*New leads in the case of Julie Novak (16) from Grunewald, missing for the past twenty years.*

*Max Bishop-Petersen/Grunewald.* Liv Keller and Philipp Hendricks met in 2019 when working at Keller's stepfather's advertising agency. The colleagues soon became best friends and flatmates, who only a year later, when the pandemic condemned the world to stay at home, launched a true crime podcast from their kitchen table. The hobby project, which started out of boredom, has now long been a serious business. The *Two Crime* podcast is now their full-time occupation and, with an audience running into the high six figures, it is one of the most successful within the genre in Germany. For the trained journalist Hendricks and newcomer Keller, careful research, empathy and respect for the victims remain top priorities.

'We mustn't forget that we're talking about real people here, with lives, families and friends who are often left behind with unanswered questions.' For not every crime can be solved; over time some become so-called 'cold cases'.

One such case is that of the sixteen-year-old schoolgirl Julie Novak who disappeared from her parents' house in Grunewald one night in September 2003. Kidnapped, so it appeared, after a ransom demand was found on a computer belonging to Theo Novak, former director of the clinic for heart, thoracic and vascular surgery at the Charité Hospital. But the telephone call they were hoping to get from the abductor never came and Julie Novak is still missing after twenty years.

This could now change, as far as Hendricks and Keller are concerned, because the two podcasters have reopened the case and their research has uncovered new leads.

'Sadly, we have to agree with Julie Novak's father, who complained at the time about the police's sloppy investigation,' Hendricks says. 'Those responsible became fixated on the idea that Julie Novak ran away from home, and even claimed there was evidence of domestic abuse. A very one-sided approach, especially as it meant that the wider group of people, Julie's friends in particular, faded from the spotlight far too quickly.'

Hendricks and Keller are not revealing any details about the new, potentially groundbreaking leads, which they claim to have uncovered in the course of their investigation. Instead they intend to make public their research in the coming weeks in a reportage that has been the result of much hard work. There is only one point on which the podcasters insist there is no room for doubt: 'Julie was the victim of a crime.' Hendricks and Keller are likely to have investigated more thoroughly the people close to the missing schoolgirl, people who have shunned the glare of publicity for years, opting instead for privacy. For example, the girl's ex-boyfriend, for a time the chief suspect, has spoken about the case only once – in an exclusive interview with the *Berliner Rundschau* in November 2004, a year after Julie Novak disappeared. Daniel W. (now 42) said at the time, 'Julie was a fighter, not someone who could be easily abducted from her house, locked up somewhere and detained for a long period of time. She would have resisted with every fibre of her body and found a way out, from the deepest cellar or any other type of prison. No question about it. It would have taken tremendous force to break this girl.' When asked what he thought had happened to his ex-girlfriend, W. replied, 'As well as being a fighter, Julie was a total free spirit. I think she ran away. She was impulsive and always dreamed of the sea. As much as it pains me, I could imagine that Julie met someone new and wanted to be free of the control her parents exerted over her when she was together with me.' W. emphasised how much he had loved his ex-girlfriend and continued to treasure her even after their separation. But he also expressed his indignation at having been made a 'scapegoat'. 'Julie's father attacked and threatened me, even though the police had let me go without any charge. As if I'd been to blame for his daughter's decision to run away. That certainly wasn't my fault. I'd never have done anything to her.' Although W.'s alibi for the time of Julie Novak's disappearance later turned out to be false, the chief investigator of Grunewald task force, Konrad Bergmann, said at the time, 'At present we don't see any reason for Herr W. to continue to be a subject of our inquiries.'

Asked about the alibi that W. originally was given by a witness who later retracted it, W. terminated the interview. Today the forty-two-year-old works as an orderly in a care home, as revealed by a now-inactive profile on a dating site. A screenshot in *Abendblatt*'s possession shows a short text in which W. says he is searching for a new partner. W. describes himself as 'faithful' and 'someone who cares and will always be by your side, for better or worse'. Daniel W. – a man who appears to have long forgotten his once 'great love' and is living a normal life, while Julie Novak's relatives still have no answer to the question of what happened to their daughter and sister. Which is preposterous, according to the podcasters of *Two Crime*: 'We humans can cope with a lot,'

Hendricks says. 'Even the most dreadful certainty is better than an open end.'

You can find more information about the case on our website, as well as at www.twocrime.dertruecrimepodcast.de.

Any information relating to the case can be shared there – even anonymously. At the time of her disappearance, Julie Novak was 1.70 m tall and slim. She had long red hair and was probably wearing white pyjamas with a blue cloud pattern. When asked about potential new evidence, the department of public prosecution said that at present it sees no reason to reopen the investigation into the case.

'Hmm,' the officer sitting opposite me says. My knees are shaking; I'm perched on the edge of the chair in front of his desk. *Hmm* – is that all? I watch in disbelief as, after not even half a minute, he lowers the newspaper I gave him as proof. He cannot have read the article in such a short space of time, that's impossible.

'Don't you understand?' I cry, turning the back of my head to him so he can see. I had to go to hospital for stitches! There's still blood and disinfectant in my hair. I was brutally attacked last night, behind my own house! By someone who clearly knows where I live! The officer remains unmoved. He invites me to file a charge against an unknown person. I shake my head and immediately regret it. Every movement sends my skull buzzing and grating. I'd hoped to be able to talk to Konrad Bergmann when I entered the police station and asked for help at the glass box in reception. But Bergmann has retired, as I found out before they sent me to one of their colleagues. To this guy here, who seems to have not the slightest sense of how serious the incident was last night. I turn back to reach for the paper that is lying flat again – and ignored – on his desk. From my viewpoint, the text is tiny and upside down, but I know exactly what to tap my finger on.

'It was him!'

The officer glances at the name my finger is hovering above. 'Max Bishop-Petersen,' he reads out slowly, then his eyes return to me. 'The journalist who wrote the article? Why would he attack you?'

I wince. Maybe I'd hoped I wouldn't have to tell the whole story, because that would have meant admitting I'd been the one who'd provoked the attack on me. I remember sitting with Queen last night and feeling ashamed about the anger that had gripped me and led to that fateful knee-jerk reaction. I decide to tell the story, but leave out the moment of madness, because I don't want to hear now that I'm partly to blame. That it's alright Bishop-Petersen crept on to my premises and knocked me to the ground. That it's alright because after all, I was the one who'd made the first move. But it's not alright. And the incident could have resulted in a cracked skull rather than just a cut. I'm the victim here and I could have died. I could've lain dead by the bins and maybe I'd have only been found a few days later. Not that I'm so desperate to cling on to life – but what would have happened to Queen? Nobody would've looked after her and fed her; she could've died too.

'It says in the article, and this is the truth, that I only once gave an interview. To the *Berliner Rundschau*. And the interviewer was no less than Max Bishop-Petersen. He'd contacted me via Facebook, which I used to be on. He seemed to be different from the journalists who, in the first few weeks after Julie's disappearance, hung around outside our house, hassling us. At the time we were still in the online phone book, with our address. And now they were there in their hordes, with their SLRs and TV cameras, screaming their questions over the garden fence: *Where is Julie? What did you do to her?* It was hell. I thought it best to say nothing because I was worried they'd twist my words and this would just make everything worse. After all, the mob had been there watching when Theo Novak, Julie's father, turned up outside our house and gave me a black eye when I came back from shopping, because he must've thought he could beat the truth out of me. And none of the journalists intervened. Not a single one! They all just gawped and kept gawping. They even spurred Novak on! Eventually I managed to escape his clutches and get into the house. He tried to force his way in to see if Julie was there. Luckily I was able to shut and lock the door just in time. Of course I immediately rang the police afterwards. They had to come and break up the siege. I mean, the head of the task force, Bergmann, had already made it known that I was no longer a suspect. And if I wasn't a suspect then I was innocent, at least in the eyes of the law. Nobody had the right to trespass on my property and assault me. Novak was charged and the journalists then kept their distance, although there was no let-up in the reporting. They wrote what they liked. For example, that I'd been controlling of Julie during our relationship, desperately jealous, and that I'd stalked her after we broke up. All nasty allegations. At some point, around a year after she disappeared, I found Bishop-Petersen's message on Facebook. He came across as sympathetic. Said he couldn't imagine what it must be like for an innocent man when a suspicion like that stuck to you. And, like an idiot, I promptly fell for it. I thought I'd finally found someone who was interested in my point of view. Besides, he assured me that if there were specific things I didn't want to talk about, he'd leave those questions out. So I agreed when he offered to meet me at a café. I also did it for the sake of my mother, who was already very ill at the time. I pictured myself reading Bishop-Petersen's article to her, and then she'd have it in black and white that her son hadn't done anything wrong. That I was a good person and it wasn't my fault that we'd got into such a dreadful situation. But Bishop-Petersen didn't stick to his promises and when I tried to abort the interview, he came running after me. From the café where we'd met to my car in the carpark. Afterwards I complained about him to his editor-in-chief. But she just claimed glibly to have known nothing about any interview between Bishop-Petersen and me and promised to carry out an *internal check*. I didn't believe a word of what she was saying. I reckon she was just trying to stop me making trouble for her rag. *Internal check.*' I laugh. 'Of course the article appeared anyway, but I felt they were paying very careful attention to what they printed. Maybe they'd even hired a lawyer to be on the safe side. I consulted a lawyer too and showed him the article. He said it was all fine and there was nothing we could do about it. Nowhere in the text did it mention explicitly that I'd abducted Julie or done anything else to her, only that I'd been briefly investigated by the police. This was fact, not libel. And so I had to swallow it, but I resolved never to let myself get taken in by a bastard like that from the press again. Eventually the focus shifted to other subjects and I did have some real peace. Peace on the outside, at least, but when the anniversary of Julie's disappearance came around, I was panic-stricken once more and I prayed that it wasn't all going to start from the beginning again. Like now.' I lean back in my chair, exhausted by my breathless account.

There's a pause, then the officer again says, 'Hmm.' But at least he picks the paper back up to have a proper read of the article. When he's finished, he says, 'Why do you think it was this journalist who attacked you last night? Even if it's true that at the outset his boss had no idea he was planning the article with you, maybe he later had to answer for himself internally . . .'

'Maybe he *did* have to. I mean, he's no longer working for the *Berliner Rundschau*. Although of course I don't know if his switch to the *Abendblatt* had anything to do with my complaint. After the article appeared, I made a greater effort to check for his name anywhere, but I soon realised that no more of his articles were being published – not in the *Berliner Rundschau*, at least. I must admit, however, that I eventually stopped reading any newspapers at all.'

'And let's not forget, Herr Wagner, that we're talking about a newspaper article from 2004. Even if Herr' – the officer checks the paper to get the name right – 'Bishop-Petersen got into trouble with his boss because of you, why would he wait almost twenty years to take revenge, if that's what you're getting at?'

I say nothing.

'Did you see him clearly?' the officer asks.

'I didn't see anyone,' I reply, my head bowed. 'It was dark and I was attacked from behind.'

With a sigh, the policeman checks his watch. I chew my lip. I could just leave and let the officer take his lunch break – no hard feelings, it's just a cut, not a fractured skull, it's really nothing. But then I think of my Queen, and when I do that, it's enough for me to picture her lying in the house, had something serious happened to me, getting ever weaker. Hoping at first that I'll be home soon, then realising this won't be the case. And I decide: not this time. This time I'm going to stand up for myself, even if it means admitting to my part in the matter. Wanting my voice to sound firm, I clear my throat and say, 'No, Bishop-Petersen wasn't taking revenge for something that had happened almost twenty years ago. But because of a thoughtless knee-jerk reaction on my part yesterday afternoon.'

# THEO

I thrust the splayed deep into the earth. The ground is hard and hopelessly overgrown with whatsit. My Vera, she's right: it looks a right mess! Especially since the gardener left. I'm sweating and panting but I don't shy away from the hard work, I never did. I come from a humble background, and yet today I'm the most important man at the Charité. You don't get that far if you're not prepared to work hard. Vera's going to be delighted when the garden looks beautiful again. This thought spurs me on too. She's forever complaining that she has to do everything here at home and so can't focus properly on her charity stuff. That's while I'm saving lives – as if that were nothing! But digging the garden, well, I can see that really isn't Vera's thing. She's dainty and not tall – she only comes up to my chest. Weed that grows by the lake, from the family Geraniaceae, seven letters: Erodium. Yes, this is something for true professionals. Sitting beside me is Julie, on the ground in the middle of the lilac-coloured flowers and clumps of earth. Her long red hair shines in the sun like fire.

Her arms are around her bent knees and she's gazing at the water. She's keeping me company while I attend to the niggled garden and telling me she's got problems with her boyfriend.

'He should keep his trap shut,' I growl in between two digs of the splayed. I really thought all of this was behind us. I mean, I'd called him and made it perfectly clear that he was to keep away from my daughter. He's far too old for her and he's a stupid arse-wiper too. Julie needs to concentrate on her schoolwork; she's got a lot on her plate at the moment. She wants to be a marine biologist. That's not going to work if she creeps out of the house at night to meet this Wegner.

'No,' Julie says. 'He's right. I've really messed up. And why?' Out of the corner of my eye, I can see her clutching her long hair. 'Just because of this. It's crazy. I've put our entire existence on the line because of my bloody hair.'

'Your hair is beautiful,' I make it clear. This Wegner doesn't have a clue. Julie tells me how she wasted a whole day at the hairdresser's instead of sitting at her computer researching the topic. It might sound silly, she says, just a single day wasted, but in view of how tight their schedule is, she urgently needed that day. So she made life easy for herself and copied it. She felt like a secretary doing dictation as she sat there at daybreak, typing what the two girls from *Murder Talk* were saying.

'What was I thinking?' she says, giving me a sad look. 'Did I really imagine nobody would notice? How naïve can you be? I ought to have known better, I mean, I'm not twelve anymore.'

No, she's sixteen, my Julie, and will soon be entering Year 11. Leaning on the handle of the splayed for a quick break, I give her an encouraging smile.

'When we make wrong decisions, it's not intentional, but because at that moment we simply don't know any better. You've identified your mistake, so make something of it. Limit the damage and then do your best to go on.' I think I found a good solution to the problem; as a parent you bear a large amount of responsibility. You have to be strict, but at the same time you must never give your children the feeling that you don't love them anymore just because they've done something wrong. 'So you can do it *better*,' I add with emphasis. 'The most important thing is that you've learned from this and that the mistake wasn't in vain.'

Julie merely buries her face in her arms that are braced on her knees. 'But that's the thing,' I hear her mutter. 'I can't put it right. How would I go about it?' She looks up at me once more, her eyes welling with tears. 'Our social media channels are bursting with messages and comments from people who've noticed how similar my transcript was to *Murder Talk*'s. A real shitstorm! That's why I was so anxious about the reportage, because I knew full well that I hadn't actually prepared anything, only copied it all. That I'm nothing but a fraud! Of course I've done the research in the meantime, as best as I could. I've sat in front of my laptop for nights on end. But it's too late.'

She cries. I drop the splayed and sit next to her in the grass. Her head falls on to my shoulder. I've no idea what subject she's talking about or which piece of homework pacifically. And I thought her boyfriend was called Daniel. But if his name is Phil, that must mean the thing with that Wegner is over for good, which is a huge relief. There's just one thing confusing me as Julie's hair tickles my nose. Because this seems to be about her hair and a visit to the hairdresser, even though her hair looks the same as ever. She was born like this, with a little red fuzz on her head. But I don't want to appear unobservant, something Vera always accuses me of, only ever focusing on my work, though she was recently at the hairdresser's too. I didn't notice any difference – red is red, after all, and we can only be thankful for most red things. Red blood cells, for example. Without them there wouldn't be enough oxygen transported along the blood vessels to our organs. But Vera said, 'I've had my roots dyed, can't you see? The grey has gone.' Me: 'I love you even when you're grey. I'll always love you.' First she rolled her eyes, then gave me a wink and said, 'You pulled that one out of the bag, you ignoramus.'

Now I examine the top of Julie's head but can't spot anything.

'Highlights?' I say, venturing a slightly clumsy guess; I mean, I don't want to look like an ignoramus. I feel Julie shake her head on my shoulder, then she lifts it and looks at me.

'Shall we promise to be absolutely honest with each other? No matter what happens?'

I nod, even though I thought I could take this for granted between us. Apart from her slipping out at night to meet that Wegner.

'I did it for Phil. He kept saying how much he'd like it if I had red hair, and eventually I couldn't ignore the comments anymore. And because I hadn't done my research in advance, properly studied the photographs, I didn't realise that it might not have been the best time to change my hair colour.' There's a greater intensity in her eyes and she shifts away from me slightly. 'I remind you of Julie, don't I?'

*Click.*

i leap up, grab the splayed, i have to work, i have to dig the garden, not because vera wants me to, but because claus dellard, that arsehole, is letting it all go wild, just look at it now, what is anyone to make of this, i bet he thinks i haven't noticed how he's treating my property, i bet he thinks i don't notice anything anymore, just because of his batched diagnosis that my head supposedly doesn't work anymore, but i notice full well, i mean i'm not blind, i also noticed how he went sniffling around vera, that, that, i notice everything, i'm perfectly clear in the head, that isn't julie, it's lisa keller, who i'm filming a reportage with, and lisa didn't have a clue what she was talking about when she recorded that whatsit, whatsit, podcast, so she helped herself to their rivals' stuff and only later, when it was certain that there would be a reportage, did she do some research herself and this is what's called fraud, rightly so, and now she has to suffer the condolences, but now, and this is what's called education, she needs encouragement, so she can make up for it and so she does her best from now on, so that it hasn't all been in vain—

'Herr Novak?'

'Don't disturb me, I'm digging!'

'I just wanted . . .' She gingerly touches my arm. I allow her to, though I don't interrupt what I'm doing.

'I'd rather you told me what's going to happen now!'

Lisa takes her hand back and rubs her brow. 'First I have to go to the studio to record another episode with Phil. Then I intend to find out what the deal is with the karate instructor Julie had an argument with shortly before she disappeared. I really need to interview him, if only so that Phil . . .' She pauses briefly. 'Oh well, I've told you all that already. He found out that I copied the

*Murder Talk* episode.' She lowers her eyes. 'But it's true what you said: I made a mistake and all I can try to do now is limit the damage by focusing on the investigation and make every effort to turn it into something really good. Because if the reportage works, nobody will care two hoots what happened before. All the hate will be forgotten.' She sighs. 'I've got to deliver – it's my only chance.'

I mutter and thrust the splayed into the dry earth.

'We have to find Julie.'

'I know, but I can't guarantee that we'll succeed, Herr Novak. We can only try.'

'Call me Theo.'

'OK.' She smiles. 'I'm Liv.'

Liv insists on driving me home. I'm quite happy because Reinhard still hasn't brought my car back. I'm never lending him anything again, that freeloader, if it means my only option is the bus. Or a taxi. It's not that I can't take the bus. Any fool can take the bus. But it takes a lot of time working out the right connections on the internet and writing them down on the yellow bit of paper, only to end up calling a taxi that costs me thirty euros. Rip-off merchants! You've got to be joking! Now that I've put down the splayed, I remember why I actually came back here before I noticed how niggled the garden looked. Someone had been in Julie's bedroom. Someone who might have had something to do with her disappearance. I also remember that it was on my mind for the rest of the day yesterday. Liv had driven us back to my flat and then went to her meeting with Konrad Bergmann, that old bundler. After she'd gone, Sophia and I spent a long time talking about the video footage that Liv had shown us. About the flowers and candles which had been there the night before and suddenly vanished the next day. I kept telling Sophia that it might be a lead, and reminding her we were going to remain hopeful. Sophia didn't say much, she just cried the whole time. Hope – as I realise, I'm not a fool – is just a feeling and not a fact, nothing concrete. But Vera, my Vera, she would say that there's something in it when a feeling manifests itself so strongly. That we should listen to it. No, we *must* listen to it.

So I tried to palm Sophia off on to Reinhard. I called him and he came to my flat to pick her up. Of course I asked him about my car too and told him he ought to buy one of his own. But all he said was that I should look out of the window: that was his car there. He also said something about a precautionary measure but I wasn't listening anymore. I just wanted him to take Sophia away so I could have some peace. She didn't want to go at first. She probably didn't think I could hear when she whispered with her husband. Sophia told him that she couldn't leave me on my own at the moment – who knows what I might get up to? So I sat at the kitchen table and busied myself with a patient file. Having a low quantity of blood, nine letters. Ha ha, I bet they were trying to trick me into making a misdiagnosis. Anaemia only had seven letters. Oligaemia, that was the correct diagnosis. Or ischaemia, a synonym. Also nine letters. But no, that didn't fit with the word running across – clear outer layer at front of the eye, six letters: cornea.

'I really need to concentrate here,' I thundered at Reinhard and Sophia, who continued their whispered discussion.

'Come on,' my son-in-law then said, taking Sophia by the arm.

'The woman from the adoption agency is coming tomorrow to take a look at our house.' This clinched it and finally, finally I had my peace. I dropped the burrow and watched Sophia and Reinhard get into their car outside and drive off. It really wasn't mine and I wondered if Richard often did this – ask other people to lend him their car, just to make it look like he had a huge fleet of vehicles. Show-off. Just like that Claus Dellard. I drove a Porsche so of course he had to go one better with a Ferrari. As if something like that would impress Vera. I went to the computer in my room and looked for the way to Grunewald. First I had to take the underground to Adenauerplatz, then a bus to Hagenplatz and the rest of the way on foot. I nodded at the computer screen. Adenauer, a good man. What would have become of post-war Germany without him? I thought it was only right he'd been given his own square. Although the way there and then on to whatsit, Grunewald, seemed unnecessarily compromised. So I called a taxi. Thirty euros the greedy driver wanted from me – rip-off merchant! You've got to be joking! It was already dark when he let me out at our old house, but that was fine by me. Maybe the person who Liv and her boyfriend had almost stumbled on would only come back at night for fear of being detected. And maybe this time it would be me who caught him in the act. But I certainly wouldn't let him go, oh no. I'd grab him by the collar until he started wheezing. If necessary, I'd beat the living haylights out of him until he talked: where was my Julie?

Opening the gate as quietly as possible, I snuck to the house. But then I hit a problem. My head. My stupid, damaged head knew that there was a key somewhere. But where? I pictured Sophia talking about a spare key that Vera had hidden somewhere. But

## DARLING MINE

I couldn't find it. I looked in all the possible places – under the old terracotta pots where no flowers had grown for years, just cracked old soil, and behind the shutters on the ground floor. Nothing. I began shaking the door and even threw the full force of my shoulder against it; I just wanted to get inside. There was another way in, I remembered. A broken window, I remembered. The boiler room? Yes, the boiler room. I hurried around the corner to that very cellar window. But my body wouldn't fit through the narrow opening and I hated it, I hated it, this worn-out, stiff, useless body. In the past it would have been a doddle getting through there. I was junior runner-up in front crawl at SV Albatros from 1967–69. Three years in succession! Maybe it was the memory of this, or more likely desperation, that drove me down to the boat shed. This door was locked too, but even when we lived here, the padlock had been more of a joke than a security measure – easy to pick. I dragged one of the two old rowing boats from the shed to the shore, made it more comfy with a tarp I also found in the shed, and crept in. Given my size there was no way I could lie down, but I had to sleep somewhere. Or I wanted to. Down here by the lake had always been my favourite place. One day I wanted to sit there, by the jetty, and take my last breath as I stared at the glittering water, the endless, indivisible blue. I listened to the gentle waves in the mild breeze, to the trees and Julie, who hummed a song for me as I used to do sitting by her bed when she was a little girl, some tune I'd made up. Sometimes she'd say, 'Daddy, that isn't a song.' I'd reply, 'Just because you don't know it, that doesn't mean it doesn't exist.' I'd learned this from Vera, who often said such things, most of which I thought were rubbish. All that mythological, isotopic stuff. I would argue using biochemistry or some studies, and of course I won every discussion – ha! But secretly I loved it that Vera was the way she was. So believing in her own way, so hearty and soft. I thought it would be good for Julie if she got the best of both of us for her path in life. My logic, my doggedness, my strength, and Vera's heart, which beat in a different way, not just as an organ in her chest.

That's how she was, our Julie. And I hope she's still the same. She will be the same, I'm sure of it.

I was woken at daybreak by the birds squawking and the pain in my neck. I sat up and couldn't believe it. What did it look like here? Everything overgrown, completely abandoned. I jumped out of the boat and fetched the splayed from the shed. Julie was here too. No, Liv, it was Liv. She hadn't been looking for me but she found me all the same. Me or a place where you could be sad for a while in private. We're friends now.

'I spoke to Konrad Bergmann yesterday,' she says when we're in her car on the way to my flat in Spandau.

'Task force halfwit,' I growl as I fiddle with the buttons for the radio. Maybe I'll find the station that played the song from the school ball. Tchaikovsky's 'Warts of the Flowers'.

Liv laughs. 'Grunewald task force, to be precise. Do you remember the thing about the broken cellar window? The question of whether the kidnapper or kidnappers could've got into the house that way?'

I growl once more. Music today is ghastly. Vera wouldn't like it either.

'He told me that traces from the cellar window – dust and

spiderwebs – were found on a sweatshirt and tracksuit bottoms in a washing basket in Julie's bedroom.'

'Hmm.'

'Is that all you've got to say? Do you know what that means, Theo? It was Julie herself who climbed through the cellar window. Not that night, of course, or the clothes wouldn't have been found in her room. Logically she would have been wearing them. But it means that she must have climbed through the window on a different occasion.'

'Not only once.' I sigh. I still haven't found the right station.

'You knew that?'

'I suspected that she often slipped out at night to meet that Wegner. Maybe she was worried we might hear if she used the front door. I even caught her once.'

'But you never told Bergmann that.'

'Bergmann is an obnoxious moron. He thought in any case that she'd run away. If I'd told him that this had been a regular occurrence, he'd have shelved the file even quicker.' One, two, three, one, two, three – I've found the station! It's just not playing the right waltz.

'Hmm, I see,' Liv says. 'He also told me that your house was full of neighbours when the police arrived and you were going to get some friends to take Sophia away.'

'That's right, I remember.' I move my right index finger in time to the waltz – one, two, three. 'Sophia, she looked pretty in Julie's dress too.'

'Yes, I can imagine. But what was the problem with Sophia the morning after Julie disappeared? Why did you want to get her out of the house? Why were there so many other people there?'

I screw up my eyes.

'There weren't that many people. There was just . . .' I screw my eyes up further. Claus Dellard comes into my mind, but that can't be right. What would that arrogant bastard be doing at our house in a situation like that? 'I can't remember exactly. All I know is that Vera didn't want Sophia there when the police arrived. She cried so terribly, Sophia, because she was terrified about Julie.'

'You wanted to protect her.'

'Yes.'

Liv puts her hand on my knee. When I look at her, she smiles. 'You were good parents.'

'Not good enough though, eh? Otherwise the reportage wouldn't be necessary.' I lower my finger. The orchestra on the radio doesn't need me; they continue to play on their own. But my daughter, she needs me.

'We have to find Julie, Liv.'

She nods.

I'm a bit sad when I'm standing outside my block of flats in Spandau and watch Liv drive off. Or maybe I'm just tired after the uncomfortable night in the boat. I climb the stairs to my flat. Someone has peed in the stairwell again. I hope it wasn't me; that would be extremely embarrassing.

The flat is empty – of course. I think I ought to give a lecture. So many people always turn up when I give a lecture. I mean, I am the director of the clinic for heart, thoracic and vascular surgery at the Charité. I'm a luminescence in my field, a real luminescence, not a self-proclaimed one like that arrogant Claus Dellard. I'm even known abroad and I'm forever getting asked to give lectures somewhere. I expect my inbox is already overflowing again with invitations. I go into my bedroom and switch the computer on. I knew it! One hundred and thirty unread emails. Most of them not serious; I send them to the recycle bin. Until I suddenly come across one which makes me gasp for air. But I can't. My breathing, my heart – for a moment everything stops.

## 3. SKYEARTHBLUE

### LARA

The moment I began to feel the effect of the sedative, I was finished. The devil had won. He was in the detail as well as in the bigger picture. He was everywhere and his power was unlimited. I sank into my fog as if into a quagmire and this time I was sure I'd never surface again. He'd keep my body alive, no doubt. Like a trophy, a stuffed animal whose head the proud hunter nails to the wall, he'd bring me *home*, lay me on the bed and lock the door. Three meals a day, sometimes none, depending how often I gained consciousness. *Consciousness*, or whatever was left of it after all the tablets he'd get down my throat from now on.

I was even more amazed, therefore, when I came to, to find myself again beneath the rustling canopy of leaves, again surrounded by the shallow ripples of the lake, again in the sun. I was still in the hospital and this woman – the doctor or nurse – was again standing beside my bed. *Isabel*, I recalled. That's what he'd called her. She was just hanging up an infusion bag on the mount above my head and to the side. I squinted carefully past her in an attempt to detect his presence. Just because I couldn't see him – as I now knew – didn't mean he wasn't there, or that he wouldn't appear at any moment.

'Isabel,' I whispered, tentatively and hoarsely. She didn't hear me the first time. 'Isabel,' I tried again, probably only a touch louder, but it felt as if I were screaming and I made myself jump.

'Lara,' Isabel said in a friendly voice, turning to me.

'Shh,' I said, wanting to put a finger to my lips. But my arm, my entire body was still leaden and I couldn't move anything. Isabel gave me a look of surprise but sat obediently on the side of the bed nonetheless. She appeared younger than I'd thought the first time. Mid or late twenties, maybe, with shoulder-length blonde hair and rounded, rosy cheeks. The picture of health, unlike me with my bones sticking out everywhere and my pale skin stretched thinly over them.

'Is everything OK? Are you in pain, Lara?'

*Lara*. I wince again, even though it ought to be obvious that he would have told her a name. Every patient needs a name and mine was Lara. Like Lara Antipova in *Doctor Zhivago*.

'Don't you worry,' Isabel continued. 'We've just got to do a few more tests, like taking a bit of your blood. That's why we can't give you a higher dose at the moment, but—'

'No!' I interrupted her anxiously. 'No pain. Have to . . . stay awake. Help me!'

Isabel narrowed her eyes.

'Is he here?' I blurted out quickly before she could waste the little time we had on anything else.

'Who?' she asked, turning her head to the door.

This was enough of an answer for me. 'What's the date?'

'It's 3 August.' She paused, startled, while my eyes filled with tears.

'Which year?'

'2023. Lara?'

Isabel felt for my hand, which had cramped to a fist in the blanket. I'd suspected it must have been years. I'd sensed my body decline, I'd watched several winters rage outside my barred window. But: 'Almost twenty years?' I hadn't expected that. I'd been his prisoner for twenty years. A noise rose from my throat; I sounded like a wounded animal.

'Please,' I begged her, croaking. 'You have to listen to me very carefully now, OK? Will you do that, Isabel?'

She nodded, puzzled.

'Thank you,' I said, attempting a smile.

Maybe I had actually been given one more chance, a truly final one.

## LIV

Phil's mood seems to have improved considerably, Liv notes, when they're sitting opposite each other in the studio in Knesebeckstrasse. They're just about to begin the recording about the Vlado Taneski case, but there are a few things to sort out beforehand. That's what Phil said, at least, and it disconcerts Liv. Her stepfather, Heinz, also had the knack of formulating things in the friendliest way. Subliminal threats whose impact was greater the more calmly he uttered them. The determination that Liv had felt after her conversation with Theo is in tatters and the feeling from yesterday evening is suddenly back. One that had kept her awake all night in front of the laptop. At least at breakfast she'd been able to tell Phil how she'd googled Julie's karate instructor, Jason, until the early hours and come across some old newspaper articles about the successes of KSVG, including a photograph showing Jason with his pupils. She'd recognised Julie and Sophia in the photo too by their red hair. Much more importantly, she'd found Jason's surname in the caption: Willmers. KSVG itself had been wound up around five years ago, so she couldn't contact the club itself to get more information on Jason, but she googled his name and found a telephone book entry: Jason and Maya Willmers, together with an address in Grunewald. She called the number before Phil got up. But the line was dead.

'That doesn't mean anything,' she told Phil at breakfast with deliberate panache. 'They haven't necessarily moved just because the number isn't active.' Phil didn't react. 'Maybe they just don't have a landline anymore,' she added hastily. 'Wouldn't be a surprise in the age of the mobile phone, would it?' Phil merely shrugged and went back to buttering his roll. She felt incredibly stupid, stupid and alone. Not only had she spent the entire night researching Jason Willmers, she'd also specially put on the T-shirt Phil had given her for her birthday and worn her hair down, just as he preferred it. Everything to appease him, to show him what an effort she was making. Not a syllable, just the monotone scratching of his knife because of the hard butter. Liv couldn't bear it any longer. She had to get out, wanted to get away from here. 'See you in the studio later,' she just about managed to utter before getting up and leaving the flat. She got into the car and drove around as if on autopilot until she ended up at the Novaks' old house. Likewise on autopilot, she used Theo's trick to get through the iron gate. She wandered through the garden down to the lake, past the two young girls with red plaits who were there in her imagination. Eventually she stumbled across a very real Theo, bent double and asleep in an old rowing boat. He cut a sad picture, especially as Liv assumed that when he woke up he probably wouldn't remember how his addled brain had brought him here. She briefly considered leaving again, but the sight of him looking so vulnerable in that uncomfortable position stirred her heart, a heart that craved genuine intimacy. Liv would have loved to have had a father like this, or any father, particularly now when she felt so alone and lost. Like the old man lying there in the boat. They recognised each other, Liv thought, the lonely, the desperate, those bruised by life. They magically attracted each other. Just as she and Phil had once attracted each other, in another time, in another life, as it now seemed. Cautiously she reached for Theo's shoulder and touched it, tentatively at first, then almost insistently, to wake him up. Without asking what had brought Liv here, he leaped out of the boat, ran to the shed and came back with a spade. He told Liv he needed to spruce up the garden, then got down to work. This wasn't what Liv had hoped for, but she accepted it all the same. While Theo began digging clumps of earth like a madman, Liv told him about her argument with Phil. It did her good to talk about it, even though she assumed Theo was taking in only half of what she said. Nonetheless, he was here and that in itself helped Liv feel a little less lonely. How lovely this was, how restorative!

But it doesn't last, this feeling, Liv realises now, having driven Theo home. Sitting opposite Phil in the studio, she feels herself slumping again internally – despite, or maybe because of, the friendly tone that Phil suddenly strikes. Liv hopes that they'll get the recording over with quickly and then she can head off back to Grunewald to find the Willmerses. At the moment anything seems preferable to walking on eggshells in Phil's presence.

'I've been having a bit of a think,' Phil says to her, pushing a piece of paper across the desk. 'In fact, I've also prepared something too.' Liv bends forward slightly to see what he's written. 'People think we plagiarised *Murder Talk*, right?' Phil shifts forward too and taps his finger on a particular section. 'What they can't know is that the whole thing was deliberate.' He grins.

Liv skims the text she's going to have to read out and stifles a sigh. What Phil obviously believes to be a master plan to appease the community, is to her mind disgracefully tenuous and ludicrous. Does he really think that the people who were smart and attentive enough to catch her out are going to fall for this? Never in a million years, Liv thinks. Nonetheless she nods. She'll do everything Phil wants her to – the key thing is that he's friendlier towards her and that she can leave the studio as soon as possible.

'Excellent,' he says with a satisfied smile. 'Let's begin recording, then.'

PHIL: A very warm welcome to you, dear crime gang, to another episode of *Two Crime – The True Crime Podcast* with . . .
LIV: . . . me, Liv Keller and . . .
PHIL: . . . me, Philipp Hendricks. What we have for you today is the first part of an absolutely unbelievable story of revenge, which – and we promise you this – even right to the end, you won't realise is actually about revenge. But before we embark on today's case, Liv has got something to say to you. Liv?

LIV: Yes, that's right, Phil. Over the last few days, we've received many messages on our social media channels relating to the episode about the Julie Novak case. Some of you have pointed out that my account of the case was very similar to that of our dear podcast colleagues at *Murder Talk*. Well, all I can say is . . . congratulations! Because this is exactly what we were hoping – that you really do listen to us closely. You see, recently we've learned, to our horror, that all too often audiences don't listen attentively to these stories, nor appreciate that those who feature in them are actually real individuals. Instead, people listen while they peel potatoes, clean or go to sleep. We deliberately based our episode – which, as you now know, is a prelude to our major reportage – on the *Murder Talk* one because it was important for us to find out how focused you are when you listen. And, guys, we're bowled over. You've proven that you're the best community we could wish for to accompany us on our project. You don't let our podcast wash over you, you have a genuine interest in discovering what we've got to say. By doing this, you endorse our claim to be the best and most responsible true crime podcast out there. Thanks for that!

PHIL: That's the truth, guys: it was all intentional. An experiment, if you like. So congratulations from me too, and huge thanks! But now to today's case – or at least to the first part of it. And Liv, maybe the starting point for this reminds you a bit of us, the way we're now approaching the Julie Novak case. Let's go back in time to 2004, to North Macedonia. For years, the little town of Kičevo has been haunted by a serial killer who has a thing for older women. The police appear to be watching on idly until local journalist Vlado Taneski decides to investigate the killer's gruesome deeds, thereby writing the story of his life.

LIV: Oh, wow. Sounds exciting.

PHIL: Uh-huh. And just you wait. So, we're in Kičevo. Picture this as a bit of a bleak place. Around 30,000 people live here, many in run-down blocks of flats leftover from communist times. But the majority of the residents aren't bothered by this; they're very attached to their homeland and they love to wallow in memories of the old Yugoslavia, a world away from capitalism. Like the journalist Vlado Taneski. Working as a local reporter for *Nova Makedonija*, the biggest daily paper in Macedonia, Vlado writes about the area around Kičevo: short articles and reports about local politics, air pollution from the mining industry in the region, or that year's maize yield. Vlado, born in 1952, is married to a lawyer with whom he has two children. The four of them live in Vlado's parents' house. In 2002, when Vlado is fifty, his father dies in the summer, followed half a year later by his mother. When in 2004 his wife gets offered a job in the capital, Skopje, Vlado decides not to move with her and the children, but chooses to stay faithful to Kičevo, the town of his birth. The couple come to an arrangement whereby she will live in Skopje with the children during the week and they'll see each other at weekends. For the family this is a major upheaval. Both Vlado and his wife throw themselves into their work. And towards the end of the year, in November 2004, something happens that will soon take up almost all of Vlado's time and energy: the sixty-four-year-old cleaner, Mitra Simjanoska, disappears. Mitra has just finished shopping at the local market when she vanishes without trace – until mid January, so two months later, when her dead body is found. Mitra was beaten, raped and tortured. But, as the forensic department establishes, she was strangled to death only two weeks before the discovery of her body. This means that Mitra was kept captive for more than a month after her disappearance, before finally being killed. Fortunately, the police soon have an idea who might be responsible. Two young men have recently been arrested: Igor Mirčeski and Ante Risteski. It has already been proven beyond doubt that in December 2004 – between the time of Mitra's disappearance and the discovery of her corpse – they attacked and killed an elderly man in his house in the neighbouring village of Malkoetz. Not only did the two men rob their victim, they physically abused him, including subjecting him to sexual torture. For example, they—

LIV: No, Phil! Please, no details!

PHIL: OK, you're right. Suffice to say that the old man died a terrible death at the hands of his tormentors, and that this type of abuse would tally with Mitra's death too. But Mirčeski and Risteski, who have confessed to killing the old man, swear that they have nothing to do with Mitra's murder. Nor does the male DNA found on Mitra's body match that of either man. The public prosecutor nevertheless charges the two of them because he's convinced of their guilt. The court agrees and both men are sentenced to life imprisonment.

LIV: Even though the DNA wasn't a match?

PHIL: Yes. I suspect they had a keen interest in clearing up the Mitra case as quickly as possible to reassure the population, and so pretty much ignored the circumstances surrounding the DNA. Anyway, as court reporter for *Nova Makedonija*, Vlado writes about this case. He too is convinced at first that the murder of Mitra has been solved with the imprisonment of Mirčeski and Risteski. Or at least this is what he writes in his article about the trial. Initial doubts surface, however, in November 2007 – three years after Mitra was killed – when a lady from Kičevo disappears: fifty-six-year-old Ljubica Licovska, who – wait for it – worked as a cleaner, just like Mitra.

LIV: Seriously?

PHIL: Absolutely, and not only that. Ljubica's body isn't found until February 2008, three months after she went missing. She too was beaten, tortured and abused – and evidently strangled not long before her corpse was discovered.

LIV: Which means she was also kept prisoner by her abductor for weeks on end.

PHIL: Correct. Now Vlado writes an article in which he highlights the parallels between the two cases, including strong criticism of the work of the police and department of public prosecution. For, let's not forget, with Mirčeski and Risteski, they'd already arrested Mitra's supposed killers. Vlado's article becomes a leading story that soon spreads across Macedonia. In the meantime, the authorities are coming under pressure because people agree with Vlado: the parallels between the murders of Mitra and Ljubica are too close for the cases to be unrelated. The investigators, however, have no idea where to begin, and in the eyes of the public, they soon look like utter clowns.

LIV: For good reason. After all, it was proven that the two prisoners killed the old man. And they admitted it too.

PHIL: Exactly.

LIV: And so it's right and proper that they should be in prison. But to pin another murder on them, whether out of laziness or prejudice – that's appalling.

PHIL: And the public sees it the same way. Nevertheless, months pass in which the police investigation is idle, until another woman disappears on 7 May 2008: the sixty-five-year-old cleaner Zivana Temelkoska. Although in this instance, her body is found a week after she goes missing.

LIV: OK, that's new.

PHIL: But that's the only thing which is different. Otherwise the body has the same signs of abuse as those of the first two victims. Which is to say: Zivana was also raped, tortured and finally . . .

LIV: . . . strangled.

PHIL: You said it. Vlado files another report for *Nova Makedonija*. In his article he writes: *Kičevo is gripped by fear after another woman's body was found at the weekend*. He calls the murderer a *serial killer*, the *Monster of Kičevo*.

LIV: What? Why are you looking at me like that?

PHIL: To be honest, I'm waiting for you to come out with one of your pithy comments. Like, the killer could've been someone unsatisfied with his cleaner's work . . . No? What's up, Liv? You not feeling well?

LIV: No, nonsense. I just think . . . No, I don't feel like it.

PHIL: Guys, I think you can hear that Liv isn't quite herself today. She's completely absorbed in the research for the Julie Novak case. We'll be able to reveal more soon, but for now all we can promise is that it's going to be groundbreaking. And for you, Liv, I've got a little tip if, like now, you're urgently in need of some relaxation. Because our partner this week is HolyGlow, the complete relaxation ritual for the home, including body mousse, body lotion, a set of incense sticks and the access code to the exclusive HolyGlow Aura website, which has guided meditation for any time of day and every mood. And the best thing is that, with the code *twocrime10*, all of our listeners get a ten per cent discount. Not bad! But now back to our case. Vlado's articles get a huge amount of attention. Readers throughout the country now know his name, they know him as the man who – unlike the police – has dedicated himself wholeheartedly to the victims of the Monster of Kičevo. And Vlado realises that he has to press on. So he embarks on his own research and questions the relatives. He learns, for example, that Zivana, the last victim, was lured from her house by a trick. Apparently, a neighbour tells him, Zivana got a phone call saying that her eldest son had been injured in a car crash and admitted to hospital. When she raced out of the house, she met the neighbour and told her briefly what had happened. After that, nobody saw the sixty-five-year-old again. When Zivana's son, who was supposedly lying injured in hospital, came home that evening and didn't find his mother there, he asked the neighbour if she knew where she was, and learned of the strange telephone call.

LIV: My God, that's terrible. Not only is he insanely worried about his mother, he finds out that *he* is the reason why she left the house in the first place and ran slap bang into the arms of the killer. That's doubly awful.

PHIL: For this reason, he and Zivana's other relatives are now obviously very grateful for Vlado's efforts. Not least because they know each other – the family live just around the corner from Vlado. He also interviews one of the team investigating the cases and later writes: *According to the police, there have meanwhile been several suspects, all of whom come from Kičevo. After various interrogations, however, they were all released. It has also been confirmed that traces of the killer were found on the victims' bodies, which are now being analysed.* Soon it is established that the traces of blood and DNA definitely come from the same male individual, but the question remains as to who this is. Liv, if you were investigating this case, what sort of killer do you think you'd be looking for? What sort of profile would you draw up?

LIV: Well, I . . . I'd think that, like the victims, he'd be from Kičevo. And that he probably knew them, because – as Vlado found out from the relatives and later the neighbour – the third victim was lured from her house by a telephone call.

PHIL: But he could've found the number in the phone book too.

LIV: Yes, but he also knew that she had a grown-up son. So he must've known her, or at least been watching her for some time. Apart from that, I'd say he's smart and not lacking in self-control. Although he kills regularly, he does it at intervals of several years. He wants to kill again, but he doesn't have to do it all the time. So it seems to be an urge, albeit one that he's able to keep in check for long periods of time.

PHIL: Not bad, Liv. Anything else? Have a think.

LIV: Well, we're talking here about a small town of 30,000 inhabitants. And he kept the first two women imprisoned for a couple of months without anybody noticing. How does he manage this? I'd say that he probably lives alone. Or at least he *operates* alone.

PHIL: What makes you think that?

LIV: Well, for one thing, an accomplice always implies a risk, especially in such a small town of 30,000 people, where, as I imagine, there are plenty of problems such as unemployment and so on. I expect people often go to the pub, drown their frustration with others, and maybe they get a bit talkative. And you know the saying: three can keep a secret if two of them are dead. Apart from this, I think the victim profile is too specific for it to be favoured by several perpetrators.

PHIL: Do you hear that, guys? Our Liv is gradually getting into gear. But it's true what you say: all the women were around sixty years of age and they all worked as cleaners – that's really specific.

LIV: The killer's a man too, no doubt about that. He raped and tortured his victims.

PHIL: Right.

LIV: And he's strong because he strangled them. I would guess he's middle-aged and has a personal problem with older women. With his mother, perhaps?

PHIL: That would be classic, almost a cliché.

LIV: But it's often the case, isn't it? Many of these stories have classic motives. That's nothing new. And you already let on to us at the start that this is about revenge. Revenge is a really old motive.

PHIL: And a very human one too.

LIV: The urge for revenge is human, perhaps. But not its execution.

PHIL: Unless the urge becomes so strong that it dominates your whole life. Imagine someone hurts the person you love more than anything else in the world. Are you sure you'd be beyond taking revenge?

LIV: No, but the guy is a serial killer. Maybe he has a very specific hate object and he takes his revenge on them again and again, by targeting victims who are a proxy for this one person.

PHIL: Bingo, Liv! That's exactly what the police think too.

LIV: Oh, are they still involved? I'd rather got the impression that Vlado was the only one really trying to find out what had happened. And, most importantly, who was responsible.

PHIL: It may seem that way, yes. And of course the police aren't at all happy that Vlado leaves them standing there looking like ignorant fools. Now they don't have any choice but to investigate under severe pressure – but Vlado keeps thwarting them, sometimes publishing information the police want to keep under wraps. For example, the fact that the third victim, Zivana, was strangled with a phone cord and her body was then tied up with it.

LIV: I see. So now it gets political.

PHIL: Spot on. And then, all of a sudden, another person disappears.

LIV: Let me guess. A woman around sixty working as a cleaner?

PHIL: Nope. This time it's Vlado himself who goes missing.

LIV: What? Please don't tell me that the police have taken him out of action because of his articles?

PHIL: It's much bigger than you think, Liv. Much, much bigger. But I'll tell you and our dear crime gang more in the next episode.

LIV: Please! I want to know how it ends!

PHIL: I'm afraid you're going to have to be patient. We'll be back next week at *Two Crime – The True Crime Podcast* with . . .

LIV: . . . me, a frustrated Liv Keller . . .

PHIL: ... and me, a very patient Philipp Hendricks. Yes, sorry, guys, that today's episode is a bit shorter than usual. But we're very busy with our research into the Julie Novak case at the moment. And you know how important it is to us to do our work carefully. So, see you next week for part two of the case of the journalist Vlado Taneski. Until then, stay safe and sound – and don't forget our discount code *twocrime10* for your order with HolyGlow. Ciao, ciao!

# THEO

*Click*, it goes inside my head. *Click*, like an old-fashioned toggle switch. Light on, orientation. I'm sitting on an examination couch. I didn't sit down on an examination couch. And I certainly would never do it in a vest. What would people think?

'Take my cloat off at once!' I bellow at the man in front of me.

'Theo . . .'

How does he know my name? What's going on here? I pounce from the couch straight at the man. He stumbles backwards, panting, 'Everything's fine.' But that's not how he sounds, as if everything's fine. He pants, a sign of agitation, I think. $C_{23}H_{29}N_{30}$. Tricyclic antidepressant, calming, mood-lifting, providing relief from anxiety and tension. Opipramol, yes! He could do with that now. I'd have given it to Vera straightaway, but not him, he can forget it. He's a thief! He's wearing my cloat. My arms shoot forward – they're in good shape, I was three times junior runner-up in front crawl at SV Albatros from 1967 to 1969 – and they hit him, my arms, causing him to teeter another step backwards. He deserves that, the man! He's a thief and a kidnapper! He beat me unconscious with the splayed from my own garden and then he dragged me here. I hurry to the door, but then it hits me – *click* – now I know. The man isn't a dangerous stranger, but an arrogant bastard. I turn around. He's recovered and has come after me. Now we're standing so close to one another that the tip of my nose is almost touching his forehead. He's a fair bit shorter than me. I bet that's secretly always bothered him.

'I have to go,' I say firmly over the top of his head. 'It's an emergency.'

'You're the emergency, Theo.' He raises his right hand and presents me with a slim folder, a patient file. 'Do you remember what happened earlier on?'

Yes, I do. It was just a very brief out, like a wink, like the press of a button – light off, light on. The email. But I'm not going to tell Claus anything because he's not trustworthy. Liv, I need to see her. It was her I wanted to see earlier, before I suddenly found myself here. With Claus Dellard, the arrogant bastard, the lardy-da who considers himself a luminescence and thinks he knows everything about me and my condition. My condition, don't make me laugh. Claus Dellard, now there's a condition. No, an illness, the creep. But I mustn't quarrel with him now, no matter how much I'd love to.

'If you say so,' I answer with a gruel. 'My shirt, please.'

Claus points at the examination couch, then turns away and hobbles off to his desk. Cherry wood, maybe even maharaja. Show-off.

'What's wrong with your leg?' I ask as he sits down awkwardly. In truth I don't really care and if I had to sprinkulate, I'd suspect he slipped on his own trail of slime. But it feels good to point out to him his own infirmity, this, this smart-arse with his con-sheeted ways.

'A minor incident with ... with an emergency.' He forces an inane smile. 'It was nothing.' I'm about to smile to show him that he can't be such a luminescence if he comes out of an emergency with a limp. But then it dawns on me that he just called *me* an 'emergency' and I leave it. I shoved him, today at any rate, and maybe more often than that. I wouldn't want to hear that it might have been *me* who injured him. So I just say, 'Hmm,' and 'My Vera, she didn't like effeminate men.' I tense my biceps accordingly. Claus doesn't react. Of course he doesn't. He knows full well that he's a wuss. Instead he opens my file, takes a burrow and begins scrabbling with it. I expect he's writing more rude things about me in his stupid folder. I have to remain composed, lucid and focused. This was always my greatest strength; it's why Vera loved me. I go over to the couch and grab my whatsit, my whatsit, my shirt. Behind me I hear Claus sigh, once, twice. The third time he does it, I spin around, with one of my arms still caught in the sleeve.

'Listen, do you have some sort of problem?'

He looks up. His glasses are perched low down on his nose, pressing his nostronauts together. 'Hmm?'

'What's up, I asked.'

'I didn't say anything.'

'No, but you're sighing!'

'And?'

'I don't have time for this sort of nonsense now.' I wriggle back out of the shirt – wrong sleeve, start again. All of this is Claus's fault; he's distracting me with his stupid sighing. Don't let yourself get worked up, Theo. The email. I have to see Liv. Stupid sleeves, stupid Claus.

'Just so you know, I didn't want your money.'

'What money?' Claus asks. *What money?* Huh. He's behaving as if he always went around with a hundred thousand in his back pocket. Which is peanuts if you consider the value of my house. But for hard-working people, for people who don't come from wealthy families like he does, it's a goddamaged fortune.

'You screwed us over! Don't think I don't realise it. You were just lucky we didn't have time to find another buyer who, unlike you, would have paid a fair price for the house.'

'Are you talking about all those years ago?'

'You exploited our plight, and on top of that, you had the cheek to play the goody two toes to Vera!' My right arm, still helplessly trying to find its way through the opening to the sleeve, begins to move as if it had a mind of its own, making little circles in the air. I could break Claus's silly arrogant nose with a single punch, then he really would have a reason to gramble. I'm strong, I was with SV Albatros. 'She was ill, you arsehole!'

'You mean—'

'The hundred thousand you gave us for the house! It's worth ten times that much! And the most scandalous thing of all is the way you've let it go to rack and ruin!'

Claus shakes his head and makes another attempt to say something. But not yet, matey, I haven't finished yet, oh no.

'Yes, you didn't consider that, did you? I was there, you see? I've seen with my own eyes what you've done to my house! The garden is completely wild—'

'Theo!'

'And inside, it stinks, it's all moulderry!' Now then, that hit home. I master the second sleeve and get to work on the buttons. I have to see Liv. Liv looks like my Julie. Liv is my friend. Liv will help me.

'Theo . . .' Claus again. I look at him but only briefly. Buttonholes are the work of the devil. 'I never bought your house. I just gave you a loan.'

I stop short. And stare. Claus puts down the burrow and now adjusts the framed photograph that's on the left of his desk. I screw up my eyes.

My memory.

Vera and I in the kitchen. But I hear her say it! I hear her say that Claus wants to give us one hundred thousand for the house and he's promised not to let anyone move in for the time being. And I hear myself grouse. But I know too that Vera's right. We'd first have to find another buyer who could quickly come up with enough money to pay us a decent price.

'No!' I protest to Claus. 'That's not what happened! You wanted the house! Just like you always wanted everything that was mine!'

'I offered to buy the house, that's right. But you didn't want that. You thought the eight hundred thousand that I could offer you at the time was inadequate. So you asked me for a loan instead.' He looks once more at the photograph in front of him and sighs, yet again. 'Which I've never asked for back, by the way.'

I rub my head. Is that possible? I replay it in my head, this memory of Vera and me in the kitchen. We're talking about whether we have to sell the house to Claus and I say, 'The price, Vera!'

That's right.

Just: *the price*.

Nothing about a hundred thousand.

I keep remembering.

Standing there at the kitchen window, my hand pointing at the lake. Saying, 'Out there, Vera! That's where I intended to sit and die one day!'

Vera: 'I know.'

'It's what I said the day we moved in. This is the place we're going to live for the rest of our days. This here is our home!'

Vera beginning to cry. The two of us know. If she doesn't start her therapy in the US quickly enough, the rest of our days is now. Me lowering my hand. The kettle boiling.

'Fair enough,' I say when I pour the water for Vera's tea. 'You're right. We need the money. We need Claus. But we're not going to give him the house!'

'What, then?'

'I'll bite the bullet and ask him to lend us some money. A loan, Vera. A hundred thousand, that ought to do us. And as soon as you're better and I can start work again, we'll pay it back. OK? I'm not having him think that we're freeloaders.'

Yes, it's true.

Claus is right.

That's how it was, nothing else. Why didn't I remember that immediately?

'Whether you believe me or not, Theo,' Claus interrupts my thoughts, 'I didn't hesitate for a second to help you. And I didn't care about ever getting the money back. I wanted Vera to be able to have her treatment. I really hoped that—'

'Be quiet, Claus,' I growl. 'Please.'

He nods. 'I just want you to know that nothing has changed as far as I'm concerned.' He turns the framed photograph he's been fiddling with all this time towards me. The picture shows him and me in the sunshine by the lake, an arm around each other's shoulders. On my free arm I'm balancing the three-year-old Sophia, who still looks like a dwarf. A baby, even when she was a small child. In the foreground Julie is doing a handstand in the grass, while Claus's son is holding her legs, supporting her.

Such a thin boy, all shin and bones, and thick glasses on the arrogant nose he's inherited from his father. I can't remember his name right now but I know I always found him a bit ugly. Julie, on the other hand, doted on him, I remember that too.

'As far as I'm concerned,' Claus continues, 'you're still the best friend I ever had. Even if you might have forgotten that.' He returns the photograph to its original place and points at the file. 'And I'd like to be there for you now too.'

I don't know what to say at first. Claus and I might have been friends at some point; somewhere deep inside me, I sense that he's right. But I've stopped liking him and I'm sure I won't start liking him again just because he's shown me an old photograph. I have to leave, I have to find Liv. The email, the email, the email. There's just one more thing I have to know before I go.

'Does that mean the house still belongs to me?'

'No, Theo,' Claus says, sounding completely tomfounded. 'Of course not.'

'But . . . if you didn't buy it back then . . . who does it belong to now?'

## LARA

The devil came into my hospital room several times a day and I always pretended to be asleep. I could sense him, as he sat on the edge of the bed, watching and waiting for my eyelids to flutter, for a finger to twitch or for me to make any movement at all. But I just lay there, as if dead, as he always liked me to be when I was under the influence of his medicines. I didn't have to make much of an effort; my body automatically went stiff in his presence. I imagined him getting increasingly nervous. Usually *he* was the one who determined the state I was in. But now that I was in hospital, with all the other staff around me, he'd forfeited a portion of his power. Sometimes, when she was in the room too, he asked Isabel about my condition, whether I wasn't gradually making progress, surely I must have detoxified by now? I heard Isabel stammer, refer to the doctor in charge and also how she was bold enough to offer her personal opinion that I ought to put on a little more weight before I was discharged. I realised that what I'd been able to say to her so far had, at the very least, unsettled her. It hadn't been the whole story. For one thing, it was still a huge effort for me to speak at all. But I also had to be circumspect. What if he were suddenly standing in the doorway again and heard me trying to get Isabel to be my accomplice? She knew what my real name was now. And that I'd been abducted. By him, the devil.

She thought I was befuddled to begin with, maybe even mad, just like he did. She said things like, 'Relax, you'll feel better soon, Lara.' She was like this a few times and I felt deeply frustrated. But then it occurred to me I could prove I was telling the truth. 'Please, just search my name on the internet.'

The next time she came into my room and stood by my bed, she was as white as a sheet. She took my hand and looked me in the eye with sheer horror. Isabel was going to help me, I knew this now. I just mustn't think of what he might do to the two of us if he got wise.

## LIV

Liv ran away from home once too. She was fifteen at the time. She'd packed a few things in her rucksack and climbed out of a window because she was worried it would make too much noise if she unlocked the front door in the middle of the night. Her bedroom window was on the ground floor of Heinz's house. The room was pretty much next to his study, while the bedroom he shared with Liv's mother was upstairs. Heinz often worked late into the night, whereas her mother usually went to bed around nine.

Liv had concocted a plan, or at least run through a few alternatives in advance. She'd take the train to Hamburg and from there go on to London. Where she would have gone on a school trip a few months earlier if Heinz hadn't cancelled. Officially she was ill. Flu, well there's nothing you can do about that. In truth, as he'd whispered to her the night before he rang the school, his breath moistening her ear, he didn't want to be without her. She'd heard that many men like him stopped doing what they did when their victims reached puberty and their bodies developed accordingly. But Heinz was different; her new physiognomy only seemed to excite him more.

She was going to go to London, therefore, if only because Heinz had denied her this experience. But she didn't make it any further than the main train station in Berlin. There she was picked up by two security men who found it odd that a girl of her age should be hanging around on platform seven shortly after one in the morning. They took Liv to an office, gave her a cup of hot chocolate, and tried to persuade her to reveal her personal details. When she refused, they told her that in this case they'd have to notify the police. Liv got scared and, a moment later, a telephone was thrust into her hand.

When Heinz picked her up, she braced herself for the tirade that would be launched the moment they were sitting alone in his car. But he remained quite calm. What's more, he smiled at her while she cowered in the passenger seat and said, 'So you think you're old enough to fend for yourself, do you?' Liv didn't respond. 'I understand, Livi. When you grow up, you hanker after new experiences, that's perfectly natural. I'm sure I'll be able to help you with this.' And that smile again, that furtive look.

The next morning at school, Liv felt even more ashamed than usual. Moreover, the hard wood of the chair made it almost impossible for her to sit quietly in lessons. But she didn't confide in anyone. Not the security men at the station, nor the teachers the following day. Shame, she thinks, shouldn't be underestimated as an emotion. Shame stops people from asking for help. Or maybe, like in Julie's case, admitting your mistakes. Perhaps she did run away after all. But if that were the case, Liv reasons, there's no way she could have done it on her own. For Julie was sixteen when she disappeared, and so just a touch older than Liv, who'd been picked up at the station after barely an hour. No, she thinks. A girl that young sticks out if she's wandering around certain places at certain times of day. Unless she's in the company of an adult. Daniel Wagner? Liv shakes her head. Bergmann said Wagner had an alibi. Albeit one that the witness in question, one of Julie's friends, later retracted. And Phil's right: the sort of stamp the police saw on the back of Wagner's hand when he was questioned can last. Liv works out her next steps. Talk to Jason, the karate instructor. Find the boy from Julie's group of friends and talk to him about the alibi he gave for Wagner before retracting it. Talk, talk, talk, in the hope that the answer to the puzzle lies in one of these conversations. What she mustn't do is get bogged down; she has to take one step at a time, calmly and without distraction. This is why she'd headed straight for Grunewald after the recording with Phil, to Jason Willmers's address. And she's almost there when her mobile rings showing an unknown number.

Sophia.

At the end of the phone call, Liv immediately turns around. Her new destination: the Charité.

When she blusters into the waiting area, Sophia is sitting on one of the chairs with her knees up. Beside her is a young man with dark skin, his arm around her shoulder. Sophia has been crying again, as Liv can see even from a distance.

'What happened?' she asks, still breathless from her own haste.

As if on cue, Sophia leaps up and falls into her arms. Liv doesn't know how to react to begin with, but then returns the embrace rather clumsily.

'He ran out into the road, screaming, and almost got knocked over,' she sobs into Liv's shoulder. 'He's absolutely fine, but who knows what might have happened if the neighbours hadn't intervened?'

'I don't understand. Why did he do that? Why did he run into the road?'

Sophia takes her arms from Liv and looks at her. 'He wanted to come after you when you drove off. He was calling your name the whole time.'

Liv doesn't understand. Or maybe she does. Theo must have had another of his episodes, where, at the flick of a switch, he's flung from reality. Just like yesterday, when he tried to jump out of Liv's car on the motorway, or this morning, when he started digging up the garden of his old house.

'I'm so sorry,' Liv says softly. She's literally waiting for Sophia, who was just hugging her, to have a change of heart and heap reproaches on her. But nothing of the sort happens. Her father is in a bad enough state as it is; Liv's being around all the time, badgering him to talk can only be agitating poor Theo even more.

'Come on, darling,' says Sophia's companion, who's now joined them. 'Wouldn't you rather sit down?' Sophia nods but makes no move to return to her seat.

'This is Richard, my husband,' she says to Liv, who politely holds out her hand. Richard's handshake is restrained and warm.

'Delighted to meet you.' Liv doesn't really know what to do now; she looks around, at a loss. Theo, she guesses, is being examined now. She really wants to ask Sophia how the near-miss happened, why – as she said – he wanted to go after Liv. At the same time she doesn't want to look like the inquisitive journalist who's only ever thinking about her story. In the middle of this uncomfortable silence, Richard offers to get them some coffee, which they gratefully accept. Sophia smiles dreamily as he walks down the long corridor to the cafeteria.

'We're trying to adopt a baby.'

'Wow, that's great.' Liv smiles too. 'And really exciting too, I bet.'

Sophia nods, wandering over to the chair she was in when Liv had entered the waiting area.

'Richard has wanted a child for ages,' she says when she's sat down. 'I wasn't keen at first, but now it's my greatest wish too. Do you have children?'

'No, and I don't think I ought to have any, either, to be honest.' Liv lowers her gaze and there's a twinge in her chest. 'My own childhood wasn't particularly nice. Sometimes I get the impression that only now, as an adult, I'm catching up on certain things, or even having to learn them for the first time. Finding myself, for example.' She laughs. 'But there are still a lot of things I get wrong.'

'I'm familiar with that.' Sophia nods pensively. 'I don't know how much time I've wasted trying to replace Julie for my parents. I even toyed with the idea of studying marine biology, like she'd planned to, but then I plumped for medicine. That only lasted two semesters. I can't stand the sight of blood.'

'I'm the same.'

'You produce a true crime podcast.'

Liv shrugs. 'The core of our work isn't in forensics. We're more interested in the psychology behind the crimes. Of course we come across the odd crime-scene photo, but that's not the focus.'

'The small but important difference between theory and practice.'

'Yes, sort of. I read on some forum that you trained in social pedagogy.'

Sophia shakes her head. 'That information is pretty out of date. It's true that I started training. Because of my mother, probably. She did a lot of charitable work, you know. For homeless people, for example, or for children and young people with psychological disorders. But I didn't manage more than an internship in that field. I don't feel particularly comfortable when too many people are around me anyway, but if, on top of that, they come with their dreadful personal stories, I'm out. I can't listen to that sort of stuff.'

Liv nods thoughtfully. Sophia comes with her own dreadful story, she thinks. And it's easy to forget that 'the loved ones' referred to in reports of criminal cases aren't just the parents. They also include siblings, grandparents, uncles and aunts, friends and so many other people whose lives are upended from one day to the next and who often can't return to normality. Liv gently lays a hand on Sophia's arm.

'I can understand that.'

'No, I really don't think you can,' Sophia responds. But, to Liv's relief, she doesn't sound reproachful.

'So, what do you work in now, if you don't mind my asking?'

'Statistics for the building authorities. Numbers are self-explanatory. Everything's straight, there's no doubt and nothing to discuss. There's something calming about it, I think. I like it.'

Liv nods once more, with her hand still on Sophia's arm, who's staring straight ahead at the door of one of the consultation rooms. Probably the one where Theo's being examined. Liv also notices how pale Sophia is. Not just now, because of the shock.

Sophia is always pale. Her skin is almost translucent, with small reddish rashes; she has a pointed chin and her dyed black hair looks dry. Liv wonders if this is the right time to ask Sophia whether she'd be willing to do an interview too, then decides against it.

'Thanks for calling me,' she says instead, and means this honestly.

'Please don't get me wrong. I never had anything against you personally. It's just . . . I just want my father—'

The door to the consultation room swings open. Theo Novak comes stomping out, straight towards them. Within seconds he's grabbed Sophia and lifted her to her feet.

'You lied to me!' he bellows at her.

Sophia shakes her head and wriggles. Liv is just about to intervene when Theo lets go of his daughter as abruptly as he took hold of her. He hurries down the corridor out of the waiting area, before turning around after a few metres and calling out, 'We need to go, Liv! We really need to go! I've got to show you something!'

Liv glances again at Sophia, who looks shocked and bewildered, before setting off after Theo, who's almost at the lifts already.

'What's the matter, Theo? What's happened?' Liv asks, as she hears Sophia croak from a distance, 'Dad?'

# DANIEL

Earlier, at the police station, I told the officer about yesterday, my moment of madness, my unfortunate outburst, which I'm still ashamed of. I told him about how I'd marched into the *Abendblatt* building, a copy of the rag under my arm, to speak to Max Bishop-Petersen. I spoke to the woman at reception, who wanted to know if I had an appointment. When I told her I didn't, she picked up the phone and asked who she should call. Slapping the paper on to her desk, I turned to the article and snorted, 'The person who wrote this pack of lies!'

The woman raised her eyebrows. I could see she was considering hanging up again. But then she sighed, dialled a number and was soon connected to Bishop-Petersen.

'I've got a Herr—' She broke off and looked at me.

'Daniel Wagner,' I growled. 'Page twelve. He knows.' She passed the information on, said 'Uh-huh' a few times, then hung up.

'I'm sorry, Herr Wagner. Herr Bishop-Petersen has an editorial meeting now and he doesn't have any time for you.' Having anticipated this, I asked to speak to a managing editor. 'Sorry,' the woman apologised again. 'I'm afraid that's not possible either without prior arrangement.' She turned back to her computer and started typing. As if I were no longer there. But I was. Yes, I fucking well was!

'Please,' I tried, a general 'please' that I hoped she'd understand. *Please let me speak to Bishop-Petersen. Please don't ignore me. Please feel my pain. Please give me back the last twenty years of my life.*

After a moment the woman did actually look up again. She gave me a sympathetic smile before demonstrably pushing the newspaper towards me, then continuing to type undeterred. With this she was telling me I had to go. But I couldn't. I felt my face starting to burn with anger. An anger that at once took hold of my entire body and scorched my composure.

'Listen to me: I want to talk to that arsehole! And right now!'

Snatching the paper, I rolled it up roughly and whacked the desk with it several times. Shocked, the woman pushed herself back in her chair, leaped up and started shouting. For help, perhaps, or security. I can't remember because I couldn't hear anything anymore. Blood was rushing in my ears like a torrent; I merely saw her gaping mouth and could only guess at the sounds coming out. There was uproar. People clustered by the reception desk, someone pulled me away, shoved me and I stumbled. Then I was suddenly outside, in front of the building. Whimpering and alone.

The police officer who'd listened to my story looked at me blankly.

'But if you didn't see Herr Bishop-Petersen in person yesterday, why would he have attacked you later on out of revenge?'

'Because he's trying to intimidate me!' I cried. 'He must've heard about the fracas at reception! He's worried about his job!' I realised how absurd this sounded, how overblown. Would a newspaper editor really get his hands dirty, risk being charged by the police for assault, maybe even manslaughter, just to silence the enraged subject of one of his disgraceful articles? And besides, as the officer rightly pointed out, the article wasn't anywhere near as bad as I thought it was if you weren't the subject of the piece.

'I just *know* it was Bishop-Petersen who attacked me,' I said, sounding abject. 'I mean, it's only a hunch, but it's so strong and—'

'Herr Wagner,' the policeman sighed. 'I can't file a charge merely on the basis of a hunch.'

'But who else, after all these years, would suddenly—'

'Herr Wagner,' he interrupted again, with a shake of the head this time. 'I can offer to call Herr Bishop-Petersen, but—'

This time it was me who shook my head. 'Don't bother.' With that, I picked up the newspaper from his desk and left.

Nobody was going to help me. What could be done, in any case? I had nothing of substance against Bishop-Petersen. I couldn't even say with certainty that he attacked me. And yes, perhaps I had become slightly paranoid because the attack had taken place so soon after my visit to the newspaper's offices. Then there was my disappointment in Frau Lessing and the thought of Anna, who must've already spread my story – or her version of it – throughout the care home. Fortunately for me I was off sick because of the injury to my head. But my boss's voice on the phone when I told her this morning about my sick note! Her tone hadn't escaped me. This empty 'Hmm, hmm, I see, well, look after yourself and get better, Daniel.' I bet I'd get another call from her before the end of my sick leave; I could virtually hear her explaining how she could no longer keep me on. Someone who'd behaved like I had couldn't be trusted to work in my sort of job. Nobody wanted me.

I recalled Vicky, a pretty young woman I'd met a few years ago on a dating platform. How determined I'd been to shed the past and start again from scratch! Vicky was a single mother with a two-year-old boy. Even better, because at a stroke I now had my own family! We met for coffee, ice cream, at the playground, at hers. These were innocent hours, no urges to satisfy, a yearning at most. I wore again the aftershave that Julie had liked so much, Subtil Pour Homme, went jogging to get in shape again, and made an effort with my hair. Although I no longer looked like a young James Dean, I could pass muster as a dedicated partner and father of a small child. I was happy, or at least something close to it.

After a few weeks, however, I realised Vicky found it strange that we'd never met at my house. So I finally brought myself to invite her over. Her son was at his grandparents' that evening, which meant we had the whole night to ourselves. After dinner, which I'd cooked, Vicky wanted to go to the bathroom upstairs. Despite my directions, she got the wrong door. Which was locked. When she asked me about this, I told her that it had been my mother's bedroom. Vicky hesitated. Perhaps she was expecting me to unlock the door to show her. But I was uncomfortable with that idea; it felt too personal, and maybe that's why I reacted slightly angrily. I'd developed feelings for her, I really had. All the same, she wasn't Julie. She was Vicky, who got a call from her parents a quarter of an hour later to say her son was crying for his mummy and would she please come home. Vicky, who I never heard from again, never. I'd fallen for her once more, that whore by the name of Hope, dressed up in her finest robes. I'd fallen for the prospect of being able to fall in love again, have a family and a home that consisted of more than a roof and a few walls.

Sometimes I thought about moving away. Away from Berlin, maybe even leaving Germany. But I stayed. The mere thought of the effort it would take only made me more exhausted. Here I still had the house at least. And my Queen. And maybe I secretly abandoned the hope that one day I would wake up and something would have changed as if by magic. That didn't happen, obviously, at least not in the sense that my life was unreservedly good. But these past few years had been tolerable. Bearable. Queen and I had enjoyed our peace. Until everything came washing up again suddenly, with the podcasts and Bishop-Petersen's article.

I rub my brow. I don't know how long I've been sitting in my kitchen staring at the computer screen in front of me. I was just going to check to see whether the article had been picked up by other media outlets yet. And of course a few online forums were already posting quotes from it. Then it struck me that I should write Bishop-Petersen an email. Maybe I wouldn't send it, but maybe I would. I wanted to write from the soul, explain to him what his article was doing to me. So I put his name into the search engine to find his email address.

Now I'm sitting here, staring at a number of photos, all of Max Bishop-Petersen. Only the man in these images isn't Max Bishop-Petersen. Or at least not the Max Bishop-Petersen who interviewed me all those years ago.

## LIV

Where's her car, or do they have to take the bus? Any old fool can take the bus, it's not that, but it would waste unnecessary time, and they need to hurry, hurry, he urgently needs to show her something. Theo literally pushes Liv out of the Charité building. She finds it as hard to keep pace with him as she does to follow what he's saying. Julie, something about Julie. And Sophia, who's a liar. He knows this from Claus Dellard who he refers to as 'that arrogant bastard', but who Liv now knows is Sophia and Julie's godfather. And who, it turns out when Theo tells her about his MRI scans, is probably his doctor too.

'My car's in the underground carpark,' Liv pants, then asks, 'Why did Sophia lie? And what about?'

'The house!' Theo calls out, spinning in a circle a few times as if disoriented.

Liv understands this, at least, and points towards the carpark. Theo nods and goes hurrying off, Liv behind him.

'What about the house?'

He suddenly stops as if he'd been struck by lightning and looks at her. 'Claus didn't buy the house! He just gave us a loan! But the house, I signed it over to Sophia, years ago!'

'What? Why?'

'Because I've got debts!' He shakes his head, his pupils flicker, his arms thrash about. 'We could still be living there, Liv! Instead I'm in this hovel in Spandau and Sophia's bought this shoebox of a dump in Weissensee!'

'She'll have had her reasons,' Liv surmises, and feels stupid the moment the words have left her lips. *Stupid, stupid, stupid little Liv.* Of course Sophia will have had her reasons, just like everyone has their reasons to do what they do, for better or worse. Perhaps she couldn't face the prospect of continuing to live in the house her sister disappeared from, because every room, every door and every wall had absorbed memories over the years that aren't easy to bear. Liv knows this. After moving out of her parents' house, she's never set a foot in it again. She does agree with Theo, however, that Sophia lied. More than that, she put on a real show pretending to look for the front door key yesterday. For if the house really does belong to her, she would surely know where the key is. That's if she doesn't already have a spare one that she keeps on some ring at home rather than beneath a loose step by the house. Liv decides she's going to ask Sophia about it. At the same time, she feels that Sophia might be able to provide her with a rational explanation. For the very reason that sometimes you could go back, but on a different level, you simply can't. Or, more accurately, you don't want to. Liv thinks of the conversation she just had with Sophia in the hospital and the realisation that she still suffers terribly from Julie's disappearance. How much she yearns for a normal life, with her husband Richard and a baby, and how much she loves her father even though he often makes things so difficult for her.

'I'll talk to her,' Liv says reassuringly, putting a hand on Theo's shoulder. 'I'll find out, I promise.'

'How could she?'

'I think she was just trying to protect you.'

Theo shakes her hand off. '*Protect, protect.* Do I look like a man who needs protecting?' He cranes his neck, perhaps to look taller than he already is. With the next movement he bends his arms, squaring his shoulders and tightening the wrongly buttoned shirt across his chest.

'Even the greatest and strongest sometimes need protection,' Liv says, smiling. 'And that's perfectly OK. It doesn't make them any weaker.'

'Hmm,' Theo mutters. 'We need to go.' He refuses to tell Liv the reason for all the hurry and fluster until they're in the car because, he says, he doesn't want to risk anyone overhearing them. But even after instructing her to drive to his flat in Spandau, he remains tight-lipped.

Liv tries again. Glancing over at the passenger, she ventures a circumspect, 'Theo?'

'Julie,' he says, only just audibly.

'Julie? What about her?'

Theo doesn't reply. It occurs to Liv that she's never asked him what he thinks happened to his daughter. She knows that, unlike the police, he's excluded outright the possibility that Julie might have run away from home of her own free will. He'd already made this plain in the television interview he and Vera did, when he held the family photograph up to the camera as if it were proof. But he'd never tried to provide an explanation for the bizarre ransom demand. Or for the fact that there were no signs of a break-in, and no unfamiliar DNA or fibres around the cellar window – seemingly the only possible way to enter the house. *You can't simply assume that people will tell you everything they know*, she hears Phil's voice in her head. *You need to ask the right questions.* Maybe, Liv thinks, she didn't dare bring this up with Theo because she wanted to gain his trust first. After all, she couldn't know how quickly things would develop, especially the relationship between the two of them. She realises that now he does trust her. For it was *her* name he called when he went running out into the road. *She's* the one he wants to share with whatever it is he's being so secretive about. Also, it now dawns on Liv, the ransom demand of thirty thousand euros no longer seems so measly if you know that Theo has got debts. Debts that may have also existed then. That's what he himself confirmed yesterday: the Novaks led an extravagant lifestyle, with cars, holidays, and staff to look after the large house and grounds. But this would mean that the ransom demand had been written by someone who was aware of the family's financial situation. Maybe it was Daniel Wagner, after all? Liv remembers the photograph in the newspaper showing Theo attacking Daniel Wagner outside his house. He must have thought Wagner was guilty at the time; he wouldn't have gone for him so brutally otherwise. He hasn't reiterated his suspicion in Liv's presence, however. Apart from the growl he gave after the interview yesterday, when Wagner's name cropped up in conversation with Sophia.

'Theo, this is driving me mad,' she now says, glancing over at him. 'Please don't keep me on tenterhooks. What do you want to show me?'

But Theo says nothing. His head is leaning against the side window and he's looking up at the sky. Is he thinking about his wife? Julie? Beetroot? Liv accelerates, breaking the speed limit. She doesn't want to risk him losing the thread again and forgetting what was so important that he ran after her, shouting, and was almost run over.

The drive to his flat in Spandau takes a good half hour. Liv is already getting her camera ready as they're climbing the stairs. When they enter the flat, she's taken aback by the chaos that's mushroomed in just a single day. The coffee cups from yesterday's interview are still on the table; the tablecloth has shifted and is bunched up. A plate is on the table too, with a gherkin, half of it cut, as well as a pile of dry cornflakes. On the rim of the plate, to either side, are a knife and fork in tarnished silver with curved handles. Where a napkin might have been is a roll of loo paper. And scattered on the floor are towels and items of clothing. Liv is hesitant about keeping the camera rolling, but then decides to do it. Rather than the mess, she focuses on Theo's back, which she follows to his bedroom, to his computer. When he moves the mouse, the dark screen flares up and shows an opened email. Theo turns to Liv, his eyes glassy. His voice cracking, he just says, 'Read.'

No salutation, Liv notes. Just the text, just a single word:

skyearthblue

Liv lowers the camera. She looks at Theo, confused and also somewhat disappointed. Is that all? Is that what Theo almost got run over for?

'Skyearthblue?'

He nods wildly. 'That's *her* word.'

'Her . . . ?'

'*She* made up that word!'

'Who?'

'Julie!' Theo's voice is strained; his face has turned red at a stroke. 'Julie made it up. *Skyearthblue!* Nobody else has ever said that!'

'Slow down, Theo,' Liv says, pointing at his bed. Again she's worried that the tension might send him into a state where she can't follow him anymore. 'Just sit down and then tell me everything in detail. This is really important now, do you understand?'

He nods wildly once more.

'Julie was still a little girl when we moved into the house, four or five perhaps. I remember going down to the lake with her for the first time. It was a summer's day, very sunny and a koboldblue sky. I stood with her in my arms on the jetty and said, "Look at that. Isn't it magnificent? You can't see where the water stops and the sky begins. Some days it's all as one." "That's a beautiful colour, Daddy," she replied. "The blue, do you mean? Yes, you're right, a beautiful colour." "Skyearthblue," she then said, clapping her hands.' He looks at Liv expectantly. 'That's *her* word,' he adds again, presumably in case Liv still hasn't understood.

'Do you think—'

'*Her* word, Liv! It's *her* word!'

'Like a code?' Liv points the camera at the desk, keeping it running as she takes a closer look at the email. Just this one word: *skyearthblue*. Liv checks the sender, *Nutcracker11*, then the email provider. No proper name anywhere, nothing. A word and an email address. She turns to Theo. Is it possible? Could he be right? She looks at him; she has to say it – or better – he has to say it, as if that would make it real. 'Do you think that this email could only be from Julie?'

Theo just stares at her.

'Does the sender ring a bell? *Nutcracker11*?' Liv probes. But nothing more comes from Theo. His face, bright red a moment ago, is pale again. Almost as if he were feeling slightly nauseous. Liv knows that she mustn't lose him now.

'Nutcracker,' she repeats, at which Theo begins to move his right hand as if he were conducting.

He starts counting, 'One, two, three . . .'

Theo, who wants to dance. Liv, who, according to him, didn't pay enough attention in dance class, who stumbles and knocks her shin against his bed. Who can't free herself from his clinch. Liv, who's almost in tears because she doesn't know what to do. Theo is far away, somewhere in his world, at his daughter's school ball. Humming, he twirls her around. Liv finds his grip on her hand too tight and that around her waist even more so. It's no longer Theo's voice humming a melody in her ear, it's a different one. Liv begins to tremble. Suddenly everything's spinning. She issues a 'No!', soft and pitiful at first, then another that sounds archaic, and then she pushes Heinz away with every ounce of her strength; he staggers back and lands on the floor. Only now it's Theo lying there again.

'Oh God, I'm so sorry!' Liv says, rushing over and grabbing him by the arm to help him back up. 'I didn't mean . . .'

Theo's bottom lip is quivering. 'No, I'm sorry,' he says quietly. 'But death doesn't care if it's Christmas or Easter or holiday or the school ball. I'm the director of the clinic for heart, thoracic and vascular surgery, that's my job.' When he's back on his feet, he gently puts his hand out to her cheek. 'Don't be angry with me, my angel. I'll make it up to you.'

'I'm not angry with you,' Liv replies. 'It was my fault, not yours.' She takes him back to his bed so he can rest for a while. To her relief, he doesn't offer any resistance. She lifts his legs on to the bed and removes his shoes. Then she waits until he's closed his eyes, leaves the bedroom and goes into the kitchen. Liv takes out her phone and presses the call icon for the number Sophia contacted her on earlier.

Sophia arrives on her own, which Liv is glad about. Richard, her partner, made a good impression on Liv – so friendly and caring. And it wouldn't have occurred to her on the phone to ask Sophia to come without him. But it's better this way. When they were in the Charité carpark earlier, Theo had made it clear that he didn't want anyone hearing anything. He won't be pleased that Sophia's here, especially after the argument about the house. But now Liv needs someone at her side. She feels out of her depth; she lost her cool when Theo grabbed her to dance. Her cool *and* her grip on reality, just like him.

She pours Sophia a cup of the coffee she made while waiting for her. She's not going to tell her about the email immediately; first she has to be sure that she hasn't got Sophia wrong. So all she tells her for now is how Theo started conducting silently, only to force her to waltz a moment later. Sophia nods as she listens to Liv. She's only too aware of her father's sudden outbursts.

'It's not easy, I know,' she says, agreeing with Liv. Then she knocks back a large gulp from her cup, as if it were schnapps rather than coffee. Now Sophia feels emboldened. 'Although I'd really like to know what's going on here. I mean, put yourself in my shoes. I'm at work when my godfather calls me from the hospital to say my father's been admitted. Claus asks me if I know a Liv, because apparently she's the reason he was almost in an accident. So I race to the hospital, I sit there and I'm torn between the relief that nothing serious has happened and the fear of where all of this might lead. And when he comes out of Claus's room, he screams at me, then marches off with you, but without further explanation.'

'The reason he screamed at you was because you didn't tell him your old house is still in the family's possession. That you own it.'

Sophia audibly swallows. 'Oh . . . that.'

Liv raises her eyebrows.

'He signed it over to me shortly before my mother went to the US for her treatment.'

'Because he had debts.'

'Yes, my parents were broke. But my father lacked understanding. He absolutely refused to sell the house because he didn't want to accept the truth. He saw their financial difficulties as a temporary phase.'

'OK, I see,' Liv said. 'But why did you let him believe he'd sold the house to your godfather? Why can't he live there anymore? Why did you pretend to go looking for the key when we were there yesterday, when as the owner, you knew full well where to find it?'

'I wasn't pretending, that's not quite right. In the past I kept reminding him that he'd signed the house over to me. But he kept forgetting. As if he didn't want to accept it. Or as if it was easier for him to focus on Claus as the bogeyman, than to admit to himself that he'd gone through all his money.' Sophia runs a hand through her long black hair, which – as in the hospital – is down on her narrow shoulders and unbrushed. 'OK, sorry, no, that was unfair. Mostly it was the costs arising from my mother's illness that ruined him. Either way, eventually you get tired of going over the same thing again and again. And it's not like he reacts gratefully if you remind him of something. He gets angry very quickly, so that you're almost scared of him. Or so sad that it breaks your heart.' She picks up her cup and blows on it, even though the coffee's gone cold by now. 'There's no handbook on what to do when grappling with this illness, Liv. And it's exhausting, for God's sake. It's so bloody exhausting, because the person who's ill treats you like an enemy. When all you're trying to do is help.' She looks up again, seeking direct eye contact. 'Would you have ever put a foot in that house again if you'd been in my shoes?'

Liv shakes her head.

'But nor could I have let him live in it alone!' Sophia adds. She makes a hand movement as if to encompass the room – the sitting–dining area with kitchenette, but most of all, the chaos prevailing here. 'Look at this! And, as for the key, yes, of course I've got one. It's in some drawer at home. But ask me which one and I've got no idea. I have no use for that key.'

'But why didn't you just sell the house then? Surely that would have solved two problems at once: you'd have been rid of the house, and your father would've had some money.'

Sophia puts her coffee cup down.

'Do you want the honest answer? I didn't dare. I mean, you never know what else might enter his mind one day. I thought that if at some point he remembered he'd signed the house over to me and I admitted I'd sold it, he'd kill me.' She opens her eyes wide, as if horrified by what she's just said. 'All I'm saying is that it's hard enough for me to maintain an emotional connection with him. Often he pushes me away and that hurts so much, Liv. I will sell the house, I definitely will. But not until he . . .' The sentence remains unfinished, but Liv knows what she's getting at. She stands up as if on cue and goes over to Sophia. Sophia, who seems to sense what Liv has in mind, gets up too and allows herself to be hugged. With her hand on the slim back, Liv can feel the bones of Sophia's spine. Earlier, when she was waiting for her and trying to get some ideas down in her notebook, she wondered whether Sophia might not have been responsible for the altar in Julie's old room. Sophia had lied, after all, about the sale of the house, and as the legal owner, she also had access to it. Perhaps, Liv had thought, Sophia had built the altar to have a place where she could grieve. But now that she's holding Sophia in her arms and feeling her vulnerability again, the idea seems absurd. Sophia hasn't been inside the house for ages and it would probably have stayed that way if Theo and Liv hadn't forced her yesterday. All that Sophia wants, Liv concludes, is to be there for her father for the rest of his life and ride out what that entails.

'I'm so sorry,' Liv whispers, feeling Sophia nod silently on her shoulder. Letting go, she says, 'There is actually a specific reason for your father's behaviour today.' Sophia nods again, like someone who's been asked if they're ready to hear a dreaded diagnosis. 'He got an email from a *Nutcracker11*,' Liv explains. 'And he thinks this email might have something to do with Julie. In fact, he even thinks that Julie—'

'*Skyearthblue*,' they suddenly hear from the direction of the bedroom. Theo is standing in the doorway. He's holding, rather awkwardly, Liv's camera, which she'd left on his desk. The small recording light is still on. Theo comes over to the table and hands the camera to Liv with the words: 'Here, you're going to need it.' Then he turns to Sophia, who looks like she's paralysed with shock. 'It's *her* word, Sophia. The email, it's from Julie. She's alive.'

## DANIEL

I stare at the picture of Max Bishop-Petersen, which has blurred before my eyes. Colourful lights are exploding in my head, like yesterday when I was knocked to the ground. My chest feels as if there's a metal band tightening around it. I hear myself gasp for air and whimper. I hear the voice of my mother telling me that I mustn't give up, mustn't give up, mustn't give up. That I'm a good boy, and that the anger, the anger, the red anger doesn't suit me. She says I don't have to prove anything to her, she doesn't have to have it in black and white, she knows anyway. Nobody has to put it in print for her. She believes me, she knows me. I start seeing images, all the images in my head. Julie, who's so beautiful and who I want back. Vicky, who I hear nothing more from than a permanent ringing when my calls go unanswered. Anna, with the newspaper under her arm, sneering at me; and Elly Lessing, sitting up in bed, the picture of health, and saying, 'My husband always said, "Elly, you can never really know what's going on in another person's head."' Images, images, all these images. I see the throng of reporters outside our house, I see the flashing of their cameras. I see Novak's contorted face and feel the tightness, the pain preventing me from breathing after his fist has hit my face. I see myself in the mirror, with my black eye, gingerly touching the discoloured inflammation with trembling fingers, crying. I'm a weed, a loser, such a pitiful, useless arse-wiper. I see the face of a thin, pale boy. *Why, why, why?* And then Julie again. *How could you? We're the two people from Bowie's 'Heroes' who, who kiss and love each other forever, even when everything around them is being blown to pieces.* I see my life, this bombed-out crater, and I hear them laugh, they're all laughing, loudly and clearly, as if they were here, all of them gathered together in my kitchen, standing around here laughing at me. But that's enough now, finished, I've had it. I slap my forehead, I need to concentrate, turn my gaze back to Bishop-Petersen, memorise his face. I close the laptop and run upstairs to Mother's bedroom.

I can already hear Queen moaning through the closed door. 'You have to take your Queen for regular visits to the vet, Herr Daniel,' Frau Lessing says inside my head. 'You really must.' I say, 'Queen is on top form,' and it's true. Queen is fine because I look after her. Just like I've always looked after everybody. I take the bunch of keys from my pocket, put the correct one in the lock and open the door, doing everything as quietly as possible. And I'm right: Queen is moaning in her sleep. There's nothing wrong with this, it's perfectly normal, she's fine. Just to be sure, I wait there for a moment, but her breathing is calm and regular. I smile. I love listening to her breathe; it soothes me every time, reminding me of what's really important in life.

'I'm going to make sure it's over for good,' I whisper, promising her that I'll hurry. I leave the room and carefully lock up again. Then I hurry down the stairs, rush out of the house and get into the car.

Max Bishop-Petersen. Face pink like a pig – how fitting! – only thinner. Brown, shoulder-length hair, thick eyebrows, piercing blue eyes. I've memorised his face so I'll recognise him. I check the clock on the dashboard and speed up. Half past five. I steer with one hand; with the other I google the paper's telephone number on my phone, then press CALL. As I'd hoped, just a few seconds later the voice of the woman at reception resonates from my car's speaker. I mumble the name Theo Novak because it's the first one that comes to mind instead of my own. I can't risk the woman remembering me as the guy who started the commotion by her desk yesterday. I ask if Bishop-Petersen is still in the office and she says yes, although he's just gone into an editorial meeting. That's enough for me; I hang up and put my foot down. If what the woman said is true rather than a stock excuse to keep potential nuisances away from Bishop-Petersen, I should make it. The editorial meeting should last at least half an hour. I mean, you need enough time to tie up all the lies and package them accordingly.

I park in a side street near the offices. Then I wander around outside, far enough away to avoid being conspicuous, but always with the entrance in sight. I wait and decide not to go away until he comes out, even if it takes the whole night.

I'm going to nail him.

## THEO

My father was a hunter. He always knew what to do. He always had a plan. Like during the plague of wild boar in 1954. They were really belligerund, those animals. They marched into people's front gardens, trampling and eating everything in sight. Afterwards he got an award, my father, made of bronze, that had a plank with his name on: Wilhelm Adalbert Novak. He wore a dark green felt hat, my father, which he'd have on even during family mealtimes so that none of us forgot who we were dealing with. I can't come up with such a felt hat quickly, only a fishing cap I found in my shoe cupboard. Even so, it's perfectly clear: whoever's wearing the hat has the say, he makes the plan. Which is very important right now because there's a right hellobello at my kitchen table. Sophia thinks that someone's having a joke with this email; she reminds me of all the disturbed people who've pestered us down the years. Those calls in the middle of the night, disguised voices claiming to be Julie's kidnapper, nutters who thought they *were* Julie. People who weren't content with playing tricks down the phone, but turned up at our house instead. A medium, a private detective, several would-be Julies, in various stages of derangement. People who left animal entrails outside our front door, along with crazed messages. People, people, always people – some we were able to laugh about, some who seriously started to worry us.

'I wasn't afraid of anyone,' I point out, thrusting my fist into the air.

'I was,' Sophia says, and that's downright rude, with no rustification. I look at her, she looks at me. I look at her and keep looking. I wait. I'm not having anyone say she didn't have the opportunity to set things straight. At any rate, Liv is filming all of this with the video camera for her reportage. She records that Sophia was afraid, which means my daughter doubted my ability to protect her. But I did protect my family! I always protected them! I – *click*.

Get out! i bellow, then everything becomes a jungle, everything gets mixed up, i've grabbed sophia and am now dragging her to the door, i want her to go, now, she's got to leave, get out of my sight, the door hits her shoulder and she pretends it hurt, i can still hear her wailing even after i've closed the door behind her and then she rings, she rings again and again, and hammers her fists against the door and calls dad! let me in again, dad, dad, please! and liv wants to grab the door handle behind me, but i don't let her, i pull her into my bedroom and liv squeals and leaps about as if i was going to do something awful to her, but i've never intended to do anything bad to anyone, on the contrary i've saved thousands of people's lives, i've repaired thousands of hearts, only a couple slipped through my fingers, only a few i wasn't able to protect, julie, i didn't protect her, i failed there, i know i did, i can hardly forget it, how could i, and this makes me angry, but i'm even angrier at sophia, who i always protected, vera and sophia never, ever had to be afraid, i was always there and i always did my best, or not, and despite this sophia comes up with such nonsense and i don't need that now, it's absolutely the last thing i need, for now it's time for action, so I drag liv to the computer and let her watch me type my reply to nattcracker11's email, and i nod to liv, full of determination and with my hat on my head, i nod like my father before he went into the forest to take on the wild boar, that was in 1954, then i press send – *click*.

## LIV

One hundred and forty-seven episodes. One hundred and forty-seven and a half, to be precise, if you include the first part of the new one about the Vlado Taneski case, which they recorded this morning. Every week a new story and hundreds of photos, this vast pool of licence-free, martyred faces, which Liv can't tell apart any longer. Almost 150 criminal cases, too many to remember every one. And yet a few names immediately come to mind, something that surprises even Liv. Victims of crimes, victims who'd often developed Stockholm syndrome or been subject to some other dreadful brainwashing. Victims, some of whom were kept captive by their kidnappers for years and decades, over time being granted more and more freedoms. Colleen Stan. She'd just turned twenty when, in 1977, she was abducted by a seemingly friendly couple with a baby. Abused as a sex slave, she spent the first few years of her imprisonment locked in a wooden crate beneath her tormentors' bed for up to twenty-three hours a day. Later she looked after the household and child and, in 1981, after being kept hostage for four years, was even allowed to visit her family. The kidnappers were convinced they had complete and utter control over their victim. And they were right: the frightened Colleen didn't breathe a word to her parents about the torture she'd suffered. On the contrary, after visiting her family, she returned to her abductors for a further three years before she worked up the nerve to escape in 1984. Or Shawn Hornbeck. Yes, Shawn Hornbeck! Kidnapped as an eleven-year-old in 2002 and kept prisoner for the next four and a half years, over time he was allowed by his abductor to leave the apartment unsupervised. Shawn had friends he went cycling and played video games with, and he even had internet access. He had the opportunity to follow the developments in his case. Eventually he plucked up the courage and left a post on the website that his mother and stepfather had set up to gather clues about Shawn's disappearance. 'How much longer are you planning to look for your son?' he asked, even adding his real name – Shawn – followed by the name of his kidnapper. His parents didn't understand the clue, and it was eventually the abduction of another child that led police to the kidnapper and thus Shawn.

What interests Liv right now is that the podcast has already featured a few survivors who were allowed out during their ordeal, where there were people who they could have theoretically asked for help. Or those, like Shawn Hornbeck, who were permitted to go online and could write messages to their relatives. Is it really so inconceivable, therefore, that the email is from Julie?

Liv takes her left hand off the wheel and rubs her brow, behind which she can feel a dull throb. The heat, the lateness, the circumstances – especially the circumstances. Sophia is right: the probability that some loony has been made aware of the case by the podcast and newspaper article, and wants to show off, is more than high. Particularly as the Novaks, as Liv understands, came across a number of would-be Julies who turned out to be attention-seekers or mentally ill. On the other hand, Theo made a crucial point: how could a stranger know the word *skyearthblue*? Liv's first thought was that he'd mentioned this word in some interview, then forgotten. To be sure, she googled Julie's name, adding *skyearthblue*. No results.

Can it be true, then? Can it really, really be true? Liv doesn't yet dare believe it completely. Nor does she dare tell Phil. While all she's got is just another ramshackle theory, she's going to keep working systematically, sticking to her plan: talk to Jason Willmers, Julie's karate instructor; talk to the witness who first gave Daniel Wagner an alibi, then retracted it later; and talk to Daniel Wagner himself.

Slightly doubtfully, she looks at the passenger seat, where Theo is sitting with her laptop on his knees. She's set up a hotspot for him with her mobile, because Theo only has an old Nokia that can't do anything but make calls and send texts. Now she can hear a click every few seconds as he refreshes the page with his inbox. The video camera is stuck to the dashboard with black gaffer tape, winking at them with its little red recording light. It probably wasn't Liv's best idea to take Theo with her to Grunewald, to Jason Willmers's address. But she couldn't think of anything else. This way at least she has Theo somewhat under control. And she'll also be there if he gets a reply from *Nutcracker11*. For Theo wrote back to *Nutcracker11* while Liv, with a shaky hand, pointed the camera at his computer monitor. Despite his clumsiness, he typed so quickly that Liv didn't have a chance to discuss the wording with him.

*i remember everything*, he wrote. *you need help.*

Liv thought it sounded like a statement, almost a reproach. In her opinion it would have been better to ask questions: *Do you need help? Where are you? How can we be sure it's really you?* But too late – before Liv could think clearly, he'd already sent his reply. Again Liv had suggested they notify the police, who might be able to trace the email via the IP address. But Theo rejected this outright; he didn't trust the police anymore. Didn't she know someone else who could do that? She was, after all, a true crime podcaster.

'I only report on crimes,' Liv told him cautiously. 'I don't solve them.' The expression on his face took her by surprise. 'I mean,' she added hurriedly, 'normally I don't solve them. Because that isn't my job, do you understand? And so I don't know any hackers or other experts who could help us with this.' Theo harrumphs but doesn't comment further.

'I've never asked you outright what you think happened on the night of Julie's disappearance,' Liv says now, after looking to check that the gaffer tape will hold and that the recording light is still on. She hears another click as Theo refreshes the page again, then a mournful sigh.

'I've been through it in my mind a hundred times.'

Out of the corner of her eye, Liv can see him wipe his face. He's lucid, she thinks.

'I don't believe the kidnapper went up to her bedroom. I tell myself that we would have heard this, because our bedroom was right next to Julie's. And surely she would have offered some resistance. She would have screamed and kicked, wouldn't she? Julie was very slim, but athletic too, because she did a lot of sport. She'd have also done well at SV Albatros, with her strong arms and powerful lungs.'

Liv nods.

'She would sometimes get up at night,' he goes on. 'I caught her once. I was coming home late from an emergency operation and I heard noises from the cellar. So I went down and caught her just as she was climbing out of the window.'

'Does this mean you think she also did that on the night in question?'

'No, I don't think she planned to slip out at all that night. The thing with that, that, whatshisname ... that was all over. But after they broke up, I bumped into her in the kitchen a few times at night. Maybe her sleep patterns had been so changed by her night-time sorties that she woke up automatically. She'd be sitting at the kitchen table, usually with a cup of hot chocolate or tea. I sat with her and we'd chat for a while until she sent me back to bed as if she were the adult. *You need your sleep, Dad*, she would say, sounding like her mother. *You've got to fix another few hearts tomorrow.*'

Liv grins, then says, 'What would you chat about on those nights? Do you remember?'

Theo shrugs and there's another click on the laptop keyboard.

'All sorts of things. Fish.' He smiles dreamily. 'She wanted to study marine biology, you know. Or we talked about her friends. School.'

'Daniel Wagner too?'

Theo's head shoots to the side and he stares wide-eyed at Liv. 'It was him, wasn't it? I always thought it was him. But I wasn't allowed to say it anymore.'

'You weren't allowed to say it anymore?'

'Yes, there was ...' He screws up his eyes as if having to

concentrate hard. '*Just leave it, Theo,* my Vera said. *That's enough now. In the end they'll get serious and you really will go to prison.*'

'Do you mean there was a cease-and-desist order?' Liv says. 'Or a charge?'

Theo nods. 'Yes, exactly!'

'Which one of the two?'

'Both, I think.' It sounds like a question, then he rams his right elbow against the passenger door. Liv gives a start; the laptop wobbles on Theo's knees. 'Oh bloody hell!' he barks. 'My Vera had such a good memory – she'd be able to tell you! Julie too! She could remember all types of fish!'

'It's alright, don't worry,' Liv says. 'Do you want to check your emails again?'

'Nutcracker,' Theo says, obeying. 'Tchaikovsky. It's where "Warts of the Flowers" is from. No new emails. Do you think Julie is still angry with me?'

'Why should she be angry with you?'

'You're right. Why? I mean, I'm head of the clinic for heart, thoracic and vascular surgery, that's my job! And it gives us a good life, doesn't it?'

Liv looks over at Theo and smiles kindly. He's slipped away from her a bit again. Into a world only he understands.

'Yes,' she says, driving the last hundred metres in silence to the Willmerses'.

Theo is to wait in the car and keep refreshing his inbox. Liv tells him it's an important job that only he can do. And that it's not going to take her long. She reaches behind her to get the black sports bag with the rest of the camera equipment and her notebook, which she takes out along with a pen. Then she hangs the cord with her mobile around her neck, leaves the car, pocketing her keys, and wanders up to the small, two-apartment house, its front garden surrounded by a neatly trimmed hedge. *M & J Willmers* is on the lower of the two bells, which Liv now presses. There's a buzz: the door clicks open. As Liv enters the house, she's greeted by pleasantly cool air and takes the stairs up to the Willmerses' flat. A woman in a linen skirt and with short, dark hair is in the door. Liv puts her in her late forties.

'Hello,' Liv says. 'Maya Willmers?'

'Oh.' The woman laughs. 'I thought you were the postman. I've been waiting all day for a package.' She checks her watch. 'Well, I don't imagine he's coming now.'

'It is late, I know. But I hope you don't mind if I take up a few minutes of your time.' Liv squares her shoulders. 'My name is Liv Keller and I'm a journalist. I'd like to talk to your husband.'

The laughter vanishes from the woman's face and she crosses her arms defensively.

'Liv Keller. *The* Liv Keller from that crime podcast?'

Liv nods, confused. 'Yes, that's . . . that's me. And I . . . Well, it's about the Julie Novak case, the girl who went missing. She was one of your husband's pupils at KSVG.'

'I know. And?'

'Well, I've got a few questions.' Liv shifts from one foot to the other. 'May I put them to your husband? It would really help me in my research for—' Liv doesn't get to the end of her sentence because Maya Willmers makes a disparaging sound. Nonetheless – and this surprises Liv more than the fact that Frau Willmers knows her podcast – she motions to her to come in. On the way to the sitting room, Liv takes the phone from her neck and pushes it into the back pocket of her jeans. The room is decorated simply, but in a modern style, and what's most striking is that it's so tidy it looks to Liv like the backdrop for a furniture catalogue. Even the fleece blanket on the pale corner sofa has been folded as meticulously as if it had been taken straight out of its packaging and not used once.

Maya Willmers invites Liv to sit, goes over to an immaculately polished glass cabinet and takes out a framed photograph. She goes back to Liv and hands her the photo.

The picture shows a man in his late twenties with shaved blond hair. He's tanned and wearing a tight white T-shirt that shows off his muscular upper arms. He has his hands on his hips and is beaming, while the palm trees and sun in the background give the picture a holiday feeling. The man is immediately familiar, of course he is. It's Jason Willmers. Liv recognises him at once, having come across his photo on an online article last night about KSVG. She looks up at his wife, puzzled.

Crossing her arms again, Maya Willmers says, 'Ask him any question you like. He's incredibly patient, you know. You see, he's dead.'

'What?' Liv looks again in disbelief at the picture she's holding, then back at Maya Willmers's expressionless face.

'And while you're at it,' Maya continues, 'ask him who his killer is. But wait! You already know that, don't you, Frau Keller?'

## DANIEL

The later it gets, the more I'm nagged by the thought that there might be another way out of the newspaper's offices that Bishop-Petersen could have taken. A few times I begin to go back to my car to drive home. But I don't make it further than a few steps before turning around again. No, not this time, I tell myself. I can't put up with it any longer. I'm not going to. I've done my best to withstand my pain and control my anger. Luke 6, verse 29 – I hear my mother's voice. *And unto him that smiteth thee on the one cheek offer also the other.* I did offer my cheek, the one and the other. I let myself get beaten up, the whole of my body and my soul. I took the blows because they seemed like the currency of my love for Julie. But enough is enough. It's shortly before nine and dusk is settling timidly over the office building. Half a dozen cigarette butts have collected at my feet. I bend down to pick them up and chuck them in a bin I've seen a handful of metres away. This is the second time I've wandered these few steps. But I'll be damned if I leave any evidence of my presence behind. I know what that leads to. Just when I've resumed my original position, I see him come outside through the revolving door: Max Bishop-Petersen, with his piggy face, the brown hair he wears in a bun, and that look in his blue eyes, which even from this distance I can feel pricking me like a cold needle. Bishop-Petersen is thin, gangly and not particularly tall, I note. You need to get lucky, at least once. I start moving, I follow him at a distance around the building to a carpark that's closed off by a barrier. Bishop-Petersen wanders to his vehicle, a black Alfa Romeo Giulietta, and I hesitate briefly, because this is exactly the same car as mine. Life likes to have a laugh. I hastily look around for potential witnesses or any CCTV that might monitor the carpark. As I can't see anything, I quicken my pace. A moment later I shove Bishop-Petersen, who's about to get into his car, against the door frame, one hand thrust firmly into his shoulder, the other sticking the barrel of my weapon into his back. It's only a paltry lighter, but Bishop-Petersen gasps so loudly in horror that I don't imagine he can tell the difference right now. Leaning into his ear, I growl, 'Get in!'

## LIV

On the internet Liv had found a case from Germany that sounded exciting. There weren't many sources, maybe three or four newspaper articles, plus various postings on one of the relevant crime forums. It was the story of Justin V., a sports teacher from Berlin, early thirties and very popular with both pupils and colleagues. One autumn afternoon in 2003, having just taught a class, he suddenly disappeared. As if a hole had opened up in the school's sports hall, where he took his lessons, and swallowed Justin. His cause of death was – and this must have been the reason why Liv jumped at the story – a gym mat. Completely absurd, unbelievable, crazy. But that's exactly what happened. Justin vanished and was found the following day upside down in one of the blue mats – one and a half metres wide, five metres long, rolled-up and fastened with Velcro. Dead from positional asphyxia – that's to say suffocated – with a pool of blood around him which, also due to his upside-down position, had gathered in his extremities and eventually leaked through his eyes, mouth and nose. Nobody died in such an absurd, unbelievable and crazy way, was Liv's first thought. With this very thought in mind, she'd embraced the case and featured it in their podcast. The episode was full of doubts about the post-mortem findings – which ruled out foul play – and the police's conclusion that Justin's death must have been a tragic accident. What Liv found much more interesting was a post on a forum that – given the way it read – must have been written by someone close to Justin, a friend perhaps. This individual didn't believe the investigators' theory either and wrote that Justin had often argued with his wife because she was pathologically jealous. Another member of the forum fuelled the post with a rumour that Justin had had an affair with a female pupil. In their podcast, Liv and Phil suggested the following hypothesis to explain the mysterious circumstances surrounding the teacher's death: Justin's wife, already jealous to the Nth degree, had got wind of the affair. After the lesson on that fateful day, she waylaid Justin in the gymnasium, killed him in an argument and stuffed his body in the rolled-up mat. Liv and Phil realised, of course, that she would need superhuman strength to accomplish this. But there were stories of parents who had salvaged their children from under wrecked cars weighing tonnes, or from the debris after an earthquake. If the circumstances required, the consensus was that strength was purely a question of will rather than something that could be measured scientifically. Liv recalls how furious she and Phil were that this had never occurred to the police. That they seriously believed Justin had accidentally fallen into the mat and then suffocated. For what reason could that have possibly happened? And how? None of it made any sense.

All of this dawns on Liv now. This and the fact that the photo that Frau Willmers has given her looks familiar, not because of another picture from an article about KSVG, but because she's seen this exact same photo of a man with shaved dark blond hair, in a tight white T-shirt, palms and sunshine in the background. The only difference is that the face in the photo Liv saw had a black bar covering the eyes. And that the name – Justin V. – was accompanied by an asterisk in Liv's sources, meaning that it had been changed by the editorial team.

'Justin V. is . . .' she stammers.

'My husband, Jason Willmers. And I'm the woman you called a murderer in your podcast.'

'No, wait!' Horrified, Liv leaps up from the sofa, still holding the framed photograph of Jason Willmers. 'We never said it like that!'

'But you explored that very scenario: what if his wife killed him in a fit of jealousy?' Maya Willmers's jaw is twitching; it's obvious she's trying to sound more measured. 'Do you not realise the effect saying things like that in your podcast has? What just one sentence like that – a teeny-weeny bit of speculation during which you and your partner work yourselves up into a fury – what it does to the person concerned? Don't you see that a name change isn't enough on its own to prevent the person from being identified? We've got neighbours, Frau Keller! Friends and colleagues. Of course all of them knew that Jason was a sports teacher, that he disappeared after lessons one afternoon and the following day was found rolled up in that mat in the sports hall! How many other people do you know who all those things have happened to?'

'You're right,' Liv mutters, her head bowed. Nobody else had ever died in such an absurd way; the case wouldn't have been half as interesting otherwise.

'You see! And so, even if you stick with the changed name the newspaper used for its article, it makes no difference. It doesn't let you off the hook – you're accountable all the same.'

Liv is still looking at the floor. Of course she knows the rules about reporting crimes, which vary from country to country. An individual's right to privacy is weighed against the general public interest. Criminal cases in the US, for example, provide a high volume of useful sources, including photographs of crime scenes and victims, some upsetting, and the names of those involved are not changed. In Japan, or Germany for that matter, the guidelines are much stricter, protecting not only the identity of the victim, but that of the perpetrator too. Asterisks and the editorial note, 'The names have been changed', black bars over the eyes, and a lack of those details which are sometimes necessary for a properly researched transcript, but are simply not accessible. Liv and Phil have been forced to discard several exciting stories because the documentation was just too thin. If you want to be halfway serious podcasters, there are only so many gaps you can fill with your own assumptions and speculation.

'Unlike you, the newspapers at least stuck to the facts,' Maya continues. 'Have you read the articles?'

Liv nods apprehensively.

'Was there anything in them suggesting that Jason's death might be anything other than an accident? Or that the police interrogated his wife as a suspect?'

Liv shakes her head. 'No, it's just . . .' She looks up. 'Of course we asked ourselves what kind of an accident it could have been for someone to end up in a rolled-up gym mat.'

'That's precisely the point. You asked *yourselves*. And not anyone – like the police press office or me, for example – who could have given you the answer at once. But I'll tell you, I'll tell you what happened.' Maya Willmers sits on the edge of the coffee table, looking towards the window, beyond which the world outside is gradually getting dark. Liv is pleased she can only see the woman in profile now; she doesn't have to look her in the eye anymore. Liv sits down again, for which her shaking knees are grateful.

'Jason was usually late,' Frau Willmers says, smiling. 'Almost always, in fact. It used to drive me up the wall, but that's what he was like. He often cut it so fine for lessons, too, that he didn't have time to go into the changing room to put his things in a locker. By things, I mean his outdoor shoes and a tote bag with his wallet, phone and car key. We once had an argument about how careless it was to leave all this stuff just lying about, seeing how many people have access to the sports hall. So, from then on, he'd put the bag in one of the rolled-up gym mats. A pretty smart idea, he thought.' Her smile gets broader, only to fade a second later. 'Picture it: the mats were lined up in rows, around a dozen in total. Jason would get on to the trolley with the small mats and from there on to the rolled-up big ones. At the end of the lesson, when his pupils had left the sports hall, he climbed back up, bent into the opening and fished out his things.' Maya Willmers looks at Liv. 'The police concluded that on the day in question he somehow slipped and got stuck in the hole. They re-enacted the whole thing, because of course people were wondering why he didn't call for help. They found that even if he'd screamed his head off – and he probably did – the mat would've muffled it all.' She gives a bitter laugh. 'Do you know what the really absurd thing is? I was actually worried about him at the time. He wasn't in a great place mentally, and I think this is why the accident might've happened in the first place. It really shook him up when Julie Novak went missing.'

There's a brief silence. Liv ponders how, after all the embarrassment of the last few minutes, all the shame she's felt, she can delve deeper into the subject of Julie without provoking Maya Willmers again. But before she can think of something, Maya Willmers shakes her head and continues, her gaze focused back on the window.

'And the claim you made in your podcast about the supposed affair.'

Liv crumples internally; instead of getting the opportunity to talk about Julie, she suspects the next tirade is on its way.

'You called me pathologically jealous,' Maya Willmers says unnecessarily, before turning to Liv again. 'I wasn't jealous. I was totally horrified.'

Liv can't breathe. Has Maya Willmers just admitted that her husband had an affair with one of his pupils? The argument with Julie flashes in her mind. Supposedly, Julie called him an *arsehole* and kicked her bag along the kitchen floor when she came home from karate. Could it have been her – Julie – who Jason Willmers had an affair with? Could he have had something to do with her disappearance? His wife has just said that he suffered mentally afterwards. That Julie's disappearance affected him badly. Was this because he was responsible, perhaps?

Liv is breathing again, but it's hesitant and shallow. 'Are you saying that—'

'That he had an affair?' Maya Willmers nods sadly. 'Yes. One day I came home from work earlier than usual. In the hallway was a black sports bag I hadn't seen before. And there were also certain noises, if you know what I mean. I followed them up to the bedroom. Can you believe that? In our bedroom!' She leaps up and wraps her arms around her body. Tears are running down her cheeks. 'He wasn't really like that. He loved me.' Her tone is almost imploring, as if she's begging. Liv moves her lips. She wants to say something but she doesn't know what.

'And he wasn't a paedophile either. He'd never been interested in young girls before. I mean, I hadn't noticed anything like that. He didn't give them weird looks or watch strange films, or that sort of thing.'

Liv moves her lips again, but still nothing will come out.

'And she was only fourteen,' Maya Willmers then says.

'Four . . . teen?' Liv stammers. Did the affair with Julie last that long? Was she already together with Jason when she was dating Daniel Wagner? Liv coughs; she's swallowed her own spittle.

Maya Willmers nods. 'Jason was absolutely horrified when he saw me standing there in the bedroom. He was as white as a sheet. And the girl started howling. I felt like grabbing her by the hair and hauling her out of the bedroom, but she was crying so terribly. I think she was very ashamed. It took me a moment to realise that *she* wasn't the guilty one. She was just a stupid adolescent child. I told her to get dressed and get her bag. Then I drove her home.'

'When was that exactly? Do you remember?'

Maya Willmers laughs. 'Do you think I could even forget? It was the Wednesday before her sister vanished. But I never did anything to my husband. We argued, of course. And I threatened to tell the girl's parents, the school and KSVG. But it wasn't necessary. I knew he'd been so deeply shocked that he'd never do anything like that again. He wouldn't even dare think of it again.'

'Wait,' Liv says breathlessly. 'The sister. The girl who vanished. Are you talking about Julie? Julie Novak?'

Maya Willmers's face contorts, a mixture of anger and surprise. 'What do you think we've been talking about all this time? But look, that's exactly what I mean. Nothing but misunderstanding all the time. People have forgotten how to listen, so what you end up with is the sort of shit you put out in your podcast. The other guy was the same. He didn't understand either. He—'

'Wait, wait!' Liv can barely keep up.

'What other guy? And the sister! Are you saying it wasn't Julie who—'

'The guy? You know who I mean. You slagged him off too in your podcast. First I thought: serves him right after the scene he made here. But then it struck me that he's just as much a victim of your unprofessional reporting as me.'

## LARA

I was sorry that I'd infected Isabel with my nervousness, or so it seemed. Her cheeks, always slightly pink before, looked pale, almost white, and she'd developed the habit of constantly peering over her shoulder. For good reason, because the devil continued to turn up in my room all the time, causing Isabel and me to flinch.

He wanted to know how I was and how many more tests had to be done that day. When Isabel stammered her way through the list, he pointed out that, according to the doctor and my medical notes, some had already been done.

'Yes,' she countered, 'but the patient still isn't putting on enough weight.' This too merely earned a shake of the head from him. I could sense his impatience slowly turning to anger. I sensed it even though my eyes were closed, which was meant to simulate how deeply I was asleep. Even this seemed to stir his mistrust. He questioned the dosage of my medication. Fortunately this didn't ruffle Isabel either. She argued that I was so thin and reacted to the medication accordingly. But he wasn't stupid; who knew about dosages if not him? Isabel had to put up with his overt doubting of her competence, in which he managed – despite the anger I detected in him – to strike a tone that was almost caustically friendly. I knew this tone, I'd known it for so long, and yet it gave me goosepimples each time. Isabel too, probably, because she didn't respond. I pictured her standing before him, looking silently at her feet to avoid his piercing gaze, before he left.

But there was in fact a problem with the dosage; that hadn't been a lie. The thing was, Isabel, who'd understood she mustn't sedate me anymore, was only with me for certain shifts, not all of the time. There were other staff – people who didn't know what Isabel knew and did everything by the book. This meant they kept giving me infusions that were a setback for my lucidity. I would go to sleep for real, wasting valuable time. Each time Isabel came on shift it took her quite a while to wake me. Sometimes she had to grab my arms and shake me before I'd come to. But maybe worse than that was the fact that I was still weak and found it difficult to articulate myself. I stuttered and rasped through everything she needed to know – my story and my plan.

My new plan.

For this we had to wait for Isabel to switch from the day shift to night. Not only was it quieter on the ward at night, there was less danger of him turning up unexpectedly. I asked her to bring a wheelchair, as I still wasn't able to walk on my own. What I really wanted was for her to push me out of the building, haul me into her car and drive me to my family. But that wasn't an option; it was too risky. If we were caught, they would notify him. Of course they would. And Isabel would probably lose her job. So we set our sights a bit lower, or closer. The staffroom at the end of the corridor. An office with everything I needed to contact the outside world. My family.

'Wouldn't it be better to call the police?' Isabel asked as she helped me out of bed and into the wheelchair.

'Absolutely not,' I protested, my voice hoarse and faltering. 'They . . . they're in cahoots. My parents . . . my parents have to come.'

'Shit,' Isabel said, probably more to herself than to me. I imagined she was wondering how she'd ended up in this situation. I knew that feeling, knew it only too well. She wanted to be back home, on the sofa, back in her pleasant, unspectacular life that had come to an end the moment she'd searched my name on the internet at my request.

'You're going to be famous,' I said, attempting a joke so she didn't change her mind. 'The only person . . . who believed me.' Trembling, I touched her arm. Isabel, who was bent over, lifting my feet on to the footrest, looked up and smiled encouragingly.

'You've almost made it, Julie. You'll be back home soon.'

I smiled back gratefully.

'Nobody's going to lay a finger on you, I promise,' she added. Then she pushed me out of the door and down the corridor to the staffroom. I noticed I was still smiling, I smiled the whole way there. For the first time in years, I felt happy. After all, I couldn't anticipate how firm the promise was that Isabel had just made. And that it would take only a couple of minutes for this guarded happiness to be followed by the worst nightmare.

And then all the blood.

# 4. VLADO

## LIV

Liv leaves the Willmerses' house as if in a trance. Her body is moving by itself, accomplishing the necessary steps autonomously. Her head gives a polite and automatic nod at the last words Jason's wife Maya utters as Liv goes down the stairs. The request is for her to be fair, for once at least. For her to keep what she now knows to herself. Jason is dead, there's no reason to discredit him and, by extension, Maya again for something that happened almost twenty years ago. She's been through enough, suffered enough. Liv's head just keeps nodding, even when she's at the entrance door downstairs. Her thoughts are going crazy; her mind is trying to order the new information, all the small pieces of the puzzle. It wasn't Julie who had the affair with the karate instructor, but Sophia. Sophia! Liv's hand goes up to her mouth, stifling a gasp of shock that's been waiting minutes to finally leave her mouth. It's as if it didn't dare come out in Maya Willmers's presence. Or was it the shock, the disbelief at Maya's revelation? After several tries, Liv manages to push the handle and step outside into the now dark grey dusk. Nobody knew about the affair, or at least nobody knew the details. There were merely rumours about Jason having something going with a schoolgirl. Where did these come from? She'd asked Maya this too, but only got a shrug in return. 'Neither I nor my husband spoke to anyone about it. I didn't confide in a friend or anyone else and nor did Jason. He knew full well that what he'd done was wrong. Neither of us was going to risk losing everything just because of that.'

*Just because of that*, Liv thinks. As if it had been a slip-up, a silly little mishap. But when a grown man gets involved with a child, that's no mishap. Even if, from a purely legal point of view, it's no longer a crime when they're fourteen, so long as the adolescent isn't coerced, it's still a major moral fuck-up.

And Sophia, of all people. Liv remembers hugging her today. Twice even: once in the hospital and later in Theo's flat. How fragile she felt, her T-shirt and trousers baggy on her thin, bony body, her dyed-black hair dry, almost dead, sitting on her narrow shoulders. How obvious it seemed to Liv that the problems Sophia kept bottled up manifested in her appearance. Sophia, who already looked as if she'd given up or was on the verge of doing so. And yet she's got a loving husband and is planning to adopt a baby. Maybe this was her last attempt to save herself. Perhaps because something wasn't right, even before Julie's disappearance – then the thing with her sister, her mother's death and finally her father's illness tipped her over the edge. Maybe that thing which hadn't been right was in fact Jason Willmers. A grown man who'd shamelessly exploited the confusion that comes with puberty.

Liv realises she's still standing outside the Willmerses' house. She hasn't taken another step, as if her body appreciates that all her energy is needed by the head at the moment. Maya Willmers said that she didn't tell anyone about the affair. But what if Sophia did? What if she told Julie, who then confronted Jason Willmers after the karate class? Maybe even threatened to expose him if he didn't keep well away from her little sister? What if that had been the reason for their argument? Then Jason Willmers would have definitely had a motive to kidnap Julie. The timing would make sense – a few days before Julie's disappearance, Maya caught Jason and Sophia in flagrante, while Julie and Jason had a row the evening before she disappeared. Liv gives a start. Not only would Jason have had a motive to kidnap Julie, he would have had a motive to kill her too. But now he's dead himself. And despite it all, there's the email, the email with the word *skyearthblue*.

Liv gets moving but only manages three or four steps before another man suddenly bursts into her thoughts and she stops again: Daniel Wagner. Maya didn't remember his name immediately. She called him *the guy . . . you slagged him off too in your podcast*.

'Do you mean Daniel Wagner?' Liv had asked. 'Julie's ex-boyfriend?' Maya Willmers nodded and told Liv that he'd turned up at their place a few days after Julie went missing. Maya had watched the scene from the kitchen window. Jason had just got out of his car, having driven home from work, when this man suddenly approached him. She saw something that looked to her like a heated discussion, judging by the frantic gesturing. But it didn't come to blows, Maya said. Obviously she asked her husband what that had been all about. He replied that the guy was the ex-boyfriend of Julie, the girl who went missing. Playing the amateur detective, he was questioning everyone she knew. Maya hadn't thought there was anything unusual, not at the time, and certainly not now, in retrospect. The evening when

Jason didn't come home, she'd also phoned around a few friends to see if they'd heard anything from him. And if he hadn't been found dead in the sports hall the following morning, she'd have continued making inquiries, perhaps with greater urgency.

'Did you phone the Novaks too?' Liv asked.

'I thought about it, certainly. Because of course I wondered if there might be some irate father who'd got wind of the thing between Jason and his daughter and was now out for revenge.'

'But?'

'You know what?' Maya Willmers said. 'To be honest I thought it was too early to start panicking. Jason hadn't come home after work, which was unusual, and I admit this made me angry. But I thought he'd just fancied going out for a few beers after all the shit with that Sophia girl, the atmosphere at home and then the disappearance of the Novaks' other daughter – and had got hammered. Looking back, I'm glad I held back. Imagine I'd panicked and told the police about the affair. I'd have made a fuss about things that had nothing to do with Jason's death, but would've haunted me for the rest of my life. I'd have merely provided more cannon fodder for people like you.'

Liv had to concede that she was right. All stories told second- or third-hand have their gaps. The true story can only ever come from the person who's experienced it. Even then, who's prepared to tell their story without gaps? People have secrets and they need them for their own protection. Liv understands this, but she's still disappointed. In Sophia. Sophia, who, during their conversation about Julie and the karate instructor, behaved as if she could barely remember his name. Yes, Theo was there, which meant she might've been too ashamed to come out with the truth. But she could've broached the subject when she was alone with Liv. Taking her phone from her trouser pocket, Liv stops the recording function she'd activated when she entered the Willmerses' house. Then she calls Sophia's number.

Sophia answers after two rings. Without so much as a hello, she asks outright, 'Is my father OK? Has something happened?'

Liv is taken by surprise. 'No, no,' she replies quickly. 'But I need to talk to you.'

'Is it about that email again?'

'No. Can we meet?'

There's a brief silence down the line.

'Hello?' Liv says, to make sure Sophia's still there.

'It's already gone half nine, Liv, and I've got to be out early tomorrow. I have to go to work and I bloody well have to be on time after all I've missed the last few days, including the little detour to the hospital today.'

'What about after work?'

Another short silence as Sophia seems to be thinking. 'I'm probably going to have to do overtime. Quite a lot has piled up.'

'Doesn't matter. I can do evenings too. Just get in touch when you've an idea what time you'll be clocking off. Then we'll arrange something.'

'OK, and if there's anything with my father . . .'

'I'll let you know immediately,' Liv finishes Sophia's sentence. The next moment she jumps when a hand touches her shoulder. She whips around. Standing there is Maya Willmers, who has followed her out of the house.

'God, you gave me a fright,' Liv gasps. Maya Willmers says

nothing; she just hands her something. Liv's notebook, which she must've forgotten on the Willmerses' sofa.

'Oh, thanks!'

'I've written my phone number in it in case you want to tell me you've deleted the episode about my husband,' she says ambiguously. Liv nods uncertainly, but Maya Willmers has already turned around and is heading back to the house. To be on the safe side, Liv moves a few further steps away before using her phone again. She's about to call Phil's number but then decides to send a message instead. *Do you have any idea how I could get in touch with Daniel Wagner?* Liv has already searched online. One look at the photos of all the social media profiles she'd come across was enough to tell her that there were plenty of different men with the same name. She hesitates before sending the message. Is she really expecting a serious answer? Or will her question just be further confirmation for Phil of how incapable she is of even tracking down a person who lives in the same city and whose house has featured several times in the papers?

Liv does send it. She really has to stop making her mood dependent on Phil. Just as she's about to put her mobile back in her bag, she hears a message come through. Phil. Liv's surprised by how quickly he's replied. *Where did you find it?* Liv types back, and again has to wait less than a minute. *Old phone book entry*, Phil writes. *Still under his mother's name. Fingers crossed, Liv! You'll smash it!*

Liv smiles. No silly comment, no barb. Maybe Phil's reconsidered and realised how harsh he was on her. Maybe everything will be alright between them again. Liv is abruptly torn from her thoughts when the thundering voice of a man in the distance catches her attention. It's Theo, she realises, who ought to be sitting in the car with the laptop on his knees, waiting for her. Instead he's wandering off in the direction of the main road that borders this residential area, holding the laptop above his head.

'Shit!' Liv exclaims. She runs after Theo. When she gets close, his bellyaching becomes clearer. He's swearing at the laptop.

'Theo!' Liv shouts. 'Stop! Where are you going?' Making a grab for his shirt, she catches a hem. Theo stops with a jolt and turns to her, bewilderment in his face. 'It's me, Liv,' she says, trying to sound as calm as possible despite the effort of running to catch Theo up. Only now does he put his arms down, and with them the laptop. Liv's first thought is that it must be the disappointment which has upset him. Disappointment that there's no new email. The realisation that they were wrong and it wasn't Julie who'd written, but another nutter playing a trick.

'I'm sorry, Theo. We won't stop, though. We'll keep trying to find out what happened to Julie.'

Theo looks at her, his eyes wide open. 'All of a sudden it was gone!' he says, sounding desperate. He turns the laptop to Liv. The page that was showing his emails now displays an error message. No internet connection. Of course there isn't, because the hotspot Liv set up was via her phone, which usually works up to a distance of one hundred metres. But Liv was in the Willmerses' flat for quite a while, probably too far away to maintain the connection.

'Wait, I'll set it up again. Let's go back to the—'

'No police!' Theo interrupts her gruffly, before wincing at his own volume. He looks around quickly. 'That's what she wrote,' he adds at a whisper. Liv can't believe it.

'She . . . You mean you got another email? From *Nutcracker11*?'

'Two!'

'Two emails?' Wedging her notebook under her arm, Liv takes the laptop from Theo and sits down with it on the edge of the pavement. She reactivates the hotspot, gets him to enter his password for the expired session and finally accesses his inbox.

He's right.

Two new emails. Liv's heartbeat fills her entire body. The throbbing in her neck is so great she can hardly swallow.

*No, no help. No police*, she reads in the first email.

*Please, Dad, keep this to yourself*, in the second.

Liv stares at the screen. This is impossible. It can't be true.

Think of Shawn Hornbeck, she reminds herself. The abducted boy with internet access, who left a message on the website set up to find him. Her fingers descend almost independently on to the laptop; they just have no idea what to write. She needs proof, something that no stranger could know. Wanting help, she looks up at Theo. Who's gone. Liv's eyes dart around. That fucking main road! Theo is just a light dot on the background of traffic lights and the evening rush hour. Liv shuts her laptop and sets off. This time it's harder for her to follow because he's got a big head start. She has to stop several times – because she's lost sight of him; because she almost drops the laptop, notebook and phone while she's running; because some pedestrian light is red or she's hindered by a car. She doesn't catch up with Theo until he's outside a mobile phone shop, shaking a locked door.

'What are you doing?' She doesn't mean to shout but can't help herself. Theo looks at her; he's spaced out. Not now, Liv thinks, please, not right now. She can only guess that he wanted to go to the mobile phone shop because they know about the internet and might be able to trace the emails. Liv can't actually ask him, because Theo's not saying anything, merely gaping. Delicately linking arms with him, Liv leads him away from the entrance to the shop. His body is stiff and sluggish, his steps slow and tentative, like those of an old man who can barely keep himself on his feet without help. He needs to sit down, snap out of it. Liv spots a bench further down the road, which they head for and sit down on. Liv moves so close to Theo that their thighs touch and she'd at once be able to detect the slightest movement, any attempt on his part to do another runner. She opens the laptop again. Some proof.

'Julie,' she says slowly. 'Think of Julie, Theo. What's the first thing that comes into your head?'

He smiles, then tears shimmer on his face. Theo begins humming a tune, which Liv has heard before. No, several times. Her fingers fly across the keyboard.

*Tell me what the last song was we danced to at the school ball or I'll do it: I'll call the police. I'm serious.*

Send.

Liv takes a deep breath. Putting the laptop beside her on the bench, she places a hand on Theo's knee and rubs his back with the other. He lets her do this as he just sits there and continues to hum, sobbing gently. It's not long before Liv is crying too. What a fucking awful illness. What a fucking awful situation. It's all too much.

Liv has brought Theo home and now he's sleeping. In truth she doesn't have the time to hang around here. To wait until he wakes, make sure he doesn't get up to anything. On his dining table is the laptop, open. Every few minutes Liv refreshes the page with his inbox. In between she jots a few thoughts down in her notebook or checks her phone. She's tried to contact Sophia, but she's not answering. Maybe she's asleep – it's almost half past ten. Liv knows Sophia wanted an early night, but she did say to get in touch immediately if there were any problems with Theo. Liv likewise keeps checking the chat with Phil, where she sees Daniel Wagner's address again. She urgently needs to speak to Wagner. But the truth is, she's afraid to. She doesn't want to prejudge him, assume he might be dangerous because he's Julie's ex-boyfriend and was for a short time under suspicion of having been involved in her disappearance, even though he was released soon afterwards. On the contrary, why would he have turned up at the Willmerses', if not on the hunt for Julie? What could he have wanted from Jason? No, it's something else that makes Liv feel uncomfortable. Recalling how they talked about him in the podcast covering Julie's case. If Maya Willmers, who they only discussed under a different name, was so angry, how would Daniel Wagner react to her if she turned up at his door asking for a conversation? Liv would have to explain herself, only she doesn't know how. And it's also doubtful that Wagner would be satisfied with a few apologies muttered with a bowed head. She has to be prepared, Liv thinks, prepared for everything. Wagner mustn't see her as incompetent and vulnerable. The alibi, she suddenly thinks. If she can convey to him how deeply she's researched the case he might take her seriously. Once more she takes her notebook and flicks to the page where she wrote Konrad Bergmann's phone number.

It keeps ringing for so long that Liv is about to hang up. Bergmann is probably asleep too, she thinks, when he finally answers.

'Hello, Herr Bergmann. I'm sorry for ringing so late. It's Liv

Keller here. You remember, we did an interview yesterday about the Julie Novak case.'

Bergmann laughs. 'Yes, yes, don't worry. Of course I remember.'

*Of course*, Liv repeats in her head, rolling her eyes at her stupidity. Not everyone she interviews is suffering from dementia. 'Right, erm . . . I thought of a few questions afterwards and I was hoping you'd still be awake and might have a few minutes to answer them for me.'

'No problem, I'm more than awake. But I was about to go off fishing. As we pensioners do. You have to go either very early or very late to the lake – that's when you've got the best chance of a decent catch.' He laughs. 'But fire away, I'm sure the little fish will be happy to wait a few more minutes.'

'OK, well, it's about Daniel Wagner, or the alibi he had for the night Julie went missing.'

'Yes, one of Julie's friends spotted him in a disco by the station. Hold on a sec, I don't want to make any mistakes.' Liv hears a rustling – Bergmann's probably looking through the case file again. 'On the night in question, he saw Daniel Wagner there more than once,' he continues. 'Around midnight, then again at about five in the morning, shortly before the disco closed. We judged the information to be credible because Herr Wagner still had the entry stamp on the back of his hand the following day.'

'Yes, exactly. You mentioned that yesterday. But tell me this: is it theoretically possible that the witness got the day wrong and that the stamp was older? Or that Daniel Wagner left the disco unnoticed between midnight and five o'clock in the morning?'

'To do what? Quickly kidnap the girl then return to get himself the alibi?'

'So it's not possible?'

Bergmann sighs. 'Purely theoretically, yes, but in practice . . . Well, we thought the likelihood of that was pretty low. It was a such a short period of time and would have required meticulous planning. Not only would he have had to abduct Julie Novak, but take her somewhere too. And the place certainly wouldn't have been in the immediate vicinity.'

'You mean it would have to have been a remote spot?'

'To minimise the risk of discovery, yes, of course.'

'I see. But what about the other possibility? That the witness might have got the date wrong?'

Bergmann chuckles down the phone. 'Funny you should mention that. Because it's exactly what the witness claimed when he later retracted his confirmation of Wagner's alibi.'

'What?' Liv, who's been wandering around the dining table, deep in thought, now sits on the nearest chair. 'And you didn't take that seriously? It could mean that—'

'It means nothing, Frau Keller,' Bergmann interrupts. 'The boy was an attention-seeker.'

'What?'

'He got a taste for being at the centre of it all. It's as simple as that. He saw what a furore Julie Novak's disappearance caused, especially when the relationship between the girl and her ex-boyfriend, Herr Wagner, was all over the media. The little shit just wanted to get in on the action. This sort of thing is fairly common: people who have nothing to do with the case get involved for egotistical reasons and then lie through their teeth. But in my career, you learn to gauge how credible people are. And this boy definitely wasn't. Later he even gave an interview to the press, saying how toxic the relationship between Julie Novak and Daniel Wagner had been. Don't get me wrong, if that had been my daughter who'd got mixed up with a much older man, I'd have read her the riot act. But, from a purely objective point of view, there was nothing wrong with that Wagner, he was just unlucky.'

Liv shakes her head. 'But that boy, Julie's friend. When he made his first statement, giving Wagner the alibi, you believed him.'

'At that stage, the whole circus hadn't got going yet. Julie's parents hadn't done their TV interview and nor had the papers reported on the father beating up Wagner outside his house.'

'Uh-huh.'

'Apart from that, I'd bet my right kidney that the boy was infatuated with Julie. He saw Wagner in the disco and told us this truthfully. Later, it must've dawned on him that he had the chance to get one over on Wagner by withdrawing his alibi. Did I just say I'd bet my kidney that he was in love with Julie? Ha ha, let's make it my liver instead – I might as well get rid of that.' Bergmann grunts at his own joke while Liv, pulse racing, writes in her notebook.

'Could you tell me the boy's name? I'd really like to talk to him.'

'Frau Keller,' Bergmann says in a schoolmasterly tone. 'You know about data protection.' With this, he says goodbye, as he puts it, 'to see the fish'.

No sooner has Liv hung up than the door to Theo's bedroom opens. He steps out of the room, his duvet rolled up untidily under his arm, the fishing hat back on his head.

'Why did you let me sleep, Lisa?'

Liv puts down the phone and pen. 'You were so tired, Theo. It's important you get some rest from time to time.'

'Another email?'

Liv shakes her head, then she realises that she was so absorbed in her conversation with Bergmann that she forgot to refresh the inbox. She reaches across the table and pulls the laptop towards her. No new email.

'I'm afraid not,' she says, looking from the screen to Theo, with the duvet under his arm and hat on his head. 'What are you planning to do?'

He looks at her in disbelief, as if he'd already explained one hundred times what he was planning next, and she hadn't listened properly one hundred times.

'I refuse to sleep another night in this tiny, uncomfortable wooden bowl.'

Liv hesitates. 'In this . . . ?'

'We need to get to the observation post!'

When Liv continues to appear at a total loss, he bellows, 'To the house! Imagine if the arsehole comes back! Oh, but let him, just let him come back, please be my guest! Because I'll be waiting for him!' He chucks the duvet over the back of a chair and wanders past Liv to the fridge. A second later she hears scraping sounds, interspersed with strained groans. It's Theo inching the freestanding fridge, about a metre high, forward across the kitchen floor.

'What on . . . ?' Liv begins as he reaches into the gap he's opened up between the fridge and the tiled wall. But she doesn't get to finish her question before Theo brings out an old hunting rifle.

## DANIEL

Bishop-Petersen drives; I tell him which way to go. Out of the corner of my eye, I can see his fingers trembling on the wheel and him venturing the occasional glance to the side. He's scared and can't disguise the fact. In this I'm better than him. At least I hope I am. I clench my jaw to control my facial expressions and stare at the road straight ahead. My mouth is desperate to say thousands of things, but I'm even refraining from speaking for the time being. The more unsure Bishop-Petersen feels, the less he's able to assess the situation, the better it is for me. I know I'm making a mistake; I knew it the moment I pushed my lighter into his back and forced him to get into the car. But I can't go back now, neither of us can.

'Where are we driving?' he asks softly, and I enjoy the unmissable plea in his voice, his begging me not to do him any harm. I don't react, I torture him. As he tortured me. All I say is, 'You wanted the truth. I'm going to show it to you.' Originally I thought about making him park away from the house so nobody would see his car in the drive. But that would mean us having to walk a bit and I don't want to risk him trying to escape on the way or screaming for help to the entire neighbourhood. Besides, we drive the same make and model of car. It's even the same colour. You'd have to actually focus on the number plate to notice the difference. And who does that? Who would've ever been interested in the details when it comes to me and my story? So I make him drive right up to the house, banking on the fact that the few steps to the door won't be enough for him to pluck up courage and devise a plan to escape. The way he can barely climb out of the car confirms my suspicions. His entire body is trembling; he's actually shaking. He even stands by the driver's door like a good boy, holding on with one hand for support, as he waits for me to wander around the car. I put a hand on his shoulder to show him the way with a discreet amount of pressure. And yet, as I'm making heavy weather of unlocking the door one-handed in the gloom – the nearest street lamp isn't particularly close – something seems to flash in him. He can't be sure what will await him once we've entered the house. But he appears to suspect that he's going to be at my mercy, whatever that entails. And it's true. It's a small house, but old, with thick walls that swallow all sound. The external metal shutters are rolled down; I almost never raise them. A judder shoots through Bishop-Petersen's body and his head darts in all directions, no doubt looking for a way out. But before he can take any action, I've opened the door and shoved him into the dark, narrow hallway. I press the light switch, put the key into the lock on the inside and turn it to the right deliberately slowly. Bishop-Petersen gasps.

'Wh . . . What are we doing here? What are you going to do to me?'

Before I answer, I take my time removing the key from the lock and putting it into my trouser pocket. 'I want to clarify a few things with you. Please give me your phone.'

'Things? What things?' He's nervously shifting from one foot to the other. 'I mean, we don't know each other, do we?'

'Don't we? Don't you know who I am? Your phone, please.'

Tiny impulses on his part hint at a shake of the head.

'Daniel Wagner,' I introduce myself. 'From page twelve.'

Something happens in his face; slowly he seems to understand.

'You remember?' I follow up. 'The newspaper article you wrote for yesterday's edition of the *Abendblatt*? That was you, wasn't it?'

'Yes, yes, it was. But . . .'

'But?'

Bishop-Petersen waits for a moment then puffs up his chest. 'Listen to me, Herr Wagner. If you're unhappy with the reporting, then we should talk about it.'

'That's exactly what we're going to do,' I agree.

'I'm sure I don't have to remind you that we have freedom of the press in this country. Besides, I didn't make anything up and, talking legally here, I can at any time provide evidence for my sources . . .'

'*Talking legally?*' I laugh. 'That sort of thing doesn't interest me anymore. I understood years ago how that goes. Being in the right and getting justice are two completely different things. And the people out there – your readers – couldn't give a toss. As far as they're concerned, the printed word is the unshakeable truth.'

During my interjection, Bishop-Petersen puts his arms out and moves his hands up and down, again and again, in a gesture probably meant to placate me. But I'm calm, I'm so calm and collected that it surprises even me. There's nothing left of the gawky *arse-wiper*, who back in the day was intimidated by a simple phone call from his girlfriend's father, nothing left of the man who just then in the passenger seat had difficulty concealing his own uncertainty, thrusting his hands beneath his legs so that the man next to him wouldn't notice how badly they were shaking. It's as if I hadn't only accepted the fact that there was no going back on my decision, but that I was starting to enjoy it too.

'A right of reply?' Bishop-Petersen suggests, still moving his outstretched hands up and down. 'If that's what you want, we can definitely talk about it.'

'That's a good starting point.' I smile. 'But what I'd also like to know is: who did the interview with me back then for the *Berliner Rundschau*?'

Bishop-Petersen narrows his eyes.

'Back then?'

I nod. 'About a year after Julie's disappearance, I was contacted via Facebook by someone with your name and the promise to tell my side of the story.'

Bishop-Petersen blinks in confusion. 'I can tell you for a fact that wasn't me.'

'Of course it wasn't you. I know that now – you're nothing like the man I met all those years ago.'

'I mean, well . . . someone must've been having a little joke. A very poor one, of course,' he adds quickly.

I take a step towards him; instinctively he recoils and his back hits the coatrack. In shock, he turns around, then back to me. Oh, his eyes, his stupid little piggy eyes, the terrified look in them, his ashen face, his sagging features.

'Don't take me for an idiot,' I say, still in a perfectly calm voice, which comes astonishingly easily. It's a sublime feeling to be in the more powerful position, to not be the victim for once. 'I mean, the *Berliner Rundschau* published the article! And you were on the editorial team.' I take another step towards him; again he steps back, but this time he only grazes the coatrack.

'An intern!' he cries in panic. 'I'm thirty-nine, Herr Wagner! I was only doing an internship with the *Berliner Rundschau* back then. I made coffee and did photocopying! They'd never have let me write an article! And certainly not such an important one!'

'So who would have used your name for that piece?' Another step, first me, then Bishop-Petersen, and my voice now straining with impatience.

'What do I know!' he shouts, then suddenly comes for me. His weight knocks me backwards and the back of my head crashes hard against the front door. Sensing his opportunity, Bishop-Petersen wrestles me to the floor. The wound on the back of my head screams. A hand digs into my face, pressing my nose to the side; I feel the blood run over my top lip. A second hand is on my trousers, by the right front pocket where my keys are. At a stroke I realise what it will mean if he now manages to leave my house. What will be in store for me. I wrench my mouth open, shout and bite at the same time, mobilise all my strength, all the suppressed anger. I taste blood, I sense his resistance wane, I push him away from me, I get up, I stand there, looking down at him, I wipe my face, the blood, sweat and tears. Then I feel the back of my head. The wound is still bleeding.

'I'm sorry,' I say. 'But I can't just let you go like that. You won't understand otherwise. And now I'd like your phone.'

## THEO

Lisa, she's quite horrifired and as white as a sheet again. Iron, how often do I have to say it, girl? I go towards her, rifle in hand. That's how my father conquered them, the goddamaged animals during the plague of wild boars in 1954. Meat is a good source of iron, as is beetroot. But she doesn't seem to want to listen to me. Even though I'm a doctor. And I'm also wearing a hat. A man with a hat always has a plan.

'A double-barrel shotgun, made by Sauer & Sohn,' I say, holding the precious item out towards Lisa, at which she immediately takes a step back.

'Theo.' She sounds really terrifuddled.

'Not ideal, I know,' I admit, sticking my finger into the top barrel. 'Even if I had the right ammunition, the thing is so old that the trigger's stuck. Hasn't budged a millimetre since the 1970s. But . . .' I change the position of the rifle in my hands to a diagonal one – the barrel is now bottom left and the wooden stock pointing top right – and swing it a few times. 'It's good enough to give someone a nice thump.'

'Are you saying it doesn't work anymore?'

'No, dear lady, I'm afraid not.'

'Are you sure?'

I put the rifle to my shoulder, aim and pull the trigger in such rapid succession that Lisa's mouth stands open in astonishment.

'You see?' I say. 'It doesn't fire.'

Despite this, Lisa crumples to the floor as if she'd been shot. Plop! Her legs give way and she ends up on her bottom. Circulation, probably. It's poor in patients with iron deficiencies. Vera, she had poor circulation too because of her illness, leukaemia. The new treatment sounded promising; my US colleagues were able to convince even me, and for a few weeks it really looked as if everything would be good again, or as good as it could be without Julie. This was the last thing Vera said as she lay in her hospital bed, her hand in mine, consuming the last of her strength: 'Julie . . .'

I lower the rifle, grab the duvet from the back of the chair and say to Lisa, 'We've got to go.'

Alright, she's not the quickest. Because the penny only seems to drop when we're in her silver sardine tin on the way to Grunewald. Of course we've got to lie in wait. After all, she was the one who saw it with her own eyes and filmed it with her video camera, someone in Julie's room at night. Someone who might return. Of course we've got to be there, ready to bash his head with the Sauer & Sohn until he finally comes out with the answer to: 'Where is my daughter?' It's also what I ask the stupid computer that Lisa's put on my lap again so I can check my emails during the drive. Lisa says it would be better to wait for a response from nutcracker instead of banqueting on the fact that it really *is* Julie who's written the emails. I said, 'Blah blah,' and then, 'OK,' because I think that we've chewed over this thousands of times already, always ending up with the question of how a stranger could know Julie's word: *skyearthblue*. I also don't want to distress Lisa anymore. This is not the sort of situation for young women with iron deficiencies, but men with hats and rifles.

'Where is my daughter?' The screen remains stubborn, showing no change in my inbox. I shake the laptop lid slightly.

'Please be careful, Theo,' Liv says. 'We still need that.'

'You just concentrate on the road,' I retort. Lisa almost killed us when she jerked the steering wheel while we were doing 100 km/h on the motorway. I think she's in a bit of a bad mood, perhaps because the rifle's not working properly anymore. She thought I should have left it at home, but of course that was out of the question. I'm not going one step further without it. Maybe she's also miffed because it didn't occur to her that we should lie in wait overnight in my old house. But it doesn't bother me; I know how to deal with this sort of thing. Vera could be distracted with flowers when she was sad or misgruntled. And Sophia, I'd take her to the merry-go-round at the funfair and buy her a toffee apple afterwards. That would put a smile back on her face. Only Julie couldn't be molliculed so easily.

I can't help but laugh.

'What?' Lisa says.

'Julie,' I explain. 'When she was annoyed with me, she sometimes wouldn't speak to me for a fortnight. Vera or Sophia had to tell me everything, even though we were in the same room.'

'Did that happen often?'

I shake my head. 'Only a few times.'

'Do you remember when?' She reaches for the homemade gaffer-tape contraption on the dashboard that her video whatsit with the flashing red light is stuck to. Maybe she's checking that it's still in working order despite the way she's driving.

'Like when you stopped her from seeing Daniel Wagner?' she asks when I don't give an immediate answer.

'No, that was Vera,' I say. 'But I thought she was right. Julie was too young for him. And far too good as well. Julie and I argued about other things. Like her mother, she was of the view that I was missing too much because of my work. But that wasn't true, at least not most of the time. I swear I always took time off when my daughters had something important on. It's just that if my pager beeped, I sometimes had to leave a bit earlier. She often didn't understand that, just like Vera. But death doesn't care—'

'I know,' Lisa interrupts me, probably to stop me from getting worked up. 'You were the director of the clinic for heart and thoracic surgery at the Charité.'

'Vascular surgery too,' I add for the sake of thoroughness and I see Lisa nod.

'Does this mean you didn't have a problem with Julie and Daniel being together?'

'No, I did. As I said, I thought Vera was right, so I rang the idiot on her behalf and clarified the matter. But I also thought that the relationship would soon unravel of its own accord. I mean, Julie always had plenty of admirers; she was so pretty and smart, she could wrap anyone around her little finger.'

'And yet, after she went missing, you went straight to Daniel Wagner's house and attacked him. Why, if you thought he was an idiot and you hadn't taken their relationship seriously?'

I have to think about this, but then it comes to me.

'Vera and I, we both agreed that he was the only one it could have been.'

'Why?'

'Well, the others, they were still boys, they were much younger. But he . . .' I look over at Lisa. 'Vera was right. He was an adult, he should have realised himself that he was far too old for Julie. What normal, grown-up man seriously believes that a sixteen-year-old is his great love? That's sick.'

'But you moved away from your suspicion.'

I harrumph. 'There was this order preventing me from going near him. So we hired a private detective to shadow him.'

'You . . . ?' Lisa swervers slightly. 'And you're only telling me this now?'

'It was nothing! He didn't find out anything! For weeks he shadowed that whatshisname, whatshisname . . .'

'Wagner.'

'Yes, him. He kept tabs on him for weeks, with no result. Whatshisname . . .'

'Wagner.'

'Yes. He didn't leave his house anymore. He barracudaed himself in there with his mother, the roller blinds down. He didn't even go out shopping. I don't know how they managed.' I begin to tremble and the computer on my knees starts moving. 'Do you think it *was* him, after all? Has he got my Julie?' I reach for the steering wheel and shout, 'Turn around! We're going to see him! We're going to pay him a visit right away!' The computer on my knees tips to the side; Lisa pushes my hand away. I scream that she should bloody well turn around. That he's taken us for a ride, this, this . . . that he's led us on a merry dance these past twenty years, that he's kept me at bay with the help of the police and the public prosecco office who stamped that document which would have sent me to prison if I'd nobbled him again, that he's not an idiot but the devil who had her and might still have her, Lisa, goddamaged, I scream, she screams, we scream and then a whatsit, a whatsit, a bang.

# DANIEL

I almost feel sorry for Bishop-Petersen, the way he climbs the stairs ahead of me, turning around all the time to peer over my head at the front door, as if hoping for a miracle, hoping that someone might burst through the door at any moment and come to his help. That's what hope is like, it makes people do ludicrous things, seducing them with the theory of a possibility that in truth doesn't exist. But reason isn't in our nature. One time he glances back, the tip of one of his shoes gets caught on the runner and he stumbles. With a nod of my head, I motion to him to keep going. He hunches his shoulders as if caught in the act, turns around and obeys. There are thirteen stairs, only thirteen, but the way up probably drags if you don't know what's waiting for you at the top. Once again I can't hide a slight feeling of satisfaction. When he lay on the floor after our tussle, he acted as if he'd been seriously wounded, clutching his ribs and begging me, with some feigned wheezing, to take him to hospital. Nobody would find out about what had happened here, he promised. But I only needed to take one determined step towards him and he was back on his feet like a young fawn.

Once we're at the top, I say, 'Second door on the left.' The one Vicky had mistakenly tried during our rendezvous. As ever, the room is locked; the key is together with the one for the front door on the ring I now fish from my trouser pocket. Bishop-Petersen stares wide-eyed, first at my fingers, then the lock. I try to unlock the door as quietly as possible and whisper to Bishop-Petersen, as I point the way through the open door, that he should keep all noise to a minimum.

The room is dark – not pitch-black, just dark enough to keep out the outside world. There are a few slits in the upper part of the roller blind, through which during the day a moderate dose of sun can pass, and at night a little light from the street lamps, to maintain a sense of time and orientation. The fact that the landing light is on too helps Bishop-Petersen get a general impression of the room. He's ventured a couple of steps into it and now stands as if his body is rooted to the floor. Only his neck and head are slowly moving in every direction. I stand beside him so I don't miss anything, watching his gaze grope its way from the darkened windows opposite to the rest of the room. His eyes skim the photographs, the older ones that are still in frames and show me as a boy with my mother. And the more recent ones that I printed out and pinned to the walls. Often they're the same photos side by side, five or six at a time. But I thought the picture was so beautiful, Julie was so beautiful. How many times have I got cross with myself for not having taken more photographs from the time we were together? My favourite picture is one I took when we were in the rowing boat on the lake by her house. It's a close-up of her face, slightly overexposed from the summer sun. Her head is slightly lowered; she's concentrating on the Pasternak novel she's reading to me. A breath of wind is blowing a few shining red strands of hair and there's a carefree smile on her lips. Bishop-Petersen's mouth is slightly open but he's not saying anything. His eyes keep wandering to the wardrobe. Hanging from the right door is an old wedding dress on a clothes hanger. Its story is sad and short. My mother was in love with my father, who I never met. She wanted to marry him, but as he was already married at the time, he'd have had to leave his wife first. Instead, he left my mother and moved away with his family – to where pepper grows, as my grandfather used to say. My mother sewed the dress herself when she was still full of hope, but she never got to wear it. I didn't even know it existed until that fateful day when, from her bed, she instructed me to take it out of the wardrobe. 'For Julie,' she said, her voice cracking, smiling weakly.

As if he could read my thoughts, Bishop-Petersen steers his gaze from the old wedding dress to the dried bunch of flowers in the vase on the bedside table. I hear him swallow, and I keep watching as now, almost in slow motion, he turns to what he must have already spotted out of the corner of his eye. His face stiffens as if paralysed.

'I want to know who met me under your name for that interview,' I say as calmly as I can in the circumstances.

## LIV

The shock is worse than the damage a verge marker can do when it collides with the front bumper of a small car. The dent is huge, and inside the car the airbags hang limply over the steering wheel and dashboard. But she and Theo aren't injured, that's the most important thing. They've escaped with a few proverbial scratches. The flashing yellow lights of the recovery vehicle and the blue ones of a police car are dancing a wild canon in the darkness. Liv has to explain how the accident happened. She says an animal suddenly darted across the road, causing her to lose control of the car. Why she says this, she has no idea; the words just come out. Maybe she's afraid that Theo – who was responsible for the accident by grabbing the wheel – would be taken away and locked up, or he'd undergo an examination to check his mental state. Something that would result in her being separated from him. Not to mention the rifle in the footwell at the back of the car. It doesn't work, but still. Fortunately she doesn't make a suspicious impression, and Theo keeps his mouth shut too, which means there's no reason for the police to conduct a detailed search of the interior. All the same Liv has to take a breathalyser test. Of course she's sober, but in the presence of the two police officers, her heart is pounding like crazy. As if she really did have something to hide. And in a way she does. She's got some striking new leads in a criminal case: three bizarre emails; a sports teacher who had an affair with the sister of the missing girl, and who died no less strangely; an argument between the missing girl and said sports teacher; and, not least, some possible inconsistencies in the alibi of the missing girl's ex-boyfriend. Maybe she has nothing, nothing at all, but maybe she does. She just can't put it together to make a coherent picture. Her head is buzzing from all the information, as well as from having bashed into the airbag half an hour ago. Liv is terrified about telling Phil, because all the annoying insurance stuff will now be heading their way – or rather, they're going to have to explain to their sponsor, Autohaus, that she caused an accident. She's fed up to the back teeth and – once again, this time more than ever – she's hopelessly out of her depth.

At least the police officers are nice, and for a brief moment Liv wonders whether she ought not just tell them everything and ask for help. It would be child's play for them – or for their colleagues from the right department – to trace the emails back to the sender, and perhaps that would lead to everything else being cleared up.

To top it all, the officers ask her if there's anything else they can do. Liv turns to look at the recovery vehicle, which has already loaded her car, and where Theo is sitting in the passenger seat of the driver's cab, wearing his hat and a high-vis vest, with the laptop on his knees again and her mobile hanging on the cord around his neck to keep the hotspot activated. With a sigh she tells the kind officers, 'No, thank you. We'll be alright.' Liv is happy when the police car drives off. The recovery service takes them to the dealership that provided the car for *Two Crime*. It and the adjoining workshop are of course closed at this time of night. They wait until the huge vehicle has driven off before fetching their things, the rifle included, from Liv's car. The dealership is in a business park, too far out of town to walk. In any case, Liv has no idea where to go right now. The Novaks' old house in Grunewald where they were going to lie in wait? Back to Theo's flat to sort themselves out first? They can't take a taxi because of the rifle. Phil's out of the question too. For one thing, he doesn't have a car. But also she doesn't fancy launching into a heated discussion about the accident in the middle of the night and outside a deserted car dealership. Sophia, then. Liv, who's taken her phone back from Theo, is just about to press the call icon when she hears him shouting. Still wearing the high-vis vest which, in the meagre light of the industrial estate, is nonetheless glowing an almost absurd neon-yellow, he's sitting a few metres away on the steps to the customer entrance.

'Liv! Liv, come quickly!'

*Liv*, she thinks. The fact that he's calling her by her proper name seems to be a good sign, an indicator of a brief moment of lucidity. She isn't angry with him because of the accident. Because, as she tells herself, it wasn't Theo who grabbed the wheel, but his illness. It was also his illness that aimed the rifle at her in his flat earlier. Theo is a good man, a loving father who'd do anything for his daughters. As much as she can understand Sophia, who is in despair at how difficult things have become with him, Liv probably wouldn't hesitate one second to change places with her. A sick father is still a father. She's beside him in a jiffy, already guessing that there's a new email.

She's right. *Nutcracker11* has answered her question about the last song at the school ball. Answered it *correctly* with: '*Waltz of the Flowers*' *by Tchaikovsky*. The email also says: *Please, Dad. You mustn't say anything to the police.*

Theo looks at Liv. 'She's frightened,' he whispers with a quavering voice. 'She's frightened for her life.' Then, without waiting for a reaction, he turns back to the laptop and begins to type. Liv wants to say that they ought first to discuss what he's going to write. Because, thinking about it now, she's no longer so sure that mere knowledge of the last song at the school ball is clear proof that *Nutcracker11* really is Julie. Sophia could know about the song, friends of Julie who did dancing lessons with her – or Daniel Wagner, or whoever – but she can't think of these others because Liv still knows too little about Julie's friends and acquaintances back then. But who of these people might have a reason to write the emails? Not Sophia, that much is clear. Nor Daniel Wagner, especially not if he had anything to do with Julie's disappearance. No. Liv is convinced that if it's anyone else apart from Julie writing these emails – particularly now, with the case having come to the public's attention again after so many years – they must be doing it for that very reason: that the case has suddenly been rekindled. Someone wanting to get their oar in for some reason. Like the boy from Julie's group of friends who Bergmann told her about. To get attention or because they take pleasure in giving the relatives the runaround, for some sick reason delight in their suffering. The fact is, it would have to be someone who knew Julie well enough that they're aware of the significance of 'Waltz of the Flowers'.

Theo's finished. He holds the laptop to Liv so she can see what he's written.

julie,

this is your dad. You know, YOUR DAD who's always loved you and wanted to protect you so long as he was alive. i swore this the day you were born, my angel. I can't remember everything because my head sometimes quarrels with me, but i still remember enough. And a memory is more than just an image in your mind. it's a feeling in your heart. Even if your face is beginning to fade, I will know forever how much I loved you. i will know what it felt like when i had you in my arms while we were standing by the lake and you, still so small, looked into the distance and invented skyearthblue. I will know how proud i was of each of your stages of development. i think I taught you how to ride a bicycle. and how to swim. I comforted and encouraged you when there was a problem at school or with one of your friends. you were always one of the most important people in my life, more important than many others, and even though sometimes you refused to believe this, definitely much kore important that medicien. and i want to apolgolise, Julie. For those moment s when you got the impression that something was more important to me, even just a touch more important. I have to be honest, I would still need to leave early from your school ball if i were director of the clinic for heart, thoracic and vascular surgery and my pager went. Because I swore I would save lives. But I would talk to you differently, not only say that i'll make it up to you, but really do it. I know you think that some things simply can't be put right or repeated once the original moment has passed. And youre right. Of course I can't change the past and undo those times when I've disappointed you. But Julie, I'm old now. You're mother isn't here anymore. i can't folllow her until I've found you. give me the chance to spenf a little more time with you while i can. That would be my greatest wish. For all those times you felt i let you down, give me the chance to be there for you now. Please. Let me help you. Let me take you homw. tell me where you are. You mustn't be frightened. Your Dad is coming to get you. I promise.

Less than an hour later, Sophia arrives at the dealership. Liv had to try half a dozen times before she finally answered her phone. No wonder, given how late it is. She looks puffy from sleep, her eyes are small and the retinas are reddened. Liv is expecting another rocket, as if she, not Theo, had been responsible for the accident in which they could have both been badly injured. But, like Liv, Sophia seems merely to be relieved that nothing worse did happen. All the same, she tries to persuade her father to get checked out by his doctor, Claus Dellard. He's just as stubborn in rejecting this as he is in defending the fact he's got the old rifle with him, as well as the plan for Liv and him to spend the rest of the night in the old house. The minimal resistance from Sophia might be down to her lack of sleep. Or is it the realisation that Theo will get his way anyway? Maybe it's both at once and, after the last few gruelling days, she's so drained that she just can't fight anymore. Who can empathise with her, if not Liv? Which means she's even more astonished when Sophia parks a road away from the Novaks' old house and says she intends to join them too. Sophia isn't comfortable about this, as Liv can see from the uncertain way she approaches the house, and even more so in Sophia's face when they stop by the iron gate.

'You don't have to do this,' she tells her, as Theo, the rifle clamped under his arm, goes about his old trick of pulling, pushing and giving a big shove of the shoulder to open the gate.

'I know,' Sophia says. 'But I can't stop thinking, that—'

'The *skyearthblue* email really might be from Julie,' Liv says, finishing her sentence and nodding. 'I feel exactly the same.' She gives her lip a quick bite. Should she tell Sophia that there have been more emails from *Nutcracker11* since? She's quite reluctant to do this after the disappointment that Sophia told her nothing about her relationship with Jason Willmers. Shame is the word that comes to mind again. Would she have told a stranger about it if she were in Sophia's shoes, and in Theo's presence too? No, certainly not.

'We need to talk in private,' she says, rubbing Sophia's shoulder as they follow Theo through the iron gate. Liv uses her phone torch to help them find their way to the house and ends up pointing it at the lock.

'The key?' she asks cautiously.

'The key?' Theo asks back. Liv exchanges an embarrassed glance with Sophia, who then puts her father in the picture. 'You do have the key, Dad. Have you forgotten?'

Theo shakes his head resolutely. 'I don't have a key! If I had one, I wouldn't have spent the night in that uncomfortable boat!'

'Erm, yes, you do, Theo,' Liv now says mildly. 'You put it in your pocket when we were here yesterday. You said it belonged to you.'

'I don't have a . . .' He sounds irate as he puts the rifle in Sophia's hands to check his trouser pockets. Then he says, 'Oh.'

Of course he's got the key. But they don't say any more about it.

Theo calls it the *observation post*. It's the place to the left of Julie's bed, invisible at first to anyone who comes through the bedroom door. Nothing inside the room suggests that anyone's been here since. The altar is still nowhere to be seen, as if it had never existed. Theo hopes nonetheless that the intruder will return. Liv, however, doesn't think that will happen after she and Phil almost caught the person. But Theo won't hear of it. He sits on the floor beside the bed, his back against the wall, the rifle pressed diagonally across his chest with both hands. From time to time he has to tighten his grip when, overcome with tiredness, the rifle threatens to slip from his hands. Liv and Sophia are squatting together on the other side of the room, behind the door. Beside Liv on the black sports bag with the camera equipment is her laptop that she opens at regular intervals to see whether there's been another email, only to close it again quickly afterwards. She's worried that the glow of the screen could give them away in the darkness, or worse, be visible from outside through the window.

'I went to see the widow of the karate instructor,' Liv whispers to Sophia, who instantly flinches. 'We don't have to talk in detail about your relationship with Jason Willmers if you don't want to.'

Sophia shakes her head. 'No, I don't want to.'

'I respect that. But there's one thing I beg you to tell me, for Julie's sake, and I swear on my life that I'm only trying to find out what happened to her. There's no ulterior motive, OK?'

'What do you want to know?'

'Did your sister know about you and Jason Willmers? Could the argument she had with him just before she disappeared have been about you? Did she maybe tell him to keep away from you?'

'No. She didn't know anything.'

'You didn't tell her?'

'I didn't tell anyone anything. Jason told me I mustn't. He said nobody would understand, and I was still so young . . .' In the dim light Liv notices Sophia put her hands in front of her face. 'I was so stupid. I'd have done anything he asked me to.' She stifles a sob. 'Please don't say anything to my father.'

'Don't worry, I won't. I just want to find out whether Julie's disappearance has anything to do with Jason Willmers.'

'No, I . . . I didn't see Jason again after his wife caught us. She dragged me out of the house by the arm, chucked my bag in the boot of her car, drove me home and, as I got out, made perfectly clear what would happen if I didn't keep away from her husband.'

'What?'

Sophia doesn't reply immediately, she merely swallows loudly.

'Did she threaten you?' Liv probes.

'She'd make my life hell, that's what she told me.'

'She'd make—'

Sophia gives a quiet and bitter laugh. 'Clearly it didn't need her involvement.'

'What do you mean?'

'Did my sister go missing or not?' She gestures to the other side of the room, where Theo is sitting beside the bed with the rifle. 'Or do you get the impression that we led a normal life again afterwards?'

'Hmm,' Liv says pensively.

'Oh shit!' Sophia slaps a hand over her mouth.

'What's wrong? Have you remembered something?'

'My husband! I need to let him know I'm with my father and won't be coming home tonight. He'll get worried otherwise.' Liv can feel movement beside her – Sophia's hands searching the floor. 'My phone, I can't find it,' she says. 'I can't see anything.'

'Wait, I'll put my torch on.' Liv reaches for the sports bag beside her. She notes that a few frayed strands of the cord that her phone is attached to have got caught in the bag's zip. In the darkness Liv struggles to separate one from the other. She curses silently, at both the cord and the bag.

The bag!

Liv stops short.

'Everything alright?' Sophia asks.

'The black sports bag,' Liv says, sounding as if she's in a trance. 'You and your sister.'

'Yes?' Sophia sounds confused.

'You looked similar.'

'Well, as similar as sisters tend to, with an age gap of a couple of years.'

'You both had long red hair.'

'Liv, I really don't see what—'

'It was your bag the ransom money was supposed to be packed into according to the note on your father's computer.'

'What are you getting at?'

'The black sports bag was yours, not Julie's.'

'Yes, but . . . yes, you're right. Julie took my bag to karate because one of the straps on hers was broken. Then she kicked it across the kitchen floor because she was pissed off . . .'

'I don't mean that.' Liv looks at Sophia. In the darkness she can't see more than a rough outline of her face. 'What if there was a mix-up?'

'With our bags?' Sophia still doesn't seem to have understood.

'No,' Liv says, a little louder than she intended to, causing Theo to grunt a snore from his corner. 'Between you and your sister.

Maybe it wasn't Julie who was meant to be abducted that night, but you! Look,' she goes on when Sophia shows no reaction. 'In the ransom demand, that may have been intended as a distraction, it just said: *We have your daughter*. Not: *We have your daughter, Julie*. Do you get me? Julie's name doesn't appear once.'

'Yes, I understand that. But you don't seriously think that Maya Willmers . . .'

'No.' Liv touches her forehead, where a bump has come up over the past few hours since the accident. Sophia's right: Maya Willmers is a petite woman. It's impossible to imagine that she could have been physically so superior to the athletic Julie that she could have overpowered her. Maya would have needed a weapon at least. Liv shakes her head. Nonsense. With or without a weapon, Maya Willmers would have definitely noticed the difference between Julie and Sophia. Unless . . .

'What if she hired someone? Someone who'd never met you or Julie before, and so had to rely on Maya's description? This bedroom is closer to the staircase than yours. Maybe it was the first one the kidnapper ended up in on his way through the house. In bed lay a young girl with long red hair. What other description could Maya Willmers have given him?' Liv gasps for air, breathless and shocked by what she's just said.

'Oh, God!' she says when she realises what she's just told Sophia who – if Liv is right – would have been kept captive for twenty years in place of Julie. Assuming the emails really are from her sister and she's still alive.

## LARA

Those last few moments when Isabel pushed me down the corridor in my wheelchair. A guarded happiness when I thought of my family, freedom. And how mistaken I was. It was like watching a film. Images separated by flashes of black, cut to the dull thump of a heartbeat. The door to the staffroom opening. Ba-dum. The image of a person looking very relaxed as he reclined in the chair behind the desk – ba-dum – and the realisation that this was a put-up job; he must have been waiting for me there. Ba-dum. A frantic pan from his face to Isabel's, now full of sympathy, the eyelids downcast with shame and a faint quiver of the lips. She'd fooled me into coming here. She'd allowed herself to be pulled over to his side with some kind of lie he'd told her. She was so stupid, so stupid, so stupid. She'd read everything online, hadn't she, but still she was helping him rather than me. Ba-dum. Then me, wide-eyed and mouth open to scream, thrashing about with my arms and trying to get out of the wheelchair – ba-dum – him, picking up the telephone on the desk as if in slow motion, holding it out to me with a smile and inviting me to take it – ba-dum – me again, the movements of my weak, sick body, faltering, eyes fixed on the telephone. Ba-dum. A trap, I knew it. A trap like everything here was a trap. Isabel, who'd pretended to be on my side but really was on his. *I've heard you'd like to call someone, Lara.* Ba-dum. A trap, a trap, I knew it, I knew it, I stared at the receiver in his hand. Ba-dum. *Don't you have the guts?* Ba-dum. With a shrug he put the receiver back down. Ba-dum. *Some people prefer to write rather than telephone. Would you like to write to someone, Lara?* He turned the computer screen a few centimetres towards me, his hand brushing the pen pot in the process. *Come on.* Ba-dum. Pan back to Isabel, holding me under the arms to help me out of the wheelchair. Ba-dum. Supporting me as I robotically stepped over to the desk, to him, to the computer. Ba-dum. Zoom into the pen pot. Focus on the scissors poking above an assortment of pens. Ba-dum. On my hand, which moved in a flash despite my condition. On the scissors in the air. Ba-dum. On me launching myself across the desk, however my sick body managed it. Ba-dum. He and I colliding. Ba-dum. The scissors only grazing his shoulder until I'd found my balance – ba-dum – then being thrust at full force into his thigh – ba-dum – and the blood, the blood, all that blood spurting on to his trousers, on to the floor, on to our faces. Ba-dum. My body sliding off his and his sliding from the chair, both of us landing on the floor. Ba-dum. Him screaming, his hands trembling, unsure whether or not to pull the scissors out of his leg. Ba-dum. Me taking the decision for him, then the blood spurting even more, like a little fountain, vertically into the air. Ba-dum. Him screaming, writhing, pressing the palms of his hands on his leg. Ba-dum. Me using the desk to pull myself up, and now heading towards Isabel with the bloody scissors and on wobbly knees. Ba-dum. Her too shocked to do anything apart from take a step backwards and bash into the wall. Ba-dum. Me telling her that she's got to get me out of here at once, and knowing she'd obey because there was no longer any doubt what I was capable of, what I was prepared to do to get my life back after all these years of being locked up. Ba-dum. Me, smiling, exhausted, wiping my blood-smeared face with the back of my right hand, the scissors still firmly in my grip, while my left hand reached for the support of Isabel's arm. Ba-dum. Us leaving the room where he was lying on the floor in a pool of blood. Ba-dum. Dragging ourselves down the corridor with the slow steps my body was able to manage after such physical effort, and me thinking how strange it was that, despite the reduced number of staff at night, we didn't meet a single one of Isabel's colleagues even though it would have been almost impossible not to hear his screaming. Until I realised it couldn't have been a coincidence. That the two of them must have planned it like this, so that they could lure me into their trap when nobody was around to witness it. What they hadn't expected was that I'd succeed in turning the tables.

Just as, right then, I hadn't expected that the man lying in a huge pool of his own blood on the floor of the staffroom was far from dead.

## LIV

The night was empty, without shadows, without creaking stairs, without one of those moments when your whole body becomes a heartbeat, you forget to breathe and for a few seconds you're nothing but adrenaline, sweat and function. No intruder, no opportunity for Theo's rifle to be used. Liv feels justified; she didn't think that the person she and Phil almost caught here would return. Why would they? And in truth she was relieved, because it meant she'd been right in both her prognosis and gut feeling. Right for the first time in a while, after many days of doubt and self-castigation. Theo, by contrast, had a grumpy start to the day. He was perfectly lucid and knew why he'd lain in wait last night with Liv and Sophia in Julie's old room. Even though he kept nodding off, causing Liv to worry that he'd wake up this morning and not be able to remember a thing. That he might start yelling at her and Sophia in his confusion and the shock at waking up here. Instead he was grumpy, but it was a peaceful sort of grumpiness, a disappointment at not having been able to use his rifle. He'd have loved a showdown like in a film when the goodies finally take down the baddies. Liv felt sorry for him, as she did for Sophia, who had spent the rest of the night as if numb with shock now that Liv had stumbled across a possible connection between Julie and Jason Willmers or, more precisely, his wife, Maya. This was understandable because, if Sophia had been the intended victim, she was in some way to blame for whatever Julie had been forced to suffer in her place. Not objectively to blame, of course, but in her own mind. After Liv offered her theory about a possible mix-up, Sophia had gone to the bathroom. She wanted to be on her own for a moment and message her husband. Liv could only imagine Sophia crouching on the tiled floor by the shower, bent double with guilt and shame, typing with jittery fingers to Richard that she was spending the night with her father and wouldn't be back until the morning. Liv could have wept at the injustice of this: it always seemed to be those who already had problems who were burdened with more. For the time being, they didn't say anything to Theo about this new theory. He needed to get over the restless night first.

They've now gone their separate ways. Sophia drove both Theo, who needed to get some sleep, and Liv home. In the car they checked Theo's emails one final time – still nothing new from *Nutcracker11*. Liv offered to keep an eye on Theo's inbox, but he didn't want that.

'In case you're worried I might forget to check regularly,' he said, 'you're wrong. I never forget my Julie.' Liv realised it was good for him to have something to do and she asked him to ring her at once if *Nutcracker11* sent another message. He promised.

Now Liv is back home. She gives a start when the coffee machine responds to her pressing of the button by making its usual buzzing sound. At this time of the morning it sounds loud. It's just after six o'clock and Phil is still asleep. He knows nothing about the accident or her new theory about Maya Willmers. He doesn't even know where she spent last night. But he didn't get in touch either and ask why she hadn't come home. Liv takes her cup, puts the bag with her camera equipment over her shoulder, clamps the laptop under her arm and leaves the flat quietly. She's going to head up to the attic, to the spartan place where it all began for the right reasons. To the time when they were genuinely concerned about the cases and the people involved rather than the numbers of listeners. Liv sets herself up there, taking the sheet down from the shelves, putting the old whiteboard back up, looking for and finding one of the special pens to write on it, and she starts to make notes. In the middle at the top is Julie's name. Beneath it, all the other names of people who've cropped up in the case so far, including Daniel Wagner, Jason and Maya Willmers, and an 'X' for the unidentified witness who gave Wagner the maybe-or-maybe-not alibi. She's just about to connect the names with arrows to highlight the individual relationships to Julie and infer potential motives when her phone signals a message from Phil. Where is she? *Attic*, she writes back curtly.

'Wow,' is the first thing she hears him say when he enters the den. 'Let me get a photo for social media.'

'Are you crazy?' That's all she needs right now – the public getting an insight into her research. Besides, what does she look like? She grasps her hair that feels like it hasn't been washed in ages. She's also still wearing the T-shirt she had on yesterday and she really needs a shower. 'Just look at me!'

But Phil's phone is already aimed at her. 'That's the point. You look like you'd die for this story.' When Liv angrily puts her hands on her hips, he corrects himself. 'Or at least like you haven't slept in days. Believe me, you'll get a ton of likes.' He waggles his hand. 'Just stand a little bit closer to the whiteboard and don't look so terrified. Don't worry, I'll pixellate the names, obviously.' He moves the phone to get the right angle, but after a quick glance at the screen lowers his arm again.

'Is that a bump on your head?'

'C'mon, Phil, I just want—'

'Done! We can post it right away. Together with the statement you read out on our last recording. You know, about the plagiarism.'

Liv is taken by total surprise when, out of the blue, he puts his arms around her. As stiff as a rod to begin with, she eventually relaxes, breathing in Phil's familiar smell and closing her eyes for a moment. How much she's missed this, how much she's missed *him*.

'Right,' Phil says, already breaking out of the embrace. 'I was actually looking for you because we need to go to the studio to record the second part of Vlado Taneski. I want to start editing today. But now . . . this looks like a right little detective's den.' He looks around, from the names on the whiteboard to the trestle table with Liv's laptop and her open notebook. He goes over to the table, having spotted a little yellow sticky label in her book.

He removes it from the page full of scrawls and reads out loud the address on it. It's the one he sent Liv yesterday by WhatsApp and she wrote down. But on the small yellow pad on Theo's kitchen table rather than in her notebook. A sticky note like that could easily be moved from one page to the next; it wasn't an obligatory fixed point on her to-do list, but something that could be comfortably postponed.

'You haven't been to see him yet,' Phil presumes correctly, his tone indifferent.

'No, I haven't found the time.' Or the courage, she adds in her head. Interviewing Daniel Wagner still seems to be the greatest challenge. He could be a criminal. Or someone who has been treated like one for many years because of people like her. Someone who might be profoundly nasty, or at least very angry. The prospect of facing him gives Liv a queasy feeling of inferiority. Like with Heinz all those years ago. Liv knows what it's like to encounter someone with a brooding anger. A hopeless undertaking, every time. 'But I did pay a visit to the wife of Jason Willmers yesterday,' she continues. 'And you're not going to believe this, but—'

'Who the hell is Jason Willmers?'

'Julie's karate instructor, that's who! I told you that shortly before she disappeared she had a—'

Phil's hand slaps the note on the table. Then he stroppily grabs the pen for the whiteboard, where he rings Daniel Wagner's name.

'You're wasting your time, Liv! It was him!'

Liv takes the pen from his hand. 'You don't know that! When I was talking to Maya Willmers yester—'

'Forget this Tanja Willmers!'

'Maya!'

'What about the boy who retracted his alibi for Wagner?'

'Bergmann refuses to reveal his name or number. Data protection.'

Phil sighs, then turns on his heel. 'I'll sort it,' she hears him say before he leaves the attic.

When he returns, he puts another Post-it into her hand with a Berlin landline number. 'Here, call this.'

'Did Bergmann . . . just like that?'

'Go on, call it.'

Liv picks up her phone and dials the number. She's almost relieved when there's no answer after three attempts, because the mood swing in Phil, who was just hugging her, to the Phil who's now standing before her with his stony face, his impatience and his discounting of the possible lead from her meeting with Maya Willmers, hits her hard.

'I'll try again later,' she promises.

He nods. 'OK. Let's go, then.'

'We could record it here.'

Phil pulls a face.

'Alright, alright,' Liv says. 'But we'll need a taxi.'

'Why taxi?'

'Erm.' Liv lowers her eyes. Phil's going to go ballistic when he hears that, on top of everything else, their car is now a wreck too. 'A lot happened yesterday.'

## DANIEL

I had to go to the police station twice to be interrogated about Julie. Once on the day after she went missing, and the second time after my alibi had fallen through. About a week later I found myself there again, this time because of her father and his attack on me. On the fourth, fifth and sixth occasions, I went to the police of my own accord. I wanted the journalists to disappear from outside our house and I wanted to get a reporting ban put on all those who'd not only smeared me – even though the police had released me without charge – but also printed photographs of me without permission, screenshots from my Facebook account that was still active at the time, or the profile I'd submitted to a dating site. Maybe I was there a seventh, eighth or ninth time too – eventually I stopped counting, and so I don't know what number visit it was yesterday, when I went to report the recent attack on me and was just sent home again. There's only one thing I know with any certainty: I've now spent so many hours at that police station that if you add them all up, they become days.

'Admittedly,' I say to Bishop-Petersen – we're sitting at my kitchen table; I've made coffee for the both of us – 'the first few times were the longest. I even had to stay overnight. Let's say it was around fifty hours in total.' I can see him starting to shift around in his chair. 'And then the third time I was there because of Theo Novak, who'd beaten me up outside my house and before the eyes of all those journalists. It was quicker that time because I was the victim. Three hours. Or let's say four, seeing as I had to go to hospital too, to have my injuries examined and treated. What does that make, Herr Bishop-Petersen?'

'Fifty-four,' he answers hesitantly. I think he's got an idea where I'm going with this. He asked me when I was going to let him go. He's got a wife and two children, he says. I don't. That's exactly what I told him before beginning to calculate the time that I, just like him now, wasted in a place I didn't want to be. Of course he and his colleagues aren't to blame for my interrogation as Julie's ex-boyfriend; obviously that was protocol. But they've played their part in preventing me from being able to lead a normal life ever again. In stopping me from having a wife and two children who'd now be worried if I didn't come home after work.

I shake my head and sigh. 'Thinking about it now, I realise that not all of this can be put on to you, tit for tat. But I've got to start somewhere, haven't I?'

Bishop-Petersen looks at me with bloodshot eyes. 'You're not going to let me go, are you? Not after fifty-four hours, sixty or at any point. You're never going to let me go.'

I smile. 'I've already told you what I want: the name of the guy who did that interview with me for the *Berliner Rundschau*.'

'But why? I mean, he wasn't the only person to write about you.'

'You still haven't understood, have you? He had the opportunity to tell my side of the story. And if he had done that, I might have switched from being the suspect – as far as the public were concerned – to Julie's boyfriend who loved her more than anything. And who, after all the suffering that Julie's disappearance had inflicted on him too, deserved a bit of a break.'

Bishop-Petersen's shoulders stiffen and his eyes look up at the ceiling, to where my mother's former bedroom is.

'How do I know you'll keep to your word and let me go if I give you the name?'

'Hmm.' I pretend to think. I stall for time by leaning back in my chair, crossing my arms and glancing at the ceiling too. Only then do I look back at him and say, 'You can't know that, you're right. But there's one more thing I can tell you from experience: there are no guarantees in life, for anything. Take Julie and me. I'd thought this was a great love affair. But it can't have been, can it? I mean, she wouldn't have just accepted our break-up so easily otherwise. She would've fought for us, against everything and everyone. Just like I was prepared to fight. Well.' I shrug. 'It's your decision as to whether you're willing to take the risk, Max.'

'Herr Wagner, please! Someone will be looking for me. I didn't come home all night and I've failed to turn up for work this morning.'

I nod; he's right. Although now that he's said it, I find it strange that he claims to have a wife and two children. Because his phone, which I took off him last night, hasn't rung once since he's been here. Surely there would have been a call if someone at home was worried. The newspaper, well, maybe his colleagues are used to him turning up a bit late from time to time, or not at all because he's making up his garbage while working from home.

'What's your wife's name?' I ask, now suspicious.

Bishop-Petersen moves his lips, but no sound comes out.

'You're only a good liar when you're writing, then,' I tell him with a grin. But I put my hand in my back pocket, where I've been keeping his phone, and push it across the table to him.

'Call your office and tell them you're working on a story. And call your mother too, for all I care, or whoever else might *really* be worried not to have seen you for the past few hours.'

He hesitantly reaches for the phone.

'Don't do anything stupid,' I add.

## LIV

PHIL: A very warm welcome to *Two Crime – The True Crime Podcast* – with ...

LIV: ... me, Liv Keller and ...

PHIL: ... me, Philipp Hendricks. Today for you, we have part two of the case of the Macedonian local reporter Vlado Taneski. But before we begin, a big thank you to everyone who reacted so positively and appreciatively to the statement we made last time regarding the episode about the disappearance of Julie Novak. We – or Liv, who's taking the lead on this one – are still up to our eyebrows in the reportage and, guys, let me tell you: it's going to be spectacular! But now back to the Macedonian journalist Vlado Taneski. Liv, would you give us a brief summary?

LIV: Yes, OK, erm ... Just interrupt me if I miss anything important ...

PHIL: You bet.

LIV: Good, right, then. Within the space of about four years, three women, all of them over fifty-five and who work as cleaners, go missing in a small Macedonian town. Their bodies aren't found until weeks or even months later. Before they died, all the women were kept captive, beaten and sexually abused, until eventually being strangled to death. Vlado is the first person to identify the parallels between the cases and he doesn't tire of reporting on them. Very much to the annoyance of the authorities, who had actually arrested two men after the first murder and declared the case closed. Vlado embarks on his own research and becomes a national hero – unlike the police, who remain idle.

PHIL: Thanks, Liv, excellent. Do you remember where we stopped last time?

LIV: How could I forget? It was a dreadful cliffhanger. Because the next person to disappear after the three women is Vlado himself.

PHIL: You'd also proposed a theory about this, if I remember rightly.

LIV: Yes, that's right. It immediately struck me that the police might have got Vlado out of the way because of his negative reporting. I mean, he kept criticising the authorities for their poor investigations, or not even investigating at all. But there's another possibility, of course.

PHIL: Which is?

LIV: What if, in one of his articles, Vlado wrote something that made the killer anxious? If he showed he was right on that person's heels?

PHIL: You mean the killer went for Vlado because he was afraid of being exposed?

LIV: Maybe Vlado had written something that might be dangerous for the killer . . . It could've been some tiny detail, and he wasn't even aware how close he'd come to the killer with it.

PHIL: Wow, that's impressive. Believe it or not, it is about a detail. And this detail is a telephone cord.

LIV: A telephone cord?

PHIL: Uh-huh. In an article about the third murder, that's to say the last one, Vlado wrote that this woman had been strangled with a telephone cable. The same cable her body was tied up with, by the way. It was found at the site where the body was dumped. But this is a piece of information that the police have deliberately kept quiet from the press and the public. All the authorities said was that the victims were strangled. Not what they were strangled with, because . . .

LIV: It's something only the killer knows!

PHIL: Exactly.

LIV: No?! Are you telling me that Vlado himself . . .

PHIL: Was the killer? That's now what the police try to find out. You might recall that traces of blood and DNA were found on the women's bodies, which were shown to have come from the same man. Only they didn't have a suspect these traces were a match with. So you were right with your first theory: it was the police who got Vlado out of the way. Or, more precisely, he was arrested as a suspect and the traces compared to his DNA and blood. And what can I say? A match!

LIV: I don't believe it.

PHIL: Yes! Three independent DNA tests were carried out and they all led to the same conclusion. Besides, women's clothes were found at Vlado's house, which relatives identified as belonging to the victims. And now it gets really gruesome: the clothes the women were wearing when their bodies were found belonged to Vlado's mother.

LIV: Does that mean he kept the women captive in his house

before murdering them and forced them to wear his mother's clothes?

PHIL: Precisely. When the police dig around in Vlado's past, they find out that his father didn't care much for the boy and often struck out at him. But his mother – who worked as a cleaner, by the way – was apparently far worse. Ex-neighbours describe her as a 'wicked woman' who was authoritarian, cold and violent towards her son. Despite this, Vlado loved her very much. For example, Vlado's wife tells of how he often argued with his mother when their family lived in his parents' house. At the same time, he would get irate if his wife dared say anything against his mother. Because of the endless arguments and her mother-in-law's meddling, she was keen to move out, but Vlado wouldn't have any of it. His mother would be sad if he left her, he explained. Even after his parents' death, Vlado stayed in his childhood home while – as you remember – his wife moved with the children to the capital, Skopje.

LIV: And so she had no idea what Vlado was getting up to at home.

PHIL: Nobody did. Vlado is described as a loner who barely had any friends. The investigators assume that his motive was revenge for the rejection by his mother. He never got over her coldness. After she died, he kidnapped the other women as proxies and took out on them his frustration that his mother had never given him the love he'd craved so much.

LIV: Sounds like something out of a bad film.

PHIL: Yes, sometimes the truth is shockingly simple.

LIV: True, but *so* like a cliché? I mean, I really can't believe that he then wrote about his crimes in the newspaper.

PHIL: The desire for maximum attention, I'd say. An ego trip. Smarter and more cunning than any other.

LIV: And, in a way, it meant he got double satisfaction.

PHIL: Exactly. As a journalist, Vlado was in high esteem, at least as far as the public was concerned. His colleagues, on the other hand, didn't particularly like him, to put it mildly. For example, there was this incident even before the first of the murders took place. It had come to the attention of one of his colleagues that Vlado often lifted entire chunks of this man's texts for his articles, pretending that they were his own. Shortly after this colleague confronted Vlado about this, he received a telephone call with a murder threat. He's sure he recognised Vlado's voice on the other end of the phone. Putting this all together gives us the following motive: Vlado killed out of a deep-seated hatred for his mother, and at the same time, he was determined to advance his career.

LIV: Oh God. Who does things like that?

PHIL: Well, Vlado himself professes his innocence. He says the police were keen to pin something on him because he'd stepped on their toes once too often with his reporting.

LIV: OK, the clothes that were found in his house – they could have been put there by someone else. But back to the telephone cable that only the killer could've known about? If, for example, an anonymous police source had revealed this detail to him, he could have mentioned this in his defence. Plus, his DNA was found on the victims.

PHIL: That's what the police claim, at any rate. For something else happens that – despite the apparent, obvious motive – sows doubt. Three days after his arrest, on 23 June 2008, Vlado is found dead in his prison cell. Apparently he drowned himself in a plastic bucket of water.

LIV: I'm sorry? What?

PHIL: Yes, there was a bucket of water in his cell, which he supposedly stuck his head into to kill himself. Also, a suicide letter is found under his pillow, in which it says he didn't kill the women and he loves his family. Those who doubt this version of the story claim the letter could have been faked and that Vlado might have died when the police were trying to force a confession out of him through waterboarding. Criminologists, however, take the view that Vlado, unable to cope with the disgrace at having been exposed, wanted to escape his punishment and protect his family.

LIV: Sounds plausible. There's just one thing: is it actually possible to drown yourself in a bucket of water? I imagine that if I were to stick my head in, my body, when it noticed it was being starved of air, would automatically give the impulse to pull my head out again.

PHIL: Yes, that's the question. But there is, of course, another very clear sign of his guilt.

LIV: Which is?

PHIL: After Vlado died, the murders in Kičevo stopped.

LIV: Good, that certainly suggests that he was the killer . . . Or . . . the real murderer was simply clever enough and had sufficient self-control to realise that, having found the perfect scapegoat, he had to stop.

PHIL: It's possible. Are you going to come down on one side or the other?

LIV: Hmm. Well, all in all, I do actually believe it was Vlado.

He obviously had major psychological problems and also he wanted to prove himself professionally. That's clear enough for me. Clearer, at any rate, than this huge tangle of conspiracy theories. Like you said earlier, the truth is often simple and the solution so straightforward that, for this very reason, we think it must be wrong. Our desire for there to be more behind it blinds us to the obvious.

PHIL: I agree. Vlado meets all the criteria for being the killer. And so I think we can consider the case closed. Vlado Taneski is the Monster of Kičevo. End of.

LIV: Crazy. And the fact that he actually wrote about all of it . . .

PHIL: Really clever, although in the end not clever enough, as it turned out.

## LARA

I remember how the time dragged and the hospital corridor seemed to go on forever. I wanted to run but couldn't. My body was spent; I felt it might shatter at any moment and then I'd be lying here, in the corridor, in the middle of my own fragments. I could manage but one step after the other, and only this because I was using Isabel for support. Isabel, the traitor. Who'd led me to believe I'd soon be back home and was not ashamed to abuse this sacred word – *home* – by following *his* definition. For how long did I have to put up with it? How often had he tried to convince me? *This is your home, Lara*, accompanied by that repulsive smile.

But my home wasn't the room where he kept me captive. It wasn't the bed I lay on, pumped full of medication so he could keep me under control. My home was in Grunewald. I stopped and screwed up my eyes in an attempt to remember the address, and briefly panicked when I realised again how badly all those years of overmedication had damaged my brain. Eventually my mother's voice came to my help. She lovingly told me our address, adding, 'We're looking forward to seeing you.'

I nodded into nothingness and tightened my grip on Isabel's arm to signal to her that we had to be quicker. Mum, my lovely, beautiful mum. She'd cook me my favourite meal so my body soon recovered its strength. Dad, my silly old dad, the best dad in the world. We'd go swimming in our lake. And Sophia, my sweet, pain-in-the-arse little sister. I'd have a go at her if she borrowed my clothes again without asking, got them filthy and just stuffed them into my washing basket. We'd argue, but end up laughing together, like sisters do. I sense the tears running down my cheeks at the thought of how happy they'd all be to hug me. How they'd weep out of gratitude for my return. I'd survived him, I'd survived the devil. That's exactly what I was thinking when an alarm went off, resounding piercingly down the hospital corridor. In shock, I dropped the scissors and screamed at Isabel, 'We've got to get away!'

'We can't, Lara,' she said. 'The alarm automatically locks the ward. We can't get out of here now.'

In the background I heard a loud panting. We turned around. In the door to the staffroom stood the devil on wobbly legs and drenched in blood. But it was mere seconds before his strength deserted him and he collapsed. Just the sight of him, the fact that he was still alive, caused my legs to give way too and I ended up in a heap on the floor. Isabel took advantage of this to grab the scissors. Then she ran over to him, removing her apron as she went. She crumpled up the material and, kneeling beside the devil, pressed it on his thigh. I saw him shake his head feebly, as if to say, *You'll never do it. You'll never escape from me.*

'Hang on in there,' Isabel told him. 'Help is on its way,' and so it was. A moment later people came rushing from all directions, sheer commotion. Some rushed at the devil, others at me. And I knew he'd been right again. I'd never escape his clutches. I belonged to him. Forever.

## LIV

Liv is back home in her small den in the attic. As she'd expected, Phil wasn't thrilled about the accident, but his reaction was remarkably mild. He even offered to look after the matter from here: the repair, the insurance stuff, sweet-talking Autohaus, their sponsor. That's nice of him, she thinks, and very considerate given all the things that are still on their agenda She's finding it hard enough to work her way across the individual threads, to gather them all together in some form while they're seeking to move off in every different direction. Liv looks at her whiteboard, at the 'X' that stands for the unidentified witness in connection with Daniel Wagner's alibi. However Phil managed to wheedle the telephone number out of Bergmann, at least here she's been spared a big chunk of work. She just has to call the number and ask 'X' what Wagner's alibi was all about. Did he see him in the disco on the night that Julie went missing or not? And why did he give Wagner an alibi in the first place only to retract it later? Pure attention-seeking?

It rings, once, twice and several times more. Liv is almost ready to give up when someone finally picks up. First all she can hear is someone panting, out of breath, as if they've hurried to answer the landline.

Then comes a woman's voice: 'Yes, Dellard?'

In horror, Liv yanks the phone from her ear and hangs up. Dellard.

*Dellard, Dellard, Dellard* throbs inside her head.

That's the surname of Theo's doctor – and the godfather of Julie and Sophia. Could that have been his wife on the phone? Liv drops on to one of the folding chairs; the frame squeaks. Bergmann said that the witness was one of Julie's friends. Dellard's son, perhaps? Liv takes the laptop. She types 'Prof Claus Dellard Berlin family' into the search engine.

'Are you planning to put your sleeping bag up here?' Liv jumps. Phil's standing in the doorway to the attic, a grin on his face. But not for long when he sees how aghast Liv looks. He crouches down beside her chair. 'What's up, Liv? Are you not feeling well?'

'The telephone number Bergmann gave you.'

'Yes?'

'It's the Dellard family's landline.'

Putting the laptop back on the table, she gets out of her chair and steps over to the whiteboard. With a cloth she rubs out the 'X' and replaces it with a name: Benjamin Dellard. Then she turns back to Phil. 'Benjamin Dellard is the son of Professor Claus Dellard, head of neurology and psychiatry at the Charité, as well as Theo Novak's doctor. Plus, he's the godfather of Julie and Sophia! And his son, Benjamin, was not only born in the same year as Julie, he was, according to Bergmann, a good friend of hers.'

Phil says nothing, though he looks alert and attentive as he sits down on the chair that Liv was just sitting in.

'Benjamin Dellard was the boy who said he saw Daniel Wagner in the disco, but then later retracted his statement. And who at the same time gave a newspaper interview in which he spoke about how toxic the relationship between Wagner and Julie was. But now comes the absolute bombshell: Benjamin Dellard is dead! I found the death announcement online. The date of his death is given as 27 October 2003. This means he died three weeks after the interview – seven weeks after Julie's disappearance. Why didn't Bergmann mention that? It can't be a coincidence.'

Phil rubs his chin. 'No, you're right,' he says to Liv, who's shaking her head in disbelief. For the first time in days, he seems to be properly listening to her.

'You think so too?' she asks, just to make sure. When Phil nods, she continues. 'I can't tell you how Benjamin Dellard died. In the announcement, it just says something about *prematurely* and *unexpected*, but—'

Phil leaps up unexpectedly, grabs the whiteboard pen – just like he did this morning – and again circles the name Daniel Wagner. 'And I'm saying *that*. Or how else do you suppose a sixteen-year-old boy might die after becoming involved in a criminal case shortly beforehand and picking a fight with the chief suspect?'

'Are you saying Wagner killed him? You're not serious.'

'Liv.' Phil gives a dry laugh. 'How long have we been doing this podcast now? How many cases have we worked on? Who, if not us, ought to know what people are capable of?'

'Hmm,' Liv says pensively. 'At any rate, there's no point in me asking Bergmann how Benjamin Dellard died. He'd just mutter something about data protection again. But nor can I turn up at the Dellards' door and say, "Hi, I'd like to know how your son died."'

'If in doubt, you could.'

'No, Phil, no way.' She thinks of her experience with Maya Willmers and how bad she felt talking about her husband's death. A feeling that only subsided when Sophia told her of the threat Maya had made to her.

Liv takes the pen off Phil and taps Maya's name with it on the whiteboard. 'If I'm being honest, I still think that this is the right lead. I can't explain it, it's just a feeling, but . . .'

Behind the lenses of his glasses, Phil narrows his eyes. 'Why are you so scared of a confrontation with Wagner?'

Liv is hesitant. 'No, I . . .'

'Yes,' Phil says, cocking his head. 'Unlike the other people here,' he says, pointing to the names on the whiteboard, 'if you exclude the Novaks, Wagner has been on our list since the start. And yet you still haven't been to see him.'

'I didn't know how to reach him.'

'I gave you his address,' he says, pointing at the trestle table where the yellow sticker is.

'Look, there just hasn't been any time to do it. I'm stumbling from one situation to the next. And, Jesus, Phil, it's all too much.' She throws her hands out. 'You said yourself: I'm barely sleeping and I haven't had a shower. My head's all over the place, for fuck's sake, but you do nothing but complain, and you shout at me when I make a mistake. And I could vomit when I hear you say *we* and *our reportage* in the podcast. Because the fact is, you're letting me do all this shit on my own even though you know it's far too big for me!' She's talking ever more rapidly, and all of a sudden, exhausted tears come. 'I'm not a trained journalist, I'm Liv who's just trying...' Phil gives her a hug, a tighter one than this morning. She sobs into his chest. How good this long-overdue outburst feels. And just like a few minutes ago, when she got the impression that he was properly listening to her, now too he seems to be aware of her again, for the first time in ages.

'I'm sorry,' he mumbles into the top of her head. 'I'm sorry, Liv. I don't want you to feel let down by me. I'm the last person who'd leave you in the lurch, you know that.' He moves away from Liv so he can look her in the eye. In his gaze is the silent memory of the past. How he saved her from Heinz and helped her build a new life. Now he's really back, she thinks. The Phil she knows and loves.

He takes a tissue from his trouser pocket and gives it to Liv, who wipes her nose. 'Let me edit the Taneski case today, and after that, you can count on me again, OK? I'm not going to leave you high and dry, I promise.'

Liv nods. 'And I'll sort out Wagner.' She takes the Post-it with the address from the table and sticks it to the whiteboard, right beneath Wagner's name. 'But I want to be prepared. I want to know what happened to Benjamin Dellard before I put it to Wagner that he had something to do with his death.'

Phil nods. It's only when he's left the attic that it occurs to Liv she must have enjoyed their moment of intimacy so much that she missed the opportunity to tell him about another important development in Julie's case: the emails from *Nutcracker11*. Liv slaps her forehead and immediately regrets it. The bump she got from the car accident makes itself painfully felt. This evening, she thinks, she'll ask Phil this evening to set aside some time so that they can work through all the experiences and findings together thoroughly.

She takes a taxi to Spandau to see Theo. He knows she's coming; she rang him shortly beforehand to say so. When she arrives, Sophia is there too and has been for quite a while, Liv suspects, for the flat is tidy and smells of detergent. Theo is sitting at the dining table, which has a fresh tablecloth. Sophia hasn't yet put away the ironing board, which is standing by the window. Theo hasn't touched the cup of coffee or piece of cake in front of him. He seems withdrawn. His hair is tousled, his hands are on his lap beneath the table and his eyes are fixed on the plate with the cake.

'He's sad,' Sophia says softly to Liv as the two of them look at Theo from the doorway.

'No new emails, then?'

Sophia shakes her head. 'I told you: someone's been playing a trick.'

'But the word? *Skyearthblue*? How could anyone else know that?'

'Maybe my father said it to somebody one time,' Sophia says with a shrug. 'But he's absolutely convinced the emails are from Julie. Now that there haven't been any more, he thinks she's still angry at him.'

'Yes, he's mentioned that to me before. What exactly does he mean?'

'In truth she was rarely angry at him. It was usually when he missed something because of his work,' Sophia says with another shrug. 'You know: *I was the director of the clinic for heart, thoracic and* vascular surgery, that's my job, no, it's more than a job. You see, death doesn't care if it's Christmas or Easter or holiday or the school ball.' While a faint grin appears on Sophia's face, tears well in Liv's eyes once more. What on earth is wrong with her? She swiftly wipes her eyes.

'And he made such an effort with his last reply to *Nutcracker11*,' Liv says, placing the hand that was just wiping away the tears on her breastbone. 'It almost broke my heart when I read it.'

Sophia nods. Taking a step towards Theo, she says, 'Look, Dad, Liv's here. I'm going home now, OK?'

Theo looks up from his untouched slice of cake. His eyes are red, Liv sees as she comes over to sit with him at the table.

'Don't worry,' she says to Sophia with a smile. 'We'll manage.'

## THEO

'Theo,' Liv says when Sophia's gone. It's a shame, she never has time for me. I hope she's going to the hairdresser, I don't like her black hair. Vera wouldn't have liked it either. Liv puts her right hand on the table and wiggles her fingers at me. I bring out my right hand too, from under the table where, along with my left hand, it's been holding on to my hat. I asked Sophia if she could iron it for me, my hat, like she ironed the tablecloth. But she didn't want to. She just gave me a strange look and I thought: she doesn't like my hat, she can't stand it. So I quickly hid it on my lap under the table.

'Your fishing hat.' Liv smiles.

'It's a hat,' I say. 'Not the sort of one my father wore. But better than no hat.'

'Would you like to put it on?'

I shake my head. 'Just look at it. It's all crimpled. I can't go around wearing that.' Liv takes it off me and goes over to the ironing board.

'This is the least of our problems,' she says, getting to work.

When the hat is back on my head, I eat my cake. I told Liv that she should have some too. I had four siblings, I know how to share. But I don't have to do that anymore as all of them are old, stupid or dead. Liv looks delighted.

'I'd like to discuss something with you, Theo.' You shouldn't speak with your mouth full, but I don't say anything. Liv seems hungry. 'Do you feel up to it?'

What sort of a question is that? She's ironed my hat, hasn't she? And now it's back on top of my head. When my father wore his hat, nobody was allowed to doubt his ability to do anything. The knives would have been out otherwise.

'You bet!' I say unambigabbly, tapping the side of my head to signal to her that today is a good day. Apart from the fact that Julie hasn't replied to my email, which is worrying me. I tried to explain everything to her so she wouldn't be angry at me. 'Do you mean this, this, you know?' I say, nodding at the fridge where my father's rifle is back in its hiding place, just waiting for me to take it out again. I would have kept it close at hand on the table, but I thought that if Sophia wanted to take away my hat, the rifle would probably be the next thing. I don't understand the girl. Julie was very different. She liked her grandfather's rifle and the stories I told about it. How he sorted out the wild boar back in 1954 and got an award as a result. I raise my fist. 'We can go any time.'

'No,' Liv says. 'I need to talk to you about something else first. We need information, do you understand? You can't embark on a mission unprepared.'

Yes, I do understand. My father didn't march into the woods to take on the wild boar without a plan. So I nod.

'It's about the Dellard family,' Liv begins, cocking her head, as if to test whether my brain is really working as well today as I claimed.

'Claus Dellard,' I say. 'He wants to be a luminescence in the field of neurology and psychiatry.' I make a disparaging sound. 'He's a silly arrogant bastard.'

'Do you remember Benjamin Dellard too?'

'Benjamin, Benjamin, Benjamin,' I say to myself like a verse I'm trying to learn by heart. And it works, just like when I did it with 'Erlking' in the sixth year. 'Do you mean that thin, pale boy with the glasses and arrogant nose? Yes, that's right, he was called Benjamin. I was only recently wondering what his name was when his father showed me a photograph from the past. Claus and I, we used to be something like friends, but that's a long time ago now.'

'You really do remember!' Liv seems scarcely able to believe it and she's beaming. I tell her she's got cream on her lips from the cake. Vera was great at baking; what she made tasted better than what you get from the bakery these days. If Sophia had peered over her mother's shoulder a bit more rather than sitting howling in her bedroom all the time, she wouldn't need to go out and buy this oversweet filth. I just hope she learns in time before the woman from the adoption agency hands over the baby.

'Theo?'

'My Vera, she'd have been a wonderful grandmother,' I say with a smile. 'She was great with children, not just our own. She volunteered in a youth centre, you know. There were a few real nutters there, but she even got on with those and never lost her patience.'

'Benjamin Dellard,' Liv says. What makes her think of him?

'Claus's son? Yes, he was a nutter too. I never understood what Julie liked about him. A show-off like his father. After she disappeared, he gave an interview, did you know that? They didn't mention his name because he was still a minor, but I knew at once that it was him. All of us did.' I stop. Now I remember too why I started arguing with Claus back then, why we no longer posted together for photos by the lake. 'I drove to Claus's because I wanted to take that little git to task. It wasn't what he'd said in the interview – some of it was actually true. Julie really had changed when she was together with that, that Wegner. But Vera and I, we thought that whatshisname, Benjamin, had no right to give his opinion on it. But Claus didn't let me see his son. I told him he was a bad father – his son wouldn't have done something like that otherwise. He simply didn't have the boy under control. And that interview wasn't the first time this was obvious. The boy, he always wanted to belong, be part of the crowd. He would go out at night, hang around discos, and he drank.' I think. Yes, now it's all coming back to me. Benjamin, Benjamin, Benjamin. 'Sometimes he'd disappear for a few days and this drove Claus up the wall each time. We didn't really take it seriously anymore though, because he always turned up eventually, the silly little idiot.' I can see Liv's writing in her notebook; I don't know why. I mean, her video camera has been flashing away on the ironing board ever since she gave me my hat back. I crane my neck. She could be a doctor with that handwriting, it's a dreadful scribble. She looks up.

My Vera had beautiful handwriting and she wrote beautifully as well. I mean the words. She always took great care over her choice of words. She read a lot too, something that Julie got from her. She loved *Doctor Zhivago*, the film, but the book even more so.

'Benjamin,' Liv says.

'Benjamin?' I really don't know what's got into her today. Judging by the way we're leaping from topic to topic, she must really be a bit discombombobulated. Bet it's the iron deficiency. If you're lacking iron, it can cause tiredness, exhaustion, poor concentration and forgetfulness. 'Do you mean that little nutter who killed himself in the sewer shaft?'

## LIV

Liv drops the biro she's been using to jot down what Theo's been saying. 'He did . . . what?'

'Yes,' Theo says, nodding vigorously. 'There was a newspaper report about it too, wasn't there?' He appears to be thinking. 'Yes, I remember. But hold on, you wouldn't have been able to find it. No names were mentioned in the article. And it was only a brief report anyway because it was obvious the boy had committed suicide. Journalists aren't allowed to write about suicide at length otherwise some other loony will do the same, and then you have problems with the law. I had problems with the law too, once, because of that, that Wegner boy. He wanted to have me done for bodily harm, not nice. I had to be very careful in everything I did after that—'

'Wait, Theo,' Liv interrupts, having got over the initial shock. 'Stick with the sewer shaft.'

'It wasn't the sort you have to climb down, but like a sort of subway that leads to the sewer system.'

Liv nods. 'OK, OK, I get it. What I mean is, what exactly happened? To Benjamin Dellard?' she adds as a precaution, in case Theo already is too distracted again.

'Oh yes, Benjamin. Well, he'd gone AWELL again for a few days, and Claus and Hanne were having kittens because it wasn't long after the Julie thing. Claus said it might be the same people who'd now taken Benjamin. He said, *Think, Theo. Did we ever share a patient where something went wrong? Someone who was out for revenge?* I told him he had a screw loose. Nothing ever went wrong while I was the director of the clinic for heart, thoracic and vascular surgery at the Charité. God knows what his statistics were like, but mine, well, there'd never been anything, such nonsense. He wanted to go straight to the police too. But then his own wife agreed with me and accepted that this wasn't the first time the boy had gone off. In my opinion, he was just trying to get attention. My Julie had vanished and everyone had gone mad. The whole city was talking about nothing else. I thought that the arrogant little shit wanted to have some fame too by hiding somewhere for a while. But then the people from the water company found him, two or three days later. He was lying dead in the sewer. They also found two empty schnapps bottles by the entrance to the shaft. First he'd got drunk and then topped himself with a knife.' With his right index finger, Theo draws an invisible line across his left wrist and says, 'Rrrrrip. The interview had brought him a whole heap of trouble, and even before that, he'd been a bit, you know . . .' With the same index finger, he now makes a spiral movement by the side of his head. 'Claus and Hanne were devastated, understandably so. First they said it couldn't be suicide because nobody would choose to crawl into a sewer to kill themselves, where it stinks and is teeming with rats. But then Hanne said her son might have felt worthless and that he belonged there.' Theo shrugs again. 'I mean, it was pretty rotten of him to sit in front of the press and talk like he did. But nobody would have wished him dead.'

'Does this mean that Benjamin's mother was able to accept the situation? What about his father? Did Claus reproach you and Vera at the time? Because you were responsible for the hassle after the interview? Is that why your friendship broke up?'

'No.' Theo shakes his head. 'Claus exploited the situation by coming on to Vera. He was so racked with grief and needed comfort.' He rolls his eyes. 'Stupid arrogant bastard.'

'Do you think he'd talk to me? For the reportage?'

Theo crosses his arms. 'That's all I need – that old bastard sticking his arrogant nose into my business even more.'

As a sign of her understanding, Liv forks another piece of cake into her mouth, if only not to contradict him. She's going to have to talk to Claus Dellard or his wife, whether Theo likes it or not. She needs more information about the alibi that Benjamin gave Daniel Wagner before retracting it. Even though, for some inexplicable reason, her gut feeling is still with Maya Willmers possibly having hired someone who was supposed to kidnap Sophia and got Julie instead, it's time to devote herself to a name that was on everyone's list from the beginning: Daniel Wagner. No matter how much the idea of this meeting fills her with dread.

## DANIEL

I've turned off the Wi-Fi and pushed my laptop over to Bishop-Petersen. He's going to write and I'm expecting nothing less than the best article of his life. The rhythmic clatter of the keys is like a mantra; when it stops occasionally, I look up. I'm weary and almost nod off in my chair. As the tiredness comes, so do the doubts. I don't feel well.

'Keep writing and no silliness,' I instruct him, anxious not to let my voice betray anything of this new feeling. As a precaution I put his phone back into my pocket before I leave the kitchen. I wait by the door for a few seconds to make sure the clatter doesn't stop. It doesn't – fortunately for him and me.

I cross the hall and sit on one of the bottom stairs. Maybe only now am I realising what I've done. As I play back the last few hours in my mind, I can hear how I'm breathing more and more heavily, until I'm panting.

Then it hits me.

The moment I was standing in my mother's bedroom with Bishop-Petersen. Relishing following his gaze through the room, hearing his breathing. Only his breathing, in otherwise absolute silence. I get to my feet and run up the stairs. Fiddle the keys out of my pocket and put one in the lock. Yank open the door. Rush at her, lying there in the same position as yesterday evening, in the same absolute silence. A silence that's wrong – there shouldn't be silence. Queen's not breathing, she's not breathing anymore.

## THEO

'Vera!' I blink.

Vera doesn't come. We've never been to such a grotty hotel. The bed creaks when I move on it. I grab the back of my neck, which is stiff from lying on the cheap mattress. I know we need to save money, but this is going too far. I turn my head towards the window. No blue sky, not even a few palm trees, just the ugly grey of a wall. What kind of holiday is this? Is someone standing in for me at the clinic for this?

'Vera!' There's something trickling my ear when I sit up. I reach for the spot and pull a small yellow sticker from the headboard. I recognise the handwriting. *Everything's OK, Dad. You live here. I love you very much, Sophia.* That must be . . . ! I scrunch up the note, jump out of bed and turn around in a circle.

'Vera?'

Vera doesn't come. We've never been to such a grotty hotel. How did she manage to talk me into coming to this dosshouse? How does she manage to get her own way every single time? Exhausted, I sink back down on to the bed and wait. Wait for Vera.

Vera doesn't come. I cry a little.

Ah well, I think after a while. I don't have to cry because everything's alright. I live here and Sophia loves me very much. My father taught me to be grateful for what you have. He was a hunter and a hero, my father. He always knew what to do. He always had a plan. Like during the 1954 plague of wild boar. He always wore a hat, my father. I look around for my hat and find it on the desk. Whose idea was it to cram such a large piece of furniture into such a small room? I bet it was Sophia again.

I'll tell her you can't cram such a large piece of furniture into such a small room. A large piece of furniture like that needs to be free-standing, with lots of space around it so it looks magnificent. I'll tell her, I'll tell her as soon as she comes back from school. I go over to the desk and put on my hat. In doing so I knock the mouse and the screen lights up. My email inbox. And a new email. I swallow, because I've just been crying and now I'm laughing. I laugh out loud and with great excitement.

I remember everything now. Julie. And Liv. And nutcracker. I look for my glasses and sit down to read.

> Thanks for your message, Dad. In truth I wanted to avoid all of this, but I realise that's not possible anymore. I know you're looking for me. But that's not necessary, Dad. I'm fine where I am, and happy. I was never in danger. I simply followed my heart – do you remember what Mum always said? That the heart is never wrong because it's much cleverer than the rest of us. I know I've caused you all a lot of pain, and I want to apologise profoundly for that. But please accept, and respect, that this here is my life and I'm deciding for myself how I lead it. Please leave it at that and don't notify the police. They'd arrest me, Dad! Don't allow that to happen. Please, Dad. You've got to stop looking for me.
>
> J.

Liv!

I have to call Liv right away. I call Liv right away. I shout 'Liv!' down the phone, tell her that Julie's written again, saying she's fine but this can't be right, and that she apologises for having disappeared and caused us pain, but that Julie would never have caused us such pain because she loved her family and, more importantly, that she'd never write something like that, none of it, that the only reason she wrote that must be because someone's forced her to and is looking over her shoulder, and that she says she'd be arrested if they found her, arrested, yes, but why arrested, in heaven's name, she's never done anything to anybody, she's the victim here, my Julie, who says she's fine but that can't be right, that simply can't be—

'Theo! Theo! Theo!' Liv shouts down the phone. She must be very excited too that Julie's written again, finally she's written again, but what she's written, well, I simply don't believe that she would voluntarily write something like—

'Theo, please! Please, Theo, just listen for a second!'

'Yes.' I need to get my breath back anyway and I have to sit down too because my chest is feeling very tight, my breathing is all over the place, as is my heart, I breathe, breathe, breathe and am otherwise quiet, but Liv doesn't take advantage of this, she doesn't say anything. 'Kindly say something now, Liv!'

'I really need to talk to you, Theo. But it would be better if we did this at mine. Do you think you could come here? Shall I call you a taxi?'

I don't believe I'm hearing right. 'I can call a taxi myself. Any fool can call a taxi!'

Liv sighs. 'Please get dressed if need be and wait outside. I'll order the taxi now, OK? The driver will have my address. You don't need to do anything except get in. And when the driver stops, you get out again and ring the bell marked Keller/Hendricks, OK?'

'Do we need the rifle?'

'What? For God's sake, no! The rifle stays at home.'

\*

Get dressed, trousers too. No rifle. Wait outside. Taxi comes. Get in. Any old fool can go by taxi. It's just the journey takes a while and I feel nervous in a way that I seldom do. Which is fortunate, because they'd never have appointed a bag of nerves as director of the clinic for heart, thoracic and vascular surgery. And my Vera, she'd never have fallen in love with a bag of nerves either.

'Everything OK?' the taxi driver asks. I quickly take my hand from my chest. I don't want him thinking I'm in pain so he takes me to hospital, to Claus, that arrogant bastard.

'Yes, everything's fine. Are we going to be there soon?'

We're there, we are. I get out. Ring the Keller/Hendricks bell and wait for the buzzler. I keep going up the stairs until one of the doors opens and a man peers out.

'Herr Novak?' he asks, looking a touch confused.

'I want to see Liv,' I reply. 'She urgently needs to talk to me.'

The man offers me his hand. 'Phil Hendricks. Nice to meet you in person at last. I'm Liv's partner on *Two Crime*.'

'Oh,' it dawns on me, 'that's you. You mustn't argue with her all the time. She only committed plagiamisery because she had to go to the hairdresser. But she's making up for it.' I look past him into the flat. 'Where is she? Where's Liv? She told me it was urgent.'

Fips turns around, then back to me.

'Not here, that's for sure. But I think I know where we'll find her.' He leans behind the door, takes the key from the lock inside, closes the door behind him and says, 'Come with me.'

We climb more stairs until we get to a metal door. Behind it is the unconverted attic and I think that this Fips has a screw loose. But then he tells me they used to work up here and Liv has started using the space again recently. We go almost as far as the end of the corridor until we get to the right compartment. The wooden slatted door is open. And inside, from one of the whatsits, whatsits, beams – oh my God!

# 5. LIV, LIFE

## THEO

He's useless, this Fips, I can tell that at once, whereas I'm firing on all cylinders at the flip of a switch. My head is perfectly lucid, my actions are determined and effective. I'm a doctor, I'm saving a life. I lift her legs up to reduce the strain on her neck, I lift with all my strength. I yell at Fips to get a knife or scissors – come on, hurry up, do it, you useless bastard. He's still saying we need to untie the knot, but that's just wishful thinking – the knot of the orange rope around her neck is so tight that it would be pointloose to, to . . . it would just waste valuable time. Finally he understands and runs off. A few seconds later I hear him ringing at a door one floor below. That, at least, I think, at least he didn't go back to his own flat, which is several floors lower, to fetch something to cut with. I hear him, loud and concise. Liv. That she's hanging here. That she's tried to kill herself. That he's got to cut her down from the beam. That we need an ambulance. Meanwhile I'm hoisting her up with just one arm now, trying with my other hand to reach between the noose and her neck. Air, air, she needs air, she has to breathe. If you don't breathe, you die. If you don't breathe, you're dead.

'We're going to get through this, Liv,' I tell her. 'We're going to get through this, girl. Everything's going to be fine.' I am a doctor, after all, I know what I'm doing, i've saved thousands of lives already, only a few slipped through my fingers, there were only a few i wasn't able to whatsit, whatsit, protect, julie, i didn't protect her, i failed her, i know that, but i'm not going to fail you, liv, i'm going to save you, you're going to survive, little one, don't you worry, i'm here, i'm going to help you, did you know, by the way, that 'liv' means 'life' in swedish, i know that, 'life' in swedish, three letters: l–i–v, you'll live, liv, you have to, just hang on in there, only a little longer, the ambulance is almost here, and by then fips is back with the knife, and the neighbour he got it from has come up too and i've cut you down from the beam, i've laid you carefilly on the floor, loosened the noose around your neck and begun the resusurration procedure, i can do that, you never forget it, trust me, i'm a doctor and look, the paramedics are already here, the paramedics are taking over and the police are here soon afterwards, and it's thonging with people in the little room, and everyone's saying you did it intentionally, you didn't want to go on living anymore, but what's that supposed to mean, what rubbish are they saying, you'd never do that, no, that wasn't you, i'm absolutely sure of it and i know i'm right when my eyes shoot around and see the name circled on the whiteboard, daniel wegner, no wagner, he did this to you, liv, was he here because you found out that it was him with julie, he was the one who abducted her, there! stuck beside his name is a little yellow note, that must be for me, because i'm the person yellow stickers are left for all over the place, sophia's continentally doing it, and on this one there's an address, is that his address, liv, is that the address of that, that, whatshisname, wegner, wagner, it must be so i quickly grab it while nobody's looking, they're distracted by the thong of people, I grab the note and slip it into my trouser pocket, then i talk to the police because they want to know how we found you, and i tell them, but i don't say anything about that, that, you know, wegner, because this is something personal, they'd only cock it up again, so i promise them that tomorrow, tomorrow morning i'll go to the station and give a more detailed statement, blah blah blah, but they understand, they understand that i'm old and now need a moment to myself after i found you here, hanging from the beam, and as i'm saying this, i put a hand on my chest, my heart, that helps, and how it helps, for they don't want the paramedics to have to do a second job here, then i leave the attic and the building, and i run along the street and stumble because my lungs are on the verge of calypso, then i keep going, panting and bent, until eventually i see a yellow car, a taxi, and any old fool can hail a taxi and ride in it, or not, can ride to the address that's on the little yellow sticker you left for me, and during the ride, during the ride i realise, as i come round, that my breathing's getting calmer, my lungs and my heartbeat too, and I think, he didn't do it without paying a price, now the writing is on the wall, now i'm going to nab him, i'm shaking, i'm shaking, my fist cramps around the note with the address, the exertion is painful, but then ...

... I feel your hand laying itself gently on top of mine. And your head dropping on to my shoulders. And your hair tickling my cheek. And you tell me you're with me. And my fist relaxes, and the shaking gets better.

'We're going to get through this, Liv,' I whisper.
'We're going to get through this, Theo,' you whisper back.

The house, I know it. I would have recognised it at once because I was here before and nothing has changed. I just wouldn't have remembered the address. But who would after twenty years? The front garden is divided from the pavement by a knee-high wall, and a concretian path leads to the house itself. The driveway is to the right of the house and covered in gravel. I remember, I remember how the gravel started flying everywhere the moment the front wheels of my Porsche touched the driveway, so I stopped right there rather than getting scratches on the paintwork. I'd come to take him to task in front of all those journalists. The roller blinds are down – nothing seems to have changed there, either. My Vera, she said later, 'Believe me, you didn't get the wrong man. Anyone who lives in the dark has got something to hide.' She was right, I know this with utter certainty now, after he tried to kill Liv. I get angry, angrier, angriest. I shouldn't have been deterred by that stupid crease and resist order. I shouldn't have let him get away, then none of this would have happened. My finger pokes at the bell. Come on, scaredy-rat, you arsehole! Open the door! I look at the drive; it's empty. I keep ringing anyway. Ring, ring. Nothing happens. But I can't just leave again. No, I'm not going to leave. I examine the stone steps up to the house, in the hope he's done what Vera did and hidden a spare key there. No! Then I wander once around the house. I'd be happy to break a window, I wouldn't care. I just can't because of the goddamaged roller blinds. I can't get in, I can't get in. But I have to. I pat my body in search of my phone and find it in the breast pocket of my shirt. Liv, I have to call Liv. Maybe she's got an idea. It takes an age for her to answer.

'Theo?' the voice says on the other end of the line. It's not Liv's voice but a man's. 'Theo, it's Phil here. Are you there?'

'Of course I bloody well am, I was the one who called!' Halfwit. 'Give me Liv, I need to talk to her.'

Fips says nothing; I just hear him breathe and gurgle weirdly. Now I remember and have difficulty holding on to the phone. The reason why I'm here in the first place. Liv, she's dead. We arrived too late. Nobody could do anything for her. Not even me.

My Liv.

My Julie.

My Vera.

One hand still holding the phone, I feel around me with the other, catching nothing but air a few times, but then I do eventually feel it, the whatsit, the wall. I have to hold on, I need to get through this. This, this, whatshisname, this, I've got to nobble him, nothing else to lose, I've lost them all.

'Theo?' Fips asks. 'Theo, where are you?' I tell him: outside the house of this, this, whatshisname. He doesn't understand who I mean when I scream into the phone, 'Where do you think I am? At the house of that bastard who did that to Liv!'

'Stay there,' Fips says. 'Do you hear me? Stay there and don't go away! I'll be with you very soon!' He hangs up.

I awkwardly sit down on the step outside the front door and look at my phone. So we'll never talk to each other again, Liv. We'll never set out, the two of us, on the hunt for Julie, aliases, friends. The two of us, Liv, what a team. I put my hand up to my head and take my hat off. You ironed this for me. Look, I haven't forgotten. Not yet, Liv. You're still here. And I'm crying for you. I'm really sorry, Liv.

I don't know how long I sit there like that. It's only when I hear a car approach and immediately afterwards a door closing that I look up. Fips is here, he's come by taxi too. I quickly wipe away my tears and put my hat back on. He's pale and jittery, is Fips, but I couldn't care less if he suffers from an iron deficiency. He's not you, Liv. At least he seems to want to make himself useful. He takes a card out of his wallet and tries it on the lock. It doesn't work and I lose my raggle.

'Just break the goddamaged door down!'

Fips looks at me, baffled. I size up his body. He's young and strong. Finally he seems to understand and launches himself with full force at the door. He howls. Nitwit.

'OK, OK,' he says quickly. 'That isn't going anywhere.'

'Give it another try!'

He looks around and shakes his head. 'We can't risk a neighbour seeing us and calling the police. Come with me.' I follow him around the house.

'I've already looked around,' I point out.

He stops by one of the closed roller blinds. 'This is quite an old house. If we're lucky . . .'

We are. The roller blind can be pushed up to about half the height of the window. Fips breaks the glass behind it with one of the drainage stones around the house. Then he puts his hand through the fist-sized hole next to the window handle. He howls again, and again, but eventually he manages to open the window. He wants to go in alone, without me. But I'm not having that, no way. So he has no choice but to help me up, getting kicked in the process – too bad, it takes me a while, it's a real effort, but I have to get inside this house, nothing's going to stop me. And then I'm in, I'm in, Liv, I've done it, I'm standing in the middle of a sitting room and Fips comes in after me, but I don't really care, because he's not you, because – even more crucially – he sat around being useless in your goddamaged flat a few floors below while you were fighting for your life up in the attic. When I realise this, I grab him by the collar and drag him beside me.

'Herr Novak, what the . . .' He pants when my grip gets tighter.

'How could you not know what was going on up there? How could this, this, you know, just wander into your building and hang Liv from the bloody beam?'

'What?' He opens his eyes wide. 'Theo, Liv did it herself!'

'No!' I snap right in his face, briefly fogging up his glasses. 'Liv would have never . . . she'd never have! Why should she?'

'She had problems, Theo. She had . . .' His eyes fill with tears. 'I'm grieving too, Theo. But—'

'Nonsense!' I tighten my grip even more; now my fingers are cramping beneath the material of his collar. 'Nonsense, nonsense, nonsense!'

'But Theo—'

'If you believe, if you seriously believe that she did it herself, why are you here, eh?' I let go of him but not without giving him a shove. He's right, a simple-minded twerp like him couldn't have protected you anyway, Liv. It should have been my job. Mine. And I failed, I failed again. I want to cry. But I can't do that now, I can't, I have to pull myself together, stay composed and lucid. I have to find him, this, this, you know, and as he doesn't appear to be at home, I need to search for a clue as to where he might be.

We look around. Sitting room, tasteless, doilies on the back of an imitation velvet sofa, oak wall unit, probably veneer. Strange smell. Dusty and a bit sweet, like rotten fruit. From the sitting room into the hallway, into the kitchen. Fips says we shouldn't turn on any lights; instead he waves his phone torch about. On the kitchen table is a laptop. When I see it, my heart thumps briefly. Because I see you, Liv, you with your laptop, which went everywhere with us. Fips is immediately euphoric and pounces on the device. Password-protected, he says, bad luck. I keep going, turning the light on even if he doesn't like it, up the stairs into a bathroom with dark green tiles, on to another room, the door wide open, a bedroom, but what on earth, photographs, photographs all over the walls, goddamaged, of Julie, my Julie, I shout for Fips, this room, a wedding dress hanging on the wardrobe, a bed with a light-blue shiny satan throw, and on the floor, at the foot of the bed, Fips! Fips! he has to come, he needs to hurry, at the foot of the bed is a cage, a huge cage, a cage which is so big that—

'Holy shit!' Fips, here he is, finally.

I point at the cage, but he can see it for himself, of course, he wouldn't have come out with holy shit otherwise. We infect the cage, measure its length with a long stride, and the height that comes halfway up my thigh. It seems to be made of steel; none of the bars budge a millimetric when you shake them. Fips bends down to the open door, takes out a sponge liner, a woollen blanket and another piece of material that, when Fips unfolds it, turns out to be a man's T-shirt. He holds the shirt to his nose and says, 'Perfume.' We look at one another.

'What does all of this mean?' I ask.

By way of an answer, Fips looks back at the cage, this huge-size cage, big enough to—

'No!' I roar, heading for the wall with the photos of Julie. I start tearing down one after the other until Fips grabs my arm.

'No!' He's roaring now too, the lout. 'Those could be evidence!'

'Evidence?' My voice has become very quiet and fearful. Because I've already guessed what all of this means, I can guess, I don't need to ask Fips. I know myself that the cage is big enough for what's currently unravelling as a nightmare inside my head. I know it, but the thought of it is so painful, it hurts everywhere, this thought. For I also know who this, this – Wagner's his name – Wagner, god-damaged, I know who this Wagner kept prisoner in there. Who he kept locked up in there like an animal. I look again at the wall, at the photographs still there, then at those I've ripped off, scrunched up and thrown on the floor, and finally at the one I'm still holding. Suddenly, everything makes sense. The laptop in the kitchen. That's where she wrote to me from. Maybe he let her out of her cage occasionally to eat, maybe she had to do the housework for him.

I grind my teeth and snarl at Fips, 'We're going to fetch my rifle.'

'Your ... ? And then?' Fips turns around 180 degrees. 'He's gone!' he says, pointing to the empty cage. '*They're* gone,' he corrects himself. 'How do we know they're going to come back?'

'We don't. But *we're* going to come back, with my rifle, and search everything here thorightly until we find a clue as to where he's taken her.'

Fips nods excitedly. 'That's exactly what we'll do. Let's get your rifle. This time he's not going to escape.'

## DANIEL

I'm steering my car because I know how to steer a car. I'll find the way home because I know the route. Over the Bluetooth connection, I'm playing again the podcast episode about Julie's disappearance. Liv Keller and Philipp Hendricks are currently poking fun at the picture the press took of me and my black eye after the altercation with Theo Novak. *Our wannabe James Dean. Also known as Grapefruit Eye.* I could speak along with the text, but I just move my lips silently from time to time, like in a dubbed film.

I wipe my eyes. When I'm able to see clearly again, I spot in the distance a yellow vehicle outside my house, a taxi, and two men about to get in. I keep driving to find out more but cut my speed, keeping far enough away that the two men can't see who I am.

Then I laugh. I laugh out loud, over the tears, because eventually Bishop-Petersen couldn't help but talk, and at least now I'm a bit wiser. Even if I'm still unsure as to how all of this fits together. I keep laughing when the back doors close on either side and the taxi drives off. I laugh because I know who's sitting inside, who must've come to pay me a visit and who evidently feels the same need to clear up this matter once and for all. It's Theo Novak and the journalist who duped me with his interview for the *Berliner Rundschau*: allegedly Max Bishop-Petersen, but in reality Philipp Hendricks, as I found out from the real Bishop-Petersen. Philipp Hendricks, whose voice is now saying on the podcast, 'Or – let's say I'm the kidnapper now – I'm anything but the dilettante everybody thinks I am. Maybe I'm even really smart! Maybe I've been playing my game for twenty years and the other players haven't realised.'

## THEO

Outside the taxi is waiting, inside I fetch the good old Sauer & Sohn from its hiding place behind the fridge. Fips is skipping around with his phone, filming. At first this bothers me and I gruel a bit. Then I recall that Liv filmed everything too. She would want it this way and, besides, Sophia has tidied up the flat. It's still small and a goddamaged hovel, but at least the washing-up's been done. The police bagged up the proper camera equipment and took it away for analysis. They're always analysing things, as if they were seriously trying to solve a case. But given the way they talked in the whatsit, the attic, about Liv, saying it looked like she'd hanged herself from the beam, I don't have much hope. I do have a rifle and a hat, however. I have a plan. No, I have a mission.

'We should have smuggled the rope past the police and taken it with us,' I say to Fips, as I rub my thumb to clean an unpolished spot on the barrel of the rifle. The good old Sauer & Sohn ought to shine when I whack it around that bastard's head. 'And then hang him up by his own goddamaged rope!'

Fips shakes his head. 'He didn't bring that, Theo. It was our rope. We used it in one of our podcasts to try out techniques of tying oneself up.'

I gawp until my left eyelid starts twitching. The rope was just lying around up in the attic because Fips, this loser, didn't tidy up properly. Then I realise that this whatshisname – Wagner, he's called; Wagner, for heaven's sake – would have killed Liv even if Fips hadn't served up the murder weapon on a silver platter.

'He's going to pay,' I say unwaveringly, holding out the rifle to Fips so he can get a good picture of it.

'Fuck!' he exclaims and I think this is him expressing his enthusiasm. But he's not looking at the rifle. He's looking at his phone.

'Wagner's written! A message via the *Two Crime* website! Here!' He turns his phone to face me, but the writing is too small for me to be able to read it without my grasses.

'What does it say?'

Fips clears his throat. 'Be honest, Philipp: aren't you totally worn out by this? Twenty years is a hell of a long time. Let's bring it to an end. You'll find me at the lake, by the Novaks' old house. Bring the old man too. Regards, D. Wagner.' Fips looks up. 'Showdown, Theo.' Only now does he look at the rifle in my hand. 'Do you have anything you can pack that into?' He nods at the window, probably indicating the taxi driver. I think for a moment.

'My fishing bag?'

Fips nods. 'Perfect. Where is it?'

'Well, where do you think?' I ask back. Now Fips seems to be waiting for an answer. Which I can't provide. I just say, 'Start looking, for God's sake! The flat isn't that big!'

While he goes off, I hurry to my computer in the bedroom to refresh my inbox. No new email from Julie, I see. Of course not – she hasn't had another opportunity to write to me. This whatshisname, Wagner, must have caught her. And then taken her away. I slap my hand over my mouth. Is he bringing her to our meeting at the lake? Has he got her with him? Am I about to see Julie, my Julie again? I start shaking.

'Vera!' I call out. But Vera doesn't come. There's a tugging in my heart; it knows why. It also knows why Liv doesn't come – hers is the next name I call out. I knock my fist into my head. Stay lucid, stay with it. It's never been as important as now.

Instead of all the other people I'd rather have with me, Fips comes running into my bedroom. 'Got it!' he says, breathlessly, brandmanaging the fishing bag. 'It was scrunched up in the vegetable drawer in the fridge.'

'Told you so,' I reply, getting up. 'Let's go, there's no time to lose.'

## DANIEL

I've never been a James Dean, I was never wild, have never gone out in my life apart from two or three times, and I'd only drink one beer at most to steady my nerves. I lived with my mother, I cooked, I cleaned. I only ever tried to be a good son, a good friend, a good person. I didn't have any grand dreams. I wanted a wife and a family. I'd ensure my children grew up better than I did, in our cramped, old, dismal house, with Bible-bashing grandparents whose every expression made it quite clear that they didn't like the fact I existed. With a mother, who for a long time was unable to love me, probably because I reminded her that she'd never worn the wedding dress she'd sewn herself. It wasn't until she got ill that she developed a little love for me. Maybe it was just a bit of desperate gratitude, I don't know, I can't ask her anymore. For most of my life I've been solitary. And yet, despite this, I know what love is. How beautiful it is, how painful, and that both of these are inseparable. Unlike my family, I've never believed in God, and yet I had belief, otherwise I would have surely taken my life ages ago, after everything that's happened to me. I believed and I hoped, again, again and again. I never gave up. Shouldn't everything have eventually turned around, if only because of that? Shouldn't I have been rewarded for my perseverance? No, life isn't fair, there's no compensation, no justice. A life can be unfailingly bad, pointless and sad. Hollywood lies, as does the Bible.

I'm sitting on the grass beside my car, by the boot, my back leaning against the wheel, staring out at the lake. It looks as if the sun is falling into it, heavy and burned out from the day. How I can empathise with that. I'm so exhausted myself, so feeble. But I tell myself that by the time it gets dark, everything will have been settled. That the night is already sneaking up on the day, ready to take it by surprise. Tomorrow morning I'll wake up and, for a few seconds, I'll be able to believe that I'd just had a bad dream. These will be the best seconds of the entire day, I know this already.

I hear the sound of an engine in the distance. I left the iron gate open after we came in earlier so that they don't have to go to the trouble. I drove past the house at walking pace, unable to take my eyes off it, wondering which of the cellar windows it was that you always crawled through to meet Jason Willmers in the middle of the night. He denied it when I confronted him; he said he didn't know what I was talking about. He lied, and how he lied. I mean, I'd seen you with my own eyes, darting across your garden. I saw you getting into his car. I watched it all, completely hidden and from a distance. I saw the two of you and he dared lie to my face. But I was a coward, I shied away from a physical confrontation, having already been given a black eye by your father. So I replied to Willmers that I was looking for you and told him to tell you to contact me, so we could meet and talk. I'd deserved that, hadn't I?

I keep looking at the lake and now I smile.

Do you remember when we went out in the boat? Me with the oars, you sitting opposite, reading *Doctor Zhivago* to me? It was the summer of my life, my darling. I felt like a character out of a novel or a film; everything I did with you was so surreally lovely. And I was under the illusion that it would stay like that forever. Hope, the whore, I laugh bitterly.

They're coming, Queenie. They're here. I can already hear their muffled voices, and then one of them calling out, 'Wagner!'

With a sigh I get to my feet, wander around the car and take a few steps towards them.

Theo Novak looks terrible. His gigantic size makes a caricature of his face, which looks sunken even from a distance. And he's doddery. There's little left of the man who beat me up back then in front of all the journalists. Walking beside him is Philipp Hendricks. He's aged too, and at the same time he hasn't. He's still wearing those distinctive glasses, maybe not the same pair but a similar model at least, and he's got the same haircut. Like someone clinging on to the past, but time itself is playing a trick on him with its aging processes. Perhaps we're even similar in this respect, in an unintentional, repellent way.

I stand there, straight back and chest out. I'm not going to slip back into the anger and craziness of the last day and a half. The price was too high, far too high. On the other hand, as I know, I must be confident as I confront them, I can't allow even a hint of uncertainty to show. So I focus on the image they present as they approach me. In step, scowling, like two ridiculous cowboys.

'Thanks for coming, gentlemen,' I say when they're around five metres away. Novak is eager to rush at me, but Hendricks holds him back. They've already discussed this, he whispers to the old man. With a growl, Novak reaches behind his back and swings a long bag round to his front. I raise and lower my hands like Bishop-Petersen did yesterday, in an attempt to calm the situation. I don't want this escalating, not against me, not after everything I've been through. I want to bring things to a neat conclusion. Or as neat as can be.

'Please stop where you are,' I say. 'And listen to me.' Hendricks holds Novak back once more, without taking his eyes off me. 'The fact that you were just at my house is going to save us some time. Now you've seen how someone lives who was robbed of his life.' Novak and Hendricks open their mouths in sync, but I check them with another hand gesture. 'It's my turn, gentlemen. After twenty years, it's finally my turn.' I take a deep breath, then I begin, 'I had a visit from your former colleague, Herr Hendricks: Max Bishop-Petersen. We had a bit of a chat. And, as I found out, both of you were interns at the *Berliner Rundschau* in the early 2000s. But while Bishop-Petersen was happy to carry out the usual intern tasks – making coffee, photocopying and doing bits of research for the paper – you wanted to make your mark with a major scoop. The only problem was that you'd already been in trouble once when you took it upon yourself to rewrite the finished text of a long-standing journalist. Your days were numbered. You were desperate to save your reputation, but more than that, you wanted a really big story. So you talked Bishop-Petersen into' – I make air quotes with my fingers – '*lending* you his name to contact me online. You must've thought that if anything went wrong and the managing editors got wind of it, you'd be booted out for good, while Bishop-Petersen, who till then had proved himself to be the model intern, would get off with a warning. Am I right so far?'

Novak, who's been listening attentively, looks at Hendricks. 'You've had dealings with this man?'

Hendricks says nothing for a moment; he seems to be thinking.

'Max agreed to it,' he says finally.

'Of course,' I reply, then laugh. 'I bet you convinced him that if the scoop worked, the two of you would be made as journalists. You'd have immediately secured a well-paid job, because you were the first person who'd got an exclusive interview with me. But our meeting didn't go as you'd imagined, because I aborted it prematurely. You wrote the article nonetheless – you couldn't let it go. But you suspected you were skating on thin ice and you were right – I complained to your editor. The *internal check*, which the woman in question promised to carry out, consisted of sacking both you and Bishop-Petersen. Of course they still printed the article.' I shake my head. 'You really are all the same, a bunch of hacks. Bigoted little arseholes. So, yes, Herr Novak, to answer your question, Herr Hendricks and I did have dealings in the past. Back in 2004, about a year after Julie went missing. A year, by the way, in which I found myself in the papers too often for my liking, partly because of you. You must remember the black eye you gave me in front of the whole world.'

'Clearly I didn't hit you hard enough,' Novak snarls, and Hendricks cautions him for a third time with an elbow to his side.

'I'm sorry I didn't listen to you properly back then, Daniel,' Hendricks says, almost at a whisper. 'But I am going to today. We have all the time in the world. Talk.'

'I'm not interested in what—' Novak barks.

'Talk,' Hendricks interrupts him.

'The cage!' Novak starts up again, but Hendricks doesn't hear him. Instead a faint grin appears on his lips.

'You're right, Daniel. Max and I were chucked out. At least he got a certificate, which meant he could apply to another newspaper as an intern. And today he's an editor, so he didn't lose much. Unlike me. But people like me get by somehow. And do you know why?' His smile becomes broader. 'It's because I never give up until I've reached my goal.'

'That's what Bishop-Petersen said about you too—'

'Enough of this nonsense,' Novak says, fiddling with the zip of his bag.

'No, Herr Novak!' I shout at him. 'This time it's not you who's doing the talking! It's *my* turn!'

Novak pauses what he's doing. I can see his jaw clench and his right eye twitch. It seems to take a lot out of him to understand that today – unlike back then – the *little arse-wiper* is doing the talking.

'You were just saying you had a visit from Max,' Hendricks says, still in a sort of whisper, though I fancy I can hear a touch of annoyance in his tone. Maybe he's worried that Bishop-Petersen has stolen the story he would so love to have. Rightly so, I think, grinning back. 'How did this come about, if you don't mind me asking?'

'I nabbed him.'

Hendricks laughs, which confuses me.

'It's up to you whether you believe it or not,' I say, trying to maintain my composure. 'I nabbed him and took him to my house. He was particularly struck by my mother's former bedroom . . .'

'The cage,' Novak whispers.

'That too,' I say. 'Inside that room is everything that was ever important to me. It's a sort of museum, or let's call it a collection. It was only there, when she lay in that bed, that my mother first really took notice of me. Hanging in that room is the wedding dress she was no longer able to give to my future wife, and also . . . Well, you've seen it for yourselves. Normally, you know, I don't let anyone in there. It's a place that belongs to me alone. And I protect it from the outside world.' I bite my bottom lip to stop my flowing tongue. I don't want to sound like a madman because that's not me. I'm not mad. And if I am, it's people like these two, Novak and Hendricks, who've made me that way. As I swallow, I notice how difficult I find it. Because the thought of the bedroom reminds me that my special place is never going to be the same after this morning. Now I've lost everything, absolutely everything. My stomach cramps, I feel sick. My body convulses and I throw up.

'Boot,' I gasp, having only been able to bring up bile. 'In there you'll see what you're responsible for.'

## THEO

'No,' I whimper and my legs give way as if an axe had been driven into the backs of my knees. *Boot*, I hear him repeat in my head. *Boot, boot*. He's brought her along, as I was hoping earlier. He's brought her along, but in the boot. And he says that we're responbible.

Fips grabs my arm and tries to help me up. I feel him shaking, he's shaking just like me. *Boot*. She was alive until that thing we were responbible for. Shake Fips's hand off my arm, I stagger off. Towards his car. My Julie, my child. *Boot.*

'Don't do it, Theo,' Fips says, taking hold of me from behind and pulling me to the ground again. The bag containing the rifle slides off my shoulder, my hat slides off my head. 'We mustn't destroy any evidence!'

'Let go of me!' I shout, but I can only free myself from his grip by going in the other direction. I pick up the bag, tear open the zip and take out my father's rifle.

'He killed her,' I hear Fips behind me. When I turn around, I see he's holding his phone. He's filming. 'He killed them all!' I stumble on, towards this whatshisname, this, this Wagner, who's just straightening himself again when I smash the stock of the rifle against the side of his head. His eyelids flatter briefly, then he falls over. I leave him there, drop my rifle and stumble back. This time Fips doesn't try to stop me. I go to the boot, he behind me with his whatsit, his phone. I push my hand under the catch, hold my breath and open the lid.

## DANIEL

Before I see anything, I hear a whistling, a shrill, high-pitched tone that seems to be coming directly from my head. I blink, but shut the lids again tightly when a liquid runs into my right eye. I try to move. My body is being stubborn. I blink again. I can see red, I'm bleeding, and somewhere over there I see the backs of two men bending over the boot of my car. Yes, that's their work. If they hadn't driven me to madness, I'd have noticed in time that she wasn't breathing. Queen is dead, my queen, my only companion all these years since. I try moving my body across the grass, try crawling away, slowly, circumspectly; everything is pain, on the inside and outside. Queen had been weak for a while, that's true. She suffered from seizures, often screaming and being sick. But I always looked after her well, I did everything for her, much better than a professional could have done, or any medicine. My trembling hand tries to reach the phone in my trouser pocket, an insurmountable task when everything is mere pain. When I went to see her in the bedroom this morning, she was just lying there, already stiff and cold. I took her out of the cage, bundled her into my arms and ran downstairs. I told Bishop-Petersen that we had to get her to the clinic and, in fact, he was quick to his feet. I don't know whether he was feeling empathy for the first time in his life, or he was just frightened about what would happen if he didn't do as he was told. But I hadn't laid a finger on him, I just wanted someone to listen finally. And understand. He drove me to the clinic and actually came in too.

'It could have been poisoning,' they said. 'Or she developed epilepsy, that's conceivable too. You should have come earlier, Herr Wagner.' And I heard Frau Lessing's voice in my head: *You have to take your Queen for regular visits to the vet, Herr Daniel. You really must.* I cried, I tortured myself. And ultimately I understood why I hadn't: I was in denial, I'd been ignoring Queen's symptoms for fear of losing her.

I was allowed a moment with her on my own to say goodbye. He'd look after everything else, he promised me. But I couldn't leave her there, in that cold, impersonal room. I had to take her with me. And so I did. I lifted her body and stormed out. Bishop-Petersen was still sitting in the waiting room. He could have easily disappeared or asked for help at reception, but nothing of the sort; he was sitting there. He was probably still in shock too. I asked him to drive us to his newspaper's offices where my car still was. Then he could go, I told him. I left it up to him whether to finish the article he'd started in my house or not, whether to print it or not. I didn't care anymore. My Queen was dead. I no longer had anything in the world. She had given my life meaning, she'd deserved better. I was so ashamed. Why had I kept her locked up all this time? Why did we only ever go out at night? Because of my fear, obviously, my paranoid fear and conviction that I had to protect her. But was it really so surprising that I felt this fear, after everything that had happened? I couldn't have done anything else, could I? Because of them, because of people like Hendricks, Keller and Novak, because of a world full of accusation and suspicion, a world full of prejudice and lies.

I roll on to my back, the phone screen blurs before my eyes, the numbers too when I try to tap them with my blood-smeared index finger. I finally manage it – 110. I say where I am, that I'm wounded and that I think they're going to kill me. Then my hand falls from my ear and the phone drops into the grass. I can't go on anymore, I just hear a roaring in my ears, everything moves away from me as if in slow motion and I almost want the unconsciousness to hurry, to be faster than the two men who are now approaching me again. Even in the gloom and with blood in my eyes, I can see the bewilderment on their faces, but also the anger. Not raw, red anger, but a silent, desperate one. It's the anger of the helpless. Possibly the worst type of anger, but definitely the most dangerous. I see their faces up close, bent over me, the expression on both of them one big question mark. And I react at once; I realise what they want to know.

'I have no idea what happened to Julie,' I say, straining with every word. 'But I didn't do anything to her. I loved Julie. How could I have ever hurt her? It wasn't me.'

And before I finally pass out, I hear Theo say, 'Who was it, then?'

## LARA

The devil. He was the living, breathing proof of a superior force who even death was no match for. You could tear to shreds his skin, his flesh, his muscles and veins, but you couldn't destroy him. Not even the slight hobble he'd recently been moving with gave me satisfaction. He carried it off almost with pride, as a memory of what I'd done. *You shouldn't have done that, Lara.*

And me, I was here again, back to square one, his prisoner once more. A sedated body in a bed, my wrists shackled, new medication, the dose perfectly calibrated. My mind was alert but useless. The connections between my brain and my body were ruined. Even the most lucid thought ended in a slobbery grunt. And the way he enjoyed parading me – *look, everyone, I got her* – the way he bragged about having caught me again and rendered me harmless. How he passed off his actions as heroic, embellished his stories and turned the heads of his simple-minded audience – today a detective with a small pad he eagerly jotted notes in. The police checked the facts. They had to find out how the bloody incident in the hospital staffroom had occurred. How all of this here, according to him, fitted together . . .

## VERA
## SEPTEMBER 2003

It was about a week after Julie went missing. There was a ringing somewhere in the distance. Somewhere in the distance is here, it occurred to Vera. Because nothing felt close anymore; since that night, everything had shifted away from her. She got up laboriously. Please don't let it be the police again, not all those journalists again. Please, please no more questions she wouldn't be able to answer anyway. She hauled herself to the front door, where she'd identified the ringing was coming from, and opened it after a deep breath. But it wasn't a police officer looking back at her, it was a girl, who seemed too young to be a journalist.

'Can I help you?' Vera asked. Days of exhaustion had shredded her voice.

The girl gave her a look of confusion, as if Vera's question was nothing short of absurd. With both hands she hastily swept her long red hair from her face.

'Don't you recognise me?'

Vera gave a faint shrug. She stared at the girl with all the concentration she was able to muster in her state. She took just half an opipramol daily, even though Theo had assured her that a whole one would be fine too, for the time being at least, so long as she didn't feel any undesirable side effects. The slowness, the sluggishness, the apathy, the feeling of other-worldliness – Vera couldn't have said whether these were undesirable contraindications or whether this wasn't precisely the best state for her to be in at the moment. But in this situation, with a girl who plainly wanted something from her, probably a very specific reaction,

Vera had to struggle to maintain any focus. The face. Yes, it was familiar. But where did she recognise it from?

'Mum?'

Vera took a step back in shock. What had that girl just said?

'Mum, it's me. Julie.'

Vera gasped. 'What the hell . . . ?' She couldn't say any more at first.

'Look, Mum,' the girl continued. 'It's me. I'm back. Now we can be a happy family again.'

Vera couldn't breathe when the girl took a step towards her.

'Stop, for heaven's sake, stop!' she said, then it struck her like a flash of lightning: 'Lara?'

The smile on the girl's face froze.

'What . . . what have you done to your hair?' Vera said. She'd only known Lara as a blonde, why did she suddenly have red hair now?

'Don't you like it? I can dye it again if you think I haven't got quite the right tint.'

Vera opened her eyes wide. And slowly, only slowly, she seemed to understand. She'd met Lara a year earlier through her volunteering; Lara had been one of the girls from the youth centre. It wasn't long before Vera had built a special connection with her and soon an idea took shape. The Novaks had until recently employed regular au pairs at home. And Lara – nice, thoughtful Lara with a difficult family background – had left school early and was desperate to earn a bit of money. She'd just turned eighteen, three years older than Julie and five years older than Sophia. A win–win situation for all concerned.

'Why not, Theo?' Vera had begged her husband. 'We'll be doing a good deed and at the same time we'll have some help around the house. You know how keen I am for a bit of assistance here.'

As ever, Theo had given in; he'd never refused a request from his wife.

And didn't Lara fit in wonderfully well? Didn't she help out as best she could, cooking, cleaning, ironing? Wasn't she always so grateful, wasn't it lovely having her around because she was so attentive, quick and friendly? And how well she got on with Julie, how amazed the two of them had been about the thing with their names: Julie Christie had played Lara Antipova in *Doctor Zhivago*. Ha ha, what a coincidence!

Or a sign that Lara belonged to them.

Well, wait a moment. It wasn't as if they'd gained another daughter. None of the Novaks had seen it that way. After all, Lara had her own family, her own mother and father, and Vera encouraged her to maintain contact with them, even though Lara moved into the Novaks' house for a while. Of course they had to recognise the boundaries – their children were their children and Lara was the help around the house. But the best and dearest they'd ever had.

And then came the big bust-up.

It was over the plans for their summer holiday in Maui. Julie couldn't wait to go diving there. She was looking forward to the manta rays, the colourful doctor fish and butterfly fish and huge groupers, while Sophia was excited about the honu, the green sea turtles. Lara appeared to be taken by surprise when Vera went through the schedule with her. They'd be on holiday from then to then, and of course during this time she'd have to move back in with her own family; she couldn't stay on her own at the Novaks' house. And it hadn't occurred to them once that they might take her on holiday with them. The holiday was a family thing; finally they'd have time for each other again.

Lara didn't seem to get this: if she wasn't going with them, why couldn't she at least stay at their house? Didn't the Novaks trust her? After all the time they'd spent together? How was this possible? What had she done to them?

Wasn't she part of the family?

Sophia was the one who said it. Maybe it was the brazenness of puberty or just the truth: 'Yes, but Lara . . . what do you want? You're our cleaning lady, since when do people take their cleaning ladies on holiday?'

And then Lara's big mistake. She slapped Sophia, an impulsive reaction to her hurtful words. Theo ordered her to pack her bags and leave the house at once. Nobody hurt his children; there was going to be no discussion of the matter. Not even Vera objected. She had the biggest heart in the world, but most of it was occupied by her daughters. The fact that Sophia – just as impulsively – hit back was irrelevant. Her parents thought it was the shock, puberty, her right. Ashamed to the core, Lara left without any resistance.

Now, a week after Julie's disappearance, there was this ring at the front door. And Vera couldn't cope with what she saw standing there: this girl with long, freshly dyed red hair and freckles that may have been painted on.

In *Doctor Zhivago*, Julie Christie had played Lara Antipova. Was Lara now, in all seriousness, trying to play Julie, only a week after the disappearance of their beloved daughter? Trying to replace the daughter of the distraught family? That was completely sick. Sick and cynical.

'Please go.' Vera couldn't speak anymore.

'We can be a happy family again,' Lara reiterated, now more emphatically, and started making her way into the house. Vera tried to push the door shut, but Lara, obsessed by her mission to return to her mother, father and younger sister, had a demonic strength. The door hit the side of Vera's head and she lost consciousness.

When she came to, she was lying on the sofa, Theo's hand on her cheek. He hadn't gone to work since Julie's disappearance; he was needed at home. He'd come into the house with some freshly picked wildflowers from the lake and had reacted quickly.

'But it's the best for all of us!' Lara screamed as the men escorted her to the police car. First they took her to the police station, but Lara continued to behave as if she was out of her mind, and was eventually admitted to hospital as an emergency case. There, too, she refused to make a statement and be examined – until one of the doctors simply told her that Vera and Theo wanted her to cooperate. So Lara cooperated.

## LARA

'The patient often talked of *the people*, which was what she called her own family. Of *the woman* – her mother – who'd been in a wheelchair since falling down some stairs,' the devil trotted out his lies, 'and of *the man* – her father – who shortly after the mother's accident was himself in intensive care. He had symptoms of poisoning after, as Lara claimed, he'd taken an overdose of his gout medicine. Organ failure; his prospects weren't good.' The devil sounded sad. 'Her own parents were afraid of her. The mother's fall occurred following a tussle with Lara and the father suspected it was her who'd given him the extra dose of his medicine. Nothing could be proven, however, especially because, as an alcoholic, the father wasn't much of a reliable witness. The authorities decided that Lara could continue to live with her parents, but should join an open group for young people with psychological disorders. This seemed to work well until Lara met Vera Novak through her voluntary work and, through her, the family that she'd probably have preferred to have. But when an incident occurred at the Novaks' after their daughter had disappeared, the public prosecutor's office decided to take a closer look at the accidents suffered by Lara's biological parents. Ultimately the court decided she should stay permanently at our clinic. But there was no evidence that she had anything to do with the disappearance of Julie Novak – obviously the police investigated this too.'

'That still leaves two cases of grievous bodily harm,' the police officer said, nodding. 'She was lucky her father survived. It could have ended up as murder.'

'Three cases of bodily harm now,' the devil corrected him, clearly feeling the need for a sorrowful sigh. 'I'm never going to be able to walk properly again. I suppose that's what you call an occupational hazard.'

*Actor!* I wanted to howl. I wanted to grab the policeman by the collar, shake him and say: *Don't you realise what's going on here? He's keeping me captive! Hiding me from my family to carry out his experiments on me. His medication experiments, his manipulation.* But nothing came from my throat save for a few gurgling sounds.

'And how exactly did the attack on you come about?' the policeman asked.

The devil sighed again. Beneath me the mattress sank when he sat on the edge of my bed.

'We're not proud that things got out of hand, but despite all the security measures on my ward, she managed to hoard pills over a long period of time, which she then used in an attempt to take her life. On this ward we're not equipped for acute medical care, so we had to transfer her to the casualty department. There she struck up a relationship with one of the nurses – without my knowledge, to begin with. The nurse's name is Isabel Rother, by the way, in case you need a statement from her too. At any rate, Lara tried to manipulate Isabel at every available opportunity, claiming that in reality she was Julie Novak and I was the one keeping her captive. She even got Isabel to read about the case online. Realising, however, that Lara didn't look anything like the missing Julie Novak, Isabel spoke to me. I then gave her a thorough description of Lara's symptoms – her hallucinations, if you like. And I'll be honest with you: I was disappointed. After all these years, I'd clearly misjudged Lara's mental state. Something like that should not happen to me; I had to be certain where we were in the therapy so I could adjust the next stages of the treatment. I asked Isabel, therefore, to engage with Lara's delusions, to *play along*, so to speak. At my behest, she pretended to be Lara's ally, up to the moment we decided that it was time for the confrontation. This isn't unusual in our work, you know. I'd often done it on a smaller scale – for example, when it came to her name. After she was first admitted, she insisted for a long time on being called Julie. I proposed the name Lara, which was on her birth certificate, and which she'd lived with for the previous nineteen years. She had real difficulty in accepting it. It was as if her head had deleted her entire existence up till then and replaced it with the biography of Julie Novak. Oh well . . .' Once again the mattress moved under me when he got up. 'As I said, I thought we'd made more progress, but the suicide attempt was a clear sign that we had to start again. And evidently this first impression proved true.' He pointed to his damaged leg. 'But we're not going to give up, are we, Lara?' As he smiled at me, I thought the same thing: I'm not going to give up either, ever. You can count on that, devil.

'Thanks, Doctor Dellard,' the officer said – then, with a last look at me, 'Get well soon, Lara.'

I felt my right eye twitch.

When he'd gone, the devil stood at the end of my bed, his hands in the pockets of his white coat. For a moment he just looked at me.

'I just want you to know that it wasn't me who reported you to the police. Because I know that you didn't *really* want to injure me. But the clinic has clear regulations regarding incidents like that when we're on duty. Don't worry, nothing's going to happen to you. You're safe here, I promise.'

As if he'd remembered something terribly urgent, he took his left hand out of his coat pocket and checked his watch. 'I've got to go. I have an appointment with a' – he hesitated – 'dementia patient.' He smiled. 'I'll see you on my evening round. Bye, Lara.'

Lara.

My right eye twitched again.

My name was Julie and one day I would get out of here. I'd kill the devil and go back to my family. Then we'd be happy again, finally. Goodnight, Mum. Goodnight, Dad. Goodnight, my little Sophia. See you soon. I managed a faint smile and fell asleep.

# 6. MEXICAN TETRA

## SOPHIA

It's gone ten o'clock and it's already dark. My body is tired, my head even more so. There's a police officer on the phone. I can barely follow what he's saying, which is probably more down to my sheer lack of energy than the information he's giving me. Conversations, protestations, doubt, tears, anger and fear – this is how I've spent the last few hours with Richard. The police officer can't possibly know any of this, and even if he did, what would he care? He's just doing his job as he summarises the key details: the police called out to the lake, to our old house, my father and another man supposedly having attacked someone. My father not in good shape, appearing confused, asking for me. Me, hanging up and telling Richard I need to go again, an emergency, and Richard, looking at me as he's been looking at me all this time. Ever since he caught me, to be precise.

'Where are you going now?' he barks. 'You can't keep breaking off this discussion.' The discussion about whether we actually have a future together.

'It's my father, Richard.'

'You've already used that excuse today.'

'It's not an excuse! We'll talk again when I'm back, OK? And without interruptions this time, I promise.' I attempt a smile, a confident, encouraging one. Because as far as I'm concerned, there's no doubt that we've got a future together. I want us to continue. I want Richard, as he's promised, to put up the overhead light in the child's room. I want us to build the cot together, paint the walls together and buy supplies of nappies. I want, I want, I will, I will, just as I said in my oath to him – *Yes, I will, for better or worse, until death do us part*. I want to be his wife, his lover, his best friend and the mother of his child. But all of a sudden, he no longer seems so sure – about me, about us.

'Fine,' he snorts as I march into the hallway to get the car key from the bowl on the chest of drawers. 'Go to your father. And you'd best take the opportunity today to tell him what you've done.'

'Richard, please . . .'

He merely shrugs and walks off to the child's room, of all places. He could go into the kitchen to pour himself a glass of wine or into our room to curl up truculently on his side of the bed. But no, he goes to the child's room as if right into the heart of my pain and my greatest fear: that the room we've been preparing for weeks for our child will never be used – because of me. Because of what I did. Me, *Nutcracker11*.

Richard caught me sending the last email to my father. All of a sudden he was standing there behind me, peering over my shoulder, reading what I was typing. And he couldn't believe it.

'Why?' he said. 'What are you doing?' As if it were that simple to explain. I tried my very best, nonetheless. I confessed to him how I'd been regularly returning to my childhood home for years.

Mostly at night, when only I and the spirits were still awake, while the rest of the world managed to do what I was no longer capable of: sleep through the night without nightmares. The old house at night was the only place I could find peace. Perhaps because I felt close to Julie there. Because the nicer, carefree times were preserved there.

Back then, before my life was shattered into a thousand pieces. Pieces that I'm still trying to gather up and stick back together today. The sleeplessness. The mood swings. My eating disorder. Of course none of that manifested itself by chance; of course it all began after the thing with my sister. Some of those nights I would sit in our old kitchen, drinking coffee that I'd brought along in a thermos and then poured into what used to be my favourite mug. I sat there as Julie had often sat there when she waited for me to return from my night-time excursions that, later, were wrongly attributed to her. The nights when I stole out of the cellar window to meet Jason.

Of course I didn't tell Richard anything about these night-time excursions. All he needed to know was that I went back to the house to grieve for my sister. And for my childhood, which was over from one day to the next. He was allowed to know that I put flowers and candles in Julie's room to create a setting where I could grieve and have silent conversations with her. He was also allowed to know that, after Liv came on the scene with her investigation, I tried to get rid of all the traces – the flowers and candles – because I suspected that her research would sooner or later lead to our old house. I mean, it had to happen, it was only logical, because it was the place Julie had disappeared from. I struggled with the idea of giving up my sacred space, which for so long had belonged to me alone. So I went – as I thought – one last time to our old house, equipped with a roll of bin bags. I was just about to clear up when Liv and her partner suddenly appeared and came within a whisker of catching me. I fled in shock, completely panic-stricken. I didn't want them thinking that I'd had something to do with Julie's disappearance. And I bet that's precisely what they would have thought, seeing how murderers always return to the scene of the crime, don't they? That night I was able to escape, but without removing all traces of me. So I had to return later that night to get rid of the candles and flowers, even though I was almost driven mad by the worry that Liv and her partner might still be there, lying in wait. But they weren't and I thought that fate had smiled on me, until I saw the video that the two of them had taken in Julie's room, proving that there really had been an altar there. Without the footage, I'd have been able to persuade my father that Liv was lying, just trying to cause upset and provoke a reaction from us for her reportage. That she was merely another one of those nutters we had to keep our distance from. I'm sure my father would have gone along with my argument. After all, we'd seen what could happen when you got involved with nutters. Even now, with Claus, who only recently had suffered a dangerous attack by that – I couldn't remember what she was called, but she used to work for us.

But Liv *had* the footage, she *had* the proof that the altar in Julie's room wasn't a figment of her imagination, eager for sensation. And when she showed us the footage, it was disastrous, because my father thought it was a lead, a reason to hope, and it made him even more determined to film with Liv. Nothing seemed to be able to deter him. I soon noticed how he was becoming ever more unpredictable and my influence on him was waning. That wasn't good, it wasn't good at all. As I'd once said to Liv, 'I mean, you never know what else might enter his mind one day.'

So I set up a new email account and wrote the first message to him, which contained just a single world: *skyearthblue*. It was only a test, a very calculated prick. I wanted to know whether and to what extent he would remember if I ventured into this one very specific area, which was bound to attract Liv's attention too at some point. I just wanted to find out where I stood and how I had to act. And, to be honest, I hadn't really expected that he would remember this word given how much else he'd already forgotten. Of course I knew it, even though it was Julie's – the story of how it came about was family folklore, a wistful *do you remember . . . ?* that my parents often told each other and me too.

But then, everything got out of control. I really wished I could have undone that stupid email, as it entrenched itself in my father's head, together with everything it could possibly mean. Then, after the argument we had in front of Liv in his flat, he wrote back: *i remember everything. you need help.*

I was seized by panic, a completely existential, overwrought fear. Had he – suddenly and as if a switch had been flipped – worked out that I was the sender of the email? Or what did *you need help* mean? That I was ill and needed more therapy, like after what happened to Julie when I was fourteen? The problem stemmed from the fact that I thought his first answer was directed at me – it hadn't occurred to me that he might think Julie was the sender. At first I considered not replying, just leaving it at that. But suddenly I felt this overwhelming fear that he might go to the police, who would be able to trace the email back to me. Although I knew he had a low opinion of the authorities, I couldn't rule out the possibility that he'd take this step if he thought I'd hit rock bottom again and needed therapy. So I wrote another email to prevent this from happening, before finally realising that my father hadn't been writing to *me* at all! He was convinced that the emails came from my sister!

This then gave rise to the next problem, because Liv, who was increasingly imposing herself on my father, also seemed to entertain the possibility that the emails had come from my sister. Again and again I thought I should simply stop, but that just made me worry that it would create more suspicion. And as if all of this weren't complicated enough, there was the thing with Richard.

So I'd had to give up our old house as my own personal space. After this, the unfinished bedroom of our future child served as a substitute, although it wasn't a conscious decision. I just needed somewhere to myself. Here I was able to compose my emails undisturbed and in secret. Over time I realised the meaning of why it was happening here. The room, with its test patches of sky-blue and bright yellow on the walls, reminded me why I was doing all of this: for our family, for our future. Sometimes, while considering what to type, I'd stare up at the bare light cables attached to the ceiling, and they'd seem to branch out, like the boughs of one of the trees in our little garden. Boughs we would fix a swing to for our child. Then these cables would move, like dancing underwater plants you encounter when snorkelling. I'd teach my child swimming and snorkelling too, and we'd be as happy as when I went with Julie and my parents on holiday to all the world's oceans. I became so used to the room and taken by it that at some point I even moved the pasting table in there to use as a desk, rather than sitting on the floor with the laptop. Of course Richard found out what I was doing; he found it 'sweet' the way I sat there with my laptop and coffee. He thought I'd rigged up a little office in the room because it's where I felt happiest. But the bedroom wasn't ready and nor did we have our baby yet. He couldn't suspect what was really going on in here – someone writing messages as *Nutcracker11* to an old man with dementia.

Until the moment he caught me.

I was on the laptop and – shit! – how careless of me to sit with my back to the door. My father had written a long email to Julie the day before. An email that had brought tears to my eyes. In my mind I could see him writing it ponderously with two fingers, his thought processes and motor skills under strain, with all the mistakes he wouldn't have made in the past and which he now no longer noticed. I'd read this email so many times that I'd lost count, and the despair that came through his words broke my heart. I'd already embarked on several attempts at an answer and deleted them all.

So I was sitting there, the email from my father on the screen, and behind me suddenly Richard, who'd crept into the room with a cup of tea for me. How long had he been standing there? Long enough, at any rate, to read what my father had written and to see that above his text I'd already started to write a reply. 'Dad,' it said. 'Once more, let me . . .' I hadn't got any further. I didn't notice Richard until he touched my shoulder, which gave me such a shock that my hand shot out to close the lid of the laptop as quickly as possible. But it was too late.

'Why? What are you doing?' he said and, when I didn't answer immediately, 'Sophia?'

How could I explain it to him? The shock alone was preventing me from thinking rationally. Yes, he knew about *Nutcracker11*'s emails; I'd told him about them because I didn't want to run the risk that my father might say something about them in his presence. I hadn't mentioned emails that might be from my missing sister? No, he'd have found that very strange. If Richard had come into the room a couple of minutes earlier, I wouldn't have started my reply and so I could have claimed that my father had forwarded me the emails from *Nutcracker11* to read. But this? Still in shock, I couldn't react quickly when Richard put down the cup of tea beside me and opened the lid of my laptop again. I couldn't think of how to explain the situation, except to come out with the truth.

'I just wanted to find out how much he still remembers.'

'But why, Sophia, what's the point? It's a good thing that he hasn't forgotten Julie!' Richard countered, utterly confused.

'No, it's not!' I hissed back. 'All it does is bring back the pain! And we've had enough of that over the past twenty years.'

Richard abruptly turned away from me and wandered round in a circles for a brief while.

'Your intention may well be to protect him. But do you realise what you've done?'

'Yes,' I said quietly. 'It's given him hope.'

'That's appalling, Sophia!'

'*Appalling* is a harsh word. I just wanted—'

'It's the only word that's fitting when you consider how unlikely it is you're going to find out anything new about Julie.'

'I'm sorry? What?' I couldn't believe what he was saying. 'That was precisely my objection to my father taking part in the interview. But you said, let him do it, maybe they'll find a new lead, and you also said that hope was a good thing.'

Richard shook his head in disbelief. 'Hope *is* a good thing, Sophia! If it's based on something real! But what you've concocted here are lies! You've planted in his mind the possibility that these emails could be from Julie! And that, Sophia, that *is* appalling.' He crossed his arms. 'Sort it out.'

'You're saying I . . . ? But how . . . ?'

'Sort it out,' he said forcefully. And he added that the Sophia he'd married, the Sophia he was planning to adopt a child with, would do this: sort it out. Ensure that her father didn't have to spend the rest of his more or less days in another blur, in the haze of possibility and a fog of questions. There was already one question he would, if the worst came to the worst, take to the grave unanswered: what really happened to Julie?

'Isn't that enough?' Richard asked. 'Do you have to burden him with further questions? Are these emails really from Julie? And, if so, where is she, how is she and can she be helped?' He shook his head. 'He's looking for her, Sophia! And he's only going to feel more of a failure if he doesn't find her! Is that what you want?' Rather than waiting for an answer, he made it clear that this wasn't what he wanted. Directing me back to my laptop, he said, 'Give him his peace.'

'OK,' I say, giving in. 'If I do that, if I sort everything out, will everything be OK again between us? Richard?'

Richard merely said again, 'Give him his peace.'

I sensed that I mustn't go over the top now. All the same I wanted to try. I had to.

'Do you think . . . I mean, could you maybe sort out the light at the weekend?' I looked up at the ceiling, from the middle of which two bare cables were dangling.

'Yes, maybe,' was the answer I got, and the hand on my shoulder tightened its grip again like a reminder of what was at stake here. I lowered my fingers on to the keyboard and typed.

> Thanks for your message, Dad. In truth I wanted to avoid all of this, but I realise that's not possible anymore. I know you're looking for me. But that's not necessary, Dad. I'm fine where I am, and happy. I was never in danger. I simply followed my heart – do you remember what Mum always said? That the heart is never wrong because it's much cleverer than the rest of us. I know I've caused you all a lot of pain, and I want to apologise profoundly for that. But please accept, and respect, that this here is my life and I'm deciding for myself how I lead it. Please leave it at that and don't notify the police. They'd arrest me, Dad! Don't allow that to happen. Please, Dad. You've got to stop looking for me.
>
> J.

Before I clicked SEND I turned around to Richard. 'Is that OK?'

He shook his head. 'No, of course not!'

I didn't understand. What more did he want?

'Now you're actively writing in Julie's name.'

'Yes, of course,' I said, still at a loss. 'I can hardly write: *Hi, Dad! It's me, Sophia. I'm sorry you thought I was Julie. No offence, I just wanted to find out how well your memory was still functioning.*'

I looked at him, waiting for a reaction. When none came, I added, '*That* would break his heart even more.'

'*That's* what a grown-up person would do. Someone who's ready to accept the consequences of their own actions.'

'Break an old man's heart? Really, Richard?'

'You know exactly what I mean.'

For a while I scraped my bottom lip with my teeth. I thought of my father, the argument we recently had about the house, how much it hurt every time I realised that his illness was pushing us further apart, and how good, by contrast, it felt when, at other rare moments, he took me in his arms and seemed to remember that he loved me.

'I'm sorry,' I said softly, and I really was. I pressed SEND, at which Richard left the room without another word. I went after him, across the hall and towards the kitchen.

'Richard, please!' I tugged at his T-shirt.

'I need to think, Sophia!'

He went off and I turned back to the child's room, its door still open, offering a view of the pasting table, the test patches on the wall and the bare light cables. Then I began to cry. No, Richard probably wouldn't sort out the lights at the weekend. Maybe this bedroom would remain empty forever. And this is exactly what he reminds me of now as he goes in, while I stand in the hallway, holding the car key: things lost. What I have already lost, and what might follow. It's serious, again and still. It never stops being serious. A faint sob struggles laboriously out of my throat. It would be a scream if I had anything like the energy. To fight, to protect, to preserve. I ought to run out of the house, drive away, tyres screeching, break every speed limit. But I don't, I can't. It's as if I'm in slow motion. What's awaiting me at the lake? What do the police want? What has my father done?

Or was that just a trick by the officer on the phone to lure me there? Have they actually traced the *Nutcracker11* emails back to me? Do they know? For a few seconds, I consider turning around. Driving away, buggering off, disappearing, just leaving. But how far would I get before they apprehended me? Or, as Liv put it in her podcast: *you can't just disappear, you have to stay hidden.* Who's capable of that, especially without any help? I decide to maintain my course. I can't go on anymore. I've tried everything to protect my father. I might have even sacrificed my marriage and my child in the process.

It's over, finished.

Showdown, the end.

# PHIL

Phil keeps feeling his right trouser pocket where his phone is. His phone with the recordings he made here by the lake. It was on the whole time, recording the story that Daniel Wagner told them. Then the big finale – Novak battering Wagner to the ground and the discovery of the lifeless body in the boot. He's got all of it. Phil's shaking with excitement and he's having difficulty controlling the expression on his face to satisfy the expectations of the half-dozen police officers around him. From time to time he can sense the hint of a smile twitch across his lips and then he turns away. These recordings are pure gold. That's why there's no way he wants to hand them over to the police, who are still asking questions. He must keep the recordings under wraps, and that's what he's going to do. Both he and Novak have to give a preliminary statement and the two of them are cooperative as they don't want to risk spending the entire night at the station. Instead they're going to be interrogated again separately in the morning, officially, in a bleak office with a buzzing neon light on the ceiling, watery coffee and a lethargic officer who will stoically run through his list of questions. Just thinking about it is putting Phil in a bad mood. On the other hand, he'd rather spend tomorrow at the police station than the rest of tonight. Besides, he needs to show the police he really appreciates the fact that they've gone for this solution rather than insisting on taking him and Novak away now, which, strictly speaking, they ought to do. After all, we're talking bodily harm here; Daniel Wagner has just been taken away in an ambulance. At first glance Phil seems to be a mere bystander in this, an inquisitive podcaster in the role of observer – surely he's got much less to be worried about. *You have no idea*, he thinks, briefly unsure whether, as so many times over the past twenty years, he should feel angry about police ignorance, or in fact relieved. The latter, he decides, feeling his trouser pocket once more. This time the latter.

'Herr Hendricks!' An officer wanders over to Phil, momentarily blinding him with a torch. 'Sorry,' the man mutters, giving a rather stupid laugh. Phil joins in. It's a sign of how the police view all of this here. This isn't a serious crime scene where it's worth going to the effort of setting up floodlights or sealing off areas with police tape. What would be the point? A senile pensioner has whacked the ex-boyfriend of his missing daughter over the head and then discovered the dead body in the man's boot. The wrong dead body. 'Could I ask you to come over to the car for a minute?'

Phil nods and follows the officer past a colleague who's currently dealing with Theo Novak. 'I want my daughter to come and pick me up,' Phil hears Novak bluster, and the policewoman replies, 'We've called her and I'm sure she'll be here soon.'

'Soon, soon,' Theo repeats laconically. 'As if death had ever waited! As if he wore a watch! Death doesn't care if it's Christmas or Easter or the school ball . . .'

'Crikey!' the officer beside Phil says. 'If you ask me, that one needs to be in sheltered accommodation and not out in the street at night on his own. Didn't that occur to you?'

Phil ignores the implied criticism; he's not going to be nudged from his role as observer into that of a guilty party. He's not Theo Novak's guardian, it wasn't his job to stop Novak from meeting Wagner. Novak is still a responsible adult so long as no official stamped document together with a doctor's certificate testifies the opposite. The boot is open after the police inspected its contents earlier. The officer shines his torch inside; the beam moves across the stiff, outstretched body. Phil looks into a pair of large, dark, lifeless eyes.

'OK, just let me get this straight,' the policeman says. 'Herr Novak thought Herr Wagner had kidnapped his daughter, and he was seriously expecting to find her dead body in the boot of this car. And he absolutely lost it. Am I right?'

Phil shrugs. Yes, that's pretty much what happened. After Wagner's psychotic monologue, and because of the huge cage they'd seen in that bedroom, they could only assume that it was Julie in the boot.

'So far as I understand,' Phil explains, 'Wagner blamed Novak for the death of his dog. The two of them got worked up and then it all escalated.'

The officer gives a prolonged sigh. A wild pensioner with an old hunting rifle, a journalist with a thirst for sensationalism and some twerp driving his dead mutt around in the boot of his car – that's quite enough absurdity for one day, and the guy probably just wants to clock off now, Phil senses.

'You do realise that you could be facing a criminal charge for having helped Novak break into Daniel Wagner's house?'

Phil nods, pretending to be anxious. 'To be honest, I didn't know what to do. Novak wouldn't allow me to call the police even though that was of course my gut reaction,' he lies. 'But I was worried he'd get furious with me and do something rash. I mean, you've seen for yourself what he's like.' Phil puts on a doleful face and points to Theo Novak, who's still arguing with the policewoman. As if to prove what Phil's just been saying, the old man now roars, 'I'm the director of the clinic for heart, thoracic and vascular surgery at the Charité! And you're wasting my time here!'

The officer sighs again. 'OK, then, Herr Hendricks. See you at eleven o'clock tomorrow morning in my office.'

'Thanks for your understanding. It's been a long day. I won't be late.' Phil nods once more, this time as a goodbye, then he turns to go. The further he walks away, the faster his footsteps become, while he keeps touching his pocket as a reflex. Phil is certain that Theo hasn't told the police anything about the recordings he made. They would have confiscated his mobile otherwise. In fact, he doesn't have any concerns about Theo. The police think he's a senile old fool, not to be taken seriously, no matter what he might come out with. And this means that he, Phil, will be able to control all of this. It's in his hands. It's still his story, only that it took an unexpected turn by the lake this evening. A turn that, even given his journalist's detachment, has bowled Phil over. For it seems as if he's been hunting the wrong man for the past twenty years.

He leaves the Novaks' property and looks for an empty side street, somewhere he can make a phone call in peace, with nobody listening in. It rings several times before going to voicemail, but Phil is undeterred. Eventually the owner of that particular number realises that Phil is not going to give up and takes the call after all.

'Do you know how late it is?' is the first thing that Phil hears.

'If you'd told me directly, I wouldn't have had to disturb your beauty sleep.'

'Phil, I—'

'Were you in Wagner's house?'

'He abducted me and kept me captive there for several hours. It wasn't my choice!'

'And you told him everything.'

'Not everything, no. Only what happened when we were interns at the *Berliner Rundschau*. That I let you talk me into lending you my name. He thinks we were just two young, ignorant arseholes trying to exploit him to make a name for ourselves. That's all, Phil. He knows nothing about Benny. I swear I said absolutely nothing about that.'

Phil clicks his tongue, thinks for a moment, then says, 'OK, listen to me, Max. Things have changed, quite a lot has happened. Liv is dead.'

'What?' Max gasps. Phil can picture his face, the wide-open eyes and Max's cheeks going red, which they always do when he's agitated and almost craps himself. 'Your partner? From the podcast?'

'The Liv you sat opposite a few days ago in the café, yes, for Christ's sake, Max! Who else?'

'But what . . . ?'

'Suicide. Or at least that's what I thought.'

'What do you mean, *you thought*? You're not saying that Wagner . . . ?'

Phil shakes his head. 'We need to meet, Max. Now, right now.'

'It's almost half past ten, Phil. Can't we do it tom—'

'Tomorrow I'm going to be at the police station for an interrogation that's likely to drag on for hours.'

'Interrogation? Why? What's happened?'

'I'll come over to yours.'

Max is just about to take a deep breath when Phil hangs up.

He takes a taxi to Kreuzberg, where for donkey's years Max has had a tiny one-room flat in a tower block. The walls are white, the furnishing is sparse. You might think Max was still an intern, without a clue or a livelihood. But maybe that's exactly what he feels like, maybe these surroundings reflect an inherent insecurity he's never been able to shake off, and which Phil can now capitalise on. Max can be manipulated, just like Liv, only, unlike her, he knows the whole story, which has its advantages and disadvantages. The fact remains, Phil needs help, someone who can be sent out there and, if necessary, sacrificed if things get out of control. This differentiates people like him from people like Vlado Taneski, the journalist they featured in their last podcast: the smart ones and the *really* smart ones. And whereas Liv believed that a person in the know was a potential risk, Phil thinks the only thing that matters is how well you're in control of that person. And this is simple when you understand what they're after. Phil is convinced that desires outweigh fears, always. For most people are profoundly isolated on the inside, just like Max.

They're sitting at a table, which for Max is both a dining table and desk because of the lack of space in his flat. Phil has his feet crossed on the table, while Max sits opposite him, small and slender, like a guest in his own flat, as Phil tells him about Novak and Wagner, and the altercation at the lake.

'I think I was mistaken, Max,' he finally admits. 'I'd never have thought I'd say this, but I'm no longer sure it really was Wagner. In fact, I'll go so far as to say that it wasn't him.'

Max offers a 'hmm', which Phil takes as a good sign in his attempt to win him over again after everything that's happened between the two of them. Or, more accurately, to win him over for his purposes. He's aware that he already got Max into big trouble in his desire to uncover the truth, that time at the *Berliner Rundschau*. He lost his internship because of Phil, and as a result he might have thought his career was over before it had really begun. Probably more serious than that was the sense of disappointment; Phil was under no illusion about this. Max had idolised him and was almost certainly in love with him, as Phil realised when they met recently in the café in Kreuzberg. In Max's eyes was that special look he had whenever he saw Phil. The desire, but the pain too. And it shouldn't be forgotten that he'd wrested that newspaper article in the *Abendblatt* from Max, which only confirmed his belief that desire outweighed everything else, again and again.

Taking his feet down, Phil leans over the table and buries his head in his crossed arms. It's a sort of test – he wants to know how Max will react. Whether he'll put out his hand to touch him. If he does, Phil will know for sure that he can count on him.

Liv functioned in a similar way; she too was driven by the insatiable desire for intimacy. It wasn't that Phil hadn't loved her. He did. And he misses her already, he misses her badly and has no idea how to go on without her. But he also knows that his way of feeling love has changed – since that time, since Benny. He no longer feels it in his heart and stomach, but far more in his head, on the basis of a hyper-analytical logic, into which a little calculation creeps too. He doesn't want to be alone; he wants someone at his side who constantly gives him approval. Who won't leave, no matter how Phil behaves. Who's simply there and will stay there. That's what makes Phil strong and he needs to be strong, otherwise he'd fall to pieces on account of himself.

Phil waits, he waits for a reaction from Max. Which doesn't come at first. And so he needs to bring out the heavy artillery. Thinking about Benny is enough. Then the tears are genuine.

He thinks back, back to that evening when they met, out of necessity, at Benny's for the first time. This was after Julie's disappearance. They didn't have much time together, less than if they'd met at Phil's when his mother had gone out. Or at their secret place at the edge of the forest, in Phil's first car, a bright red, roaring Polo. On the odd occasion they'd take a room at the station hotel, so they could hide away from the world for the weekend. The bed would seem like a raft in the middle of the stained carpet that scratched the soles of their feet when they had to leave it to go to the small filthy bathroom. A raft carrying two castaways, far, far away from all the chaos, the anguish, the fear of being exposed in front of their narrow-minded, middle-class parents who wouldn't have understood their love. Was there such a thing as happy castaways? Benny and Phil – they were these. They needed nothing apart from each other. Only time was their enemy, time and the question of how long it would be until Benny's parents had finally had enough. For now, they still put up with their son's occasional disappearances. Benny could still endure going back on Sunday evenings, where the questions, tirades and threats awaited him. He'd be grounded, sent to a boarding school in Switzerland, a reform school, whatever they could dream up when they tried to force him to open his mouth and tell them where he'd been. How often Phil was amazed and impressed by Benny's strength and his defiance, which he took as a model. Phil himself had it easier; his mother didn't object to him spending the night with his supposed girlfriend at the weekend. Apart from those occasions when she pestered him to finally let her meet this girl, she left him in peace. And his father was always away with the navy, so he had little idea of what was going on.

'What's wrong with you?' Phil asked, puzzled, when they were lying on Benny's bed. He noticed how Benny reacted to his caresses differently than usual, how he froze. Something was bothering him and it had to be more than the fact that they were at Benny's because Phil's mother had the builders in today. Benny's bed, Benny's room that smelled like him and contained all his personal things. The film posters on the walls, the books and records on the shelves, the pinboard with all the photos, snapshots of him with other people, others who didn't have to remain hidden, the fine, blue-beige-striped bedclothes made of Viennese silk. It was – and Phil felt exactly the same – not only unusual, but slightly dangerous too. They'd locked the door, of course, in case Benny's mother came home earlier than expected. They didn't have to worry so much about his father; he was a doctor and always at work. But you never knew. What other choice did they have at the moment than to meet here? They couldn't simply disappear without running the risk of a police-led search being launched. This would definitely happen; the entire city was in an uproar after the disappearance of Julie Novak, Benny's best friend since kindergarten. Phil had never met Julie personally, but Benny had often talked about her and, judging by the many photos on the pinboard showing them together, she was the person closest to him, apart from Phil of course. She even knew that Benny had fallen in love with a handsome eighteen-year-old who was in his final year at a different school and worked at the kiosk in Herbertstrasse, where Benny often passed by after school to get an energy drink or packet of cigarettes. 'He's called Phil,' he'd told her, lowering his eyes uncertainly. Unlike what Benny was expecting from his parents, Julie had no reservations; on the contrary, she was delighted and very keen to meet Phil as soon as possible. But that never happened.

'Julie,' Benny began after a sigh, sitting up as Phil stroked him. 'I went to the police yesterday and gave a statement.'

Phil sat up too. 'What? A statement? What about? And why didn't you say anything to me?'

Benny nodded. 'Everyone seems to be gunning for her ex-boyfriend, Daniel Wagner. Do you remember? We bumped into him at Chichicoo.'

Now Phil nods too. Chichicoo was a club near the main station, colourful, loud and a bit shabby, but with good music and bouncers who never asked for ID. Something that Benny and a few of his friends made good use of.

'OK. And?' Phil said.

'I saw him, in Chichicoo. On the night she went missing.'

Phil shrugged, slightly at a loss.

'That means he can't have been involved in her kidnapping,' Benny explained. 'Because he was in the club at the time. Don't you understand?'

No, Phil didn't understand. For Benny had to be mistaken. Badly mistaken, in fact. Julie disappeared on the night of 6–7 September. As far as Phil was concerned, Benny couldn't have been in Chichicoo that Saturday night. Because this would have meant he'd gone out without him. Why would he have done that? They were a couple, even though nobody knew about them. And so you didn't go out on your own, as if you were single. In truth, they were more than a couple, because a couple were two. And they were one. The one, single great love. Phil was certain Benny had stayed at home that Saturday evening, yes, he remembered this for sure. Because Benny had said he wanted to please his parents by having dinner with them and then playing a game afterwards. Monopoly, Phil seemed to remember. Yes, Monopoly, because Benny's father Claus liked the game so much.

Fortunately all of this came straight back to Phil and he pointed out to Benny his error. He must've mistaken that evening for the one before, when both of them were at Chichicoo. The sweet barman had just given them a mischievous wink as he put two caipirinhas on the bar when Benny said to Phil, 'Look over there. That's Julie's ex-boyfriend, Daniel. Total freak. I bet he's only here because he's hoping she'll come too and he can bump into her *by chance*. He just doesn't get that she's not interested in him anymore.' He laughed. 'And besides, she's still shit-scared of coming here, little Miss Perfect.'

Now, therefore, Phil said, as they lay on Benny's bed, 'You've got to go back to the police, Benny! You have to explain that you got the date wrong. Because you did, you did. I know that for sure, because of us, because you don't go hanging about anywhere without me, where another guy might hit on you. And what's more, if you don't set this straight now, later on the police will accuse you of having hindered their investigation. That'll be really stressful, Benny. The authorities won't put up with that.' Benny looked hesitantly at Phil, maybe even a bit fearfully.

*Back then*, Phil thinks now. When he still assumed that this look reflected Benny's anxiety about the legal ramifications. Not for one second would it have occurred to Phil that it might have something to do with him. And now, too, he dismisses the thought. Not because he still thinks it's completely far-fetched that Benny could have gone out without him, but because it would hurt if that had really been the case. Yes, it would still hurt, even now.

Either way, Benny did in fact go back to the police and change his statement, saying that he might not have seen Daniel Wagner on the evening in question, but the previous one. Which meant that Wagner's alibi for the night of Julie's disappearance was invalid.

Lifting his head from the nest of his crossed arms, Phil looks at Max. 'It's perfectly clear, Max! Wagner knew Benny by sight, he knew that he was Julie's best friend. And he knew from the police that it was Julie's best friend who'd first given him, then retracted, the alibi. They should never have told him that! This was a flagrant breach of their otherwise so-sacred data protection rules! And this put him in danger, Max. Wagner waited for Benny. He waylaid him after school and confronted him. Actually, worse than that, he grabbed Benny by the collar and screamed: *Why? Why did you do that?* It was only when Benny cried for help that he let go and stormed off. I could've flipped my lid when Benny told me. I wanted to go over to Wagner's house and beat the shit out of him. But what good would that have done? Theo Novak had already gone down that route and where had it got him? So I advised Benny to put Wagner in his place in a different way. He had to go on the offensive. Besides, I sensed the newspapers would pay a nice bit of pocket money for an exclusive interview with someone close to Julie. And, after all, we needed every cent we could get if we were going to run away together after Benny had done his exams. For our new life, you see? Far away from all of those people who would never have understood our relationship.'

Max is startled but says nothing. He already knows the story, although it's different from the version Phil told him before. He hadn't mentioned that, with the interview – in which Benny had spoken of the allegedly toxic relationship between Julie Novak and Daniel Wagner, only fuelling the public suspicion against Wagner – he and Benny had seen a way of making some money. What he'd claimed to Max was that he, who was always able to sniff out a story, was trying his level best to expose an injustice. To make it clear to people, especially the police, just what a monster Wagner was. That without doubt he'd been the one who kidnapped Julie Novak. That he'd committed a crime and was playing the whole world for a fool. And that must have been true. For why else did Benny die so soon after the interview, if not because Wagner was exacting revenge on him? For Phil and for Max – because Phil always knew how to convince other people – it all made sense. Benny hadn't committed suicide – why would he have done? He and Phil were in love and they'd forged plans. Could the pressure following the interview have really been so great that it eclipsed everything else? Phil had recounted to Max, a hundred times over, this sequence of events: Wagner lying in wait for Benny again, taking him to the sewer shaft, forcing him to drink the schnapps and then slitting his wrists. How Wagner had committed the perfect crime by making an ice-cold murder look like suicide. Phil was convinced that this is what had happened. He *knew* it. Only, the police and Benny's parents refused to listen when he spoke to them about it. Of course he said nothing about his relationship with Benny, merely insisting that they were friends. But Benny's parents doubted that Phil had ever known their son. After all, Benny had never spoken about him, let alone introduced him to them. And so Phil was treated like an attention-seeking weirdo and he wasn't taken seriously. But he *knew* the truth – he thought he knew it – and he was going to prove it to them. He only needed to publish an article, with Max's help, when they were doing their internships at the *Berliner Rundschau*. Just Max's name, he didn't need any more than that. A different name from his own, which was tarnished as far as the police and Benny's parents were concerned, a name with no connection to the matter. Not to mention the trouble he'd been in with the management after rewriting the text of another journalist.

But the interview he did with Wagner as Max Bishop-Petersen turned into a disaster and Phil was forced to keep a low profile for a while. Also, just like Max, he had to find somewhere else to work.

One of his many jobs was in an advertising agency, where he met Liv. The agency belonged to her stepfather and she was employed there too. He sensed at once that she wasn't working voluntarily at the agency. They became friends and it wasn't long before they decided to launch *Two Crime*. For Liv it was a welcome exit from the agency, for Phil the perfect opportunity to find further proof of Wagner's guilt. There were a number of reasons it took 146 other criminal cases before he could actively engage with the whole affair again. First, he didn't want to be unmasked as the 'weirdo' from back then. Second, for a long time, he had no idea how he should go about this research. Because one thing was certain: he didn't have many more chances to have Wagner convicted; perhaps this was the very last. He mustn't risk anything. So when the twentieth anniversary of Julie's disappearance came up, he seized his chance.

Liv, on the other hand, suspected none of this. It had transpired that most suggestions for their podcast cases came from Phil, including the episode about Julie Novak. The detour via Julie was unavoidable because at no point had Benny's death been classified as a criminal case. And apart from a piddly report about his supposed suicide, there was no material that Liv could have drawn upon. The report didn't mention his name or any possible connection to Julie Novak and Wagner. How could Liv have worked with that? It was impossible; there was no way she could have researched it. That meant focusing on Julie's case instead – and why not? Even though Phil had never met Julie, and only knew her from what Benny had told him, she had been Benny's best friend. And in all probability another of Wagner's victims. She deserved justice too.

The problem was that Liv really messed up at first. Even when they were recording the episode, Phil thought it was a pile of crap. None of the information in her transcript was new to him; everything had been chewed over a thousand times already. Later he found out that the script wasn't even hers. Instead she'd simply copied large chunks of it straight from another podcast. So he goaded her to undertake the reportage. Now she couldn't help but research *properly*. And Phil had specifically sent her to the hairdresser with a seemingly spontaneous idea. For he'd seen photographs of Julie. There was a definite similarity between her and Liv, and now, with the red hair, it was even more uncanny. Phil imagined her meeting Wagner for an interview and him being derailed by her appearance. After all, Wagner had been searching for a partner for ages on a dating website. Phil hoped that he'd fall for Liv at once. Of course there was a risk that he wouldn't answer her questions in the first place, and of course that would have been Phil's fault, because back in the day, pretending to be Max Bishop-Petersen, he'd overstepped the mark and gone against Wagner too aggressively. Why did he nonetheless think it wasn't hopeless? The anniversary of Julie's disappearance was approaching – and the fact that *Murder Talk* had chosen the case for their podcast too, independently of Liv and Phil, was a lucky coincidence, which hopefully would give Wagner the impression that the case was being revisited, and thus his role in it too. Did he really want to go through all of that again? Or would he now take the timely opportunity to present his side of the story? The newspaper article about the reportage, which Phil had wheedled out of Max, and the fact that Wagner had been attacked, possibly by someone who thought he was guilty, was supposed to make him only more aware of how urgent it was to act. To act and, in the process, finally make a mistake after twenty years. And yes, of course it was Phil who'd hung around outside his house and clobbered him. For Phil was that someone who believed Wagner was guilty.

Sadly this, too, ended in a right old mess. Instead of focusing exclusively on Wagner, Liv just hung around with Julie's demented father. She hadn't taken the path Phil was trying to steer her down. Right until the end, she hadn't met Wagner, even though Phil had done his best to make this happen. Wagner's address was no longer in the telephone book; he'd gone ex-directory years ago. But Phil had never forgotten it, because he'd often been there after Benny's death to keep watch on the house. And the Dellards' telephone number – this was from Phil too. He hadn't called Inspector Bergmann, as he'd led Liv to believe – he didn't have to, because he'd called Benny's number thousands of times and still knew it by heart all these years later.

Now Liv is dead before she could arrange a meeting with Wagner. And Phil is left with the question of whether, and to what extent, her death might be connected with the disappearance of Julie Novak. Whether she found out, for example, about the intruder in the house that they'd almost apprehended that night. What the altar, the candles and the flowers in Julie's room meant. Who'd set all of it up and later got rid of it all. Phil could kick himself for not having acted soon enough. Why hadn't he simply listened to her?

'It was the way he was lying there, Max,' Phil says. 'At the lake earlier on, Wagner was lying on the ground howling like a small child, puking his guts out and whimpering, "It wasn't me, it wasn't me."' He shakes his head. 'If I hadn't been there myself and someone had just described the scene to me, I'd have probably laughed and said, "He's just a good actor." But he came across as genuine. A pathetic little twerp. "So who was it, then?" Theo and I asked him, and he said, "I don't know. But if you find him, please let me know. Because he's destroyed my life too." Then he passed out.' Phil sighs and looks at Max for help. 'Is it possible, Max? Is it really possible that I've been wrong all these years?'

'Hmm,' Max says cautiously. 'I have to say that I had my doubts too after I was in his house. Inside the house of a man who's crazy, no question about that,' he adds quickly. 'All the same, what he was saying sort of made sense. And he did seem to be absolutely devastated when his dog was suddenly dead.' There's a brief silence. 'And perhaps it's inevitable you'd go mad if the whole world implied you were guilty of a crime you never committed.'

'What about me, Max? Might I be mad too because I never got over Benny's death?'

Max says something but Phil isn't listening. His head is spinning. Julie's disappearance. Benny's supposed suicide. Then Liv. Phil notices he's being overcome by real weakness, something he never lets happen. He slams his fist on to the table.

'No, Max!' Max winces. 'I'm not mad! This fucking puzzle needs to be solved once and for all.'

'But what if there is no puzzle, Phil?' Max asks quietly. 'What if Benny really was under a lot of pressure? Not just because of the interview, but also because he could no longer live up to his parents' expectations. What if he simply couldn't cope anymore? What if Julie Novak disappeared of her own accord? And as for your partner . . . well, didn't you tell me she had a difficult past? What if none of these things were crimes and there's no killer at all?'

Phil shakes his head vehemently. He has to admit that his initial thought was that Liv had taken her own life. But then he thinks again of Theo Novak, who was certain that she'd never have killed herself. What if he's right? What if Liv was close to finding out something, closer than she could have known?

'We're going to start from the beginning again, Max,' Phil says, finally revealing the real reason for his visit. 'Go through everything again thoroughly. You're going to help me.'

Max gives an uncertain shrug. 'How's it going to work?'

'As soon as the police give me back the video camera, Liv's mobile, and her notebook, we'll plough our way through her research word for word. We'll check everything again meticulously and make sure we understand it all.'

'Don't you think the police are doing that already?'

'Max, you know yourself how they work. They've already concluded that Liv's death was suicide. No,' he adds resolutely. 'I remember that Liv told me something about a karate instructor. And who knows what else she uncovered that she wasn't able to tell me before she died.'

'Phil . . .'

Phil responds to the pleading in Max's voice by leaning over the table and holding out his open hand. Earlier, when Phil tested Max, his friend resisted the urge to touch him. So now Phil goes on the offensive.

'You're going to help me, Max, aren't you? The two of us, you and me. I promise you, this is going to be the story of our life.'

Max puts his hand in Phil's.

'OK,' he says with a timid smile and a nod.

## THEO

Sophia arrives late but just in time. This woman from the police, she's been gabbling on at me for half an hour about how she's going to take me to hospital because she thinks I'm in a bad way. All the other police officers have gone, just her and her colleague are still stomping in the darkness over my property, ruining everything on top of all the hammock that Claus Dellard already caused. Actually he didn't cause hammock, because he did bugger all to look after the beautiful garden, he just let it go wild. He wants to be a luminescence, that, that Dellard. But he's a lazybones, a lazybones and a wimp who can't even hold a splayed with his thin Mickey Mouse arms.

'That one!' I say to Sophia, pointing at the policewoman. 'She says I need to get checked out! But I don't need to go to hospital! I didn't get thwacked by the good old Sauer & Sohn! It was me who thwacked Wegner!' Sophia, she shoots her hand up to cover my mouth. 'Shh, Dad! Don't say a word right now!' Then, to the policewoman, 'Does he need a lawyer?'

I push her hand away, I'm not having her shouting me up too. 'But she knows already! The woman knows what happened here!' The policewoman nods and fills Sophia in. I'm not listening, I mean, I know what happened, I was in the thick of it. 'I want them to leave now!' I demand. 'They're trampling over everything!' I look around for the beautiful flowers at my feet – Siberian irises, marsh gladioli, cuckoo flowers – but because it's so dark and the policewoman is aiming her torch too high, I can't see a thing. I know they're there, the beautiful flowers, they're always there even if you can't immediately see them. Finally the policewoman and her colleague understand that they're not wanted here, and so take their leave.

'Tomorrow morning, Herr Novak, OK?' they say. 'Nine-thirty sharp.'

'It's Doctor Novak,' I growl. 'Professor Doctor Novak to be precise.'

'I'll make sure he's on time,' Sophia butts in, and nods as if she had a spring in her neck. Grabbing my arm, she drags me away from the policewomen. I shake my body; I don't want to go yet. Sophia recoils then doesn't move anymore. She stands there as if frozen. I can still make out her face at first, but the further the two policewomen wander away with their torches, the more it's swallowed up by the darkness. Now Sophia is just a silhouette, a slender, whatsit, whatsit, outline in the night.

'Sophia?' I whisper. Not that I'm scared, but there's something odd about her. Maybe she's angry at me. But what reason could she have for that? I haven't done anything! Only what, according to Vera, any good father would have done in a situation like that. 'I couldn't know that what that, that Wegner had in the boot was a dead dog! I thought it was Julie! Our Julie!' I curl my lip; I'm so worked up I think I may have inadvertently spat at Sophia. It's silent for a moment and I think that now she's even angrier at me because of the bit of spittle that may have hit her face. Then I hear her sniff and a second later there's a white light shining beside her: her phone torch. Now I can see her again. And what I see is that she's crying.

'You really don't remember, do you, Dad?' she says, guiding the beam of her torch past me to a spot by the shore. I turn around and screw up my eyes. I cock my head and croak, 'Julie?'

'Yes, Dad. She's there.'

I screw up my eyes even more to see her better, my Julie. But I can't make anything out; it's too dark. I totter a few steps forward in her direction.

'I can't see her, Sophia. I can't see her!' My footsteps become faster.

'No, Dad, you can't see her,' I hear Sophia say. 'She's under the earth. You buried her yourself.' I stop abruptly. Sophia's words are like bullets riddling my back. I begin to shake and turn back to her, staggering.

'No!' I want to cry, but it's just a sound, a flat feeble sound.

'You buried her,' Sophia repeats. 'Try to remember.'

I do try but I can't. My head, inside it there's a black hole and Sophia's words go tumbling into it, falling and falling without hitting the bottom. 'But why . . .' I stammer. 'Why would I have done that?'

The beam from her phone torch flashes in the darkness like lightning as Sophia comes right up to me. Then she says, 'Because you did what any good father would have done.'

## SOPHIA

'Hey!'

The voice caught me off guard, giving me such a shock that

I almost knocked my head against the frame of the small cellar window. Shit, I thought. Those bloody old stairs with their stupid bloody creaks. They must've given me away again. For a moment I thought about going on regardless, creeping outside, but before I could finish this thought, I felt Julie pulling on my legs.

'Stop that! What do you think you're doing?' I hissed, moving back awkwardly to where the pulling had come from. At that moment the light of a torch flared up; my sister was pointing it straight at my face. Instinctively I flung my hand up to shield my eyes. 'Are you crazy?'

Julie lowered the torch. 'No, but it seems like you are. Didn't we speak about this?'

Yes, we did. And this wasn't the first time she'd caught me trying to climb out of the cellar window.

'Who are you? Mum? Or Dad?'

'Your worst nightmare – that's who I am if you don't stop this bloody nonsense, Sophia! The guy's a grown man!'

'Oh, I see, and that idiot Daniel isn't?'

Julie shook her head in exasperation. 'For one thing, as you know, I'm not together with Daniel anymore. And besides, I'm older than you and Daniel is younger than Jason Willmers. Or is your stupid little head so stuffed full of shagging hormones that you've forgotten how to do sums?'

I'd just opened my mouth to hurl an insult of mine at her when she kept going. 'I don't want Dad thinking it was *me* again creeping out of here to meet up with Daniel. Do you have any idea what I had to listen to last time? He was so disappointed in me, Sophia. I didn't deserve that.'

'Yes, you're so perfect, we all know that.'

'I didn't say that and I didn't mean it either. All I'm saying is that I'm not going to cover your arse anymore, certainly not at my expense. Forget it.'

I made a snorting sound – *cover*, puh. She'd covered me once. I'd crept out of the window and she was just about to follow me when Dad came into the cellar and caught her. OK, she didn't snitch on me and so Dad thought she was the one secretly going to meet her boyfriend. So what? Didn't sisters help each other out occasionally? Did this mean I was forever in her debt?

'By the way, I told Willmers during training today that if he doesn't keep away from you, the shit's going to hit the fan,' she went on. 'And I'm being serious, Sophia. He's using you, and you're a stupid, naïve child who just doesn't get it.'

'I'm not a child!' I said, stamping my foot.

'Alright, then, you're just stupid and naïve,' Julie shot back at me. 'The fact is, you're not to do that shit, OK? You're making a complete fool of yourself. Crawling out of the cellar at night like a little rat, to go creeping to the Willmerses' house. How long does it take you to walk there if he doesn't pick you up with his car? Fifteen, twenty minutes? In the middle of the night, Sophia! Have you any idea what could happen? And what happens when you get there? Do you chuck little stones at the bedroom window so he wakes up and knows that his little shag is there?'

I lower my head. It was the sitting room window I threw stones at because Jason usually slept on the sofa. His wife had booted him out of the bedroom, supposedly because of his snoring. But I knew that he was only doing it so he didn't have to sleep in a bed with her anymore.

'Where do you do it, then? Behind the house, by the bins? That would be fitting: like two little rats.'

I could feel my jaw tensing. Mostly we'd drive to the woods in Jason's car. We had our peace there and it was a little bit romantic too. But obviously I wasn't going to tell Julie that. It was bad enough that she'd got wind of the whole thing anyway. Actually it was my fault that she knew. I'd confided in her because keeping a secret like that was hard. And who might understand me if not her? That's what I'd thought at least. But she didn't understand. She didn't understand anything, nothing at all about true love. She'd proven that with Daniel, who she thought was the man of her life to begin with, only to move on from him eight or nine weeks later because she didn't think he fitted into her life plans. She was a hypocrite, a vile, bloody hypocrite.

'And while we're at it,' she said, running the beam of light over my body, 'stop borrowing all my clothes then just shamelessly stuffing them in my washing basket.' She turned her back on me and made to leave the room.

'What did he say?' I marched after her, only catching her halfway up the stairs to the kitchen.

'You want to know what he said?'

'Shh!' I waggled my hands. I didn't want to risk waking up our parents.

Julie shook her head in resignation. I pushed past her so that I was now two steps above. 'Yes! Jason! What did he say when you talked to him after karate today?' I was still furious at my mother for not letting me go because of my cold. It would have been the first time I'd seen him since his wife had caught us in bed a few days earlier.

When my sister made no effort to answer me, I snatched the torch from her hand and now pointed it at her face.

'You don't want to know, Sophia.'

'Yes, I do!' I said, brandishing the torch. 'Come on, out with it!'

She gave a dramatic sigh. 'He said I needn't worry. The thing with you had been a mistake. And he certainly wasn't going to risk his marriage and job for it.'

'No! I don't believe you!'

She shrugged. 'Leave it, then.'

'He didn't say that!' Never, not Jason, the man who loved me. Who'd promised that the two of us would soon go away together if his wife kept refusing a divorce.

'Sophia.' Julie sighed again. 'You're fourteen! We're still so young. We have our future before us, there are so many lovely things to come. Life is—'

I would never find out how her sentence finished and what she thought life was. For at that moment my body made a rash movement. Later I wouldn't be able to remember if it was just a shove or if I'd lashed out with the torch too. All I could recall was her falling – this was etched into my memory forever. Her falling and our eyes meeting for a millisecond, hers wide open, mine too probably, the shock, the shock, the disbelief. And then the dull thwack at the bottom of the stairs as her head . . .

## THEO

'. . . hit the cement floor.' Sophia ends her account in tears.

But it's not true this story, it's a pack of lies.

'No, Sophia, no, that's . . . that's not true, it didn't happen like that at all. Julie, she's . . .' I blink like a madman, as if that would help tease the relevant images from my brain. But there are no such images, thankfully, thankfully. 'No!' I yell at her. What's she talking about? None of that happened. Julie, our Julie, she just suddenly went missing; someone kidnapped her in the middle of the night, abducted her from our house!

'Yes, Dad,' Sophia howls, reaching out for my face with her left hand, while her right hand is still holding the phone, its torch beam twitching in the darkness like lightning as she trembles. 'Julie was lying in the cellar, and for a moment, everything was quiet. I switched on the light, went down the stairs and kneeled beside her. I whispered her name but she didn't respond. Her eyes were still wide open and rigid. And blood was oozing out from beneath her head, more and more blood. At that moment I started to scream. My screaming woke Mum up. Do you remember, Dad? That's exactly what happened. No kidnapping, nothing else . . .'

'Your mother,' I begin tentatively, as I hear Vera in the distance. My Vera, calling my name – 'Theo!' – and sounding as it had once sounded. If I concentrate on my Vera, on my name being called, I can see us lying in our bed. And Vera rearing up with such energy that the mattress sways, as if we were on the high seas. I, on the other hand, don't move. I'm tired after a long shift; I just continue sleeping. When I do eventually open my eyes again, Vera's standing at the foot of our bed. She's flailing her arms, and words are shooting out of her mouth like missiles. They don't reach my brain; they come crashing into my head and stick there.

Julie, something about Julie.

Vera has darted around the bed and is now tugging at my arm. I hear a sound, a scream, the scream of a girl, one of my girls. I leap out of bed, out of our bedroom, Vera behind me. The screaming, it's coming from downstairs. When we get to the whatsit, the kitchen, I notice that the door to the cellar is open. Sophia, I think. The screaming, it's coming from Sophia. I've only heard her scream like this once before. She couldn't swim at the time and had toppled into the lake from the jetty. It was Julie who saved her; she was quicker into the water than me. Even though she was only five or six at the time. My Julie, my little water lily.

I scramble down the stairs, Vera still right on my tail, and when I stop abruptly near the bottom, she almost comes crashing into me. The sight my eyes take in. The images flicker in competition with Sophia's phone torch.

Julie, Sophia, the blood.

In reality, here, at this moment by the lake, I fall to my knees, just as in my memory I fall to my knees. In my memory, however, I don't land in the wet grass but on the cold hard cement floor beside Sophia, who's kneeling beside her motionless sister. I move Julie's head, I feel her pulse, I move her head again, put my fingers right into the part that's curving inwards, which it shouldn't be doing, put my fingers into the blood.

'No!' I shout, down there in the cellar. 'No!' I shout up here too, collapsed on the shore of our property, and beat the sides of my head with my fists. My old, sick head, it's playing a trick on me. This isn't true, it isn't true. Not only am I sick, now I've gone mad too, as mad as Sophia, who made up this whatsit, this scenery in the first place for my simple, stupid, sick head. And she's just not stopping; she's pulling my arms and grabbing my fists. When she does this, it's as if the flashes of light from her phone whatsit pass straight through my thoughts – there's a blaze of white then the red on the grey cement, the pool of blood that has formed beneath Julie's head, and this image is so genuine, so real, not my imagination. I put my arm out to Vera, who I want to comfort, who in reality isn't there, but who was down there in the cellar. And I understand. That very image, the image of my Vera, standing there, shaking and pale, in only her thin nightie – it came to my mind recently. In a dream, perhaps, or on the evening when Sophia and Richard were at my place, because they wanted to help me practise for the interview that Liv was going to do the following day.

*Practise*, or just make sure that I said nothing wrong.

That I remembered the truth.

In the cellar.

Now I can picture it again, now I feel it. How cold it is around us, how the walls of the cellar seem to move in, as I put Vera's hand on my chest and let her feel my heartbeat. *A lion's heart never stops beating, never, do you hear me? I'm here and I'm not going away.*

'I wasn't able to save her,' I whisper, still lying in the wet grass tonight, almost twenty years later. 'How's that possible, Sophia? How's it possible that I saved the lives of thousands of people but not that of my own daughter?'

'Dad . . .'

I want to die, right here and now, just as I wanted to die back then but couldn't, because I had my wife and younger daughter who needed my protection.

I remember it, I remember it all, it's all coming back. Vera and I debating what to do. How desperate we are. We've just lost one of our two daughters. We've lost the one at the hands of the other. What will happen if we call the police now? Will we lose our second daughter tonight as well? Will they take her away from us? Sophia is only fourteen, she's still a youth as far as the law is concerned.

'It was an accident,' I say. 'She won't go to prison.'

'Can you be absolutely sure of that?' Vera asks. 'And even if she doesn't go to prison, what if they put her in some other institution? Do you really believe they'd simply leave her with us as if nothing had happened? She's just killed her sister, Theo! She's killed her sister! Do you think anyone's going to ask about the circumstances? Wonder if it was a tragic accident? No, they'll say only one thing about us – they'll print in every newspaper that she killed her sister. Her future would be destroyed, Theo! Her whole life would be destroyed! And ours too!'

She's right, my Vera. Just as she's always right. What's happened is bad enough.

So we hatch the plan.

Vera writes the ransom note as she once saw in a crime show. She does it on my computer so that nobody will be able to identify her handwriting later. But she's so upset that she forgets a zero, and from that point on, people will forever spectaclate about why on earth the ransom demand was for such a low sum of 30,000 euros. If I'd run my eye over the text, I'd have noticed the error. And also the wording that sounded exactly like a bad film, like fiction. In reality the truth comes out in few words, whereas the liars are those who tend to embellidge their stories with as many details as possible. If I'd read through the text, I would have noticed this. If only I'd done that. But when? I can't, I've got other things to do.

'Mum said we all had to behave as if Julie had been kidnapped.'

Sophia's voice mingles with the images inside my head, which is unnecessary for, once they get going, they sluice over me, they sluice over me like a latrine of rubbish, filth and debris.

While Vera writes the ransom demand and cleans the cellar with corrosive, I wrap Julie in a picnic blanket and take her away. Oh, my God, I take her away, I carry her in my arms out into the garden, down to the lake. To here. She's in her pyjamas, the white ones with blue clouds, which she was always slightly ashamed of and yet they were her favourite. I dig her a grave, right here, amongst the wildflowers. Then I fetch a tarpaulin from the boat shed, to wrap around Julie's body too. Finally I lay her, my Julie, I lay her in the grave, very carefully. Just as I used to lay her in her bed when she'd fallen asleep in my arms as a little girl. I say a final 'Goodnight, my angel' before burying her. When I'm done, I move one of our rowing boats over the spot to hide the freshly dug earth. Then we make the emergency call.

Everything's coming back, everything.

Us doing the television broadcast and me threatening Julie's kidnapper. Everyone suddenly pouncing on that, that Wegner, and Vera saying that we mustn't ignore this – it's like a gift from heaven. Me driving to his place at her behedge and attacking him before the eyes of the press because that's what a loving father would do; he would grab hold of the allegendary abductor and beat the truth out of him. He would have a go at the police who weren't getting any results. He would hire a private detective who he knew in advance wouldn't provide any new information because there was none to be had. There's a lot he would do, this father, out of love, despair and fury. And most of all, he would, of course, protect his other daughter. He would try to deflect her feelings of guilt. He would take her to the funfair and buy her a toffee apple, in the hope of finally seeing her smile again. He would continue to love her, maybe even a little more than before, because now she was his only daughter and, apart from his wife, the only thing he still had. He would not allow her life too to come to an end with this fateful night.

'You remember,' Sophia says, the older Sophia, who at this moment is sitting beside me in the wet grass. Who's crying and sobering, just as back then. Who's now saying that she didn't want any of this. That she was the one who wrote me those emails, because she was worried I'd remembered what had really happened to Julie. And that my memories would put all of us in danger. A danger we'd tried so hard to avert for twenty years. And that now she thinks everything's finished, everything, everything's finished, that Reinhard no longer loves her because of the emails, and that she wants to die, that I'm to bury her beside her sister. Julie . . . I remember this too. I remember the spot exactly. Sophia was close, she was off by just a metric or so. I crawl over to my Julie's grave, the material of my trousers soaking up the dampness of the grass; my knees get wet, just as the palms of my hands get dirty. But what does it matter? Everything's lost anyway. Sophia crawls behind, while I'm already pulling out clamps of grass with my bare hands.

'Don't, Dad,' Sophia howls. 'I'm really sorry, I'm really sorry.' Her torso topples forward, she rolls on to her side and curls up like a baby, and I remember how small she was when she was born, a little mite. And how we were worried she wouldn't make it. Now she wants to die, she wants to die of her own free will, after having fought so hard for her life when she was an infant.

And after everything her mother and I did later on to ensure she still had a life. I stop digging, I leave it. I crawl over to Sophia and pull her into my arms.

'I'll protect you, my little sweetheart,' I promise her. 'Your daddy is going to protect you. Forever.'

# PHIL

Dear Flps

i'm writing you this email today because it's time to bring this to an end. As you know I have this illness that makes me forget my life. My life, Fips. Not just silly little things that lots of people forget once they get oo a certain age. Sometimes, if i concentreate really hard, the things I'M trying to remember do come back. Someimes it takes a bit longer. some things come in little pieces, others in big chiunks. And now I have to apologise. the worst thing is that I ought to be apologising to Liv but she's not here anymore. only you are here, giving me a bit of a connection still with her. After whast happened at the lake with that Wegner, after the fear that I'd actually find my daughter in the boot of his car, but instead of her we found that poor dog, after realising how many other loives were affected by Julies disappearance, and also that I beat Wegner to the ground, and now im going to have to face another charge. In short, when the last twenty years exploded that evening by the laked it was as if it had gone click inside my head.

Now I remember, Fips. I remember everything. And I'm going to tell you it, well aware that you can't keep this email to youtself. And you shoukdn't, either. it's time for a conclusion, and for justice. Bring the reportage to an end, for Liv. And tell the public what really happened.

The truth is, Julie is dead. She died the very night she supposedly

## DARLING MINE

disappeared. I was the one who killed her, Fips – me, her own father. I caught her trying to climb out of the cellar window again to meet her lover. I was besdie myself, so fuRious, as furious as I was down by the lake the other evening, and you've seen for yourself how furious i can get, unfortunately. I got so furious that Wegner was knocked unconscious and started bleeding.

It was the same that night with my Julie. In my anger i hit her, which made her fall so distastrously that she suffered a fracture of the skull. She was dead at once; even I as a doctor couldnt do anything for her. I – me alone – arranged everything to make it look as if shed been kidnaped. my wife knew nothing, and Sophia was far too young anyway.

I was a coward, Fips. I was terrified. I'd just lost my daughter and with her a large part of my life. I wanted to preserve the rest of it, my wife and my reamaining daughter. I couldnt look them in the eye and tell them what I'd done. So I faked the kidnaping. I lied to the police and made use of the suspicion touted in the papers that Daniel Wegner could be the one responsible. I drove to his house and beat him up in front of the press to make it lOok genuine. Because thats what you'd expect from a distraughtered father, isn't it? I even hired a private detective, fuilly aware that he wouldn't find out anything. I only did it to make the whole scenery more realistic. In the same vein i went on television and had a go at the police. All of this, I thought, was what you'd have to do if it had really happened like that, if your own child had been abducted. you had to be angry and distraught and you had to do everything you possibly could, move heaven and earth. As far as my own anger and despair was concerned, i didn't have to fawn it – it was real. I really was angry and distraught. Only my anger was actually directed at myself.

i'm very sorry, Fips.

Also for what i did to Wegner with this terrible charade. Please show him this email so he knows. I deeply regret my actions and i'm ashamed of them.

Signed, prof dr theo Novak

PS: I buried Julie down by the lake, where the marsh gladioli and cuckoo flowers grow. You will find her.

# THEO

My Vera, she always said that a person's true nature was in their heart. Deep inside it, inside *my* heart, I already knew back then that she was right. But I wouldn't have admitted it because I was dealing with dozens of hearts every day, which for me were nothing more than engines. And I was their mechanic.

My heart, Vera, it tells me I have to calm down. I need to stop seeing the forgetfulness as a punishment. It promises to preserve whatever was important in a different way, in a much more significant way than my stupid old skull would have been able to.

And so this morning I'm sitting here, on the old jetty by the lake, rather than at the police station, where I ought to be giving my statement about the incident with Daniel Wegner yesterday. They'll realise I haven't turned up. And they'll certainly know by the time Fips shows them the email I wrote him earlier at home. I don't care, Vera. It doesn't matter anymore.

I keep my gaze fixed on the glittering water, with barely a division between its blue and that of the sky, and I feel the tears on my cheeks and I think: now I'd like to forget, just once. I'd like to forget what Sophia told me. But for the moment it seems etched on my mind. I have every word at the ready, and every associated image, every feeling.

My heart, Vera, now it's tugging as if it were trying to curl up inside my chest. As if it were trying to make itself very small, to have as little surface area as possible to feel.

I slept well nonetheless, beside me Sophia, our little mite. I really had to make a scene to get her away from here yesterday. And then I was worried about what she'd do if I didn't keep an eye on her. So I took the car key from her and drove us to my flat, where we spent the night. This morning she still didn't look particularly well so I showed her the email I'd sent to Fips and said, 'Go home, back to your husband. Make up with each other. Everything will be fine.' She gave me a firm hug and said, 'Thanks, Dad.' Because she understood, she understood the purpose of my email. I want to see Julie's case concluded with a clear result. So long as Julie continues to be classified as missing, Sophia will never properly be safe.

What about me? I don't have anything to lose anyway. I'm old, Vera, old and sick, and if Wegner presses charges, I'll be sent to prison for bodily harm anyway. Sophia, on the other hand, has everything to lose. She's got a husband she loves and she might be a mother soon. Imagine that, Vera: our little girl is going to be a mother! Now she's got the opportunity to experiment for herself what it means to have a family, to experiment the greatest happiness, to understand the true meaning of life.

After I said goodbye to her this morning and watched her drive away from my kitchen window, I put on my hat and came here by taxi, to our old house. I went down to the spot by the shore and began digging. The idea of some chump from the police doing this suddenly seemed unbearable. I don't know how long it was until I'd unearthed her – maybe just one hour, maybe three. Now I lifted her out as carefully as I'd laid her in the grave all those years ago. There were holes in parts of the tarpaulin I'd wrapped around the body but for the most part it was still intract. It and the rest of the picnic blanket held her body together like a firm, warm embrace. With sedate steps I carried her through the flowers – Siberian irises, marsh gladioli, cuckoo flowers and all the wild species that grow there and which you picked to put in a vase on the kitchen table – down to the jetty. And now I remember this too, I remember why you always picked those flowers. You imagined they were a greeting from our Julie, a greeting with which she let us know that she was still with us.

We've been sitting here since, Vera. We're sitting on the jetty, gazing into the distance where there's no longer any separation between the sky and the water, where everything becomes one and is one. *Skyearthblue.* And I'm holding her in my arms, Vera. In my thoughts there is no tarpaulin, no blanket that after all this time under the ground has been just about keeping her body together. In my thoughts she's just as pretty as back then, twenty years ago. With my left hand I take the hat off my head and set it on the plank beside me. I don't need it anymore. My heart, Vera, it wants to stop being an engine. It's full of love and peace and I'm smiling.

My greatest fear was to die from forgetfulness. That one day there would be a definitive *click* like with an old-fashioned toggle switch and it would remain dark forever.

But I think I'm lucky.

My heart, Vera.

Vera, my heart.

# EPILOGUE

## SOPHIA

*Life is—*

I still wonder how my sister would have finished this sentence, with the experience and knowledge of someone who was sixteen at the time. Would she have said that life is beautiful? Wild and wide and open, like the sea she so loved? That first you had to learn how to take the waves before you could enjoy riding them? That there were currents, eddies and storms you had to counter with controlled breathing and stoical calm? That you must never panic, to avoid losing your orientation? And that, if you managed to feel at one with the sea, you also lost the fear of what lay hidden beneath the surface? The magic that lay below, with its imposing landscapes and unbelievable variety of sea creatures – a magic that could only be experienced by those courageous enough to face the depths?

Or would she simply have said: *Life is long, Sophia. So many guys are going to come along, that one day, he'll be there:* the one. No matter how she'd finished her sentence, I wouldn't have understood it. Because I was too young, too aggressive, too pig-headed.

I also wonder how my father would have finished this sentence for himself, in the moments before his death, when a whole life is concentrated on the essence, on one last feeling with which you depart this world. Is life good even when it's painful? Is it the pain itself that hones the beauty, revealing its true core?

For my part, I'd say that life is many things, but there are also many things it's not. Fair, for example. I'm the living proof of that. For many years I've suffered from what happened back then, what I have to answer for, even though I was still a child. My parents spared no effort to give me a second chance, because I was still a child. Now that I'm a mother myself, I'd do exactly the same.

But I also wonder how I'd have acted today, twenty years later, had I been in my father's shoes. He died with my guilt. And through his confession, which has been all across the media, he's made sure that finally there's peace. The Julie Novak case has officially been solved, there are no more unanswered questions that might put some nitpicking journalist on my case. This is my father's legacy: I get to live my life. Finally I get to be happy and no longer view my second chance as one of merely existing. I have to make the best of it, for him and my mother, for Richard, for Leonie – his granddaughter – who he was never able to meet, for my sister Julie, who was denied the life I've been permitted to live, but most of all for myself.

*And, Dad, I'm doing my best.*

My hair is red again and I've put on a bit of weight. On Tuesdays I go with Leonie to baby swimming and on Wednesdays to the cemetery, where her grandparents and aunt have a joint grave. Richard has forgiven me, at least for what he knows about: the emails to my father and the lies connected to these. This too – knowing what a wonderful husband I have at my side – has only bolstered me further. I will value and protect this life for the rest of my days, with all my love, strength and determination.

Daniel Wagner has given an interview. A television crew visited him at his house and discussed with him how it feels to have lived for so many years under the shadow of a false allegation. I'm not to blame for that – it was my parents' doing. They could have publicly distanced themselves from the suspicion that Wagner had something to do with my sister's disappearance. But they decided to play along with it to make their storyline more believable. They were willing to sacrifice him – for me, yes, but beyond that, for them too. For that decision to give me a second chance was also motivated by self-interest. They weren't seeking to protect just me, but the whole construct that anchored them in life and gave them meaning, purpose and structure: the family.

*Life is—*

. . . in all likelihood, what it is. A succession of big and small lies that we tell – not because we're bad, but because we're human, with all the brightness and darkness, with our light and shadow.

*Life is—*

. . . my little Leonie in the baby swing that Richard fixed to the branch of the old oak in our garden. Her bare feet, kicking cheerfully when I push her gently. Her gurgled laughter. And my darling husband, clattering the cups as he makes us coffee, the sound carrying through the open door to the terrace.

'Your phone, Sophia!' I hear him call out. I call back for him to answer it. I can't do it myself right now, I'm busy being happy on an October afternoon that feels like the summer which rushed past far too quickly, and large portions of which we wasted with arguments, fear and discussions.

'Who was it?' I ask anyway, as Richard comes out of the house. I'm still so focused on Leonie that he almost has to shove the phone in my face for me to realise that whoever it is is on the line, they're not going to be satisfied with Richard passing me a message. Laughing, I roll my eyes and take it.

'Coffee's ready,' Richard whispers, lifting Leonie out of the swing and kissing me on the side of the head before going back to the house with our daughter in his arms. He's a good father, the best you could imagine. Just like mine was.

'Hello?' I say.

'Oh, yes,' a man's voice answers. 'Sophia? It's Phil Hendricks here, the former partner of Liv Keller, from the *Two Crime* podcast. We've never met in person, but Liv might've mentioned me.'

'Phil, yes, of course. I'm really sorry, you know.'

It's silent for a moment then he says, 'Yes, it's a great loss, but ... well, such is life, I'm afraid.' I mutter my agreement. 'But I don't have to tell you that, do I?' he adds. 'It's not something you get used to, is it? You simply refuse to believe it's true. You see, my first great love committed suicide. It took me twenty years to come to terms with the fact that this person I loved so much had really ended their life voluntarily. And now Liv ...'

I wrinkle my nose, irritated by the fact that this total stranger is barraging me with his life story. 'Yes, terrible,' I say tentatively. 'But no matter how well you think you know someone, you can't read their mind. So, what can I do for you, Phil?'

'Oh, quite a bit, I hope. The police gave me back Liv's things – her notes, her phone – which is how I've got your number.'

'Ah, OK.' With my free hand I hold on to one of the ropes of the baby swing.

'Yes and, to be honest, what Liv's left behind is a bit of a mess. But I'm hoping you might be able to bring a bit of order to all of this.'

'Me?' I instinctively shake my head, even though he can't see me. 'I don't know how I might . . .'

'We could meet. How about tomorrow, for example?'

'Listen, Phil. My sister's case is now closed. You know what happened – after all, you were the one my father sent his confession to. You read it out in your podcast and, from the short-term media hype, I'm assuming you've passed it on to the press for a nice bit of pocket money. I can understand that. It must be great to have an exclusive, particularly if it solves a case which for twenty years has been one of the most unusual, unresolved cases in German criminal history. But I think that's enough now. It's finally time to put this to bed.' I can feel my hand that's holding the rope cramp with tension. I relax my grip and wave at Richard, who signals that the coffee's getting cold.

'Oh no, it's not,' Phil Hendricks says. 'This isn't about your father or your sister.'

'Who, then?'

'I'd like to talk to you about that in person. Tomorrow, OK?'

'But I said—'

'Tomorrow, Sophia.' The tone of his voice leaves no room for doubt.

I take a deep breath, then say, 'Alright. Let's meet at yours.

Shall we say eleven o'clock? My husband and daughter will be at playgroup. But just so you know, I don't have much time.'

'Three to five minutes.'

I stop short. 'I don't understand.'

'Oh, it just came to me because you were talking about time. Three to five minutes is usually how long it takes to die from acute shortness of breath. By strangulation, for example.'

'I . . . I'm sorry, but I'm afraid I don't follow.'

'It was your father, Sophia. His immediate reaction was that Liv would never have hanged herself. And, do you know what? I think he was right.'

'You mean . . . Surely you don't think that Liv . . . ?'

He makes a drawn-out sound. 'I may be wrong – I mean, I have been in the past, but . . . I just can't stop going through Liv's last day, you understand? To begin with, she was with your father. Then she went up to our attic to work. Later, as I know from your father, he called her. She sounded agitated and asked him to meet her at once. So what happened, I wonder? What happened between Liv's visit to your father and the phone call? Let me tell you. I think Liv went back through everything again, all the notes and impressions she'd collected over the days prior to that one. And maybe she stumbled upon something. What was that, Sophia?'

'Erm, I'm sorry? How should I know?'

'The thing is, I'm asking you because this morning I logged on to our mobile provider to cancel Liv's phone. Our mobiles are both on a business contract in the podcast's name, you see, so we can both access the account. Or *could*. I mean, I still can, at least. So, when I was on the site, I looked at Liv's itemised bill.

And guess who she called in the period between her visit to your father and her phone call with him?'

I grab the rope of the swing again to hold on tight. 'Oh yes, I remember. Me! She called me.'

'So, what did she want? Did she by any chance ask you for a meeting too? Or for some information? An explanation for something she'd come upon?'

'Huh, no. No, I don't think so. To be honest, I can't really remember why she called.'

'Hmm, that's a shame. How about the knot?'

'The knot?'

He laughs. 'Yes, it's crazy. The police didn't spot it but I did. My father was in the forces, the navy, to be precise. I didn't notice it at first when I saw Liv hanging in the attic with the rope around her neck. But the image burned itself on my mind, Sophia. The knot was a bowline, one of the first my father taught me because it's a fairly basic and strong knot. You must know it too, huh? Didn't you and your sister get your boat licences when you were very young?'

'No, I've never heard of it. My sister had a boat licence but I didn't. We only had two old rowing boats at home, so there was no mooring. We used to pull it to the shore or into the shed and that was that.'

'Oh, I see. Ah well, no hard feelings. We can talk more tomorrow. You know where I live.'

I sigh. 'OK, then. Even though I don't really know how I can help you any further.'

'How, actually?'

'I'm sorry?'

'How do you know where I live?'

'From Liv, of course.'

'Did you ever come to visit?' Before I can reply, he adds, 'Look, you know what? You can tell me that in your own time tomorrow. I'm looking forward to meeting you.' Then he hangs up.

That Phil Hendricks.

Perhaps he's got a fertile imagination. Or he's just seen too many bad films in his life. And in this one, Liv would've called me and cajoled me into an urgent meeting. Even though she'd caught me at a bad moment – let's say I'd just had a row with my husband, who himself had also caught me at a bad moment – I would've complied with her request and made my way straight to the address she gave me, to her flat. But rather than invite me into the flat, she'd have taken me up to her pathetic little amateur detective office, and offered me a seat on a camping chair. I wouldn't have taken the seat, especially when I saw my name on the whiteboard. I'd have crossed my arms and said, 'Right,' to get the meeting over with as quickly as possible.

'Right,' Liv would have repeated, sounding a little sheepish. As if she weren't certain about whatever it was that had fuelled the urgency of her voice in the telephone call. 'The emails,' she might have then said hesitantly. 'All this time I've been thinking about who, apart from Julie, might have written them. And for some reason this phrase kept coming back into my head, you know, your father says it all the time – that he's the director of the clinic and that death doesn't care whether it's Christmas or Easter or the school ball. And in his last email he apologised for having to leave Julie's ball early for an emergency.'

'And?' I'd have asked, at which she would've swallowed audibly.

'There was an email that I wrote instead of your father, to find out if it really was Julie he was communicating with. I wrote, *Tell me what the last song was we danced to at the school ball.* The answer that came to this was *"Waltz of the Flowers" by Tchaikovsky.* But this doesn't fit with Theo having endlessly apologised for having left the ball early.' She would have narrowed her eyes and given me a weird look. 'The two of them didn't have a last dance together because your father had to leave early to attend to an emergency. Unlike you and your father – you *did* have a last dance. "Waltz of the Flowers".'

'Come on, you know he's always mixing things up or forgetting them altogether.'

'Your father, yes. But not Julie. Julie would've written that they didn't have a last dance together. And do you know what else puzzled me?'

I would've shaken my head.

'That when I mentioned your father's last email to *Nutcracker11*, you didn't ask about it. I told you he'd made such an effort and reading it almost broke my heart. But you weren't interested in finding out what was in it. You just nodded. As if you already knew.' She would have taken a step towards me. 'Was it you? Did you write to him as *Nutcracker11*?'

'Of course not!' I would've protested. 'Why would I have done that?'

Liv would've shrugged. Perhaps because she'd already asked herself this question and hadn't been able to come up with an answer. Perhaps she'd have brought Jason Willmers into it again and would've wanted to know why I hadn't told her about him earlier. Or she'd have raked over the thing with the key to our old house again. Some minor questions that I'd already given her explanations about, and plausible ones at that.

But she'd have known this herself, she'd have known that I didn't warrant her mistrust, so she'd have backpedalled quickly.

'I'm not insinuating you did anything, Sophia, really I'm not. On the contrary, I want to help you. But if I'm to find out what happened to your sister, you have to help me too in return. You have to tell me what you know.' When I wouldn't have reacted to that, she would've continued, 'My partner, Phil, is firmly convinced that Daniel Wagner has got something to do with Julie's disappearance. But I . . . I don't know. I just can't get over the thing with Jason Willmers. I believe that's the right lead to follow. It's the direction we need to keep going in.'

'And I don't think we should go on any further, Liv,' I'd have said, my tone now noticeably gruffer. 'Don't you understand how much of a strain this shit is on all of us? I've just had a huge bust-up with my husband. Now my marriage is on the line, not to mention that after two miscarriages, I was finally about to become a mother.'

'Oh, I'm really sorry. But why did you have a row? Was it because of the reportage?'

'And then my father!' I would have gone on, without responding to her question. 'Just look at him! Look at how reduced he's become in the last few days! It's too much, too much for us all.'

Liv would've taken another step towards me and held out a conciliatory arm. 'I know how dreadful this is for everyone. But my gut feeling tells me that we might be on the verge of solving the puzzle. You've just got to stick it out for a little longer, please. Give me a few more days, OK? I really think I'm very close—'

'No!' I'd have said. 'This is now the end, once and for all!'

'But . . . surely you too want to know what happened to Julie, don't you? What are a few more days, when I assure you that we've got a serious chance of discovering her fate?'

'I said no, Liv. This is it. Over. I hereby withdraw my consent, and that of my father as well, to take part in the reportage. Is that clear?' I would've turned to go and leave the attic space. Liv would've stayed up there and, maybe confused by my hurried departure, called my father. Perhaps so he could explain to her my strangely aggressive behaviour or, more probably, to give her his permission to keep investigating, even without my consent. Maybe I would've heard the end of the conversation – because halfway down the stairs, I'd turned around when I realised how close Liv was to finding out the whole truth. And that she wouldn't stop until she'd solved the puzzle of Julie's disappearance. She'd never stop. I'd have thought of my father, who'd forgotten a long while ago what had really happened back then, but who also barely loved me anymore. I'd have thought of the argument with Richard over the emails. The fact that, even if I didn't go to prison because I hadn't intentionally killed my sister, I would find myself as a murderer in the press at least, possibly remaining one forever in the eyes of the whole world. That I'd never lead anything approaching a normal life again. As my mother had predicted.

So maybe I'd have gone back. Maybe I'd have crept up on Liv from behind. I'd have forced her to the floor and, on impulse, grabbed the orange rope that was lying there as if merely waiting for this moment. I'd have been strong, strong enough to pull up her now unconscious body. Hysterical strength, my father would have called it if I'd told him, maybe on that night down by the lake. And he'd have compared it with a mother who'd have freed her son from beneath the wreck of a car after an accident, or other such stories that he'd encountered in his time at the Charité. And he'd have wept – over Liv, but also because it would've made him even more aware how important it was to finally bring matters to a conclusion.

And of course I would've been lucky up till this point because it was assumed that Liv had taken her own life and so her body wasn't examined for any other traces. For had that been done, my fingerprints or my DNA would have definitely been found on the rope.

Yes, I would've been lucky.

An undeserved, shameless luck, perhaps, in the view of someone like Phil Hendricks, who it appears has many problems himself. Everyone he loves eventually kills themselves. That can only drive you mad. And he's just proven to me that he undoubtedly is. For of course the scenario he's possibly got his teeth stuck into is just a hypothesis and not the truth.

Because the truth is, my father caused an accident in which my sister died. And Liv Keller was a lovely, sweet soul who couldn't cope with the pressure she'd put herself under.

Sad, but true.

'OK, Phil, see you tomorrow,' I say softly, just to myself, because the phone call has already finished.

Then I smile and go over to my family. To my husband and my daughter.

*Life is* . . .

. . . what we make of it. And I'm going to cherish and protect mine, for the rest of my days. With all my love. All my strength. And all my determination.

*I promise*, Dad.

# AFTERWORD AND ACKNOWLEDGEMENTS

It's been three years since my last thriller, *Anatomy of a Killer*, was published. Three years during which I've often been asked, 'When are you going to write something new?' My answer is that I'm always writing something new and, just like Theo in *Darling Mine*, my mania doesn't take account of Easter, Christmas or the school ball. I just don't make it easy for myself when I'm writing; sometimes the subjects I deal with are really punishing, both in the extent of the research and how they zap my personal energy. But it's the best form of 'punishment' I can imagine. My aspiration as a human being and as a writer is to throw myself as deeply as possible into a project. I want to understand the themes I explore and my protagonists, but also myself, perhaps, when in this process I try to fathom why a particular project interests me at a particular time.

Sandwiched between *Anatomy of a Killer* and *Darling Mine* is my non-fiction title *True Crime: Der Abgrund in dir*, and the associated podcast which came about in collaboration with my good friend, the forensic biologist Dr Mark Benecke. There has also been what is perhaps my most daring endeavour to date, the poetry collection *Princess Standard*, together with the accompanying music album with the Cologne indie band Fortuna Ehrenfeld. Although it might not be apparent at first glance, both projects have their origin in the same thing that inspires my thrillers: my need to understand the human condition in all its facets.

And that leads me here, back to the thriller *Darling Mine*, where everything is one, where there is no longer any clear separation between the truth and viewpoint, between understanding and interpretation. My main character, Theo, once a renowned heart surgeon, suffers from dementia and is making one last attempt to find out what happened to his daughter who went missing twenty years ago. The inspiration for Theo came from Lorne Campbell, the grandfather of Phoebe Handsjuk, who died under mysterious circumstances in December 2010, and whose family, including Lorne, I was able to talk to for my true crime project. Lorne, himself a former police officer, is now in his mid eighties. Unlike Theo, he doesn't suffer from dementia, but close contact with him and our conversations made me wonder what it must feel like when a person's clock is ticking away and they know that they'll never be able to get the answer to the one, perhaps only question that has determined their entire existence. The sadness I felt when I thought about this is still with me today. Maybe *Darling Mine* is my attempt to give at least Theo some peace of mind, if I can't do this for Lorne. For even after having explored the true crime genre, I still believe that although there cannot always be clarification, very sadly, perhaps there can be some peace. The tiniest light in the darkness, the milligram of love which, hopefully, weighs more heavily than fear.

There are also some true criminal cases that have made their way into the book, which you might have found utterly fanciful when reading about them. The case of the sports teacher, for example, who died in a gym mat. Or that of the Macedonian journalist, a murderer of women, who wrote about his own gruesome deeds in the newspaper. The story of the sports teacher is based on the tragic death of the high school pupil Kendrick Johnson, while the tale of Vlado Taneski, the Macedonian journalist, is lifted straight from real life. The strange ransom demand that the Novak family receive after the disappearance of their daughter is also based on truth. The parents of the six-year-old beauty queen JonBénet Ramsey, who was killed in 1996, received a ransom letter of a similar length and just as strange, although, unlike Vera and Theo, they didn't write it. Other true cases have been echoed in the novel, albeit in a more subtle form. I discuss these, and the ones above, with Dr Mark Benecke in our new podcast that accompanies the novel and shows once more that nothing an author can concoct is crazier than what has already happened in real life and what, sadly, will happen again.

But I'm not just preoccupied by stories from this 'great' and actively brutal genre. Writing from the perspective of a man with dementia and trying to portray the illness as authentically as possible – also taking into consideration the people around the person suffering, who likewise have to struggle with the situation, day in, day out – was a matter close to my heart. For dementia is not a 'minor' topic. In Germany there are currently 1.8 million people suffering from this illness; in 2023 the global figure was 55 million. Dementia is a silent enemy and perpetrator, and nobody is invulnerable. Unlike a criminal, however, you can't sentence it and put it in prison; you can only watch it continue to wreak its harm. We're at the mercy not only of the disease, but of everything that comes with it. Besides memory loss, this includes, in the longer term, the loss of personal identity, frequently accompanied by social exclusion.

And so we return to the things that are important to me personally: understanding one another and developing real empathy. I'm fully aware that these won't cure a disease or solve a crime. But how we shape our society and how we co-exist are key questions. We need to open our hearts and maybe, from time to time, leave our egos folded up in the cupboard at home. As Theo's daughter Sophia says in the epilogue: *life is what it is*. And this is true – we're not in control of everything and, in many areas, we have to accept our impotence. On the other hand, we definitely can control how we behave on this earth, how we treat our fellow human beings, the inspiration we provide, however minor, and what we are going to leave behind one day. Something good, hopefully – the world needs that, it needs us.

At this point, therefore, I'd like to thank the people who *I* need and without whom I wouldn't be able to write. I thank my readers who have shown me so much appreciation and loyalty. I thank the booksellers who respond to my books with so much curiosity and support. My publisher, Penguin Random House, Bianca Dombrowa, Britta Clauss, Britta Egetemeier, Karin Pfaff and the rest of 'my' team. Thanks for allowing me to do what I do so unconditionally and without anxiety. I'd like to thank my agency Copywrite, Caterina Schäfer and Felix Rudloff, for preparing the way even when it's difficult. Thanks to Andrea Seibert, Sonja Schmidt and Constanze Chory, the embodiment of loyalty. And finally, in no particular order, because each and every one of you knows the specific reason for my gratitude, a huge thanks to Kalle, Mama and Papa, Isolde and Opa, Kathrin

## DARLING MINE

Bruzi, Tim Schlenzig, Lala Statello, Natalie Handsjuk, Claudia Schmidt, Lutz Heineking, Andy Baker, Juliette Braatz, Annika Strauss, Hans Grünthaler, Berit Fischer, Astrid Eckert, Christian Kalinowsky, Norman Stoffregen, Sebastian Fitzek, Mark Benecke and Martin Bechler. And, of course, thanks to you, Theo. You're the best character who's ever foisted themselves on me. I hope I was able to give you peace of mind.

To life, love and all the other good things,

Yours, Romy

'In the beginning there is always the word.'

Or an editor who understands even the wildest idea implicitly.

For you, Bianca.

Thank you for your friendship, your loyalty,
your huge heart and your quick mind.